Aubrianna

house of dark shadows

BOOK ONE OF
DREAMHOUSE KINGS

watcher in the woods

BOOK TWO OF
DREAMHOUSE KINGS

ROBERT LIPARULO

THOMAS NELSON
Since 1798

NASHVILLE DALLAS MEXICO CITY RIO DE JANEIRO BEIJING

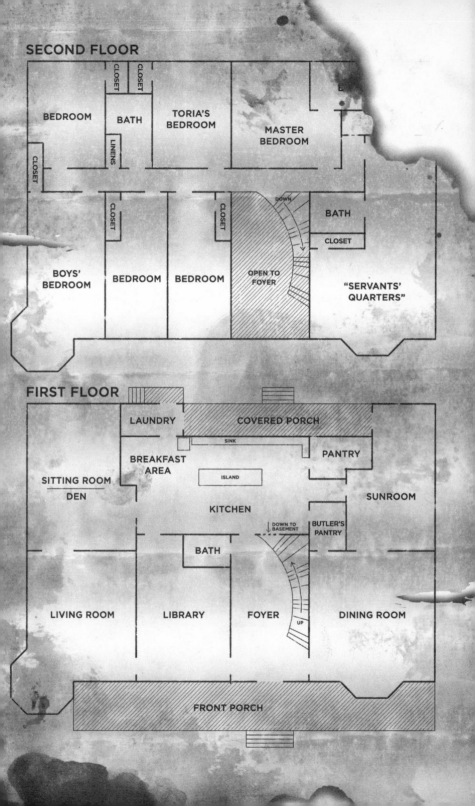

Published in Nashville, Tennessee. Thomas Nelson is a registered trademark of Thomas Nelson, inc.

Thomas Nelson, inc. books may be purchased in bulk for educational, business, fund-raising, or sales promotional use. For information, please e-mail specialMarkets@thomasNelson.com.

Page design by Mandi Cofer
Map design by Doug Cordes

ISBN 978-1-59554-712-5

Printed in the United States of America

08 09 10 11 12 QW 6 5 4 3 2 1

To my son Anthony,

whose enthusiastic and energetic spirit
makes our home as adventurous as
(but eternally brighter than)
the house in this story.

This one's for Isabella

"Ain't nothing sweeter"

house of dark shadows

"A house of which one knows every room isn't worth living in."

—GIUSEPPE TOMASI DI LAMPEDUSA

PROLOGUE

THIRTY YEARS AGO

The walls of the house absorbed the woman's screams, until they felt to her as muffled and pointless as yelling underwater. Still, her lungs kept pushing out cries for help. Her attacker carried her over his shoulder. The stench of his sweat filled her nostrils. He paid no heed to her frantic writhing, or the pounding of her fists on his back, or even her fingernails, which dug furrows into his flesh. He simply lumbered, as steadily as a freight train, through the corridors of the big house.

She knew where they were heading but not where she would end up. In this house nothing was normal, nothing as it appeared. So while she knew in advance the turns her attacker would take, which hallways and doors he would traverse, their destination was as unknowable as a faraway galaxy. And that meant her *taking* would be untraceable. She would be unreachable to searchers. To would-be rescuers. To her *family*—and that realization terrified her more than being grabbed out of her bed. More than the flashes of imagined cruelty she would suffer away from the protection of the people who loved her. More than death.

But then she saw something more terrifying: her children, scrambling to catch up, to help. Their eyes were wide, streaming. They stumbled up the narrow staircase behind her attacker, seeming far below, rising to meet her. The thought of them following her into the chasm of her fate was more than she could stand.

"Go back," she said, but by this time her throat was raw, her voice weak.

The man reached the landing and turned into another corridor.

Temporarily out of sight, her son yelled, "Mom!" His seven-year-old voice was almost lost in the shrillness of his panic. He appeared on the landing. His socked feet slipped on the hardwood floor, and he went down. Behind him, his little sister stopped. She was frightened and confused, too young to do anything more than follow her brother. He clambered up and started to run again.

A hand gripped his shoulder, jarring him back.

The boy's father had something in his fist: the lamp from his nightstand! He passed the boy in the hallway. His bare feet gave him traction.

Thank God, she thought.

He reached her in seconds. With the lamp raised over his head, he grabbed her wrist. He pulled, tried to anchor himself to the floor, to the carpeted runner now covering the wood planks. But the brute under her walked on, tugging him with them. The man yanked on her arm. Pain flared in her shoulder. He might as well have tried pulling her from a car as it sped past.

She caught a glimpse of the bizarrely shaped light fixtures on the corridor walls—mostly carved faces with glowing eyes. The bulbs flickered in time with her racing heart. She could not remember any of the lights doing that before. It was as though the electrical current running through the wires was responding to a disruption in the way things were *supposed* to be, a glitch in reality.

"Henry," she said, pleading, hopeful.

His grip tightened as he stumbled along behind them. He brought the lamp's heavy base down on her assailant. If the man carrying her flinched, she did not feel it. If he grunted or yelled out, she did not hear it.

What he did was stop. He spun around so quickly, the woman's husband lost his grip on her. And now facing the other direction, she lost sight of him. Being suddenly denied her husband's visage felt like getting the wind knocked out of her. She realized he was face-to-face with the man who'd taken her, and *that* felt like watching him step off a cliff.

"Nooo!" she screamed, her voice finding some volume. "Henry!"

His hand gripped her ankle, then broke free. The man under her moved in a violent dance, jostling her wildly. He spun again and her head struck the wall.

The lights went out completely . . . but no, not the lights . . . her consciousness. It came back to her slowly, like the warmth of fire on a blustery day.

She tasted blood. She'd bitten her tongue. She opened her eyes. Henry was crumpled on the floor, receding as she was carried away. The children stood over him, touching him, calling him. Her son's eyes found hers again. Determination hardened his jaw, pushed away the fear . . . at least a measure of it. He stepped over his father's legs, coming to her rescue. Henry raised his head, weary, stunned. He reached for the boy, but missed.

Over the huffing breath of the man, the soft patter of her son's feet reached her ears. How she'd loved that sound, knowing it was bringing him to her. Now she wanted it to carry him away away from this danger. Her husband called to him in a croaking, strained voice. The boy kept coming.

She spread her arms. Her left hand clutched at open air, but the right one touched a wall. She clawed at it. Her nails snagged the wallpaper. One nail peeled back from her finger and snapped off.

Her assailant turned again, into a room—one of the small antechambers, like a mud room before the *real* room. He strode straight toward the next threshold.

Her son reached the first door, catching it as it was closing.

"Mom!" Panic etched old-man lines into his young face. His eyes appeared as wide as his mouth. He banged his shoulder on the jamb, trying to hurry in.

"Stay!" she said. She showed him her palms in a "stop" gesture, hoping he would understand, hoping he would obey. She took in his face, as a diver takes in a deep breath before plunging into the depths. He was fully in the antechamber now, reaching for her with both arms, but her captor had already opened the second door and was stepping through. The door was swinging shut behind him.

The light they were stepping into was bright. It swept around her, through the opening, and made pinpoints of the boy's irises. His blue eyes dazzled. His cheeks glistened with tears. He wore his favorite pajamas—little R2-D2s and C-3POs all over them, threadbare and too small for him.

"I—" she started, meaning to say she loved him, but the brute bounded downward, driving his shoulder into her stomach.

5

Air rushed from her, unformed by vocal cords, tongue, lips. Just air.

"Moooom!" her son screamed. Full of despair. Reaching. Almost to the door. "Mo—"

The door closed, separating her from her family forever.

one

SATURDAY, 4:55 P.M.

"Nothing but trees," the bear said in Xander's voice. It repeated itself: "Nothing but trees."

Xander King turned away from the car window and stared into the smiling furry face, with its shiny half-bead eyes and stitched-on nose. "I mean it, Toria," he said. "Get that thing out of my face. And turn it off."

His sister's hands moved quickly over the teddy bear's paws, all the while keeping it suspended three inches in front of Xander. The bear repeated, "I mean it, Toria. Get that—"

At fifteen years old, Xander was too old to be messing around with little-kid toys. He seized the bear, squeezing the paw that silenced it.

"Mom!" Toria yelled. "Make him give Wuzzy back!" She grabbed for it.

Xander turned away from her, tucking Wuzzy between his body and the car door. Outside his window, nothing but trees—as he had said and Wuzzy had echoed. It reminded him of a movie, as almost everything did. This time it was *The Edge*, about a bear intent on eating Anthony Hopkins. An opening shot of the wilderness where it was filmed showed miles and miles of lush forest. *Nothing but trees.*

A month ago his dad had announced that he had accepted a position as principal of a school six hundred miles away, and the whole King family had to move from the only home Xander had ever known. They were going to a place he had never even heard of: Pinedale, almost straight north from their home in Pasadena. Still in California, but barely. Pinedale. The name itself said "hick," "small," and "If you don't die here, you'll wish you had." Of course, he had screamed, begged, sulked, and threatened to run away. But in the end here he was, wedged in the back seat with his nine-year-old sister and twelve-year-old brother.

The longer they drove, the thicker the woods grew, and

the more miserable he became. It was bad enough leaving his friends, his school—*everything!*—but to be leaving them for Hicksville, in the middle of nowhere, was a stake through his heart.

"Mom!" Toria yelled again, reaching for the bear.

Xander squeezed closer to the door, away from her. He must have put pressure on the bear in the wrong place: it began chanting in Toria's whiny voice: "Mom! Mom! Mom!"

He frantically squeezed Wuzzy's paws, but could not make it stop.

"Mom! Mom! Mom!"

The controls in the bear's arms weren't working. Frustrated by its continuous one-word poking at his brain—and a little concerned he had broken it and would have to buy her a new one—he looked to his sister for help.

She wasn't grabbing for it anymore. Just grinning. One of those see-what-happens-when-you-mess-with-me smiles.

"Mom! Mom! Mom!"

Xander was about to show her what happened when you messed with *him*—the possibilities ranged from a display of his superior vocal volume to ripping Wuzzy's arms right off—when the absurdity of it struck him. He cracked up.

"I mean it," he laughed. "This thing is driving me crazy." He shook the bear at her. It continued yelling for their mother.

His brother, David, who was sitting on the other side of Toria and who had been doing a good job of staying out of the fight, started laughing too. He mimicked the bear, who was mimicking their sister: "Mom! Mom! Mom!"

Mrs. King shifted around in the front passenger seat. She was smiling, but her eyes were curious.

"Xander broke Wuzzy!" Toria whined. "He won't turn off." She pulled the bear out of Xander's hands.

The furry beast stopped talking: "Mo—" Then, blessed silence.

Toria looked from brother to brother, and they laughed again.

Xander shrugged. "I guess he just doesn't like me."

"He only likes *me*," Toria said, hugging it.

"Oh brother," David said. He went back to the PSP game that had kept him occupied most of the drive.

Mom raised her eyebrows at Xander and said, "Be nice."

Xander rolled his eyes. He adjusted his shoulders and wiggled his behind, nudging Toria. "It's too cramped back here. It may be an SUV, but it isn't big enough for us anymore."

"Don't start that," his father warned from behind the wheel. He angled the rearview mirror to see his son.

"What?" Xander said, acting innocent.

"I did the same thing with my father," Dad said. "The car's too small . . . it uses too much gas . . . it's too run down . . ."

Xander smiled. "Well, it is."

"And if we get a new car, what should we do with this one?"

"Well . . ." Xander said. "You know. It'd be a safe car for me." A ten-year-old Toyota 4Runner wasn't his idea of cool wheels, but it *was* transportation.

Dad nodded. "Getting you a car is something we can talk about, okay? Let's see how you do."

"I have my driver's permit. You *know* I'm a good driver."

"He is," Toria chimed in.

David added, "And then he can drive us to school."

"I didn't mean just the driving," Dad said. He paused, catching Xander's eyes in the mirror. "I mean with all of this, the move and everything."

Xander stared out the window again. He mumbled, "Guess I'll never get a car, then."

"Xander?" Dad said. "I didn't hear that."

"Nothing."

"He said he'll never get a car," Toria said.

Silence. David's thumbs clicked furiously over the PSP buttons. Xander was aware of his mom watching him. If he looked, her eyes would be all sad-like, and she would be frowning in sympathy for him. He thought maybe his dad was looking too, but only for an opportunity to explain himself again. Xander didn't want to hear it. Nothing his old man said would make this okay, would make ripping him out of his world less awful than it was.

"Dad, is the school's soccer team good? Did they place?" David asked. Xander knew his brother wasn't happy about the move either, but jumping right into the sport he was so obsessed about went a long way toward making the change something he could handle. Maybe Xander was like that three years ago, just rolling with the punches. He couldn't remember. But now he had things in his life David didn't: friends who truly mattered, ones he thought he'd spend the rest of his life with. Little kids didn't think that way. Friends could come and go, and they adjusted. True, Xander had known his current friends for years, but they hadn't become like *blood* until the last year or so.

That got him thinking about Danielle. He pulled his mobile phone from his shirt pocket and checked it. No text messages from her. No calls. She hadn't replied to the last text he'd sent. He keyed in another: "Forget me already? JK." But he wasn't Just Kidding. He knew the score: out of sight, out of mind. She had said all the right things, like *We'll talk on the phone all the time; You come down and see me and I'll come up to see you, okay?* and *I'll wait for you.*

Yeah, sure you will, he thought. Even during the past week, he'd sensed a coldness in her, an emotional distancing. When he'd told his best friend, Dean had shrugged. Trying to sound world-wise, he'd said, "Forget her, dude. She's hot. She's gotta move on. You too. Not like you're married, right?" Dean had never liked Danielle.

Xander tried to convince himself she was just another friend he was forced to leave behind. But there was a different kind of ache in his chest when he thought about her. A heavy weight in his stomach.

Stop it! he told himself. He flipped his phone closed.

On his mental list of the reasons to hate the move to Pinedale, he moved on to the one titled "career." He had just started making short films with his buddies and was pretty sure it was something he would eventually do for a living. They weren't much, just short skits he and his friends acted out. He and Dean wrote the scripts, did the filming, used computer software to edit an hour of video into five-minute films, and laid music over them. They had six already on YouTube—with an average rating of four and a half stars and a boatload of praise. Xander had dreams of getting a short film into the festival circuit, which, of course, would lead to offers to do music videos and commercials, then on to feature movies starring the next Russell Crowe and Jim Carrey, and probably an Oscar. Pasadena was right next to Hollywood, a twenty-minute drive. You couldn't ask for a better place to live if you were the next Steven Spielberg. What on earth would he find to film in Pinedale? *Trees,* he thought glumly, watching them fly past his window.

Dad, addressing David's soccer concern, said, "We'll talk about it later."

Mom reached through the seat backs to shake Xander's knee. "It'll work out," she whispered.

"Wait a minute," David said, understanding Dad-talk as well

as Xander did. "Are you saying they suck—or that they don't *have* a soccer team? You told me they did!"

"I said 'later,' Dae." His nickname came from Toria's inability as a toddler to say David. She had also called Xander *Xan*, but it hadn't stuck.

David slumped down in his seat.

Xander let the full extent of his misery show on his face for his mother.

She gave his knee a shake, sharing his misery. She was good that way. "Give it some time," she whispered. "You'll make new friends and find new things to do. Wait and see."

CHAPTER

SATURDAY 6:18 P.M.

Their motel room was decorated like a six-year-old boy's bedroom. Athletes doing their thing illustrated the wallpaper, bed-
spreads, hand towels, shower curtain. The bedside lamp was a
cartoon-faced baseball player, whose bat held up the bulb and
shade. A throw rug between the beds was supposed to look like
a giant basketball, but time and lots of feet had worn it into
something more like a squashed pumpkin.

15

"Who do they think stays here?" Xander said, noticing someone had painted red stitching on the globe of the ceiling light in an effort to make it resemble a baseball. When he pointed it out to David, his brother thought it was supposed to be a bloodshot eye. They were sitting on the bed that, unbelievably, they would have to share until his parents arranged for something more permanent. Xander was going to make darned sure no one fed the kid beans before then.

"The décor is . . . *interesting*," Mrs. King said. Usually she found something charming or at least educational about everything. That she didn't this time validated Xander's suspicion that the motel owners were totally clueless.

"I like the soccer players," David said.

"No, really?" Xander pushed him hard enough to send him flying off the bed and onto the road-kill pumpkin.

One thing Xander appreciated about David was his determination to stand up for himself. Instead of crying for Mommy every time Xander did something he didn't like, he either turned a cold shoulder or fought back. This time he fought back. Smiling, he sprung off the floor and tackled Xander back onto the bed.

Xander rolled, so he was sitting on his brother. He grabbed David's wrists and tried to pin him. David jerked his arms free and landed a blow to Xander's stomach. Xander jabbed David in the ribs and got a solid grip on his wrists. He pinned his hands to the bed, one next to each of David's ears. He made a noise in his throat that implied the gathering of something worth spitting onto his brother's face. David began to squirm, tighten his face, and thrash his head from side to side.

"Boys!" Mom said.

"Ah, let 'em be," Dad told her. "They just spent nine hours in the car."

David heaved his legs up behind Xander and drove a knee into his back.

"Ahh!" Xander yelled.

David pulled an arm free, reached up, and grabbed a handful of Xander's hair.

Xander squeezed his eyes shut. "David . . . let go!"

"Get off me."

"*Let go.*"

Somewhere in the room, Mom pleaded to Dad. "Ed?"

"G, they're fine."

It hadn't been until Xander was in kindergarten, when the other kids had laughed, that he realized G—as in "gee whiz"— was a funny name for a mom . . . for anybody. His mother had explained that she simply did not feel like a Gertrude, and even at that young age, Xander had agreed that G was much better. In fact, the family had developed a saying whenever Mom did something bold or crazy—like getting in the face of the line-backer-sized neighbor who'd yelled at David to get off his yard or parasailing behind a speedboat in Baja: *definitely not a Gertrude.*

"Okay, okay," Xander said. Slowly, he slid off his brother.

David held on until Xander had shifted his entire weight from David's belly to the bed. David pulled his knees up to his chest, preventing Xander from jumping on again. Then he cautiously released his grip on Xander's hair. Before David could spin away, Xander spat, nailing his brother's cheek. Xander howled in laughter and bolted for the door. He yanked it open and darted into the parking lot.

"Alexander!" his mother yelled after him. "You get back here right now!"

But Dad called to them, "Not too far, guys!" giving him permission to continue on.

The door slammed. Heading for a big field beyond the parking lot, Xander looked back to see David sprinting after him. He was still wiping his face.

CHAPTER

three

The man in the house lumbered through the corridor. He could tell right away nothing had changed. It was the same dark, empty place it had been time after time. But it was his duty to check. So with a deep sigh, he moved through a threshold into the next room. His shoulders scraped both sides of the door frame. The weight of each footstep rattled the windows and caused the floor to groan under him. His eyes were accustomed to darkness, but still he squinted at the shadows gathered in each room. He grunted at them, and when he was satisfied they were only shadows after all, he moved on.

A spider dropped from the ceiling, landing on his shoulder. He swiped at it, smearing the grime and sweat already there. It darted to his chest, where he flattened it with a palm the size of a Ping-Pong paddle. Having made his usual circuit through hallways, stairways, and rooms, he heaved his heavy shoulders in a deep, sad breath and headed for the door that would take him home.

Something stopped him. A sound. He turned and retraced his steps to the front rooms. He looked out a leaded glass window. Through a patina of filth, he saw a man approaching. He was ambling through the trees slowly, cautiously. He did not move directly to the door, but cut diagonally to the side of the house.

The man inside moved with him, from window to window. The outsider returned to the front. He went toward the door but did not come close. He seemed satisfied and began walking away, his gait more confident. At the window, the man inside shifted his considerable weight from one foot to the other. A floorboard creaked.

The other man stopped to look. He appeared to stare directly at the man inside. But it was dark in the house, and if the other saw him, he gave no clue. He walked on, glancing back only once more.

For a while, the man watched his breath condense and evaporate on the window. Then he turned and went home.

four

SATURDAY, 6:58 P.M.

Halfway through the field, almost back to the hotel, Xander reached out and brushed the most obvious grass out of his brother's hair.

David smiled. "Thanks."

Xander shrugged. "Don't want to get in trouble for pounding on you."

David appraised him. "Who pounded on who?"

Xander pushed him. "Look at you."

"*You're* the one limping."

"Yeah, right," Xander said, trying to ignore the pain in his ankle.

"If the cops stop us, I'll tell them you're a mugger."

"I don't think they have muggers here," Xander said. "Besides, they'd have to be blind to not know we're brothers." They both had dark brown hair, though Xander's was longer and shaggier. Same smile. And while David had their mother's hazel eyes and Xander his dad's blue, they shared an eye shape that was sort of like a teardrop lying on its side. There were times when each of them had mistaken David for Xander and vice-versa in photographs. Even Dad had done that, but never Mom; she always knew, and without squinting at them to be sure, the way Dad did.

"It's going to be cool," David said, "us being in the same school again, huh?"

"Maybe." Pinedale was so small, it had only one elementary school and another school that served seventh through twelfth grades. It had been five years since the brothers attended the same school at the same time, when David was in second grade and Xander fifth.

"Are we going to find a house before school starts, you think?"

"That's the plan, but it's a lot to do in a week."

"Car's gone," David announced.

Xander looked up to see that the 4Runner was not in the motel parking lot. He said, "Dad probably went out for food."

"Good. I'm starving."

When they entered, Toria and Mom were sitting on Toria's rollaway bed. They were looking at brochures for what the locals thought were visitor attractions. Toria had picked them up at a gas station outside of town. She was always looking for something to read, was almost never without a book or newspaper. She even read the sports section, for crying out loud.

"Dad went for some grub," Mom said.

"When'll he be back? I could eat a whole cow," David said.

"Gross," Toria said.

Mom checked the bedside clock. "Should have been back by now. Probably making new friends. You know your father."

"McD's?" he asked hopefully.

She smiled. "'Fraid you're heading for a junk food withdrawal, Dae. None of that here. There's a café up the street. Bet you like it."

David looked at Xander, neither of them so sure.

"Did you know this is the capital of Bigfoot country?" Toria asked.

Xander made a face. "Bigfoot?"

"Yeah," she said, consulting the brochure in her hands. "There have been more sightings in this area than anywhere else in the United States. People have launched expeditions to find him, right from Pinedale."

"So?" Xander said. "Did they find him?"

"If they did," she said, "it would've been in the news. But there's a Bigfoot museum in town."

The door opened and Dad stepped in, a brown grocery bag in one arm. The smell of roasted chicken filled the room. "Dinner's on," he announced.

David said, "Oh yeah!"

They sat at a table near the door. It was chipped Formica with what looked like stickers of sporting equipment plastered all over it.

As she heaped meat and potato salad onto paper plates, Mom said, "Eat up! I want us to get to bed early. We have a busy day tomorrow."

"Doing what?" Xander asked.

"House hunting."

Xander made a face. "All of us?"

"Would you rather stay here and babysit?"

"No, thanks."

"I thought we could swing by and see your new schools too."

"Noooo," David moaned.

"Oh, come on!" Xander said. "We're in town less than twenty-four hours and we have to go see the *school*?"

Mom said, "You want to see it before your first day, don't you?"

"I can wait," Xander said.

"It won't be so bad. You'll see," Dad said, shaking a forkful of chicken at him. "Now eat."

CHAPTER

five

SUNDAY, 9:20 A.M.

The next morning, during breakfast at the same café where Dad had bought their chicken dinner, Mom wondered about the local churches.

Dad frowed and looked at his watch. "I haven't had a chance . . ."

Mom shook her head. "Mr. King, next week for sure. No excuses."

Dad smiled. "Absolutely."

Twenty minutes later, the Kings found themselves in front of Pinedale Middle and Senior High School. Xander could not find the right words to describe it. Okay, it had a nice setting—quaint, peaceful. Situated up a forested hill, it overlooked the town. On three sides the tree-covered hills continued, giving the school a lush, green backdrop. The building itself was a brick single-story. L-shaped. In the square yard between the wings were grass, several flat-rock patios, picnic tables, and a flagpole. *A lot like a park*, he thought. Still, it was a *school*.

"Pretty, isn't it?" his mother said.

"It's okay," he answered, shrugging. "Does *pretty* really matter when it comes to education?" Trying to sound enlightened.

She gave him a dirty look. "Hey, you're the one who has to look at it for the next three years, not me."

They all climbed out of the SUV. From their vantage point in the front parking lot, marked VISITORS AND FACULTY ONLY, they could see the end zone and scoreboard of a football field around back.

David pointed to the statue of an animal leaping over the scoreboard. "Their mascot's a cougar. That's cool."

"Panther," Dad said. "Pinedale Panthers."

"That's cool too."

Mom crossed the pickup lane and stepped into the grassy area. "Come on, let's have a look."

David, forgetting himself, ran to catch up. Toria followed.

Dad stepped up next to Xander. He patted his son on the back, then laid his hand on Xander's shoulder. He said, "Not interested?"

"I'll see enough of it after next week."

"I know it's tough to change schools. I did a lot of that."

Xander turned to him. "So that makes it okay?"

"I'm not saying that. Just . . ." Dad seemed to search for the right words. "I wouldn't have done this to you if it wasn't important."

"Important to who?"

"Us. The family. Me."

"That's the part I don't get. Why is it important? I thought you liked being a teacher. I thought you liked Valley High."

"I did. I—" Dad looked up at the sky. After a few moments, he lowered his eyes to Xander's. "You gotta trust me on this, okay?"

Xander turned away, pretending to watch Mom, Dae, and Toria scope out the school. *Did* he have to trust him? It wasn't really *trusting* him he had to do, was it? It was really about going along with his plan, because he was a kid and couldn't do anything else. Not yet.

He said, "Sounds like you don't have a good reason."

"I do," his father said. "I just can't . . . I can't get into it right now with you. When I can I will."

Xander bowed his head. *What is this?* he thought. Dad had a secret reason for moving all of them to Pinedale? Or was it Pasadena he was moving them *from*? Was he going *to* something or running *from* something? A hundred possibilities occurred to him at once: Was his father in the Witness Protection Program? Had he discovered a treasure map and was determined to make them all rich? Had he had an affair, and distancing all of them from the other woman was the only way to hold the family together? Nothing sounded right. But it had to be *something*. Probably it was a midlife crisis or something else equally lame.

"Son," his father continued, "don't think you're here simply because I want to be and I have to bring you along. You're not baggage or furniture. I *need* you."

"But you can't tell me why." Xander held his lips tight.

His father's shoulders slumped. He looked miserable. He said, "Not yet."

"When?"

"Soon, I promise. But don't fight me on this, as hard as it is for you . . . please." He extended his hand to Xander, wanting to seal his son's compliance with a shake.

Xander knew his dad was trying to bridge a gap. He stared at the hand, then grabbed it. He let a weak smile bend his lips.

He said, "I'll try to do better."

"That's all I'm asking for." Dad cocked his head at the school. "Wanna check it out?"

They started walking. Dad kept his palm pressed to Xander's back. Mom, David, and Toria were gazing into different windows.

"Classroom," Mom called out.

"Here's the library," David informed her.

Toria said something Xander couldn't make out.

Dad and Xander stepped onto the open area's grass. It was thick and impossibly green. It felt like an exercise mat under Xander's feet.

"I still want to go home," he said.

"I know, Son." He slid his hand to Xander's shoulder, squeezed it. "I know."

A few paces farther, Xander said, "Dad?"

"Hmm?"

"If I guess your secret, will you tell me if I'm right?"

His father laughed but didn't answer.

CHAPTER

Six

Two hours later, they had seen three properties that were for sale.

It was clear to Xander his parents were looking for something completely different from the suburban house they had left. The lots were large and thick with trees, the houses more like the hunting cabins he had seen in movies—cabins where college kids seek shelter from ax-wielding madmen or ticked-off ghosts. In those movies, the cabins were never shelter enough.

One house he and David liked was situated down a slope from the road, nearly invisible through the trees. A river—Dad said it was Weaver Creek—cut so close to the house, Xander thought they could fish from the back deck. The water rushed over boulders, making a surflike sound. All Mom could see was a deathtrap and refused to discuss the possibility of buying it.

Xander didn't mind the secluded settings. He figured that since there wasn't a multiplex or mall within two hundred miles, and given the choice of forested isolation or depressing little cafés and retail shops, he'd rather live near Mother Nature. He started to view the properties from an outdoorsman's perspective: hiking alone in the woods; dirt biking over the rugged terrain; campfires and pup tents within sight of a refrigerator and bathroom.

Each property took them farther from the school but never so far that he couldn't bike it when he had to. If he got a car, he wouldn't care if they found a place in the next county. In fact, he was starting to get into the tight, winding roads that snaked away from Pinedale in four directions. He could easily see himself behind the wheel of a '68 Corvette convertible—327-cubic-inch engine, tuned exhaust, four-on-the-floor—nudging the speedometer on each turn until the tires squealed in fear.

Dad consulted a stack of property listings, which he had printed from a local Realtor's Web site. He put the car in gear and backed out of the gravel driveway.

Mom turned in the seat. "So what do you think so far?"

"I liked the one with the river," David said quickly.

"Will I get my own room?" Toria asked.

"*You* will," Mom said, and the way she said it made Xander ask, "What about us?" He and David had shared a bedroom for twelve years, and he'd thought if anything good came out of the move, it might be finally getting his own room.

"It depends," she said. "These houses really aren't that big."

"I noticed, but there's lots of land. Could we add on?"

"Hey!" David said, clearly liking the idea.

"Whoa," Dad said, "additions are expensive."

Xander rolled his eyes. *Everything* was expensive. When Dad started talking costs, it meant it wasn't going to happen.

Dad switched on the blinker to turn left, waited for an oncoming car to pass, then pulled the 4Runner onto a narrow, paved road. The forest here was especially dense. They crowded the road and in spots formed leafy tunnels through which Dad drove.

"What if we do it ourselves?" David asked.

Dad glanced back. "Do what?"

"Build our own bedrooms." His big grin told Xander he had all sorts of ideas for a room. Xander shook his head at David and mouthed the words *no way*.

"I don't think so," Dad said. After a moment, he said, "You know, *maybe*." He smiled back at David. "That's not such a bad idea."

David made wide eyes at Xander, whose face was slack in

disbelief. Dad hadn't even said he'd think about it. "Not such a bad idea" in Dad-talk was *yes*.

The 4Runner pulled onto a dirt road. While David rambled on about skylights and secret rooms behind hidden panels, Xander studied the forest on his side of the car. Foliage and shadows limited visibility to twenty or thirty feet from the edge of the road. He would be the first to admit that he knew as much about trees and the woods as he did about Thailand, but he couldn't help but think that there was something different about *this* forest. The leaves of different trees seemed to sway in opposing directions, more like they were controlled by the trees themselves than by the wind. Shadows shifted oddly. The darkness rushed at the car, stopping just feet from the forest's edge, then it pulled way back, exposing gnarled trunks and spindly branches deep within the forest. It reminded him of the surf, flowing in and out, but much quicker and without a discernible pattern. He knew the swaying leaves and branches, as well as the clouds, could cause the weird shifting of shadows, but still something about it left him uneasy.

City boy, he thought. *Freaking out over the trees' shadows. Man, I gotta get over this.*

CHAPTER

Seven

The road simply ended. No cul-de-sac. No sign like the ones they had seen before: "PRIVATE PROPERTY. NO TRESPASSING." Or "NO MOTORIZED VEHICLES BEYOND THIS POINT." Just road . . . then trees.

Dad pulled to a stop and looked around. He rolled down the window and listened, as though the house would somehow make itself known. Wind in the trees, nothing more. He picked up the listing page and studied it.

Mom leaned forward to squint through the windshield. "Are you sure this is the right place?" she asked.

Dad nodded.

She reached for the paper, but he was already crunching it into a ball. He tossed it out the window.

She said, "Maybe it's out of sight. With all these trees . . ."

"Nah." He shifted into reverse and backed up. Shifting again, he drove sharply toward the side of the road, then reversed again.

"Three-point turn," he told Xander.

"I *know*. We covered that in—" Xander stopped. He was gazing into the woods and saw a line too straight, something too flat to be natural. "Wait. I think I see it."

"What?" Mom said. "The house?" She looked back at him, then to where he was staring. David and Toria clicked out of their seatbelts and crowded up against him to look.

"I . . . think so," he said. He opened the door and stepped out. Toria nearly tumbled out after him. Dad killed the engine, and they gathered at the end of the road.

"I see it!" David said. He ran into the woods.

"Hey!" Dad called. Too late: David was already gone. All of them plunged in, crunching over pine needles and dead branches.

Twenty paces in, Xander saw it and wondered how they had missed it from the road. It was two stories high, and it was capped by a steeply pitched roof, from which two dormer windows protruded. A covered porch ran the length of the front, casting the entry door and entire lower level in shadows. The supports were ornately carved columns. Occupying the left front corner was a round tower that rose slightly higher than the rest of the house. It wasn't really round, though. It was an octagon, with only five sides showing. At the tip of its tall spire was a black weathervane. As Xander watched, an unfelt breeze made it turn; it squeaked like a mouse caught in an eagle's talons. The exterior paint—whatever color it had once been—had been washed gray by years of weather and neglect. It seemed to Xander to be as much a part of the surrounding forest as the trees themselves.

"Oh, Ed!" Mom exclaimed. "It's a Victorian."

"Pure Queen Anne," Dad agreed.

Tendrils of mist slithered over the forest floor, around the base of trees. Xander noticed that some of it had climbed the porch pillars and drifted, almost invisibly, over the shingles of the porch roof. It reminded him of an old TV series Dean's dad had bought on DVD: *Dark Shadows*. It was about a creepy old house and a vampire who lived there. Barnabas, Xander remembered.

David was standing farther in, halfway to the house. His head was bent back as he took in the tower, tall as a silo.

Mom said, "I think it used to be green, with darker trim."

"Makes sense," Dad suggested. "One of the original tenets of Victorian architecture was that homes blend in with their surroundings."

Xander hung back as his family moved forward as one. Something on the ground caught his eye and he stepped over to it. Off to the side, away from where they had walked, shoe prints were pushed into an area of soft dirt. The prints approached the house at an angle. Xander scanned back toward the road, where they came from, then toward the house, but did not see any other prints. He wondered how long ago they had been made. They seemed fresh, undamaged by rain or wind or scampering animals.

The back of his neck tingled and he knew—*knew!*—he was being watched. He spun toward his family, but their attention was on the house. He scanned the windows, expecting to see someone looking out or a curtain falling back in place. But he saw nothing like that: no faces, no moving curtains. The feeling of being watched stayed with him. He thought of Barnabas again and a shiver ran up his spine, like a spider with cold feet.

His family had reached the steps leading up to the porch and double front doors. The wood creaked as they climbed, and Xander half-expected one of them to crash through the rotting boards.

"Is anyone home?" Toria asked.

"I don't think anyone lives here, honey," Mom said.

"Why not?" David said. "It's cool."

Wind blew through the treetops, and the weathervane *squeeeeeaked.* Xander looked up at it, and it rotated slowly to point at him.

Without knocking, Dad pushed open the door and walked in. Mom followed, then David and Toria. To Xander, it looked like the house was eating them, just popping them in, one at a time.

"Hey!" he called to the open doorway. He felt uneasy but didn't know why. It was just an old house in the woods. And the footprints could have been left by the real estate people or someone else looking for a house. He walked toward the front steps. A breeze blew past him. It was cold, and it came from the house. He looked up at the eaves, where the roof hung over the sides of the house. It looked taller, this close. He had the sense that he had not walked up to the house, but it had walked up to him, a monster sizing him up.

David's voice drifted out to him, saying something was cool.

He ascended the steps. They groaned and creaked. At the open doorway, he stopped. A curved staircase followed the wall to the second floor high above the first. To his right, a wide doorway serviced a dining room. He could see two chairs, part of a table, a buffet, and cabinets on the far wall. The doors pushed straight into the walls—pocket doors, Xander knew they were called. They were what David had thought was cool.

To his left another archway led to a study or library. Its walls were lined in shelves that were packed with dusty books. Straight ahead, beyond the foyer, a hallway led to a room where the family was gathered. From their words, he assumed they were in the kitchen: "Here's a pantry." "Beautiful cabinets . . ." "There are dirty dishes in the sink!" "Gross!"

Furniture, books, dishes in the sink. If the items themselves suggested someone still lived there, the setting quickly corrected that misconception. Cobwebs clung to the corners where the walls and ceiling met. Dust coated the floors, showing where his family had walked as clearly as if they had traipsed over the smooth beach sand. Wallpaper curled off the walls like peels from a banana. Several banister spindles were broken or missing. Grime lined the fancy carvings in the wood on the banister, around the doors, the doors themselves. Gaps wide enough to stick a finger into had formed between several planks in the hardwood floor.

"Xander!" Dad called from the kitchen. He beckoned to him. "Come on! Check this out!"

He stepped fully into the house. The air inside was cool on his skin. He turned, expecting the front door to close on its own. But it stayed open, as it was supposed to. He shook his head, chiding himself for letting an old house spook him. He walked toward the kitchen.

Behind him, the front door slammed shut.

CHAPTER

SUNDAY, NOON

Xander spun around to stare at the door. It had closed on its own.

And only after all of us had come in, he thought.

From the kitchen behind him, his dad said, "Isn't this incredible?"

"Did you see that?" Xander asked, pointing at the door, but when he stepped into the kitchen, it was empty.

"Whatta ya think?" Dad asked.

Xander turned around to see his father coming toward him from the direction of the front door. His mouth went dry. "Weren't you just in the kitchen?"

"I was. I walked around. You okay?"

"No, I mean . . . yes, but . . ."

His dad tilted his head. "Xander?"

"There's something going on." He was looking past his father to the front door.

"Going on?" Dad asked.

"Something strange. First I heard you in the kitchen, and uh . . ." Xander's head was swimming. "Then the front door slammed . . . by itself."

"It's an old house," his father explained. "Hinges start to sag and that causes doors to close on their own. Have you seen the round room, the one in the tower?"

Xander shook his head.

Mom's voice called down from upstairs. Xander would have sworn she was in the kitchen a few seconds ago as well.

"Dad," Xander said. "Doesn't something about this place seem weird to you?"

"You mean the stuff, the dishes? Whoever lived here before did a poor job packing up, huh?"

"No, I mean *really* weird."

"Like what?"

"Like . . ." Xander didn't know where to start. There was the door shutting after he'd thought about it doing that very thing. His father had chalked it up to sagging hinges. But what about hearing Dad in the kitchen when he was somewhere else? And the chill he'd gotten outside, when he felt as though he was being watched?

"Ed," Mom called again.

"Hold on a sec," his father told Xander, holding up his index finger. He went into the foyer and started up the stairs.

Xander went to the front door and squinted at the hinges. They were dirty and rusty, but otherwise looked fine. The house creaked around Xander. He thought of the way dogs sometimes whimpered when you gave them special attention. He wondered if the house creaked all the time, maybe from constant settling or from the wind buffeting against it . . . or if it was responding to his family's presence. Voices and foot-steps streamed at him from the corridors and upper landing. He could identify each voice, but not the direction from which it came. He heard David in the kitchen again, but didn't see anyone in there. Movement caught his eye, and he looked up to the second floor landing. A hallway disappeared to the left and right. Two doors were visible. One was open, and he saw David standing in the threshold, his familiar silhouette backlit by sunlight coming through a window behind him.

"David!" he called.

"What?" David said, almost beside him.

Xander jumped. David was standing at the foot of the stairs, having stepped out of the dining room.

"David!" Xander yelled, because he had to yell something. His eyes snapped back to the figure in the upstairs doorway, but it was gone.

"What do you want?" David asked.

"I . . . were you just upstairs?"

"I haven't looked up there yet."

"But I just saw you up there."

David gave him a funny look. "Not me. Look at this." He stepped closer to show what he held in his hand. At first Xander thought it was a flashlight, and then he recognized it: a toy light-saber. The plastic red tube that represented the laser had broken off, but the cylindrical handle, with its decorative rings and On/Off switch, was unmistakable. It was old.

"Some kid must have lived here a long time ago," David said.

"Or came in to play."

Xander heard excited voices coming from . . . somewhere. "I really love it, Ed. I do," his mom said.

"Even with all the work?"

"Yes, yes. How else could we afford something this big? If we ever got into a house like this, it would have to be a fixer-upper."

His parents were upstairs, but the voices seemed to be drifting from everywhere at once: the library, the kitchen, the second floor. Relief washed over him when they appeared in the upstairs hallway. Mom leaned over the railing. "It's big, boys. Seven bedrooms!"

"Seven?" David said. "What would we do with that many?"

"You can each have your own, for starters," Dad said. "Your mother's counting servants' quarters up here . . ."

"Servants!" David said, tickled at the idea.

"That doesn't mean we're going to *get* any," Dad said. "Besides, that room needs a lot of work, so we can't use it. For now, anyway."

In his excitement, David ran halfway up the stairs. "So, can we live here?"

Dad looked at Mom to answer. "We'll see what we can do."

Xander felt his stomach roll over on itself. He wanted to get out of the house, but he didn't like the idea of going outside alone. He thought of the shoe prints he'd seen. "Dad, can I show you something outside? It might be important."

Dad looked at him curiously. He gave Mom a quick kiss and clomped down the stairs. "What is it?" he asked.

Mom stopped him. "Ed, where's Victoria?" she said with that hint of worry mothers seem capable of conjuring at a moment's notice.

Everything he felt about the house made Xander panic. Instantly, he yelled, "Toria! Toria!"

His dad gave him a puzzled look, then called for his daughter.

Silence. Not even the creaking, which had seemed so loud and constant a few minutes before.

"Toria!" Dad called again. He looked up to Mom.

She said, "I haven't seen her since we came in."

"Check up there," he said. He came the rest of the way down the stairs and turned into the dining room.

Xander went the other direction, through the library. He circled around and met up with Dad in the kitchen. When they returned to the foyer, Mom was coming off the last step, worry and hope etched on her face.

"Not down here," Dad informed her. His voice had risen a notch. He appeared more concerned than Mom now.

"Ed—" she started.

Footsteps came from upstairs, running, growing louder. All of them looked. The footsteps grew closer. *They sound like Toria's*, Xander thought. A little girl's. *Please let it be her.* When the footsteps could not possibly get any closer, she still did not appear, but the pounding continued. Again, Xander glanced toward the dining room, the kitchen, the library. Considering the tricks of sound he had witnessed, he no longer assumed his sister was upstairs. And that was *if* the footsteps belonged to her.

"What in the world . . . ?" his father said.

"I looked up there," Mom assured him. She called, "Victoria!"

Dad went to the stairs. He hesitated, as if fearful of what he would find at the top.

Toria emerged from the shadows of the upstairs hall. She stopped at the railing, all teeth and dimples. "Hey, guys!"

"Where were you?" Mom asked.

Toria looked confused by her tone. She pointed. "In that bedroom, right there."

"But I looked, honey."

"I didn't see you either," Toria said, shrugging. "I think the room used to belong to a little boy."

"See?" David said, slapping Xander's arm with the lightsaber.

Dad said, "Come on down, sweetheart. It's time to go."

"Ahhh," she complained.

"Come on." Dad approached Xander. "What did you want to show me?"

"Nothing, never mind," Xander said. They were leaving anyway, and what would Dad say about shoe prints in the dirt? Exactly what Xander already considered: that they were left by someone looking for a house, just like they were. No biggie.

At the 4Runner, Xander looked around. The house was easy to spot now that he knew it was there, but he could also see how they had missed it the first time. The woods were shadowy and so was the house. He noticed there wasn't any trash caught in the bushes at the edge of the forest. Or beer bottles scattered around. He thought that was funny, since a dead end like this was exactly what high school kids looked for in a party place. Either there were too many dead ends in these backwoods or too few teenagers looking to party. He didn't want his family to be the only litterbugs, so he snatched up the crumpled property listing his father had discarded and pushed it into his pocket.

47

All the way back to the motel—a good ten minutes, at least—the car buzzed with ideas for making the house their home. Dad said it needed, first and foremost, a thorough cleaning. Mom wanted to paint, recarpet the floors, and stain the wood. Toria knew exactly which bedroom she wanted. And David grumbled about not getting a chance to scope out the upstairs. Only Xander remained silent. If they were really going to live there, he hoped his uneasiness about it went away. He didn't think he could feel this way—all tight inside—24/7.

nine

Sunday, 11:11 p.m.

Everyone else was asleep except Xander and David. They were lying in bed, facing each other.

"I don't know . . . just a *feeling*, like in . . ." Xander thought for a moment. "*Star Wars.* You know, when Han Solo says, 'I've got a bad feeling about this'?"

"Didn't they *all* say that?" David whispered back. "Luke and Leia and . . ."

"My point is the *feeling*, not who *said* it."

The only light came from a sodium vapor lamp that illuminated the motel parking lot. It slipped in where the curtains didn't quite meet and cut a shimmering line over the boys' bed. It was almost too quiet to sleep. No car horns or sirens. No hum of the city, which you didn't notice until you got away from it. Mom's rhythmic breathing told Xander she was fast asleep. Dad's slumber seemed less peaceful, and he didn't quite snore, but his breathing was loud. Xander imagined lions sounding like that. Toria was a quiet sleeper except for an occasionally rolling over. He wasn't sure which one of them was doing it. Something in the room ticked: not a clock, but like a car engine cooling down. Or like someone sitting in the corner of the room making noises with his lips.

For an hour Xander had had been listening to the subtle sounds, unable to get the house out of his head. He had tapped David on the shoulder and whispered his name. It had taken several proddings to wake him. Finally, the boy had rolled over to face Xander. Xander had asked him if he had sensed anything weird at the house. David had thought about it. He'd said it was a little creepy but couldn't offer any specifics.

Now, David said, "So what, you don't like the house? You don't want to live there?"

Xander was torn. There was a lot to like about the house: its size, that it was so isolated in the woods, that it *looked* cool.

If they had to live in Hicksville, they could certainly find worse places than that house. But then . . .

"When I was outside, before we went in, it felt like someone was watching me . . . someone *inside* the house," he said.

"You think it's *haunted*?" From the glow of the lamplight, Xander saw David's eyes grow wide.

"I don't know, but you know how in scary movies something is watching somebody or sneaking up on them, and the person feels it?"

David nodded.

"It was like that."

"You're scaring me."

Xander looked at his brother. If scaring him would make David more aware, more sensitive to the house's weirdness, he decided maybe freaking him out was a good thing.

"Remember *Supernatural*, that TV show?"

David nodded. They'd watched it together a few times.

"Those guys face off with vampires and werewolves and ghosts, but they're not afraid, they just do it."

"You think *vampires* live in the house?" The pitch of his voice had risen a notch. He was starting to sound like Toria.

"I'm not saying that." He closed his eyes. He wasn't sure what he was saying, what he wanted. A brother in arms. Someone to validate his unease. He hoped something more would come from waking David than just spooking him. "Listen, just keep your eye out, okay? If you see anything weird, just let me know."

"Weird?" David paused a moment. He said, "You mean, besides you?"

Xander could sense more than see David's smile. He wished he could be more like that, easygoing. But then, David hadn't seen what Xander had seen.

CHAPTER

MONDAY, 8:52 A.M.

In the morning, Dad announced he was heading out to talk
to the real estate agent about the house.

"Can I come?" Xander asked.

"You're not ready, are you?"

"He hasn't even brushed his teeth," Mom said. She was
sitting on the rollaway, brushing Toria's hair.

Dad rolled his eyes at Xander. He gestured toward the door

with his head. He tiptoed to the door and opened it quietly—as if anything could happen secretly in a twenty-by-twenty motel room, never mind the flood of sunlight that opening the door brought in.

Grinning, Xander grabbed his T-shirt, socks, and sneakers and hurried out. As he pulled the door shut, Mom called, "At least get some gum."

In the car, Xander asked, "You didn't notice anything strange about the house?"

Dad took his time to answer. "I think it's a *special* house, Xander. We wouldn't buy it if it weren't."

Xander bristled. Now he knew how it felt to be like Kevin McCarthy in *Invasion of the Body Snatchers*—a person who *knew* something was wrong but was chalked up as crazy because he couldn't prove it. He couldn't even count the number of movies featuring *that* character. If it happened so often on film, it must be pretty common in real life, right? He had the brief image of himself in a white padded room, arms bound by sleeves that tied in the back, yelling through a little window in the door. "I'm not insane, really!" Nurse Ratched would slam the window shut and his cell mate, Jack Nicholson, would tell him to shut up.

He said, "No, I mean—"

"You mean the sounds?" his father asked.

Hope flared in Xander's gut, feeling a little like when a roller coaster reaches the peak of a tall climb. "Yeah! The *sounds*."

"I think all that creaking and groaning was just the house settling, or getting used to having people in it again."

The roller coaster stalled. "Yeah, settling."

Dad cleared his throat. Xander noticed the skin on his forehead and around his eyes wrinkle in thought. Dad said, "And the way the sounds seem to trick you."

Back on the coaster. Xander smiled. "You noticed that?"

His dad threw him a glance. "Of course. I mean, how many footsteps could Toria have taken to get from one end of the house to the other? It's big, but with all that noise, you'd have thought she was running in place."

Xander hadn't considered that. If that had been the only trick of sound, he might have been able to accept that explanation. He could tell his dad didn't buy it either. "What about . . . *other* things? Like noises coming from a different direction than they should have?"

For a moment, Dad was unreadable. Xander waited like a man for a verdict. Finally, Dad nodded. "That too," he said quietly.

Xander felt tension fall away from his chest like a bandage that had been constricting his lungs. The way his dad had said it was all he needed to know: there *was* something weird about the house. Something that had made his father uneasy as well. And if the house's strangeness revealed itself through sound, then why not visually too? How Dad had appeared to move instantly from one side of the house to the other, the silhouette that had looked like David in the doorway upstairs.

Weren't these just the eyeball equivalent of the tricks on his ears?

"Why is it like that?" he asked.

"I don't know, Son. I really don't."

"But . . . doesn't it *bother* you?" Obviously not, since they were heading to a real estate agent to buy the place.

Dad smiled at Xander. "Not yet."

eleven

MONDAY, 9:28 A.M.

Kathy Bates, Xander thought. Not the homicidal loony from *Misery* but the little-too-happy, bubbly Bates from *Rat Race*. That's who the real estate woman reminded him of. Like Bates, there was plenty of her. She seemed to find everything funny regardless of who said it or how unfunny it was.

"Ooh . . . you just rolled in from Pasadena!" She laughed —her whimsy at the use of the word *rolled* or at Pasadena,

Xander couldn't tell. "And you're looking for a house?"

Mr. King smiled, the way people do when they're waiting for a punchline. "Well, actually, I think we found one."

"Just go ahead and make my job easy, will ya?" she said and lowered herself into the chair behind the office space's single desk. She positioned a keyboard in front of her and said, "Which one?"

"At the end of Gabriel Road."

She looked up and somehow kept her smile while forming a perplexed expression. "Off of Highway 3 . . . and Rem Way?"

A bulge the size of Xander's thumb appeared between her eyes. "I don't think . . ." She started typing, squinting at the monitor. Xander turned to look out the big front window. Across the street was some kind of lumber mill. Whole trees, stripped of branches and bark, were piled into stacks the size of office buildings. Someone was using a fire hose to spray water over the logs. Perhaps it was to keep them from burning up at the slightest spark. It didn't look safe to Xander.

A paper cup tumbled by in the parking lot, and Xander remembered. He pushed his hand into his pocket and pulled out the crumpled property listing his father had tossed away. It was exactly what Kathy Bates needed. He unfolded it and smoothed out the wrinkles. But this wasn't the house on Gabriel Road. The picture was of a smallish cabin they had not seen. Dad had tossed it out the window, frustrated that it had led him to nowhere. That was before Xander had seen the house in the shadows. *Could Dad have been looking at the wrong property listing?* he wondered. If so, how had they found the house?

Another thought occurred to him, and it chilled his skin. What if the house's power was so strong it made Dad see something on the page that wasn't there? Or maybe it had even changed the page after getting them there.

That's called paranoia, Xander thought. *Stop it!*

He crunched the paper back into a ball. He tossed it into a wastebasket by the desk.

"There's nothing here. I'm sorry," Kathy Bates said. Then something dawned on her. "You're talking about the old Konig place!"

"Konig?" his father said. He glanced at Xander.

"That ol' rundown place?" she laughed. "I didn't know it was for sale. Was there a sign?"

"No, but . . ."

Xander said, "There was a property listing."

"Really?" She squinted at him as though he had just said his name was Johnny Depp.

"Off the Internet," his father said. "I think it was your Web site."

She shook her head. "Not mine. Not if that property was listed. But then we all share the same listing service, so I don't know . . ."

"Is it for sale?" Dad asked.

She laughed. "Well, my daddy used to say everything is for sale. Let me look into it." She looked at Xander, then back to Dad. "It's pretty rundown, you know. Nobody's lived there for . . . I don't know, thirty or forty years. Way before my time." She leaned over her desk—as much as she possibly could—and whispered, "The man who lived there . . ." She looked again at Xander. "Well, I shouldn't say."

Dad turned to leave.

Xander knew he had no patience for rumors. Xander had no such qualms. He said, "What about him, the man who used to live there?"

Happy to have Xander's ear, she said, "They say he killed his wife."

Xander took a step back. He threw a shocked expression at Dad, who had turned back, interested.

"Schoolteacher. Just disappeared. After the authorities started asking questions, the man and the rest of his family vanished."

"Family?" Xander said.

"Little boy and girl. I don't know how old. Sweetest family in the world, if you listen to the old folks around here."

Xander was stunned. "And nobody knows what happened to them?"

"Some say they high-tailed it to Europe." She raised her eyebrows at him. "Most believe he took them somewhere and killed them. Then took his own life."

Dad forced a smile. "Just old rumors," he said. "Thank you for looking into this for us. I'll be back." He strode for the door.

Xander's feet felt like cement. He didn't like that a house he already thought had problems also had a gruesome history. He knew it shouldn't have surprised him. Every haunted house in every movie he had ever seen got that way by some tragic event in the past. He wanted to ask the woman what else she knew, but his dad had already pushed through the door. He nodded at her inquisitive look and hustled to catch up.

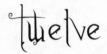

"It *is* haunted."

Night again. The same swath of lamplight stole through the curtains. The same parental breathing. That *tick tick tick* lip sound.

"What do you mean?" David squirmed under the covers.

"That toy you found? The lightsaber? It belonged to a little boy. His father killed the whole family."

David's eyes got huge, then flickered as he thought about that.

"It's like *The Shining*," Xander continued. "The hotel drove the dad crazy."

"How do you know?"

"I saw the movie."

"No. How do you know about the family, the dad who killed them?"

"The real estate lady told us. They never found any of them."

"And it's *haunted*?"

"Has to be. Look, weird things were happening there and—"

"What weird things?"

Xander hadn't told David everything. "Just some stuff. But I told you I got a bad feeling about it, then we find out about this murder." He emphasized it: "A *triple* murder and suicide. A guy *slaughtered* his own family. How awful is that?"

"*Slaughtered*? What'd he do?"

"I'm sure it was something bloody and grotesque. You don't go out of your mind and keep it neat."

Xander could almost see the vivid images bouncing around David's head.

"What do we do?" David asked.

Good question.

"Do you still want to move into that house?"

"Not if it's haunted!"

"Shhhh." Against reason, Xander still felt the *thrill* he had experienced at the house. That sense of adventure, that he was privy to some kind of secret knowledge. He imagined finding another house, one without a history or ghosts. Yeah, he'd sleep better at night, but he'd be bored out of his mind during the day. Especially in Pinedale.

"Look," Xander said. "Let's just keep our eyes open, be really watchful. If it gets dangerous, we'll go nuts—you know, scream and throw a fit or something—to get everybody out."

"I can do that." David smiled, but his eyes said he was still worried.

•••••••••

The next day, they looked at more properties, but their hearts weren't in the search, and they saw nothing they liked.

The following day, Wednesday, Mr. King pulled to the curb in front of Tall Pines Park. The boys, Toria, and Mom had staked a claim at one of the picnic tables. They'd walked from the motel to the park, stopping at a burger joint on the way. Xander and David had already devoured their fries, but Mom had made them wait for their cheeseburgers until Dad showed up.

Their father did a sort of half-skip across the grass. His smile showed where Toria and David got their dimples; Mom and Xander had radiant smiles without them—at least that's what Mom said.

Dad stopped at the head of the table. "Well," he said, "it's ours."

"The house?" David squealed. "I mean *the* house?"

"We haven't closed, of course, but the trust that owns it has agreed to a price and said we can move in right away, if we want."

Mom nodded. Xander realized she had known all along, but she'd kept it a surprise.

Dad leaned down to give her a big kiss. Xander and David exchanged a look, one with equal parts happiness and fear. Xander thought if you took a picture of them during a really scary part of a really good movie, they would look like they did now. He hoped he was right about the house being more frightening than dangerous, and he wondered, if he was wrong, if they would realize it before someone got hurt.

"So what do you say?" Dad clapped his hands. "Want to go to our new home?"

"Now?" Toria said.

"Sure." He saw Xander and David eyeing their burgers. "Bring 'em; we'll have a picnic there."

•••••• ••

Xander hadn't thought about it until now, but it was odd pulling up to their home when the only things visible were trees. There was no driveway, no garage. Who would build a home like that? At least in this age of mass transit. It made him wonder how old the house was, who had designed it, who had built it, who had lived in it.

Dad stopped where the road did. He must have been thinking similar thoughts, for he said, "There's not even a curb to pull over to. I wonder if building a carport or a drive up to the house would be too expensive."

"I don't mind parking here," Mom said.

"Wait till it rains," David said, and laughed.

Mom laid her hand on Dad's arm. "Besides, I have a feeling this house is going to take everything we have."

That made Xander shudder. He opened the door, appreciative of the sun.

David carried the food. Mom had a blanket. As they approached the house, Xander thought about how he and David would begin the inspection as soon as they were settled in. He knew the best way to unearth the house's secrets was to have an open mind. In the movies, too many people missed important clues because they were looking for something else, some preconceived notion of what they would find. Even with this in mind, he couldn't help but think they might locate the bodies of the family who had disappeared. Most screenwriters these days would have them buried in the basement. But Xander liked the old Edgar Allen Poe stories like "The Black Cat" in which people were bricked-up in walls. Not always *after* being murdered.

Dad, Mom, and Toria tromped up the front steps. Dad swung the door open with a "Ta-da."

Mom said, "We'd better get a locksmith out here, first thing."

"Already taken care of," Dad said. "I called him from the car on the way to the park."

They streamed in. Xander stood at the bottom of the steps, his foot on the first one. David tested the banister's strength, then leaned against it. "Xander," he whispered. "'Member what we were talking about? About the place being haunted?"

Xander stepped closer. "Shhh."

"I can *feel* it." He said, "Can we share a room? Just for a while?"

Xander smiled. He was glad David had suggested it first. Now he had to be careful about appearing overeager. "Let's see how it goes."

"Okay, but . . ." David's voice trailed off, and he bowed his head.

"But?"

"I don't think I can stay here if I have to sleep alone."

"There's always Toria," Xander suggested.

David made a face. "That would be *worse*."

"Than *what*? Getting eaten by vampires?" Xander started up the steps.

"Don't say that!" David moved in close to him.

"I'm just kidding, David. Don't worry about it." They

stopped at the open door. Dust moats drifted in the gloom. They were catching the sunlight and were bright as stars in a black galaxy. The others were out of sight; their voices drifted out to Xander. They were obviously talking to one another, but now it didn't surprise Xander that they seemed to come from different places in the house and from different distances away. Standing next to him, David found his hand and gripped it. He looked at his little brother, who offered no other sign of fear.

"Besides," David said, "vampires don't *eat* you. They drink your blood."

Xander thought about responding with something wise like, "Those are normal vampires; this house has a different breed." But he figured he had scared David enough—had scared *himself* enough. So instead, he said, "Fine, Dr. Van Helsing. You're the expert." And with that, they stepped into the house together.

thirteen

WEDNESDAY, 3:17 P.M.

Victoria told everyone she wanted the room that had been decorated for a little boy, even though the one across and a bit down the hall from it had obviously belonged to a little girl. "Too pink," she called it.

"Should we let her pick *either* of them?" David whispered.

"Why not?" Xander asked.

"The little boy and the little girl?" David said, as though speaking to an imbecile.

"So?"

"They were *murdered*. What if their ghosts still think those are their rooms?"

Xander shook his head. "You're worrying too much. Just watch out for anything weird. Don't let your imagination get ahead of you."

"You sound like Dad."

Xander accepted that. "Which room do you want?"

"Not one of those. What room do *you* want? It's going to be *our* room, isn't it?"

Xander stood tall, stretching his spine. Maybe sharing a room for a while wasn't such a bad idea. As they got used to the house, and as they discovered—as they probably would—that it wasn't haunted, Xander could move into a room of his own. He patted his brother on the chest. "All right. Yeah. Sure. As long as I can put my posters on the wall."

"Not *Friday the 13th.*"

"No scary ones," Xander agreed. He gestured with his head. "Let's look down here."

They moved farther away from the central staircase, past the murdered boy's room.

No, no, no, he thought, *don't start that. Simply, the boy's room.*

He stopped at the door to what used to be a little girl's room. He nudged it open. It creaked into a shadow-filled room. Faint light came through two dirty windows and thin curtains—Mom had called them sheers—that may have been white at one time. There was an old dresser and a bed with a canopy. Didn't matter: Dad had said they would not sleep on any beds or bedding found here anyway. They were probably dirty and had bedbugs.

David said, "Toria's right: too pink. Let's keep looking."

The next room was dingy, dusty, and dark. Nothing about it appealed to either boy.

They moved to the next door which served the corner room on the front side of the house. Xander pushed it open, and they took a step in. This room had a chest of drawers against the far wall and a bed with a simple wooden headboard. Like the other room, two dirty windows let in meager light. The coolest part of the room was that one corner opened up into the tower, a five-sided room-within-a-room. Heavy curtains covered the tower windows, except for the center one, which—

Someone was standing in front of it.

Backlit by the window, the figure was nothing more than a black silhouette to Xander's eyes. David had spotted the shape as well. His hand found Xander's again and squeezed painfully. Xander realized both of them had stopped breathing. The only sound was the figure's labored breath, deep and heavy. The thing shifted. Its head appeared to turn toward them. When it spoke, its voice was baritone and gravelly: "Come in, boys."

David screamed first. It was long and high pitched. Xander's quick "Ahhh!" was almost completely lost in the sound of

David's fear. They turned together and knocked each other into the door frame. They were almost into the hall when they heard a familiar voice call their names. They were through the doorway and moving in separate directions, when they heard, "Boys! Boys! Come back!" and uncontrollable laughter.

Xander stopped and looked back. David had stopped as well, halfway through the doorway at the end of the hall. The boy's eyes were saucers of shock.

From the room: "Xander! David!"

They scowled at each other. Xander took a cautious step toward the door.

Dad stepped into the hallway between them. He looked at Xander, then at David. He said, "Sorry. Really." He stifled a laugh.

David, generally calm, cool, and collected, yelled at the top of his lungs, "That's not funny!"

Dad walked toward him. "I know, I know. I'm sorry. I couldn't help myself." He hugged his youngest son, who resisted, then gave in. He looked back at Xander with a guilty smile.

Xander shook his head and pointed at David. "What *he* said."

Dad nodded. "You guys have been whispering about this house since we talked to the real estate woman. I couldn't resist."

The muscles in Xander's face felt tight. He said, "You know what they say about payback."

Dad snickered. He said, "My boys, my brave young men."

Still pressed against him, David punched his father in the side.

Dad let out an exaggerated grunt and pushed back from him. "So," he said, "have you picked out a room?"

"We're *trying*," David said. "What about beds?"

"Your old beds will be here in a few days. I just have to tell the moving company we found a place."

"And till then?"

"We'll stay in the motel."

"Not here?" Xander asked.

Dad shook his head. "We have to do some cleaning first, get the utilities turned on, make sure everything's safe."

As if to punctuate his last word, Mom yelled, "Ed! Ed!" All three of them looked one way, then the other. It was impossible to tell where she was. Dad made a decision and ran toward the main staircase. Xander and David followed. Toria came out of her room, knocking David against the wall. They clambered down the stairs together. Dad stepped into the foyer, looked down the corridor to the kitchen, and called, "G!"

Her voice came back with an edge of panic: "Ed!"

He started for the kitchen. Xander stopped him. "Dad, in here."

Mom stood in the dining room near one of the windows. Dad pushed past the kids to reach her. "Are you all right? What's wrong?"

She pointed. Dust covered the floors. Most of it had been

75

disturbed by their own shuffling around. Near the walls, in corners, under furniture, it had remained thick and as unbroken as an arctic landscape. Here, in such a spot, were two footprints. They were from bare feet twice the size of Dad's. The toes were pointed toward the window, as though someone had stood there, watching.

CHAPTER

fourteen

WEDNESDAY, 5:30 P.M.

They were sitting at a big, round table in the café. Each of them leaned in toward the center.

"The door was unlocked," Dad whispered. "That's how *we* got in. Who knows how long the house had been open to anyone who tried the front door?"

"Or how long ago those footprints were made," Mom added.

"Mom," Xander said, "they were *fresh*. There was no dust in them, just bare wood."

"They were so big," David said.

"It was Bigfoot," Toria said, with a hint of danger.

"Toria," Xander said.

"Well, it was somebody with really big feet," Mom said, "but I don't think it was Bigfoot, honey. Not *the* Bigfoot."

"But he lives here," Toria said. "I read about it."

"Bigfoot's not real," David said.

"Is too."

"Okay, okay. Whether it was a guy with big feet or it was Bigfoot, doesn't really matter, I don't want him in my house. So, listen . . ."

The waitress stepped up behind Toria. She smiled inquisitively, taking in their conspiratorial postures. "Ya ready?"

Dad smiled apologetically. "Not yet. But how about waters all around?"

"Gotcha," she said and wandered away.

All faces turned back to Dad.

He said, "Tomorrow we all go over there and start cleaning. Xander and I will go through the whole house. Basement to attic. We'll see if anybody's there."

Toria inhaled sharply and covered her mouth. *A bit melodramatic*, Xander thought, but that was Toria.

"Or if there are ways to get in we don't know about," Dad said.

David said, "I want to search too."

Dad shook his head. "I don't think—"

Xander touched Dad's arm and said, "He can do it."

Dad studied Xander's face. Maybe he was trying to gauge whether Xander was sticking up for his brother because he thought David could handle it, or because he was going to use the opportunity to somehow scare Dae. Whatever he saw in Xander's eyes, he seemed to appreciate it. He nodded, said, "Okay. It'll be the King boys then."

David smiled. "And may God have mercy on anyone we find . . ."

"Because *we* won't!" Xander finished.

•••••••••

THURSDAY, 10:49 P.M.

The flashlight beams pushed away the inky blackness of the basement. The walls and floor were stone. Cobwebs and spiderwebs everywhere. David pointed out that he heard the squeaking of rodents and the click of their claws on the stone. "I don't like this," he said.

"No kidding," Xander said.

Dad said, "We'll just take a walk around. See if there's anything obvious. We don't have to move things around, or anything."

What they had seen so far was a basement full of wooden crates, loose lumber, and cardboard boxes that had mostly rotted away, spilling their contents of old clothes, dishes, and record albums onto the floor. The electricity was supposed to have been turned on, but it hadn't been when Dad last checked. It was impossible to tell how large the basement was. Their lights did not go far, and the area was divided by stone walls that seemed to Xander to be haphazardly placed. If it occupied the same square footage as the first floor, it would be big enough to install an Olympic-sized pool or maybe a couple bowling alleys.

"So what are we looking for?" David asked.

Dad said, "Evidence that someone is squatting down here."

"Squatting? Gross," David said.

Xander laughed.

"It means living somewhere you're not supposed to," Dad explained.

"Or *doing* something you're not supposed to," David said.

This time they all laughed. Their voices seemed to cut away some of the gloom. It made the search less creepy. Their flashlights came upon a wood-plank door. Xander and David looked to Dad.

"Let's check all the rooms. Keep your eyes open for doors or recesses that might lead to a sub-basement or root cellar or to the outside."

"This is like a video game," David said.

"It's like *And Then There Were None*," Xander corrected. "That's where all these people are stuck in a house and they're—"

"That's enough, Xander," Dad said.

They stood with their flashlights on the door. No one moved.

If Xander were directing this, he would have a camera approaching them from behind while they weren't looking. He spun around, panning the light back and forth.

"What?" David said, a little too shrill.

"Nothing. Thought I heard something."

No one moved toward the door. Xander said, "Dad?"

"All right." He moved to the door. Xander's heart leaped as a black figure sprung up in front of Dad. Then he realized it was Dad's shadow. Xander's and David's flashlights had created it. Dad pulled open the door. Its hinges squealed like a rat caught in a trap.

"And don't scare us," David said in a loud whisper.

Dad's light moved around the room, then he stepped back. He shut the door. "Nothing," he said. "And how about this . . ." He used his finger to draw a big cartoon face in the dust on the door. the figure's name was "Bob," and Dad had been drawing him since he'd been a kid. Bob was the family's unofficial mascot.

When he finished, Dad smiled and nodded. "There. Now we've marked this area as ours."

"I can think of another way to mark our territory," Xander said.

"Hey," Dad said. "None of that."

Together they moved through the basement, checking rooms and corners. They saw lots of spiders and rat poop, dust and dirt, but no people or indications that someone had ever lived down there. When the stairs came back around, Xander sighed with relief.

"What do the cops say?" Dad asked.

"Clear!" Xander called.

"All right, then," Dad said. "Onward and upward." He climbed the stairs, clicking his flashlight off as he neared the open door at the top.

"No *squatters*," Xander said, making the word sound as gross as he could.

David smiled and started up the stairs. "So what about *And Then There Were None?*" he said.

Xander thought again of the camera moving in the darkness toward him, and he bolted up the stairs right into David's back. "I'll tell you later. Just hurry it up."

CHAPTER

They'd gotten through half of the first floor when Mom
called them to lunch. PB&J and potato chips in the dining
room. She had cleaned the room well, and Xander was starting to see the house's potential as a nice home. Even the table
and chairs, left there by the previous owner, had been polished
to a nice shine. They didn't look nearly as battered and ruined
as when Xander had first seen them. Dad said the hardwood

floor needed resurfacing, but it looked fine to Xander, kind of rustic and retro.

"Have you been helping your mom, young lady?" Dad asked Toria.

"I cleaned the windowsills," she said proudly.

"That's it?" David asked.

"And my room!"

Mom nodded. "Mostly, she's been in her room." She handed Dad a paper plate with a sandwich cut diagonally. "I take it you haven't found anyone lurking in our house."

"No squatters," David said and broke up laughing.

Mom gave him a puzzled look.

Smiling, Xander shook his head to show that, at least in front of his mother, he was above such childish humor. He said, "We searched the whole basement."

"Talk about creepy," David said.

"Yeah," Xander agreed, "but we didn't find anybody."

"And no place where anybody's been staying," Dad added. "Or any way to get into the house."

Nonetheless, Mom looked worried. She said, "Could we put a lock on the basement door? Just in case?"

"Sure," Dad said. "We can bolt this place up like Fort Knox." He popped a chip into his mouth.

"We're about half-finished with this floor," Xander said.

Around a mouthful of sandwich, David said, "We're even looking in the closets and cupboards."

"Like anybody would hide in a *cupboard*," Xander said, glaring at Dad.

Dad shrugged. "Never know."

"Lots of gross stuff," David said.

Mom made a face. "Gross stuff?"

Dad said, "Just grime and trash. Stuff like that."

"Rat poop!" David said.

"Eeewww!" Toria said. "I'm not hungry anymore." Xander got an image of her as a mom.

"Rats?" Mom said.

"More like mice," Dad said. "I'll set some traps this afternoon."

"And spiders," David said.

"David, stop. You're scaring Toria," Dad said. To the King ladies he said, "There are not as many spiders as you'd think for a house abandoned so long and in the woods. We'll bug-bomb tonight when we leave."

"Cool!" David said.

"They're not *real* bombs," Xander told him.

David frowned. "Oh."

"They're still cool." Dad raised his eyebrows at David. "Lots of smoke. You can help me."

David nodded. He was pushing an entire half sandwich into his mouth.

Mom surveyed her family, sitting around the table in their new home. "Well, guys," she said, smiling, "think we found our dream house?"

"Yeah!" Toria chimed.

Mouth full of sandwich, David said something indiscernible.

Xander scowled at him. "What?"

He held up a finger, swallowing painfully. "I said . . . we're the Dreamhouse Kings!"

Mom laughed. "I like it. The Dreamhouse Kings." Her eyebrows shot up as she remembered something. Pointing to Dad, she said, "Honey, don't forget your appointment."

Dad stopped chewing; his eyes went wide. He looked at his watch. He swallowed, said, "You boys continue without me. I'm meeting the district superintendent at the school. School starts next Monday, and I haven't even toured the place."

Mom laughed. "Not to mention that you haven't met the teachers, set up your office, reviewed the school calendar—"

"I know, I know," Dad said. He shrugged. "When they hired me I told them I didn't have time to do everything. They said not to worry about it." He smiled. "Getting someone of my caliber is worth a little disorganization. That's what they said."

Mom *aaahhh*'ed. "How sweet."

"So what, you want us to look for intruders *alone*?" Xander asked.

"You'll be fine," he said, glancing at his watch again. He stood. "I have to run by the motel, take a shower, and change." He grabbed the rest of his sandwich and hurried out.

•••••• ••

The sun had crested in the sky and started its descent toward the horizon by the time Xander and David brought their inspection to the second floor.

"This is great," David said. "We wanted to search the house anyway. Now we got Dad's help, and we don't have to sneak around. I hope he's back before we get to the attic. I don't want to go up there alone."

"Hey! You're not alone."

"You know what I mean."

"Let's start with the far bedrooms and work our way back," Xander suggested.

As they walked the corridor, their heads swiveled back and forth to look into each room they passed. Toria's bedroom had been swept and the windows washed. It was amazing how much light came in now that the filth was off the glass. It would be even better when they finally got to cleaning the outside.

"Shaping up," David said.

They passed the pink room and the bedroom that was going to be theirs—the corner room with the tower. *Duh.* They hadn't had a chance to do anything with it yet. It was as gloomy as ever.

"Lot left to do," Xander said.

"Yeah, but we haven't found any graves or coffins with vampires or anything like that. I was thinking the basement would be the place for those things."

They stopped outside the open door of the last room on the other side of the hall. Looking back, Xander was struck by how long the corridor really was. It continued beyond the foyer and grand staircase. All told, it was fifty feet, maybe longer. Even then, the far end of the hall bent into another corridor that led only to what Mom and Dad called "the servants' quarters." Xander would have called it a second master bedroom, because it had a walk-in closet and a private bathroom. He thought servants should also have their own kitchenette so they had privacy on their days off; that room didn't have a kitchenette. Still, he hoped it was inhabitable by the time Dae was ready for his own room—Xander would love to claim the "servants' quarters" for himself.

He said, "I don't know. I get the feeling there's more to this house than it's showing us."

They went into the bedroom and flipped on their flashlights. More of the same: dust, old furniture, peeling wallpaper.

"Hey, look at this," Xander said. His light had captured a framed picture on a nightstand. The photograph was faded, almost white, the faces indistinct. But Xander could tell it had once been a color portrait of a family: a man and woman, a little girl whose size would have made her three or four years old, and a blond-haired boy, a few years older.

"Is that the family who was murdered?" David whispered almost reverently.

"I bet." He was thinking how the fading of the photograph made them look like ghosts. In *The Picture of Dorian Gray*, a painting of a man changed to reflect the ravages of his evil deeds instead of reflecting the person himself. It seemed to Xander this picture instead continued to show the reality of the family: faded from the earth, faded from memory. His heart ached for them, for the people they never became. Even the dad, who had done the dirty deed. If the house had gotten to him, was anything he did after that his fault? Wouldn't it be like being hypnotized and forced to do something against your will? Xander resolved again to be alert against the house's power. His family would not suffer the fate of that family. He would not let them fade away.

"Weird they left so many personal things," David said.

"But not everything," Xander said. "Like they left in a hurry."

"If the father murdered them, why would they take anything at all?"

"Maybe they were trying to get away from the house. Maybe it was the police who took their clothes and stuff. Evidence."

David went to a closet. He opened the door and flashed his light inside. "Hey, what's this?" he said.

Leaning into one of the corners was a wood pole, similar to a broom handle. One end had a brass cap with a small hook coming off it.

"I don't know . . . wait a minute, yes, I do." Xander swept the light over the ceiling. He stopped on a rectangular hatch. "The attic entrance. That pole hooks the door and pulls it down. I saw it in a movie."

"We should wait for Dad," David said. "He'd want to come."

Xander smiled. "He'd want to, or you'd want him to?"

David stared at the door for a long time. Finally, he said, "I'm all right."

"Okay, then. Come on."

CHAPTER

Sixteen

Thursday, 2:29 p.m.

It was a bust. The attic turned out to be nothing but dust, mouse poop, spiderwebs, some decomposing cardboard boxes of disintegrated clothes like in the basement, and a few pieces of furniture. They opened a wooden chest, big enough for a man to fit inside, but it was just full of papers—a child's schoolwork, sheet music, stuff like that. They cautiously approached a large wardrobe—definitely where Xander would have hidden if he were a creepy guy hiding in someone else's house. But it contained only a dress and some other clothes on wooden hangers. The space up there was smaller than the other floors, probably having to do with the way the roof canted inward, he figured.

Xander was glad to have cleared the attic without relying on his father. He was also relieved they hadn't uncovered some crazy maniac living up there . . . relieved and a little disappointed. *That* would have been something to call his best friend, Dean, about. Danielle too.

They clambered down the hatch's built-in steps, then used the pole to shove the whole thing back into place. David reached up and slapped at Xander's hair and shoulders. Clouds of dust billowed off him. Xander returned the favor, then said, "Let's check our bedroom. Maybe we can clear the whole house before Dad gets home."

"That'd be cool," David agreed.

Heading to their room, Xander pointed his beam at a narrow door in the corridor wall.

"Check the linen closet," he told David and stepped into the bedroom. Corners, closet, tower: nothing, nothing, nothing. At least no intruders or hidey-holes. In the closet, he did find a garment draped over a wire hanger.

"David," he called over his shoulder, "check under the bed."

He stepped farther into the closet to examine the clothes. It appeared to be a man's suit. Old-fashioned with wide lapels and pinstripes. He remembered something like it from the movie *Bugsy*. A zoot suit, it was called. He tapped it with the end of his flashlight, igniting a small explosion of dust from the fabric. He coughed and waved his hand in front of his face. He left the closet and shut the door. Scanning the room, his brother was nowhere in sight.

"David! Where are you, dude?" He bent and flashed the light under the bed, but David wasn't hiding there. Back in the hall-way, he opened the linen closet door. It was narrow and deep. The shelves started a few feet in, leaving a space for maybe brooms or a mop bucket in front of them. His eyes went from the floor to the top shelf. Empty. He shut the door.

"David!" he yelled again. His voice echoed, then cut short, as though whatever messed with the sounds had rippled past, snagging his call. A third time, he yelled for his brother. He flashed his light into the room they had checked first. Letting out a deep sigh, he entered and opened the closet door. Again, nothing. Back in the hallway, he yelled, "David, this isn't funny. Remember how you felt when Dad scared us? Don't mess around."

His voice came back to him: *Don't mess around.* Oh, now the auditory tricks were getting outright scary. From up the hall, his own voice barked out again: *Don't mess around.* His stomach was tightening. He didn't know whether to stand still, look for David, or run like a madman to the front door.

Twenty feet away, a figure stepped out of a bedroom.

"David?" Xander whispered.

"Don't mess around," the figure said in Xander's voice and stepped closer.

It was Toria, with that blasted bear in her arms. She squeezed its paw, and it said, "Don't mess around."

"*Victoria!*" Xander yelled, stomping toward her. "Stop that! Where's David?"

"I haven't seen him," she said, frightened by his anger.

"Go back in your room. Stop messing with that bear. I mean it." He followed her into her room, checked the closet, and then he realized: one of the second floor's three bathrooms was between here and the end of the hall. He hurried to it and knocked on the closed door. "David, are you in there? Didn't you hear me calling?" He knocked again, then tried the handle. It was unlocked, the bathroom empty.

Now, not only his stomach felt constricted, but his heart.

"David!" he screamed with everything he had. He ran to the nearest door, the bedroom they would make their own.

Let him be here. Let him be here. Just lost in imagining what our room would be like.

But it was empty. And the closet was empty.

His mom yelled up from below: "Xander, what is it? Is everything all right? Is Dae with you?"

Xander surged into the hall, intent on getting Mom's help. Whether she would blame him for losing his brother didn't matter now.

Movement in the corner of his vision. He looked. David

was standing in the hall, back by the first rooms they had checked. A gash above his eyebrow trickled blood. He looked dazed.

"Xander?" Mom called. Her footsteps clopped on the stairs.

Xander called over his shoulder. "Got it, Mom! Everything's okay!"

"David's okay?"

"Yeah! Just . . . uh . . . bathroom."

Her footsteps descended, echoed in the foyer, and were gone.

Xander rushed to David. "Where were you? What happened?"

"You won't believe me if I tell you."

"Dae, what happened?"

He prodded the cut on his brother's forehead.

David flinched away. He touched it himself, looked at the blood on his fingertips. "Whoa," he said.

Xander had David's blood on his fingers as well. It frightened Xander more than a simple bonk on the head should have. "David—" he began.

David grabbed Xander's arms. "I mean it, you wouldn't believe me if I told you."

"You gotta—"

"I'll *show* you!"

"Show me what?"

"Come on." David opened the linen closet door.

"Were you hiding?" Xander said. "I checked in there."

"Shhh. Just go." He pushed on Xander's back, trying to get him in the closet.

Xander resisted, sidestepped away. "What are you *doing*? I'm not going in there."

David let out an exasperated breath. "I was going to scare you. I went in there and closed the door."

"I told you I looked."

"Something happened. I went somewhere."

"Where?"

"Just go. Please?"

Xander looked from his brother to the closet. He shook his head. "This is some kind of trick."

David's eyes got big. "It *is*! But not like you're thinking. Do it!" When he realized Xander wasn't budging, he said, "Okay. Just do what I do. Promise?"

Xander closed his eyes. "Okay, okay."

David stepped into the closet and turned around. He pulled the door partially shut, said, "Do what I'm doing exactly." He shut the door.

Xander waited. "Okay?" he said to the door. "David?" He opened the door. His brother was gone.

CHAPTER

Seventeen

THURSDAY, 2:36 P.M.

The closet shelves were empty. The walls seemed intact. The ceiling and floor showed no sign of harboring a vent or door. David was just gone. There one second, not there the next.

Xander stepped in and felt the shelves. They were solidly mounted. He poked at the walls, on the sides, and behind the shelves. They felt firm and unmoving. "David," he called. He sighed. "All right, I'm doing exactly what you did."

He pulled the door completely closed. Blackness engulfed him. The floor seemed to move as though the closet were an elevator. But his stomach didn't lurch the way it did on elevators. A wind swirled around him and was gone. He felt dizzy. Someone wrapped his arms around him and squeezed. "David?" he said.

But then he realized it wasn't a *someone*. The walls of the closet had squeezed in, becoming so narrow he had to turn sideways. Slits appeared in the closet door. Level with his eyes. Light poured in, blinding him.

"David!" he yelled, panicked now. He pushed against a side wall. It flexed a little and made a metallic popping sound. He pushed his behind into the back wall. The same kind of flexing. The same sound. He pushed his palm into the front door. It felt like cold metal. "David!" he screamed again.

A metallic *click* and *thunk*. The door opened, but its width was now no more than eighteen inches. David stood smiling, holding the door, a step below him. Beyond David, sunlight came in from huge windows. This was *not* the second-floor hallway. He peered around. He was standing in something like a metal coffin. A coat hook almost snagged a nostril.

"What's going on?" he said to David. "Where are we?"

"Step out and look."

Xander squeezed through the metal threshold and stepped down to a tiled floor. He was standing in a short corridor. To his right, the corridor met another, wider hallway, which disappeared around a corner. He walked to the corner. Windows lined one wall running the length of the hallway. What lay beyond seemed familiar to Xander, but he couldn't immediately place it. He turned to see what he had just emerged from. It was a locker, one of a series that occupied the entire wall. They were all painted bright blue.

He said, "What the—"

"We're in the school!" David said.

"What school?"

"Our school. The one we're going to next week."

Xander recognized it now. Outside the windows was the school's yard of lush grass and picnic tables. Beyond that, the parking lot. In fact, Xander realized, their 4Runner was in one of the slots. He pushed his face close to David's and whispered, "Dad's here."

"What do we do?" David asked.

Xander smiled. "Let's look around." He walked back to the locker and shut the door. "Remember this number. One-nineteen." That made him think of something. He asked David, "That *is* how you got back, right? Through the locker?"

"Yeah, that's how I got this." He pointed to the gash above his eyebrow.

The two of them rounded the corner and headed toward a set of double doors at the far end. Every forty feet or so, the lockers gave way to windowed classroom doors. The lights were off in each one. Soon, the place would be full of kids and teachers with hardly a moment of inactivity. Schools were not meant to be empty. At times like this they seemed lonely and forlorn. Almost sacred, like empty churches.

Ooh, Xander thought. *School . . . sacred . . . Two words that did not belong together.*

He felt like a trespasser. Which, he guessed, they were. He had not asked to come here. In fact, you could say, he came by force. Besides, his dad was the principal. What were they going to do to him? This was one of those times he'd rather not find out.

David asked, "Why the school, do you think?"

"I don't know."

"Do you think it was an accident, or did somebody plan it?"

"I don't know," Xander said again.

"Do you think other people know about it?"

"David, I don't know. I don't know any more than you do. Anything else?"

"Yeah, do you think all the lockers lead somewhere?"

Xander stopped.

David took three more steps before realizing Xander was no longer by his side. He looked back inquisitively.

"One way to find out," Xander said.

David took in the lockers nearest them. "Really?" he said, unsure.

"How else are we going to know?"

"Do we *have* to know?"

Xander thought knowledge was like candy: you never turned it down, especially if you didn't have to work too hard to get it. And especially *cool* knowledge: how to assemble and fire an MI6, how to get your movies to play at Sundance, which lockers were really teleportation devices.

"You don't want to know?" Xander asked.

David thought about it. His face slowly twisted into an I'm-gonna-eat-it-but-I-know-I'm-not-gonna-like-it expression. "Yeah . . . I kinda do."

Xander stepped to the nearest locker, number 76. "You or me?" he asked.

David did not approach. "Um . . . why not both of us?"

"Because in *The Fly*, two life forms teleported at the same time and ended up all mixed together. As much as I love you and all that, I don't want to *be* you."

"I think I saw something like that in *SpongeBob*. It was pretty gross."

"So . . . you or me?"

"You?" David said, closing one eye.

Xander shrugged. He put his foot in the locker.

David stopped him. "No, no, wait. I'll do it. I did it the first time; I can do it again."

Hey, if Dae wanted to. "You sure?"

David climbed in without a word. Xander started to shut the door. David stopped it with his hand. "What if I end up in somebody else's linen closet . . . or worse?"

"What's worse? Like on their dining room table while they're eating? A trash compactor? You want me to go?"

David closed his eyes. "Shut the door."

Xander pushed it until the latch clicked tight.

The scream was hideous. For the first time Xander understood the meaning of the term "bloodcurdling." He pulled up on the latch. His fingers slipped off. The scream went on. He pulled again. Got it. He opened the door. David was hunched over in the tight space.

Laughing.

"Did I get you?" he said.

Xander half-yelled, "You and Dad! What's with you?"

David looked around. "I didn't go anywhere."

"Unfortunately." Xander slammed the door. He stormed toward the double doors at the end of the hall, then pulled up. He turned back to the closed locker door, said, "David, don't keep it up. Don't make me come open that door." The latch rose by itself and the door opened. David popped his head out, displaying a sheepish smile.

Xander said, "You're getting smarter."

David stepped out and approached him.

"Look," Xander said, "all this is weird enough. This is not the time for practical jokes. Don't you think that whatever can take you from home to school faster than a blink could make you scream like you just did?"

David lost his smile. He bowed his head.

"You could have really been in pain, dying," Xander continued. "If we're going to be there for each other, you can't cry wolf. Understand?"

David nodded.

"Next time you scream, it might be for real and I won't come because I think you're joking."

"I know what 'cry wolf' means," David said quietly.

Xander gripped David's shoulder and gave him a little shake. "It's okay. Just don't do it again." When David looked up, Xander saw in his face that he really got it. He didn't want David to be like Dad with his practical jokes, especially now; and he didn't want himself to be like Dad with unending lectures. So he patted David on the back and they walked on.

CHAPTER

eighteen

As they approached the double doors, they heard voices. They looked at each other with wide eyes, looked around for a place to hide. Xander's first thought was the lockers, but David's test didn't prove anything. Any of these lockers could be portals to another place. He looked at David, whose eyes went from the lockers to Xander's face. He had considered the lockers as well and had ruled them out. And they were too far from the nearest classroom to hide in there—*if* the door was even unlocked. He pointed and David moved to the wall beside the door as Xander did the same on the other side. They pressed their bodies against the wall and waited. The voices did not get louder. One of them was Dad's. Xander came off the wall and stepped before a little wire-embedded window set in the door nearest him. Beyond the door was another wide hallway and another set of double doors. Looking down the hallway to his left, he saw his father talking to a man in coveralls. Beside the man was a rolling cart, upon which were a big red toolbox, an assortment of small boxes, and small brown paper bags open at the top. Xander could hear the rhythm of their conversation, but not their words.

Dad was smiling, nodding, probably telling the man about his family, the move here. The man laughed, stooped to reach a lower shelf on his cart, and stood again. He handed Dad what looked like a stack of wooden playing cards. Xander realized they were mousetraps. Dad said something, and the man stooped again for another stack. He turned one of the paper bags over. The clattering sound of dumped nails reached Xander's ears. The man dropped his stack of mousetraps into the bag, then held it open for Dad to do the same. He rolled up the top and handed it to Xander's father. Dad nodded and extended his hand. The man grabbed it and they shook. Dad turned and looked directly at Xander. Xander dropped down below the window, noticing David had been tiptoeing to peer out the window in the other door.

David whispered, "Did he see you?"

"I don't think so." He rose again, expecting to see Dad looming just on the other side. But there he was saying his good-byes and turning to walk in the other direction. Xander caught David's attention and jerked his head to go. They walked quietly away, toward the short corridor at the end of the hallway and locker one-nineteen.

David whispered, "How did they not hear you yelling at me?"

"Or your screams?" Xander thought about it. "Maybe they met out there after all that."

"I hope so. I guess we'll find out when Dad gets home."

"It's not our fault," Xander said, repeating his thoughts from earlier.

"We'll show him what happened. He *can't* blame us."

Xander stopped walking. He looked back at the double doors, saw no sign of anyone. He hunched down to be at David's eye level. "I don't think we should tell Dad," he said. "Or Mom," he added in case that wasn't clear.

"But . . . why not?"

It was a fair question. They were a close family, not in the habit of keeping things from one another. What was embarrassing or personal, dreams and fears—it was all fair game in the King household. Mom had said the world was tough enough without having to worry about hiding things in your own home, from your own family. "So what if you do stupid things?" she'd said. "We're humans, not robots."

Recently, Xander had done some things he had not shared with his family. Just before school finals, a friend had shown him the answer key to the biology exam. Xander hadn't asked how he'd gotten it. But he *had* studied it and aced the test. Another time, Dean had bummed some cigarettes off his older brother, and they'd smoked them behind the school. His dad would have been disappointed, but wouldn't have jumped on him too badly. Still, they were secrets he'd kept from the family. He felt both bad about that and excited to have things they didn't know about. He figured when the time was right, he'd share these experiences and the family's openness would be complete again. Until then, he'd keep these indiscretions in a little footlocker in his mind. The linen closet's fast-track to school would go in there, as well. If his little brother had never needed a footlocker, Xander would have been happy for him. But something told him they were playing with fire. The fewer people burned, the better.

"Something like this will freak them out. They might decide we shouldn't live there. Then we couldn't explore anymore. If the house has a closet like that, what *else* could there be?" He nodded as if to say, *Yeah, this could be fun.*

They went around the corner and David frowned and Xander knew why: his brother didn't like secrets, but neither did he want to move away from the house. At last he said, "Okay, it's just between us. But if it turns bad, we tell them."

Xander stood straight. "Of course."

David stepped into the locker first. Xander shut it and counted to ten. When he opened it again, David was gone.

"I will never get used to this," he said, then stepped into the locker.

Five seconds later, he stepped out of the linen closet into the upstairs hallway, where David was waiting.

nineteen

THURSDAY, 11:32 P.M.

Xander and David's late-night conversations had become habit. It helped both of them process the day's events and plan for tomorrow. So this night, like the two before, they faced each other in the motel bed.

"Do you miss Danielle?" David whispered.

"Of course."

"Maybe you'll find a new girlfriend."

"I doubt it. Maybe you will."

David smiled. A year ago, he would have protested that no such thing would *ever* happen, not in a thousand years.

They fell silent. Their parents breathed. Something ticked, ticked.

"I don't think Dad saw us," David said.

"No," Xander agreed. An hour after they had stepped back into the corridor from the closet, from the *school*, Dad had returned home. If he had seen them peering at him from the windows in the doors, he had not let on. He had simply gone about organizing the rest of the upstairs exploration. Both of his sons said they could handle it and had urged him to find something else to do. He had wandered off, moping theatrically. By the time it became too dark to continue, Mom had made short work of the kitchen and butler's pantry—that's what she called the small room with cabinets and counters between the kitchen and dining room. Toria had proclaimed her room ready for furniture and decorations. Dad had walked the grounds, finding nothing of particular interest. And the boys had finished the second-floor investigation. They were all so wiped out, Toria had suggested turning off the television midway through *America's Funniest Home Videos*. Despite its ranking as their favorite show, everyone had agreed.

But now, an hour later, the brothers were wide-awake, sharing their thoughts.

David whispered, "Do you think the closet's the only place that moves you from one place to another?"

"One place like that in the *whole world* is enough," Xander said. Then he thought about how his father had seemed to instantly shift from the dining room to another part of the house when they had first been here. "I think there might be other spots like that in the house. We just haven't found them."

"Yet," David added.

"I was thinking. What if the spots come and go? I saw that in a movie. These portals moved around. Once it was in a phone booth. Another time, in the bathroom of a Chinese restaurant. Same portal, moving around."

"That would suck."

"Yeah. What if you were taking a shower and suddenly you were standing in the middle of a football field at halftime?"

"*Naked?*"

"Shhh." Xander nodded. He could tell David was thinking about it.

"Ooh. That would *really* suck," his brother decided.

"I don't think that could happen."

"Why not?"

"With the closet and the locker, you know what to do to make it work: you step in and shut the door. In the middle of a field, what would you do to return?"

David made a sour face. "Maybe you don't."

"Well, that tells you something, doesn't it?"

"Like what?"

"Like we don't know anything about what we're dealing with. It could be dangerous."

"So . . . should we tell Mom and Dad?"

Toria popped up from the side of the bed nearest David. "Tell them what?"

Both boys screamed in whispers.

"Toria, go back to bed," Xander said.

"Tell Mom and Dad what?"

"That David feels like throwing up."

"Ugh!" She was back in the rollaway before Xander realized she was gone.

"And no," Xander said, almost touching David's nose with his finger. "Don't tell them. Not yet."

David didn't respond for a minute. Then he said, "You know how when we got back from the school, we checked the rest of the second floor and closed closet doors with one of us in it? Shouldn't we go back and do that in the rest of the house?"

"I guess."

"The basement?"

"Everywhere." Xander knew what David was thinking: they'd both been surprised when nothing turned up down there. Now they were going to give it another chance. He thought of all the rooms down there, all the doors. Lots of places to hide a portal. And if there was any correlation between the connected places—the relative brightness and friendliness of a linen closest and a school—where might a portal in the dark, creepy basement lead?

He whispered, "We need to stick together." David said nothing. His eyes were closed. "David?"

A slight snore.

"'Night, Dae," Xander said, and rolled over.

CHAPTER

FRIDAY, 11:17 A.M.

The power came on with a *pop! pop! pop!* Xander was standing at the top of the stairs on the second-floor landing when an electric light flared out from the big entryway chandelier. Then three bulbs exploded, one after the other.

"They're on!" he called.

Several lamps in the upstairs corridor came to life as well. One of them blazed bright and went out. The master bedroom suite was down the hall on the opposite side of the house from the kids' bedrooms. Dad hurried out of there now, his eyes surveying the corridor's ceiling lamps.

Down the hall in the other direction, David came out of their bedroom. "Lights on here too!" he said.

Dad said, "I see."

Xander pointed. "Some lights just blew on the chandelier."

Dad nodded as he descended the stairs, two at a time. "Old wiring, plus water and rodent damage, dirt in the sockets . . . I'm gonna throw the breakers until we know it's safe."

"Awww," David moaned.

"Won't be long," Dad said. He disappeared into the corridor under the boys, heading for the kitchen and the basement stairs.

Smoke coiled up from the blown bulbs in the chandelier. "Cool," David said.

Xander elbowed him. "That's *not* cool." He headed toward their bedroom with a bucket of sudsy water. Dad had said their furniture was arriving in the afternoon, and if they wanted to set up their room, it had to be clean first.

David followed him into the bedroom. They had positioned their flashlights on the floor and dresser to illuminate the areas they were cleaning. David had apparently dropped the broom when the lights came on. He picked it up now and began sweeping a pile of dust toward the door. Xander sat the bucket down by one of the windows. He pulled a washcloth out of the water and lathered up the glass. The windows and frames were so filthy, glass cleaner and paper towels simply didn't cut it.

David said, "When are we going to look for more portals?"

"When we get a chance, I guess."

David swept a big cloud into the hallway. Granules of dirt and other debris rained into the hardwood floor and linen closet door on the other side of the hall. He turned around, leaned on the broom handle, and said, "I thought we were going to do it today."

Xander continued to inscribe big, soapy circles on the window. He said, "You want a bedroom, don't you?"

"Yeah, but . . ."

Xander had to smile. "You thought putting your new room together would be the most excitement you'd have after we got here."

"Guess I was wrong." He looked back through the door, at the linen closet.

Xander said, "Don't even think of going in there on your own."

"I'm not."

Xander didn't like the way he said it.

Their bedroom faced the front of the house. As Xander wiped away the soap, he saw a big moving van pull up to the end of the road.

•••••••••

Until now, Xander had lived in the same house, in the same room, his entire life. That room had been too small to be creative with the placement of the furniture. The most they could do was swap the position of their bunk beds and dresser, change the posters on the walls, and alternate who got to sleep on top.

The bedroom in their new house was huge. Xander had no idea how much fun simply arranging furniture could be. Using bunk beds to save floor space was no longer necessary, and the boys quickly decided to have their own beds with no one above or below them. Each boy had wanted to put his bed in the tower. When the argument got loud, Dad had ruled that neither of them could use it. So the tower became their homework and reading area, with a writing desk and beanbag chair. They had voted to keep the dresser that was already in the room, as well as their old one from Pasadena. That way, each boy would have his own dresser for the first time in their lives.

"I don't know what to do with all the space," David said with a big grin. He was looking into one of the empty drawers of their old dresser, which a losing toss of a coin had awarded him. Neither dresser mattered to Xander, but after he ended up with the one from their new house, he wondered if his things would disappear from any of the drawers. He imagined a pile of boxers suddenly appearing on some family's kitchen counter one day.

Each boy would also get his own night table and bedside lamp. It was almost like having your own room. But not.

Dad's music pounded from the master bedroom. Most of the lyrics and high notes didn't make it as far as the brothers' bedroom, but the bass thumped in the floors and off the walls.

Xander opened a box full of rolled posters and began sorting through them. He selected one and flattened it against the wall above his bed. The edges were torn, the tips of the corners lost long ago. It was a lithograph of a tiled mosaic hanging in Naples' Museo Archeologico Nazionale that featured a scene of Alexander the Great at the Battle of Issus. Xander was named after the ancient Greek king of Macedon.

It was a family tradition, dating as far back as anyone could remember, to name King children after great kings and queens. Fortunately, the practice did not extend to marrying people with royal names. That would really crimp their pursuits of love. Still, Mom insisted there was a Queen Gertrude. Dad said only in Shakespeare's *Hamlet*, and that didn't count.

The Alexander in the poster had long sideburns, down to his jawline—the guy would have been hip today, twenty-three hundred years after his death. Xander touched his own face. He could not grow sideburns yet, just a bit of fuzz; as soon as he could, he would.

"Whatcha think?" he asked David, who had settled on the floor with his PSP. He glanced up at the poster.

"Aren't you sick of looking at that? I am."

Xander let the poster spin back into a roll. He said, "Just because you don't put up the one Mom and Dad gave *you*."

"Michelangelo's *David*? The guy's *naked*."

"It's art."

David made a disgusting sound with his lips. "I'll find a different poster of King David, thank you."

Footsteps in the hallway drew their attention. The clomping boots of the moving men. When they'd arrived, all they wanted to do was grumble about having to haul the stuff through the woods to the house. Then Dad had slipped each of them some extra cash and that was that.

"This one?" someone said.

Another answered, "No, down there. She said by the bedroom." A man came into view carrying a box. He opened the linen closet door and stepped in to slide the box onto one of the shelves. Another mover, coming up behind, bumped the door and it swung shut.

David gasped.

The door didn't latch, however, and the second man kicked it open with his boot. The first man turned in the closet and took the box from his colleague. The second man looked in at them. "Hey, boys."

Xander and David were too stunned to answer. The man gave them a puzzled look, then both movers pushed the closet door shut and clomped away. David turned from the open dresser drawer to stare open-mouthed at Xander, who returned the expression.

David said, "He almost . . ."

Xander nodded. "And another thing . . ." He walked to the linen closet door. David moved up behind him. Xander opened it. Two boxes inside. "It must only work with people."

"Good thing. We'd lose all our towels."

"We'd get them back dirty," Xander said, "along with some kid's schoolbooks."

When they shut the door, they jumped. Dad was standing there. He had turned down the music and they hadn't noticed.

"How you guys doin'?" Dad said.

"Good, good," Xander said, a little too quickly.

"Fine," David said in that higher Toria voice he got when he was scared or nervous.

Dad looked past them into their room. "Getting settled in there?"

"Getting there," Xander said, and went into the bedroom. David and Dad followed. Xander sat on his bare mattress. David sat on his, facing Xander.

"What do you think?" Dad said. "Is this going to work?"

Xander looked around the room appreciatively. "It's cool."

"Yeah," David agreed.

"So . . ." Dad looked from son to son. "Stay here tonight?"

"Really?" David said, hopping up.

Dad said, "If we can get the lights back on." He looked at his watch. "An electrician should be by anytime now."

"All right!" David said.

Xander smiled his agreement. Dad scanned the floor near the walls. "You haven't seen any mice up here, have you?"

Xander shook his head. "Did you catch some?"

"A couple in the kitchen cabinets." He put his finger to his lips in a hushing gesture. "Don't tell your mother."

"Can I see?" David asked.

"Next time."

David furled his brow. "Do they have a mouse problem at the school?"

Xander kicked his leg, then stood to make it look like an accident.

"I don't know," Dad said. "Why?"

Before David could complete the task of wedging his foot into his mouth, Xander said, "I was telling him that rodents are everywhere out here in Hicksville. Not just in old houses."

"Yep," Dad agreed. "They're everywhere." He turned to leave then stopped at the door. "Mom's got the boxes of sheets and blankets in our room. Come get some."

"Be right there," Xander told him.

When he was gone, Xander punched David in the arm. "Idiot."

David frowned. "I'm not used to secrets."

"Everybody has secrets," Xander said, irritated. He brushed past David on his way out the door. Over his shoulder, he said, "Even this house."

●●●●●●●●

Mom was sitting on her bed when Xander looked in. She was examining the pages of a photo album that was open beside her. With her hair falling over her face, he thought at first she was crying. He rapped gently on the master bedroom door. He was relieved to see a beaming smile when she looked up.

"Hey, Xander. Come sit." She patted a clean spot on the bed. Boxes and items wrapped in newspaper covered the rest.

"I came for our sheets and blankets," he said. "Dad said you had a box."

"Oh, sit with your mom a sec, will ya?"

On the way over, he glanced around. "Big," he said.

"Needs some work." She was talking about the old wallpaper, stained and hopelessly outdated. "I like it, though."

When he sat, she tapped a picture in the album. "Remember this?"

Xander about six years old, standing next to Mickey Mouse in front of Sleeping Beauty's Castle at Disneyland. Xander's face was twisted in terror, his face glistening with tears. His mouth was open so wide, you could almost see that little hanging thing at the back of his throat. *Uvula*, he thought it was called. What made it worse was David—three years old, big happy grin, holding Mickey's white-gloved hand.

Xander frowned. "You made me stand next to him. I thought he was creepy." He thought about it. "David was too young to know better, that's all."

She smiled, closed the book. She touched his hand. "I want to show you something." She stood and went to a bookcase, where a half-dozen ceramic figurines had been unwrapped and were on display. She selected one and returned to the bed. She rotated it in her hands. It was a chipped and faded ceramic rooster, about a foot high. He knew it meant a lot to her.

"Nana gave you that before she died," he said. Cancer had taken his grandmother when Xander was two. He sometimes thought he remembered her face, but couldn't be sure.

Mom nodded. "And *her* mother gave it to her. She brought it over from Portugal, when she immigrated to the States. She used to say it was the only thing they had left from the old country, except our blood." She pushed her fingers into a hole in the base of the rooster and pulled something out. It was a fat roll of dollar bills. The outside one was a twenty.

"Mom!" he said in a hoarse whisper.

She held up the roll. She said, "It was going to be a surprise, but this move has been so hard on you . . . It's for your car."

"My *car*?"

"It's not that much yet, and you have to chip in, but maybe by the time you're sixteen . . ."

"But how . . . ?"

"You know we don't have a lot of extra money. When you were born, your father and I decided I'd quit my job and be a full-time mom. That made things tight, but . . ." Her eyes scanned his face. "It was the right decision. Last year, when you started talking about a car, I realized we weren't ready for something like that. The car, gas, insurance . . ." She shook her head. "I started putting a little aside every month. I cut more coupons, didn't go to the hair salon so much."

"Mom . . ." He didn't know what else to say.

"It added up," she said, looking at the wad. She seemed as amazed by its size as Xander was.

"How much is it?" A pang of guilt rippled through him for asking.

"Almost two thousand, but I hope we'll have more by the time you turn sixteen in January."

"Two *grand*?" He leaned over the album and threw his arms around her neck. "Thank you."

"Now, Xander, you have to contribute. I only meant to—"

"I will! I will! I'll get a job as soon as I can!"

"Your bedding is right there. David's too." She indicated a box on the bed.

Unable to stifle his grin, he stood and picked it up. "Thank you," he whispered again.

CHAPTER

twenty-one

The bulbs in the bathroom emitted only a dim, yellowish glow. *Better than nothing*, Xander thought, standing in front of the toilet bowl in only his boxers. The electrician had kept the power off in some parts of the house—the basement, the library, the far hallway on the second floor. He'd explained that some wiring and fixtures needed replacing first.

He flushed. The toilet shook and rattled like an excited dog at the end of a short leash. The water in the bowl disappeared in a loud *whoosh*. It filled again with a choking-gurgling sound that made Xander believe stepping into the woods to relieve himself would prove a better experience. At the sink, he turned on the faucet. Water did not immediately come out. Rather, the faucet sputtered and spat. A trickle of water followed, slowly building to a steady flow. He splashed it onto his face and looked at himself in the murky mirror. His hair was a mess, but he didn't look as tired as he felt.

He had tried to sleep, but found himself watching the shadows of branches and leaves play across his ceiling in the moonlight. Finally, he'd tossed his bedding aside and gotten up. His clock had read 11:57. He was glad his mother had put a night-light in the hall; he might have never found the bathroom without it.

He dried his face on a hand towel, relishing its familiarity. Living out of a motel room wasn't the worst thing in the world, but it wasn't home. Neither was their new house yet. Still, as their things from Pasadena started to settle into their new locations, Xander realized these things, as much as his family, would help change that.

When Xander opened the bathroom door, David was there, clad only in pajama bottoms. "Couldn't sleep," he said.

"It's a new place," Xander said. "That's—"

Something fell over in the corridor. The boys spun toward the noise. Boxes were stacked at intervals all the way past the landing to their parents' bedroom. Another night-light glowed at the far end, making the boxes black and their square edges sharply defined. Dad had made a point of telling his kids and the movers to place the boxes against only one wall. That would keep half the hallway open to walk. Now, a box lay in that path just beyond the landing.

"Xander?" David whispered. He stepped back into his brother.

Xander whispered, "Just a box. Someone didn't stack it right."

Another sound reached them. A scraping that seemed to come from the entryway.

David pushed back even farther into Xander.

"Get off my foot," Xander whispered. David didn't budge. "Maybe it's Dad."

"In the dark?" David said.

Xander thought about the way sounds couldn't be trusted in the house. Whatever had made the noise could be anywhere. That made him spin around to look the other direction, toward their bedroom.

David jumped, said, "What?" He grabbed Xander's hand.

"Nothing. Just looking."

A door thunked shut. Somewhere on the first floor . . . maybe. Xander took a step toward their bedroom. "Wait here," he said. He tried to shake him loose, but David was having none of that.

"No way," David said.

"Then you go. The flashlights are on my dresser."

"No way," he repeated. "Turn on the hall light."

"I don't know where the switch is."

"All right," David said. "Stay here." David released his hand and walked to the bedroom. He looked back every second step. He could have been swimming, turning his head regularly to breathe. He hesitated outside the bedroom, then reached his hand around the frame to flip on the light. Moments later, Xander saw the two flashlights come on and shine against the linen closet door.

When David emerged, Xander asked, "Is the switch down there?"

The beams flashed around.

"I don't see it," David said. He hurried to Xander and handed him one of the lights. They moved down the hall toward the landing. Toria's door was open. A night-light revealed her sleeping in bed. David cast his light into the room.

Xander pushed his hand down. "Don't wake her," he whispered. At the landing, they leaned on the banister. Xander panned his light over the base of the stairs, the few feet of dining room visible to him, and the front door.

David shined his light directly below, onto the corridor leading to the kitchen. "It's like we're in a guard tower."

"Shhh." Xander's beam caught the chandelier. A thousand sparkles of white and blue light danced on the walls.

"Whoa," David said. He added his light to Xander's. A galaxy of stars exploded around them, swirling over the walls and their faces. Despite their unease, they shared a smile.

Then David's light fell from his hand. It tumbled end over end, until it crashed on the floor way below and blinked out.

"Dae—" Xander said and stopped. His brother stared wildly at something past Xander. David reached out. He found the flesh of Xander's arm and squeezed.

Xander hissed in pain. He looked over his shoulder, down the hall. Where the corridor made a ninety-degree turn toward the back of the house, a figure stood. Just like the boxes, it was backlit by the night-light. He could make out no features. Who-ever—*whatever*—it was, it appeared huge, but that could have been a trick of the light. "Dad?" he said.

The figure swayed, seeming to shift its weight from one foot to the other. Its arms became more distinct. Muscular and massive.

"That's not Dad," David whispered.

Xander turned to swing his flashlight around. At the same time, David grabbed for it. It flipped out of Xander's hand. He fumbled for it, caught it, and flashed its beam down the hall. The light captured a flash of shoulder, a foot as the person disappeared beyond the corridor's bend. David's other hand shot out, and he sank both sets of fingers into Xander's bare torso.

"What was that?" David said.

"Come on," Xander said. He moved toward the spot where the figure had disappeared.

"No, wait . . . Xander!" David was right on his heels.

"Don't you want to know?" Xander whispered.

"Not like this! Let's wake Dad. Xander! Wait!"

They were approaching their parents' bedroom on the left. It was a wonder Dad wasn't already bolting out to investigate. He suspected the noise had rippled away from their sleeping parents. Whether the house had randomly kept Mom and Dad from hearing the sounds or had done it purposely, Xander could not guess. He hoped it was not intentional.

In any event, he had the opportunity now to burst in and get their help. He pulled up beside their door. The shaking flashlight beam betrayed his nerves. He braced himself, turned to David.

"We have to look ourselves, first," he whispered. "We're right behind him. It may be our only chance to figure out what's going on."

"What's going on is somebody broke into our house."

"How'd he get in? Where was he when we searched?" He tried another tactic: "Look, if it's a false alarm, Dad's going to really think I'm crazy."

"False alarm?" David said between clenched teeth. "Didn't you *see* him?"

"That doesn't mean he's there now."

David knew as well as Xander did that the bend in the hall led only to the servants' quarters. David said, "Where could he have gone?"

"The house, Dae. It doesn't make sense."

"Then what are we doing *living* in it?" He kept looking

past Xander to the bend, so Xander didn't have to.

Xander held his index finger to his mouth. "Shhh," he whispered. "Hear that?"

Somewhere outside, a dog was howling.

"Something's got him spooked," David said.

For some reason, that bothered Xander even more than seeing an intruder. He said, "Okay, listen. If we're attacked, we go crashing into Mom and Dad's room, sound good? Let's just take a look, see what we see. *Just a look.*"

David reached past a box and picked up a shower curtain rod. He got a two-handed grip on it, shook it to test its weight and balance. "Let's do it," he said.

CHAPTER

twenty-two

Xander and David followed the flashlight beam around the corner. It found the closed guestroom door, and Xander held it there.

"Was it closed before?" he asked.

"I don't know."

Being closed was worse. It meant opening it to who knew what. Stepping nearer, he expected the door to spring open and the man with the big feet to charge out. The backsplash of light filled the hallway. Their own shadows danced around them. David was near enough for Xander to feel his breath on his back. He glanced back at his brother. Big eyes. Tight lips. He held the shower curtain rod straight up, ready to bring it down hard on any head he didn't recognize.

Xander reached for the door handle. He turned it slowly, listening to the metal inside grinding against itself. The latch disengaged from the receptacle in the frame. He pushed. A musty odor drifted out. He pointed the flashlight at the black breach. It illuminated a thin strip of hardwood floor, a slice of furniture deeper inside. He debated kicking at the door, then decided to simply push it fully open. Extending his arm, he hoped nothing reached through and grabbed him.

David tapped his shoulder. Xander did not want to turn his attention from the partially open door. "What is it?" he whispered.

"Look."

"Now?"

Instead of answering, David tapped him again.

Xander looked, saw him nod to his other side. Xander swiveled his head around that way. On the back wall, where the hall ended, a thick shadow, straight as a ruler, ran from floor to ceiling. He turned the flashlight's beam to it. Part of the wall was canted out, open like a door that had not closed fully. The wall had been paneled in vertical planks of wood.

The opening matched where two planks met, which explained why they had not spotted the secret door before.

Xander pulled the guest room door closed. He no longer thought anyone occupied the room, but he didn't want to make it easy for someone to sneak up on them if he was wrong. He tiptoed to the movable wall. Before he could get his fingers to the edge, David reached out and pushed it shut. It clicked and remained flush with the rest of the wall.

"Dae!" he whispered. "What if we can't get it open again? We don't know where the—"

David gave the wall a quick push and it popped open a crack.

Xander scowled at him. "Good thing." He pulled at the edge. It swung toward them easily, silently. He reversed a step, bumping into David and pushing him backward. The flashlight picked up another wall several yards beyond the fake one. He moved into the opening. A closed door was set in the second wall. A sheet of metal had been riveted to it, as if to strengthen it. Xander approached it, feeling David clinging to him like a wet leaf.

"Check it out," he said quietly.

Hanging from a bright metal hasp, attached to the door, was a heavy padlock. Dangling with the lock was the portion of the hasp that had been screwed to the door frame. It had been ripped out, broken when the door was forced open. Splinters of wood lay at the baseboard, a screw not far away.

"It looks new," David said.

Xander turned the handle and pulled the door open. Stairs ascended to the floor above. But he and David had already found the attic entrance on the other side of the house. He recalled how small the attic had been, how he had assumed it was because of the shape of the roof. Now he thought of another reason: there were *two* attics.

He didn't like it. This was right out of a *Goosebumps* story: snoopy visitors would find the stairs to the attic, go up, and . . . well, what happened to them wasn't pretty.

Xander's light revealed nothing at the top of the flight. The landing was deep enough to mask any door or wall that might be at the top.

David was peering around Xander, pressing his chest against Xander's back. Xander could feel the boy's racing heart, and more: he was shivering as violently as a person who'd fallen through a lake's frozen surface. Xander stepped back and closed the metal-skinned door.

He took in his brother's frightened face, wondered how much of it mirrored his own expression. He had read somewhere that bravery is not the absence of fear but the forging ahead despite being afraid. David was certainly afraid, but he'd seen his brother's bravery too many times to assume he wanted to end their adventure here and now.

"You okay?" he asked.

David nodded and actually bent his lips into a smile of sorts.

"Your call. We go up now . . . or wait till tomorrow, get Dad's help if you want."

David stared at the door, considering his options. His heartbeat continued to pound furiously against Xander's back.

At length, he whispered, "What I said before: let's do it."

Xander felt himself shiver. It was more internal than David's vibrating goose bumps, but a sign of his fear, all the same. Maybe he had been counting on David to vote them off this island, to send them home, back to bed. Perhaps his brother's fear was contagious. *Bravery isn't the absence of fear*, he reminded himself. He just wished he had something like David's curtain rod to wield. A bat would be nice. So would an MI6. And he didn't much like the idea that he was almost naked, except for boxers. Going into battle required a uniform, didn't it? At least *clothes*. Did he say *battle*? Not battle. No, not battle. Just . . . just . . . checking out a new place in their home. That's all.

Yeah, a new place behind a fake wall and a door with a broken lock, where some huge dude is probably waiting to ambush you.

Stop it, he scolded himself. *Are you going to do this or not?*

David, right behind him, had said, "Let's do it." How could Xander back out now? He'd never live it down.

He pulled open the door again, flashed the light up the stairs. Nothing lurked at the top . . . that he could see. He passed through the threshold, then mounted the first step. The second. The third.

David stayed one step below him.

Another step. A wall came into view, just past the upper landing.

Up to step number . . . he'd forgotten. Didn't matter. David kept a hand on Xander's hip. He was so close, Xander felt he was giving his brother a piggyback ride.

He stepped onto the landing. Set at a ninety-degree angle from the stairway was a long, dark corridor.

David edged up behind him. He said, "Xander, look."

On the left wall was an old-fashioned light switch: a copper faceplate through which two push-buttons, one over the other, protruded. The upper button was depressed, almost flush with the faceplate. The bottom button stuck out a half inch farther. Xander pushed this one, which caused the top button to pop out, teeter-totter style. The corridor lit up, illuminated by lights in the ceiling as well as wall-mounted lamps, spaced at even intervals on both long walls. The hallway wasn't straight; it bent slightly this way then that way, like a snake. It never curved enough to block the far end from view. And its length puzzled Xander. It seemed longer than the house itself, which was impossible. He wondered if the wall on the far end was mirrored, giving the hallway its extended appearance. The floor was hardwood, as was the rest of the house, but an old-fashioned carpet, red with an intricate black pattern, ran the length of the corridor. The bottom third of the walls was wainscoted in squares of dark wood. Wallpaper covered the upper portion: vertical stripes of old vines and leaves over an ivory background. Doors lined both sides. They were staggered so no one door faced another. Their handles glinted dully in the light.

"Holy cow," David whispered. "What is it?"

"I don't know."

"It looks like a hotel," David said.

"A hotel designed by Dr. Seuss, maybe," Xander added.

"Do you think the guy we saw is in one of these rooms?"

The *figure*. Xander's nerves were coiled on the razor edge between fight and flight. The figure had become symbolic of anything this house could throw at him. But David had kept the threat focused. It was not a row of doors that could harm them. It was what could come out of those doors.

"Well . . ." Xander answered, taking a tentative step into the hallway, "there's only one way to find out."

CHAPTER

twenty-three

The curvy corridor lay before them. It was creepy and mysterious and oddly inviting.

Both boys had stepped onto the carpeted runner. It was soft and warm under Xander's bare feet. He forced himself to start walking. David clung to him like one of those remora fish that attached themselves to sharks. It made Xander feel like the big brother he was. When it came to tackling new adventures, David was fearless. As long as he knew others had trod before him and lived, he figured he could do it too. What spooked the kid was . . . well, *spooky* things: ghosts, vampires, dark shadows, mysterious noises. The unknown.

My turn to be brave, Xander thought.

They approached the first light fixture. It was a small statue mounted to the wall: an old man, whose long beard flowed into a tunic. A wreath crowned his head. He held open a book and pointed at a page. His eyes were cut out, allowing the light from the bulb within to shine through them. Xander recognized the style of the carving as ancient Greek—one of the things about having a history teacher for a dad was you got a lot of history lessons. He suspected the man was Plato or Socrates or one of the other brainy sage-types. The top of the lamp was open. Light splashed up the wall in the shape of an ice-cream cone. The ice-cream scoop itself was a glowing circle on the ceiling. As they passed, Xander's eyes kept darting back to the decorative fixture. He half-expected the old man to turn his head, following their progress.

David jabbed him in the ribs.

"Ow, what?" Xander said. David was pointing. The wallpaper had been peeled away in four thin, horizontal furrows. The rips were as long as Xander's arm. One ended in a bunched-up wad of wallpaper; at the end of the other three furrows, rippled strips of paper hung like the tails of rats.

"Claw marks," David whispered.

"Maybe," Xander said, but that's exactly what they looked like.

They were a few feet from the first door. It was six-paneled and stained dark brown, like the others in the house. On the front of the door handle was a face: a scowling man whose tight lips appeared ready to open for a hearty reprimand. A brass plate under the handle was etched in the same intricate pattern as the carpeted runner. The impression of an old hotel was so strong in his mind, Xander was mildly surprised that no room number was affixed to the door.

"What do we do?" David whispered behind him.

"I'm thinking." He had a mind to knock—another remnant of the hotel milieu. Or maybe he thought politeness would spare him the wrath of whoever might be lurking on the other side. Instead, he turned the knob and pushed open the door. A small room lay within. A single domed fixture in the ceiling cast the room in a harsh, bright light. Xander pushed the door farther until it stopped against the left-hand wall. He could see through the crack between door and frame, on the hinged side, that no one was waiting to jump out.

Xander stepped in.

David hung back, putting more than a hair's distance between them for the first time since they saw the figure downstairs. He looked up the hall in both directions, apparently decided that being in the strange room with Xander was better than being outside it without him, and stepped in.

A wooden bench ran the length of the wall on the right. A shelf with a series of heavy brass coat hooks below it was above the bench, slightly higher than Xander's eye level. Hanging on the hooks were the accoutrements of a day at the beach: a man's bathing suit, a colorful beach towel, swimming fins, snorkel, and mask. A beach umbrella, extending from bench to ceiling, leaned into a corner. Next to the umbrella, two blue and white flip-flops sat side by side. Opposite the entrance was another door. It felt like they were in a mudroom.

Xander stepped to the inner door. Slowly, he gripped the handle. "It's locked," he informed David.

"From the other side?"

Xander looked at the handle. There was no keyhole. No deadbolt or any other hardware on the door. Even the hinges must have been on the other side, for they were invisible to him. He tried the handle again. It was as solid as a dock's mooring cleat. If it could be unlocked only from the other side, then it must also be locked from that side. The implications hit Xander like a plank upside his head. He pressed his palms against the door, holding it shut. He swung his face around to David.

"It's locked from the other side," he said, almost hissing out the words. "You can't unlock it from this side. That means—"

"There's somebody in there!" David finished.

"Can you see anything under the door?"

David dropped. He pressed his cheek against the wood floor. "Nothing. It's all black."

Xander kept leaning into the door, sure something was about to push through. He tilted his head to put an ear against the surface. Something on the other side scraped the door. He said, "Get out! Go! Now!"

David scrambled up. He backed through the open door into the hall.

"Xander?" he said, sounding like he was ready to cry.

Xander came off the door. He backpedaled out of the room, pulling the first door shut as he did.

His grip remained tight on the handle. At last, he let go and backed away. He and David stared at the door a long time.

"What'd you hear?" David said.

Scraping.

"Think it was *him?*"

"Has to be."

David scanned the other doors down the hall. "You want to check the other doors?"

"Why?" Xander said.

"If he's in *this* one, he's not in those. Maybe we'll find something to help us."

David was the video game player of the family. He tended to think this way: strategically. When Xander got stuck on *Halo 3*, David jumped in and methodically checked each possibility until he found the answer.

Xander doubted snapping a beach towel at the figure would do any good. But tools or weapons, now that was another story.

At the very least, they might be able to determine the size of the locked room by examining the other rooms. He wasn't sure exactly how that information would assist them, but didn't the hero in every movie, from war spectacles to horror flicks, gather intelligence about his opponent? Often, the solution lay in outwitting the bad guys, not overpowering them.

"Good idea," he said. He stepped past David to the next door. It was on the other side of the hall from the first. Before he could open it, David stopped him.

He gestured toward the first room they had looked into. "What if he comes out of *there*, while we're in *here*?"

Xander didn't have an answer. "You want to go back downstairs?" he said. "Go to bed?"

David shook his head.

Xander opened the door into a room precisely like the first: the bench, the shelf, the second door set in the opposing wall. The only difference were the items left behind. There was a white parka with a fur-lined hood, goggles, binoculars, a white canvas bag adorned by a fat red plus sign. Propped into the corner was a pair of beat-up skis. Beside them on the bench were what appeared to Xander's untrained eye to be two sticks of dynamite. Long fuses. Wrapped in thin red paper, stains showing through. *Nitroglycerin*, Xander thought.

"Are those real?" David asked.

"Don't touch them."

"What's with all this stuff?" David said.

Xander shook his head. "It's like a closet for storing a few things you'd need for one activity. The beach stuff in the other room, the . . . I guess *alpine* things here."

"*Dynamite?*"

Xander shrugged.

"Why?"

"David, I'm seeing this for the first time, like you."

"Check the door."

The second door was locked, as the one in the other room had been. He tried to force the doorknob to turn. Clockwise, counterclockwise—it wouldn't budge. His body rocked as he attempted to rattle the door. It didn't move or make a sound. "How . . . it's *impossible,*" he said.

"There's not somebody in that room, too, is there?"

"I hope not." He put his ear against it. He pulled back fast, almost ran, but didn't. "It's the same sound," he whispered.

"Fingernails?" David was moving toward the corridor.

Xander listened again. "More like *wind.* Something blowing around in the wind. Sand, maybe. Leaves and twigs."

"Does it lead outside?"

"Can't," Xander said. "I've inspected the outside of the house. There are some dormer windows in the attic. Nothing like this, no doors."

"Is it a *real* door?" David said.

Xander stared at him, thinking. "Like . . . maybe it's not a door at all." As David had done earlier, Xander got onto the

151

floor to look under the door. "It doesn't look like it just stops there." Remaining on his knees, he looked around. He rose and stepped to the skis. His hand was inches from them when he stopped. What if it was a trap? What if every item was booby trapped somehow? He pulled his hand away. To David he said, "Give me your pajamas."

"They're my *pants*," David protested.

"I'll give them right back."

David tugged at the drawstring, unraveling a bow. He pulled them off. In only boxers now, as Xander was, he hesitated, then handed over his pajama bottoms. The material was thin and lightweight, as Xander had expected. He dropped to his knees again and began pushing one of the pant legs under the door. "Hey!" David said.

"I just want to see if there's space on the other side of the door . . . or if there's a wall. I told you I'd—" The pajamas ripped out of his hands. They zipped under the door and were gone, so fast their final moments were a blur. Xander jumped back. He crashed into David, who had already spun halfway out of the room. Xander grabbed him and shoved him toward the stairwell.

"Go, go, go!" he yelled.

twenty-four

SATURDAY, 12:41 A.M.

The brothers tripped and banged into each other as they flew past the first door and the Plato wall light. At the landing, David tromped down. Xander turned to look back. Nothing was after them. "Wait!" he said.

David stopped. "Are they coming?" he asked.

Xander shook his head.

"What was that? What happened to my pajamas?" He was slowly reascending the stairs.

Xander looked at his palms, as if for clues. "They were just pulled out of my hands."

"So somebody *was* in the locked room."

Xander thought about it. Somehow, the way the pajamas vanished didn't feel like someone yanking them away. "There was kind of a breeze when it happened."

"Yeah, anything moving that fast is gonna make its own wind."

"Not like that. I mean right before they disappeared."

"So, what now?"

Xander smiled. "We keep looking." He started down the corridor.

"Well," David said, coming up behind him, "if you want any more clothes, use your boxers." He chuckled at that.

"Funny."

Both of them kept their eyes on each door they passed. The first one, then the second. They reached another wall lamp, this one completely different from the last. It appeared to be half of a large, ornate goblet. Lead or pewter, maybe. There was a flat base; a stem that resembled a vine-entwined column; and a chalice inlaid with colored glass pieces, cut like gems. Light not only poured from its open top, up the wall to the ceiling, but also gleamed through the colored glass. He saw now that each fixture was different, but he could not tell at this distance what each one resembled.

The next room they entered was much like the first two: bench, shelf, locked second door. The theme of the items had something to do with war. There was a smooth, round helmet; binoculars—black, not white as the ones in the Alpine room were; and a gun belt with bullets and a holster, but no gun. On the bench was a hand grenade.

Xander nudged David. "Don't touch *that*, either."

They went from room to room, finding the same arrangement of bench, shelf, hooks, and locked door. The items within reflected a wide range of activities, from mountain climbing to boating to something to do with hunting. Several times Xander and David were at a loss for what the items meant. They reached the end of the long hall and the final door.

"I counted twenty," Xander said.

David nodded. "I lost count at twelve."

Xander noted that the wall at the end of the hallway was not mirrored but decorated to match the side walls. The landing at the other end, where they had started, seemed far away.

To make their investigation complete, they stepped through the last door. Hanging from the hooks were the props from a costume play: a round shield, battered and bent; a simple helmet, equally scarred; a scabbard with a sword's hilt extending from it; a net, made of steel links; and what appeared to be an animal pelt. Xander tried the interior door, knowing what he would find: it was locked. When he turned away, his heart leaped into his throat. David was holding the scabbard, pulling the sword from it.

"David! Don't touch it!"

His face was beaming. "Why not? This is cool!"

Xander grabbed his brother's hands, preventing him from pulling the short sword all the way out. "It might be a trick," he said. He listened for any sounds that might reach him from the hall. No doors clicking open. No footsteps.

David watched him listen without saying a word. They stood like that—both boys in only boxers, sword and scabbard held between them—for a long time. It did not escape Xander how strange it was that he was more worried about the props than about their intrusion into the rooms. Rooms were rooms. A man's tools, his weapons, were part of who he was, part of what he did. To Xander, his camera said more about him than his bedroom. He did not know in what way, but he suspected the items in these rooms were more important than the rooms themselves. Because of that, if there was a trap, he believed the spring, the trigger, would be among them.

With a stillness, a quiet, he began to relax. He released his brother's hands.

David, spooked now, did not move. He said, "What is it?"

Xander smiled. He nodded toward the sword. "Let's see it." It came out of the scabbard with a metallic *shiiing!* David held it up. The blade was two feet long, thick, tapering to a fine point. It was dinged and scratched with rust and—

"Is that blood?" David asked, staring.

"Stage blood," Xander said with more certainty than he felt.

David rotated his wrist, circumscribing a figure eight in the air with the tip.

Xander cautiously plucked the helmet off the hook. He hefted it in his hands. He said, "This thing's heavy." It felt gritty under his fingers, as though it was rusting or had been lying in dirt. He checked inside, then fitted it over his head.

David laughed. "Gluteus Maximus, I salute thee!"

Xander pulled the metal net off its hook. It too was heavy, even heavier than the helmet. About the length of the sword, it was formed into a tube, open at both ends, but wider on one side than the other. Leather straps were attached to the wide end. He understood what it was. He stuck his arm into the tube up to his shoulder. His hand popped out the other end, where a metal band crossed over his palm. He tugged on the straps and cinched the ends together like a belt under his opposite arm.

"Whoa!" David said.

Xander flexed out his chest, held up his arm. "Chain mail," he said. His arm almost immediately felt the strain of the chain's weight. He lowered his hand, resting it on the locked door handle. "I know what all this—" The handle rotated under his palm. He fell to the floor as the door clicked open.

David screamed and dropped the scabbard. He squared himself to the door. He held the sword in both hands, extending his arms before him.

Xander scrambled up. He stood next to David. Light, *sunlight*, streamed through the three-inch opening. Nothing on the other side interrupted the flow of light. No shadows cast by beast or man as they prepared to push through. A sound, not dissimilar to the wind in the trees, reached their ears. Beyond it was a muted rumble, like a distant surf.

"Xander?" David said.

That spurred Xander to move. He approached the door. He cocked his head to see through. Only light. He reached out, touched the edge of the door, and pulled it open.

David sucked in a sharp breath. Beyond the threshold was nothing that could be part of the house. It was a vast landscape of sand. An unfelt wind whipped the grains into spinning dervishes that danced for a few seconds before settling again. New torrents sprang up in different spots. Nearby, rocks broke the surface of the dunes. They huddled low as if avoiding the sting of flying sand.

The heat of a midday sun radiated over the boys. *Impossible,* Xander thought. *It must be about one o'clock in the morning. Here, anyway . . . certainly not in there.* Sand blew in. Xander felt it hit his legs and then his stomach and chest. It was drifting in, obscuring more and more of the hardwood floor. He stepped closer, put his hand on the door frame. He stretched his leg past the threshold.

"Xander, don't!" David yelled.

"I'm just *seeing,*" he said over his shoulder.

He pushed his bare foot into the hot sand. It sank in a half inch. This was no hallucination, though he didn't really think it was, with David seeing it too. Xander released the door frame and took another step. He was completely out of the little room now.

"Xander!" David screamed again.

Xander looked back, grinning at the wonder of it all.

The door slammed shut.

CHAPTER

twenty-five

SATURDAY, 1:11 A.M.

David couldn't believe it.

Oh, no, no, no, no, no . . .

He tossed the sword aside and leaped for the door. Both hands on the handle. It turned. He tugged at it and it opened— six inches, no more. Something seemed to be tugging back, and he lost an inch of opening. Every muscle strained to pull the door open.

"Xander! Xander!"

He raised his foot and pressed it into the wall beside the door.

Pulled . . . pulled.

Quickly, he moved one hand from the knob to the edge of the door, wrapping his fingers around to the other side. Then he moved his other hand. He felt the heat of the sun, the tickling of the sand on his fingers and his ankle.

Where was Xander? Wouldn't he be calling? Wouldn't he push from the other side?

Grunting and straining with everything he had, he lost another inch of opening. Four inches. His knuckles were close to the edge of the doorframe. His hands were white, the blood squeezed out of them. If he eased up now, if he took a breath, the door would slam shut, taking eight of his fingers with it.

The door closed farther.

Noooo!

Now the muscles in his legs, his arms, even his stomach, were burning in pain. The door pulled in farther. His vision blurred as tears filled his eyes. With a scream of anguish, he snapped his fingers out from the narrowing crack. The door slammed with a solid *bang!* Despite his muscles feeling stretched like taffy, he seized the door handle. It would not turn.

"Uh . . . uh . . ." His sounds were cries and calls and groans all at once. He tugged, but the door held firm. He dropped to the floor, held his lips to the gap. "Xander! Can you hear me?"

In the little room, individual grains of sand began rolling across the hardwood floor toward the gap. More and more sand disappeared under the door. Believing it signaled some kind of finality, David slammed his hand down on the sand. He felt it grating against his skin. It slid out and flew out beneath the door.

"No, no." He laid his forearm in front of the gap, wedging it between door and floor. Sand whipped around his elbow and away. It formed a drift against his arm, then sailed over; some pushed under. He lay down in front of the gap. He felt the insistent tug of the wind like a vacuum. His boxers fluttered, trying to follow the sand through the gap. The grains kept flowing past, faster and faster, until he felt and saw no more and the suction coming from the gap stopped. He flipped himself around and held his eye to the base of the door. The light beyond faded and went black.

CHAPTER

twenty-six

When Xander first looked back, David was standing in the small room. He was holding the sword out in front of him. Panic made his eyes wide. The streaming sunlight made his skin pale. He mouthed Xander's name—Xander recognized the movements of his mouth, but did not hear the word come out. The wind was howling out here.

Then a funny thing happened to his vision. David—in fact, the entire rectangle of the threshold and everything it framed—*rippled*. It wavered, as though superheated air had passed between Xander and his brother. Then the door slammed shut, silently and instantly. The frame and door rippled again . . . then simply vanished.

He was staring at endless sand. Mountains in the distance. The roaring surf sound grew louder and the mountains rushed in at him. Surprised, he covered his face with his arm and took a step back. He tripped and went down. Peering over his forearm, he witnessed the mountains become something else. First, they elongated into stone cliffs. Then, faster than a heartbeat, they formed into stadium bleachers. In another heartbeat, the bleachers were crowded with people. The roar was theirs: loud cheers, unrestrained enthusiasm.

Reposed on one elbow, he rotated his head. The stadium completely encircled him. The rocks nearest him shimmered and became a body. It was cut and bloodied. The other rocks he had seen from the small room did the same, until more than two dozen corpses were scattered around the sandy stadium floor. The sand itself took on a darker tint, as though a cloud had rolled over the sun. It was darkest around the bodies and severed limbs. Xander knew it was hued not by shadow but by blood.

The top level of the stadium was lined with ornate columns. Above them, wood poles held canvas awnings, which flapped in the wind. He recognized this place. It was the Roman Colosseum. His father had shown him pictures. But the crowd did not sit in the ruins he had seen. The highest level of the oval was unbroken. The surfaces were crisp and polished, throwing back the sun in a hundred places.

When was the Colosseum finished? He tried to remember. The Emperor Titus had ordered the inaugural games in . . . in the year 80. *Not long after Jesus Christ was crucified!*

Xander pushed himself onto his knees.

The tone of the crowd changed. From within the victorious rumble came a gasp of surprise.

Xander stood. He glanced around. Sure enough, the portal was gone.

Guess I was wrong about where you could end up. Not quite a football field, but close.

The crowd closest to him began an angry chant: *"Sine missione! Sine missione!"*

They pointed at him, raised their hands, then pointed again, as if lashing at him with whips. The chanting and whipping of hands was picked up by more and more people, sweeping the stadium in two directions, outward from the section that had started it.

"Sine missione! Sine missione!"

Xander followed its progression, as clear to him as the terminator line between night and day was to astronauts. As he rotated, his eyes fell on the only other living man in the arena. His back was turned against Xander. His arms were raised as he received an ovation of stomping feet and raised voices. Flowers and petals rained down before him. One hand held a sword, the other a shield. He started strutting back and forth, pumping his sword and shield into the air. Then he caught the change of the crowd, their shift from joy to anger. He stopped. He scanned the stands on his side of the stadium.

"Sine missione! Sine missione!"

He spun and spotted Xander. He lowered his arms. He tossed back his shoulders—the gladiatorial equivalent of a bull digging his hoof into the ground, Xander decided. The man strode toward him.

He thinks I'm an opponent he missed, Xander realized. And he looked like one: almost naked, wearing a helmet and chain mail. He held out his hands. "Wait!" he yelled. "Hold on! This isn't what you think! I don't belong here!"

The gladiator was thirty yards away. He showed no sign of stopping. He began waving his sword in the air, then clanged it against his shield. The crowd roared.

Xander backed away. He tripped over something. His cheek hit the dirt. A dead man stared at him from two feet away. The top of his head had taken a severe chop. It was cleaved at his eyebrows. Xander screamed unintelligibly. He got to his feet.

The gladiator was fifteen yards from him, moving in fast. He clutched a long-stemmed rose in his teeth. A red petal fell with each of his thunderous steps.

"I said wait!" Xander pleaded.

The man spat out the stem. *"Morere honeste, sceleste!"* he said.

"What? No, wait!"

The gladiator was so close now, Xander could see the oily sweat that covered his body, the enumerable scars, the splattered blood from his victims, the green pulp from the stem dribbling down his chin.

"I'm just a kid!" Xander yelled. He turned and ran all-out to the curving wall of the arena. He found a wooden door the size of a garage entrance and pounded on it. "Help! Help!"

Where's the portal? How do I get back if the portal's not where it dropped me off?

The thrumming of the crowd rose in pitch. Xander spun to see the gladiator charging him, sword raised over his head.

Xander dropped straight down. The man brought the blade down. It thunked into the door. Xander darted out from under him. He felt a sandaled foot strike his thigh. He fell, kept moving, crawling, crawling in the dirt. He got his feet under him again. He did not look back, but stayed low and shot away. His feet lost traction, but he dug in, dug in and ran. He glanced back. He had put some ground between them. The man jogged toward him, a practiced pace that conserved energy.

Xander spotted a canopied area in the stadium. Flags and brightly breastplated soldiers surrounded several people sitting in wide, ornate chairs. One of them must be the emperor or governor or senator—somebody important. He ran for them, waving his arms frantically.

"Please! Please! I don't belong here! Please!"

Whoever the toga-clad man in the VIP section was, he seemed

to take notice, seemed to understand him. He stood suddenly. His white, closely trimmed beard turned into a hairy frown.

"Please!" Xander yelled.

The man turned to a soldier, barked an order.

The soldier stepped forward, raised a spear, and hurled it at Xander.

Xander turned his shoulder away just as it sailed past. He glared at the long shaft of the spear, wobbling from the effort of piercing the ground. Another soldier threw another spear. Xander dodged, and it impaled a body lying in the dirt. He got the message: no talking to the audience.

He darted away before another soldier used him for target practice.

twenty-seven

While Xander had tried to get help from the bonehead who'd had his soldiers attack him, the gladiator had closed the distance between them. When he looked away, the big man made a sharp turn to cut him off. His feet skidded out from under him, and he went down. The crowd let out a loud and sustained "*booooo!*"

Xander didn't wait to see what happened next. He sprinted the length of the arena, skirting bodies and body parts.

Once again, he reached a large wooden door and pounded his fists on it. He wondered how many of the dead men on the ground around him had done the same thing. This wasn't going to work.

He spied the gladiator jogging toward him. He couldn't play keep-away forever. He'd seen the movie: they'd do something to make sure he was caught. Somehow—maybe with chained wild animals or legionnaires with razor-sharp blades—they'd shrink the area of combat until he had no choice but to face the gladiator.

He ran to the nearest body—a boy not much older than Xander. The wounds made Xander fall to his knees and vomit. His panic had kept his stomach from betraying him until now. Once he'd decided to defend himself, his mind became more rational. And any rational person would have puked at the sight.

The crowd cheered with delight.

Xander wiped his mouth on his bare forearm. He spat and crawled over to the dead boy. It seemed that death had not relieved him from the desire to possess a weapon; the boy's hand held firm to the handle of a mace. Xander pried his fingers open, feeling his stomach lurch again at the stiffness of the corpse's joints. He lifted the powerful weapon, which consisted of a stocky handle, a length of chain, and a heavy shot put–like metal ball tricked out with spikes.

He clambered up. His right arm was heavy and slow, weighed

down by the chain mail and mace. He used both hands to lift the weapon. He hefted it and swung it to his left. The ball moved sluggishly, as though Xander were trying to fight underwater.

The gladiator approached.

Xander pulled the handle to his right. The ball swung with it. He had to throw his hips back to avoid being hit by his own mace, but he thought he had figured something out. Once the ball was moving, it didn't want to stop. All Xander had to do was get it going and steer it. He pumped his arms, as though he were stirring a vat of molasses. The ball swung out in front of him. It came back to his left side. When it swung out again, he pulled it toward his right. This kept the ball swinging in a semicircle around him. The problem was, he couldn't get it higher than his stomach. Still, the gladiator seemed intimidated by this display. Perhaps he believed it was a cunning trick to lure an unsuspecting foe near, at which point a fancy flick of the wrist would send the ball skyward and down on the opponent's head.

If only, Xander thought.

The chain, kept taut now, did not make the *chinking*, chainlike sound Xander expected. It was the ball that emanated the sound of danger, with a *whoosh-whoosh* as it cut through the air. At his right ear, the chain mail's metal rings scraped together, reminding Xander of pebbles dropped onto a metal slide. These sounds, and the grunting of the gladiator, occupied Xander's auditory sense. The crowd had ceased to be. Xander was in a zone that maybe his brother would understand on a very minimal level because of his gaming acumen: two combatants . . . life and death . . . nothing else mattered.

Focus would make him better than he was. Still, he was outmatched. The gladiator possessed skill and experience and bloodlust and the strength to turn these things into a killing machine. The way he glared at Xander, Xander realized he was also focused—focused on bringing down this last stubborn opponent.

As the mace reached its leftward apex, Xander heaved up on its handle. The ball arced up. It passed in front of Xander, level with the gladiator's head. This potentially fatal move was impressive . . . and completely unsustainable. As it swung out, it dropped heavily, all the way to the ground. It took Xander with it, yanking him off his feet, like a novice water-skier. He tumbled over it and wound up on his stomach, staring up at the gladiator jogging toward him. The man was laughing.

Xander scrambled to his feet and ran. He had decided to take a stand, but now was no time to learn how to use a new weapon. Especially one as exotic as an ancient mace. To his untrained and underdeveloped arms, it was nothing more than an anchor. If he had tried that last move while the gladiator was moving in for the kill, Xander would be dead now.

He spotted another body at the far end of the arena and turned toward it. The chain mail on his arm was heavier and heavier. Wearing it was like carrying an anchor. As his feet dug into the sand, he unlashed the strap under his arm and let the chain mail fall away. As much protection as it provided, he needed agility more. Besides, it may have prevented a blow from that gladiator's sword from cleaving off his arm, but without doubt, such a blow would shatter his bones. In agony, without the use of his arm, the gladiator's coup de grâce would have come swiftly.

Xander skidded next to the damaged body. A sword lay in the sand beside it. The handle was sticky with blood.

All the better to keep my grip, Xander thought. He stood and faced the gladiator, who had closed the distance faster than Xander had expected. Xander swung the sword in front of him and screamed. What came out was guttural and animalistic and represented exactly what he felt inside.

The gladiator sneered. It was the same twisting of the lips Xander had witnessed on the faces of countless bullies. It dawned on him that the gladiator was a bully to the extreme.

The man lumbered forward.

Despite his resolve, Xander took a step back. Then another. The top of a round boulder protruding from the sand caught his attention. Of course, it couldn't have been a boulder: Just beneath the sand of the coliseum arena was a wood floor. Under that was the hypogeum, tunnels and rooms where the amphi-theater managers kept slaves and animals before spitting them out for the entertainment of the crowd. The "boulder" was a shield. He sidestepped over, stooped to pick it up.

The gladiator rushed in.

Something prevented Xander from gripping the strap behind the shield. The gladiator loomed over him, raising his sword. The weapon disappeared in the brightness of the sun. With no time to wield it perfectly, Xander dropped his sword and clutched the perimeter of the shield. He lifted it over him and ducked his head under it. The gladiator's sword slammed into the shield. It felt as though Xander were trying to hold back a battering ram. Metal clanged. The impact rattled his hands and vibrated up his arms to his shoulders. Instant pain.

But nothing like it could have been, he thought. *Nothing like the sting of death.*

With the shield pushed down onto him, he saw the reason he could not wield it properly. Another arm was already in the shield's straps. It had been severed mid-bicep, at the edge of the shield. The dead fingers waggled at Xander, as if bidding him farewell.

twenty-eight

Again, the sword came down on the shield, bending it in at the center. He hoped the gladiator would not notice his fingers and lop them off. The sword struck again. A central blow that drove Xander backward, onto his butt. His legs were unprotected now, and one more blow would pitch him onto his back. The tip of the sword scraped the shield as the man lifted it out of the crease he had made.

Xander released one hand from the shield. He put all

his strength into swinging it around, aiming at the gladiator's knees.

The gladiator was no fool.

Obviously accustomed to last-ditch efforts at survival, he reeled back. The shield missed its mark. Xander lost his grip and it sailed away.

Even before the gladiator had started moving away from it, Xander had grabbed his sword and slipped a foot under himself. By the time the shield left his hand, he was already leaping forward. The tip of the blade trailed the shield's trajectory by no more than a second. It was extended farther than the shield, thanks to Xander's forward momentum. It clipped the gladiator's left shin and then his right. Little bleeding mouths opened up under both knees.

The man howled and staggered back. He did not fall. He bowed to examine his wounds. *Probably*, Xander thought, *if the man lost a leg, he would pick it up and beat his opponent with it.*

Xander saw his strike had caused little damage. He pushed himself up and again ran. There was no shame in it. He was there to survive, not honor Caesar or this barbarian game or even himself. Since he was learning about combat and weapons literally on the run, hightailing it was a *strategy*, not an act of cowardice.

He pulled up to catch his breath. Before he could turn, he heard the gladiator's footsteps, like the crunching of cereal between molars. He spun, swinging his sword in time to deflect his opponent's blade. Sparks snapped between them. The man leaned in, howling in rage. Rancid breath filled Xander's nostrils. The man's eyes were black, hateful.

Xander caught movement beneath him. The gladiator was reaching beneath their sword arms. His hand grabbed at Xander's torso, much the way David's had done not so long ago, but so very far away. This time, however, Xander's skin was slick with sweat. The man's fingers could not get a grip. Xander pulled his sword back. It came off the gladiator's weapon and dropped onto the top of his forearm. It sliced a deep groove into the man's flesh. Xander continued the movement of his hand until his sword was positioned over his head, ready to bring it down.

Xander knew the gladiator's entire life had been about surviving in battle. He would not be defeated so easily. Xander caught a flash of the man's sword as it swung up. If nothing changed, it would catch Xander below the ribcage and angle diagonally through his chest to his heart. Abandoning the possibility of victory, as close as the lashing down of his hand, Xander pitched himself sideways. He somersaulted, was up, scurrying away again.

That image of his heart impaled on the gladiator's blade made him sick and dizzy. It did not stoke the fire of determination. Rather, an overwhelming sense of defeat washed over him. It occurred to him this was how battles were won and lost. They were not always the result of superior skill and stamina. Close calls, images of impending death, and the lack of opportunities were just as instrumental in putting combatants in the ground. Xander suspected that with experience, a fighter became accustomed to these little defeats; so he would reach the point of giving up much later than Xander would.

Giving up? No, he was not there yet. He did, however, doubt his chances of getting out of this alive. After all, he was a fifteen-year-old boy, living a relatively cushy life by most standards. His opponent had lived a brutal life in a brutal world—he was a shark: Xander nothing but a minnow.

But even minnows wanted to live.

The gladiator huffed toward him. If the nicks Xander had inflicted to the man's shins had enraged him, the slice to his arm and perhaps Xander's escape had sent him into a stratosphere of maniacal hatred. Despite his wounds, the man moved faster. His sword sliced the air before him, this way and that.

In seventh grade, Xander had fought a kid who was smaller than he was. Xander hadn't wanted a showdown, couldn't even remember what had ticked the kid off. He'd easily parried some blows. Finally, to end it, he gave the boy a hard knock on the side of his head. Instead of admitting defeat, the kid had come at him with wild disregard for anything except pummeling Xander. Xander had discovered that pinwheeling arms were nearly impossible to stop. They just kept coming like a lumber mill's saw, and you were the tree.

The gladiator was coming at him like that. With swords, though, instead of scrawny seventh-grader fists.

The blades moved so fast they left gleaming arcs in the

air that appeared solid to Xander. He could hear them now, hissing through the air like the mace never had. Rage may have pushed the gladiator into this mulcher mentality, but he had not lost any dexterity in reaching it. The blades whirled in perfect opposition to each other. One coming up as the other came down. They crossed in front of the man and never so much as grazed each other.

Xander backed away. He made feeble slashes at the approaching *Pinwheel of Death*. Xander wondered how, at a time like this, he could name the instrument of his own demise like that. Definitely too many movies. Too many movie posters and trailers, with their catchphrases and taglines.

"Stop!" he yelled. "This isn't fair." He continued moving backward, keeping ten feet between him and the whirling blades. He stepped on something, twisted his ankle, almost fell. He steadied himself, lifted his leg higher, and stepped back. He had almost tripped over another body. He didn't want to see it; he'd join its former owner soon enough.

The gladiator continued after him. That nasty sneer never left his face. He could have moved in for the kill at any time. Xander thought this drawn-out prelude to his dissection was orchestrated. The gladiator was as much a performer as warrior. Xander hoped his body parts would not teleport back to the house. It was bad enough to die this way. Torturing his family with evidence of it was cosmically cruel. If his parts did make it home, would it be David who discovered them? Would they splash down at his feet back in the little room? True, it would keep his kid brother from making Xander's mistake, but could you ever recover from seeing something like that?

Xander was backing toward a wall. Soon, the only thing left for the gladiator to do was end this performance. Xander swung his sword again and again. If nothing else, he would go out fighting.

When he could reverse no farther, he screamed, another unintelligible representation of his anguish. Then, the sound formed into words—defiant, angry last words: "Come on, you fat pig! Do it!"

The blades whirled. His own weapon clashed against them. *Chang! Chang!* His wrist snapped one way, then the other as the blades battered his sword. For a moment, he wondered if he should pull his arm in so that the first hot cut would be the last he knew. Otherwise, he would watch his hand go first, then his arm, fed slowly into the ancient Roman version of a blender.

Something rumbled. The sounds of the crowd were returning to him. Their feet stomped in anticipation. As his right hand swung the sword, his left counterbalanced the weight. Held out from his side and back just a little, his fingers pressed the hewn stone of the arena wall.

The spinning blades ripped his sword from his grip. It flipped away. Something clamped around his left wrist. He was yanked into the wall, then through the threshold of one of the big wooden doors. He plunged into shadow, as the door rumbled closed. A latch snapped shut. From the other side, swords *thunked* against the wood.

Hands grabbed his shoulders, breath—not rancid, but smelling of toothpaste—blew over him.

"Are you all right?" someone screamed.

His legs felt weak. Emotion, like adrenaline, hit his heart, rushed into his face. He said, "Dad?"

"It's okay, Son. Hold on."

CHAPTER

twenty-nine

SATURDAY, 1:32 A.M.

As soon as Xander and his father crossed the threshold, the door slammed shut. Xander's face was pressed into his father's chest. Dad's arms around him had never felt so good. Xander opened one eye. He saw the bench and shelf in the small room. David stood a few feet away. He was shaking and sniffing. His eyes were puffy and red, still leaking. He had been crying, hard and long. Xander tried to smile at him. He squeezed even closer to his father, trying, for just a moment, to get lost in the man's warmth and smell, his very being. He hitched in a stuttering breath. Then he wept. It started gently, then grew into ragged sobs. Too many emotions to hold in. Relief swirled with the residue of intense fear. His *soul* felt abused and tired.

A month before school had let out, Mitch Dawson had been goofing off in his new ride, a '74 Firebird Formula. He had been ripping donuts in the school parking lot. Mitch had lost control, nailed a car, then a light pole. The Firebird had jumped the curb and rolled down the concrete embankment of a runoff canal. The whole school had run out to see. When Xander got there, Mitch was bawling like a baby. Everyone had assumed he was grieving for his totaled car, but later he had confessed to Xander that as the car was rolling, he had been completely and utterly convinced he was going to die. Through an embarrassed smile, he had said, "I stared death in the face and got another chance." Xander had nodded, but had not truly understood. Now he did.

Dad let him cry it out. He stroked Xander's hair and whispered over and over, "You're here now."

When the worst of it was over, he felt David hug him from behind. The boy slid around to include their father in the embrace. They stayed like that a long while. When Xander raised his head, David released them and Xander took a step back. He wiped at his cheeks and ran the underside of his nose over his forearm. He sniffed back what hadn't already come out. He said, "I'm sorry."

Dad squeezed his shoulder. "I am so glad you're here."

Xander glanced at David, back to Dad. "But how . . ."

"Your brother came and got me." He offered David a tight, I'm-proud-of-you smile.

Xander turned to David. He couldn't help it. He had to hug him.

David returned the squeeze, but said, "Are we a bunch of girls or what?"

"Shut up."

When Xander released him, David didn't let go. "Man, I thought you were gone forever."

"So did I. I couldn't find the . . . Dad, how did you follow me?" Then he noticed the animal pelt tied around his father's waist over his pajama bottoms. The sword Dae had been holding was in the scabbard, slung around Dad's neck, hanging under his arm. Xander had a faint memory of feeling it as he embraced his father, but he had been too lost in his emotions to care what it was.

"I couldn't get the door open," David explained. "It locked me out. Dad put those things on and opened it."

Xander said, "How did you know to do that?"

"David told me how the door opened after you put on the chain mail and helmet." He shrugged. "Not difficult to figure out."

"But why didn't you end up where I did, in the middle of the arena?"

Dad's eyebrows went up. "You can add that to my long list of questions, Xander."

"Where *did* you appear?"

"In the bleachers, on the other side of where I got you. I went through, and suddenly I was standing in the middle of a crowd that was chanting for someone's death. I almost croaked myself when I saw it was you."

Xander squinted at him. "They were chanting *sign*-something. You know it?"

"*Sine missione.* It means 'to the death.' Romans used to say it to encourage the winning gladiators to take down their opponents."

"Dad, we were in the *Colosseum!*"

"I recognized it."

"Like in Rome?" David said, catching the excitement.

"But it was *new*," Xander told his father. "Like it was twenty centuries ago."

"History is my subject, Son. Good thing I studied the Colosseum. I knew there were tunnels under the arena. When I saw where you were heading, I used them to reach the door closest to you."

"Just in time," Xander said and felt his eyes tear up again.

"Just in time?" David said. "What happened?"

Xander opened his mouth to answer but simply couldn't. He didn't know where to start, how much to say . . . "Was that real?" he asked his father.

"Felt real to *me*. And . . ." Dad poked Xander's arm.

Xander flinched away. "Ahhh."

A long swath of skin had been flayed from his bicep. It was glistening red. Blood had trickled down to his elbow.

"Ow!" David said for him.

Dad said, "Talk about a close call. You almost lost your arm."

"Arms," Xander corrected. "And legs and head."

"*What?*" David squealed. "How? What happened?"

"I'll tell you later, okay?"

David had moved beyond the terrible panic he must have felt at Xander's disappearance. Now he was fired up. But out of respect for his brother's condition, he nodded. He could wait . . . barely.

Dad untied the pelt and hung it from a hook. He slipped the sword and scabbard off his shoulder, hung it on the next hook. "These things," he said. "I'm not sure how, but I think they helped us get back." He studied them, hanging on the hooks, swinging gently back and forth. "When I got to your side of the Colosseum, they got . . . I don't know, *heavier*. I realized they hadn't gained pounds, but they were pulling away from me, like they were trying to go somewhere. When I grabbed you, I kind of went with them, let them tug me where they wanted to."

"Tug?" David said. "That pelt and sword were tugging *you?*"

Dad nodded. "That's what it was, a tug. When I gave into it, we fell back and landed here."

"So the items are what get you there and bring you back?" Xander said.

"I don't know if they bring you back or simply show you the way. Maybe we were close to the portal anyway, and they led us to it." He eyed Xander funny. "David said you had chain mail."

"And a helmet," Xander said. "I left them back in the arena. Now that you say it, the chain mail did get heavy; that's why I dropped it. Maybe it was tugging me toward the portal." His face paled. "If I needed them to get back . . . and I lost them . . . I could have been stuck there." His eyes welled with tears again. "If you hadn't come for me . . ."

Dad gripped his shoulder. "It's okay. We're here now, that's all that matters."

"Except for not helping me get back," Xander said, "is it bad I lost them? Nothing bad will happen because I didn't bring them back, will it?"

Dad shook his head. "No more questions, Xander." He lifted his foot onto the bench, leaned an arm over his knee. "I have a question for the two of you, though."

Here it comes, Xander thought. *The lecture, the scolding.* He and David exchanged a look.

Their dad said, "Chocolate or vanilla?"

If he had suddenly slapped David, he could not have elicited a more stunned expression on the boy's face.

Xander stumbled over his words. "But . . . what . . . uh . . . Don't you want to talk to us about . . . all of *this*?" He swept his hands in a wide arc trying to encompass this room, all the rooms, the hidden stairway and corridor.

Dad scrunched his brow. "We'll get to that. But let's get some sleep first. And, of course, ice cream."

"Since you put it that way," Xander said, "chocolate."

CHAPTER

SATURDAY, 10:13 A.M.

It was only a dream, Xander thought. He blinked against the sun coming through the bedroom windows.

Then he rolled over, and the wound on his arm flared with white-hot pain.

"Aaahhh!"

David stirred under his covers. He turned to face Xander. "Hurt?"

"No, I always wake up screaming." He turned the clock radio toward him. 10:13. Yow. Dad must have asked Mom to let them sleep in. She was usually all over them if they weren't up "before the sun got hot." He said, "I thought I'd dreamed the whole thing, fighting a gladiator in the Roman Colosseum."

David shook his head. "It wasn't a dream. I was there when you went . . . and when Dad brought you back."

Xander closed his eyes. Thinking about it made his stomach sour. All those bodies. His own close shave with death. Even the simple fact that life's rules—especially the ones dealing with time and space, little things like these—were not carved in stone, as he had been taught. All of it made him feel disoriented, like a kite broken from its string, whipping around in the wind. He'd just woken up, and already he was getting a headache.

"Xander, what happened over there? You said Dad got there just in time."

He didn't open his eyes.

"Are you going to tell me?"

"David, it wasn't good. Trust me, you don't want to know."

"I want to try it."

Xander's lids flipped open. "It?"

"Going someplace. Through the door."

"No, you don't want to try it. Don't say that."

"Dad did it and came right back. He wasn't in any danger."

"David, I almost died."

"But you *didn't*." His eyes sparkled with excitement.

"I didn't know you were so stupid."

David's smile faltered. Xander reminded himself that Dae had saved his life last night. If he hadn't fetched their father, Xander would have been slaughtered by that barbarian. In fact, he would have been in his grave for about two thousand years by now. That was something to think about.

Xander blinked slowly. "Sorry. I'm just saying I don't know why you would even be thinking this way, when you saw what happened to me."

"I didn't *see*. That's just it."

"Well, I'm telling you, okay? I almost died, and it was the most horrible experience of my life."

David considered this. After a time, he said, "I'm not talking about going where you went. Just *somewhere*."

Xander threw his legs out from under the covers and sat up. He thought of David and the situation he had been in, under the shield as the sword came down on it. He wouldn't have had the physical strength to survive. Nothing against him, just his age. And all those bodies . . . Xander wasn't sure how well *he* was going to handle it over time. He got up and sat on David's bed. "I know it sounds exciting; I would think that too. But it's not worth it."

David looked like he had been told Christmas had been called off. He said, "You and Dad got to do it."

"If we'd been in a car accident, would you want to do that too?"

"That's different."

"It's *not* different, David. That's what I'm trying to tell you. It's just as scary and potentially deadly. When Dad brought me back, the first thing I thought of was a friend who'd been in a car accident. I'm telling you, that's what it was like."

David's face reflected his disappointment. Xander could tell he wasn't totally convinced.

Xander said, "Promise me you won't sneak off and do it."

David said nothing.

"*Promise* me."

David's lips grew tight. The bottom one rolled out a little. His stubborn face.

"If you don't promise, I'm gonna follow you every second of every day. Even to the bathroom. I'll be like a bad smell you can't wash away."

Slowly, a smile found David's face. He said, "I promise."

"Okay." Xander pushed him playfully on the chest. He stood. He snatched his jeans off a post at the foot of the bed and pulled them on. He had showered the night before, which was really earlier that morning. He could not believe how much grime and dirt and blood the water had sluiced off him to swirl down the drain. His father had stayed with him, leaning against the sink, talking quietly. Xander knew Dad was worried about him. He had seen some of what Xander had gone through. He had also commented that he hoped the jaunt itself, to another time and place, did not have lasting consequences on their physical bodies or mental state. Xander should have reminded David of that, but he had gotten him to promise and that was all that mattered right then. Dad had said they would decide what to do about the rooms upstairs another time. For now, they were off-limits. He had also asked the boys to not tell Mom or Toria. He was afraid they would panic and want to leave without carefully considering the situation, and since the corridor was behind a secret wall, there was no need to stir up trouble.

"Let sleeping dogs lie," Dad had said.

It bothered Xander that in the short time since their move, the number of secrets in their family had skyrocketed.

"What are you going to tell Mom?" David asked, seeming to know Xander's thoughts. This was one of the topics he and Dad had discussed while he let the hot shower strip centuries-old dirt off his body. When he'd come to bed after that, David had already been asleep.

He looked at the gauze and tape Dad had applied. "Just an accident while investigating the house."

David sat up in bed. "You're going to flat-out *lie*?"

Xander pulled on a T-shirt. His movements made his arm throb. "It's not really lying. We *were* investigating the house, and it *was* an accident." He registered David's expression and sighed. "I know, I know. If it's not a lie, it's darn close. Dad said sometimes lies told to keep people safe are okay."

"Hmm. Do you think Dad has lied to us?"

Xander pulled a pair of socks from his drawer and picked up his sneakers. He'd put them on outside, on the front porch steps. He wanted to spend more time outside today. He shook his head. "I think Dad's as straight as they come."

David smiled.

As he left the room, Xander thought, *What's one more lie?*

thirty-one

SATURDAY, 11:30 A.M.

After breakfast, Xander decided he needed fresh air and sunshine. He and David set off to explore their property.

Every few minutes Xander found himself looking back through the trees at the house. He kept expecting to see something not right: an angle or addition that wasn't true; or, as before, a whole chunk of house just up and gone. If the house played tricks, it wasn't doing it today. The irregular *squeak-squeak* of the weathervane on top of the tower continually reminded him of its looming presence.

They'd been out awhile, and his hunger told him it was close to lunchtime. Some time ago David had wandered off toward the back while Xander explored the dense forest on one side of the house. Bushes and trees had gone unpruned for decades. Even at midday the area was cloaked in shadow. Enough sunlight seeped through to render flashlights unnecessary, but no one would mistake Xander's trek through the bush for a cheery walk in the park. Most interesting to him were the fallen trees. They lay here and there in various stages of decomposition. Rolling them over, when they were small enough or decayed enough, revealed swarming worlds of beetles and centipedes, spiders and worms. He always tried to find the stump of a fallen tree. Sometimes it was nearby. Other times he'd have to walk around to find it, usually up an embankment. He'd make up stories about how the trees fell: lightning, beavers, some dudes fooling around with an ax. Probably most had simply died and fallen over. But that was boring.

He had his camera out now and was filming a black beetle crawl over one of Toria's dolls in macro-lens mode when he heard David calling him. He kept the camera rolling and brought the camera up to capture his brother's progress through the woods. David moved toward him, stepping into and out of shafts of light, into and out of view. Then he veered away, still calling.

Xander considered letting him wander completely out of

sight and out of earshot. That would make a funny short film, if a bit abstract. Deciding against being mean today, he yelled, "Over here!"

"Come see something," David said, leaping over bushes and deadfalls to reach him.

"What is it?" Xander asked.

David puzzled at the overturned log and Toria's Barbie. Ants were swarming over her face, through her hair. "What are you doing?" he asked.

Xander smiled. "The doll represents Average Man—or Woman. The bugs are all the little problems that plague him. See?"

"I think I liked it better when you were making movies about skateboarders wiping out."

"I am now *le artiste*," Xander said, trying to sound as French as François Truffaut. He raised his fingers to the sky, in a flourish, thinking he looked flamboyant and artsy. He was enjoying the dual distractions of the outdoors and his cinematic aspirations.

His brother thought about that. He said, "Whatever. Come see what I found."

"Is it cool?"

"It's weird."

Xander paused. He wasn't so sure he could take any more weirdness.

"Not like last night," David assured him. "Kind of . . . just *weird*. It won't make you think you're crazy or anything." Then: "I don't think it will."

"Lead the way," Xander said.

They pushed deeper into the woods, behind the house. At times, the bushes and brambles, trees and branches were so thick they had to walk around as surely as they would a mountain. Xander watched the house recede, becoming less distinct through all the foliage. After a time, he could see it no more. The shadows were even darker here. It made Xander think of the Hansel and Gretel woods, how they got lost in them. More accurately, it resembled the woods in every werewolf movie he'd ever seen.

"How much farther?" he asked.

"Just up here."

"How'd you get this far away from the house?" David had ventured at least three times the distance Xander had.

"I thought I heard something."

"Like what?"

"Footsteps. You know, breaking branches and crunching."

"Footsteps? Out here?"

"And then laughing."

Xander stopped. "David, with everything we've gone through, you followed footsteps and laughter into the creepiest woods we've ever seen?"

David shrugged. "I didn't think anything would happen outside the house. It wasn't spooky laughter. More like . . ." He thought about it. "A kid on a playground."

"You haven't seen enough movies. Children are a vital part

of ghost stories. They lure you in, then *wham!*" He punched his fist into his palm.

David shook his head. He turned and kept going. Xander hesitated, then followed.

"See there?" David said.

Through the trees ahead, sunlight broke through. It wasn't a mere shaft but a radiant glow covering a wide area. A clearing.

Xander thought if David had found a stone altar, he was going back to the motel, with or without everybody else.

But when he stepped out of what had become an impossibly dense forest, he was both fascinated and puzzled. Fascinated because out of untamed wilderness was a meadow half the size of a football field. The ground was mostly flat and covered in a thick, green grass. No rocks, bushes, or trees marred its parklike perfection. It was shaped like an egg, its boundaries well-defined by the dark, imposing forest that completely surrounded it. Overhead, the canopy of the treetops leaned way in, forming a natural dome. At the center, an opening revealed blue sky, white clouds.

The strangest aspect of this area could not be seen, only felt. It was as though Xander had instantly ascended to the top of a high mountain. The air was cooler and felt thinner. It rushed into his lungs with ease, giving him a mild jolt of energy. When Xander was David's age, oxygen bars were all the rage. Dad was curious and took him to one. They held masks over their mouths and noses and breathed from a canister of oxygen, like you see in hospitals. Both of them had decided the gimmick was a rip-off. However, the purchased air did somehow *taste* better than regular air and had made them morning-perky. The air in the meadow felt— *tasted*—like that.

"What is this?" Xander asked.

David shook his head. "Can't be natural, can it?"

At first, Xander had thought the same thing. Now he saw imperfections humans wouldn't leave—the ground under the grass was bumpy, wavy; the trees encroached into the area just enough to give the perimeter a slightly shabby appearance. Despite the unmistakable dome of the leafy canopy, there was no evidence any pruning had occurred. If someone had carved the clearing from the forest, it had not been tended to in a long time.

As Xander's eyes scanned upward, David said, "But that's not all."

Xander laughed. His brother had stepped out twenty feet into the meadow. "Say that again," he said.

"I said, that's not all."

"Why are you talking like that?"

"Like what?"

"Your voice. It's higher pitched." David's voice had not yet started changing. When he answered the phone, people still mistook him for their mother and sometimes even Toria. While not dramatic, his voice was even higher now.

Xander walked toward him. "I've listened to you enough to know what you sound—" As he spoke, the pitch of his own voice rose. Not to an unnatural level, but the way it did when he got excited or whiny about something. "Hello? Hello? Hear that?"

"I'm talking right now," David said. He was listening to his own voice, nodding, an open-mouthed grin widening with each word.

Xander said, "Can you hear it in me?"

"Yeah!" David started howling like a wolf. His pitch rose to ear-splitting, glass-breaking levels.

"All right, all right," Xander said, covering his ears. "Stop it."

"Now look," David said, He ran out into the meadow, then back.

"Okay?" Xander said.

"What'd I do?"

Xander looked at him from the corner of his eye. "You . . . ran."

"How fast?"

"All-out sprint, dude." And then he noticed David was not out of breath. He said, "Wasn't it?"

David shook his head. "I was jogging. Now watch this." He walked away. He ran past Xander at a pretty good clip, but nothing stunning. Then he jumped. A little too high, a little too far. It was nothing most people would probably notice. But this close, and knowing him so well, Xander knew it wasn't normal. Xander took off across the field. He didn't feel like Dash, the fast kid in *The Incredibles*. It simply felt like a good run on a good day. He leaped into the air. From his own perspective, he realized it was the best jump of his life.

Directly in front of him, a man climbed through the brambles and stepped into the clearing. Xander braked and fell back onto his butt.

It was Dad. He had leaves in his hair. One sleeve of his sweatshirt was pushed up over his elbow, the other down around his wrist. Sweat had soaked through in the shape of his sternum.

"Xander," Dad said. He sounded excited. Then Xander realized it was a casual greeting, and the excited part was the tricky air making his voice higher than normal.

His father reached him and held out a hand to help him up.

As Xander rose, he said, "What are you doin' here?"

David ran up and stood by his brother's side.

"Out looking for you," Dad said. "I've got to run some errands, and I'd like you boys to stay in the house."

Xander realized Dad had not commented on the clearing at all, let alone the strangeness of the air and the way it affected their voices. "How did you come from over there?" he asked his father, pointing. It was the opposite direction from the house.

Dad looked over his shoulder as if just catching that. He said, "I heard you guys, but you know how sounds are around here. Must have gotten lost."

"Must have gotten *really* lost," David said. He reached up and pulled a leafy twig out of Dad's hair.

Dad smiled. "Are these crazy woods, or what?"

Xander said, "Were you out this way earlier today?"

"The other day I was. Found this clearing." He looked around in wonder, shook his head.

"What do you think this place is?" David said.

"More weirdness, Dae. But pretty lightweight stuff, compared. You know?" He winked.

Xander knew what he meant. Still, it bothered him to find yet another oddity on their property. It was like all the anomalies of the world had congregated on this one spot. Or—more likely—one truly weird abnormality happened here and smaller drops of strangeness splattered out from it. He pictured a dollop of paint falling from God's palette, striking the earth where the house now stood. Its splatter made things like this clearing and who knew what else?

As Dad passed them, he gave David a healthy shove. The kid fell and tumbled—farther than he should have, laughing all the way.

CHAPTER

thirty-two

SATURDAY, 11:55 P.M.

When Xander returned from a late-night bathroom run, David was not in his bed. The covers were folded back, exposing only sheets and a pillow. Had he been there when Xander got up? *Yeah*, he thought. He remembered hearing David's rhythmic breathing. It was only a little after eleven, but the day spent outside had worn them out. The boys had crashed around ten. Xander had watched the shadows on the ceiling, falling in and out of light sleep until he realized he had to visit the bathroom. Maybe David had felt the same need, and finding the bathroom occupied, went to one of the others.

"David," he whispered, in case the boy was hiding. No answer. Xander crawled in bed, pulled the cover over his shoulder, closed his eyes. They snapped open again. He threw back his blankets and jumped up.

"David?" he said, louder. "*Oh no!*"

He ran from the room and down the hall. Past the foyer. Past their parents' bedroom to where the hallway bent and went toward the back of the house. By the illumination of the night-light, he saw the false wall was angled into the hallway, leaving a gap of several feet.

"David!"

He ran through, scraping his injured arm on the edge. He felt the pain, but did not allow it to distract him. The second door, the one with the metal skin, was also open. He slammed into the doorjamb, rolled off and through, and started up the stairs. A flashlight clicked on, blinding him.

"David?"

"What took you so long?" He was sitting on the landing.

"What are you *doing?*" Xander's concern had instantly turned to anger.

"I promised I wouldn't go into the rooms without you."

"Then what are you doing?" Xander repeated.

"Waiting for you. I can come here any time I want. See?"

"What are you saying?"

"I want to know what it's like. Just once."

"David, there is no way—"

"Just once, Xander. You can help me, or not."

"You promised."

"I'm not breaking it, but I'll take it back if you don't help."

Xander's heart felt squeezed to the size of a raisin. David was honest, but that did not always translate into being *good*.

"Scoot over," Xander said. He sat beside his brother. While David played the light over the stairs, the open door below and, occasionally, down the hotel-like corridor, Xander told him about fighting the gladiator. He did not spare any detail. The bodies. The sword crashing down on the shield. The soldiers who attacked when he had begged them for help. The close calls, when he'd thought he was dead. David listened without making a sound. When Xander finished, they sat quietly. David had stilled his hand; the light shined on his sneakers.

After a few minutes, Xander felt his brother's hand on his shoulder. David said, "I'm sorry that happened to you."

"You see why I don't want you to do it?"

At first, David didn't reply. Then he whispered, "I have to. If I don't, I'll always wonder. My whole life."

"If you do, your whole life may not be very long." Xander had to admit this was consistent with David's personality. He had dirt biked and scuba dived, hit a black diamond slope on only their fourth trip to Mammoth Mountain, and had even flown in an ultralight with a friend's father. Xander was into adventure as well, but never with David's degree of enthusiasm—Dad called it "reckless abandon." David could ramble on for hours about the things he wanted to do when he became old enough: pilot a jet; bungee from some bridge on the Zimbabwe-Zambia border; and streetluge, which was like putting wheels on your back and flying down the longest, scariest road you could find. Once, when the dinnertime conversation turned to how each of them wanted to die, Xander had said "In my sleep." *Yeah, that sounded like a decent way to go.*

David had said, "I want to hang glide into a cliff when I'm ninety." *OK, that was cool,* Xander had admitted to himself. Then David had added, in all seriousness, "Or get eaten by a shark." He did not have a death wish. He would be the first to say he wanted to live a long, long time, so he could do all the things he dreamed about doing. It was more like, for David, life was most exciting when you could lose it. Xander didn't think David had actually figured that out yet. But it was true.

Now that Xander thought about it, he had been an idiot to think he could keep David out of those rooms. His little brother got scared like everyone did. He was just very adept at pushing his fear aside when doing so led to some grand new adventure.

"Look," Xander said, "if I go along with it, I pick which room."

"Not something stupid, like the one with the beach towel."

"That one sounds like a lot of fun to me."

David just looked at him.

Xander said, "Okay, but nothing with a weapon. Okay? A weapon seems like a bad sign."

"Well, if the only rooms that look cool are the ones with weapons . . ."

"No," Xander said. "No weapons, no matter what." When David didn't respond, he added, "Otherwise, I'll drag your butt to Dad right now. He'll brick up that wall down there, and if that doesn't work, I'll kick and scream till we move."

"All right, already. No weapons."

Before his brother's agreement had registered in Xander's mind, David was standing, stepping toward the corridor. He flipped the metal breaker, turning on the lights.

Xander stepped up behind him. "Do you know which room?"

"Antechamber."

"What?"

"That's what Dad called these rooms: *antechambers*."

"Whatever. Do you know which one?"

David shook his head. Xander stepped past David and opened the first door.

"That's the beach towel room," David complained.

"Uh . . . no it's not." Hanging from the hooks were an astronaut's helmet, a metallic space suit, something that looked like a pistol, but may have been a welding torch. There were a few other items consistent with an outer-space adventure.

"Whoa," David said, looking past Xander.

Xander quickly said, "There's a gun. That's a weapon."

"That's not a weapon!"

"I said, not this one." Xander slammed the door.

He opened it again, peered in. He clicked it shut, once more. He said, "You know, I think you're right. That *was* the beach towel room."

"Duh. Those beach things with the flip-flops were the first things we saw. Remember?"

Xander nodded. "Well . . . it changed."

David scrunched his nose, hitched up his top lip. "Would Dad do that?"

"Why would he? And . . ." Xander thought about it. "It's not like someone just switched the stuff around, and I don't remember seeing astronaut stuff. I *know* we checked every room."

David nodded in agreement. "Somebody put *brand-new* stuff in there."

Simultaneously, they gazed up the corridor at the other doors. About ten minutes later, they had rechecked every room. About half of the themes were ones they had seen the previous night, though both brothers thought they were in different rooms. The other themes were altogether new.

"Who's doing it, you think?" David asked.

Xander was squinting at the doors. "I don't know, but . . ." They went to every room again, verifying that none of the themes had changed since their last inspection. None had.

"Maybe they all change at a specific time," Xander suggested.

"Or when no one's around."

They were silent for a while. At last, David clapped his hands together. He strolled up the center of the carpeted runner. "Let's see. Which one . . . had . . ." Thinking, thinking. "The police badge and uniform?"

"No weapons," Xander reminded him.

"That one didn't have . . . oh, the pistol."

"You'd probably wind up smack in the middle of a bank robbery."

Xander caught the spark in David's eye before he turned away.

"David . . ."

"I know. How about that one with the rope and carabiners?"

Xander tossed his hands up. "You don't know how to mountain climb! These places don't suddenly give you new skills. They just drop you in."

David opened a door. He turned a smile on Xander, then stepped through.

"What?" Xander said, rushing to catch the door before it shut.

Khaki-colored safari hat. Compass. A vest with many pockets and loops and straps. A canteen on a utility belt. A machete. On the bench were knee-high leather boots.

"A jungle?" Xander said.

David grinned and nodded.

Xander said, "A *machete*. That's a weapon."

"It's a tool. I'll probably have to cut my way out of some bushes, that's all."

Xander didn't like it, but a deal was a deal. He pulled the utility belt off its hook and held it out to David.

The boy hesitated. When he reached for it, his hand trembled.

Xander's eyebrows went up. "You okay?"

"Yeah." His voice was high, like it had been in the clearing. His tongue clicked dryly in his mouth.

Xander thought of Richard Dreyfuss in *Jaws*, when he was preparing to go in the shark cage. He was so afraid he couldn't spit into his diving mask to keep it from fogging up. Now there was a David personality for you: scared, but willing to do it anyway.

David cinched the belt around his waist. Xander handed him the machete. He unsheathed it and gave it the once-over. He clipped it to the belt. Xander set the helmet on his brother's head. It was too big and made him look five years old.

"Dad's gonna kill me," Xander said.

David reached for the second door's handle.

"Wait!" Xander said. "Don't open that door. I'll be right back."

"What?" David said.

"Just wait, don't move." Xander hurried out of the room. Even with reining in his speed on the stairs and tiptoeing past the master bedroom, he reached his and Dae's room and was back in the antechamber upstairs in no more than a minute. He held his camcorder up to David. "Here, take this."

"I don't want that!" David protested. "What if I need my hands? What if I lose it?"

Xander let the camera drop to the end of its long leather strap. He slipped it over David's head so it hung around his neck.

"I'll turn it on now," he said, flipping the power switch and pushing the record button. "If you think about it, point it at something. If you don't, we'll still have proof you went some-where. You might not want to burp or do anything too embar-rassing, though."

"Like scream?" David asked. He opened the inner door.

The antechamber instantly became more humid. A botani-cal fragrance wafted in. Beyond the threshold, fat, green leaves swayed in a breeze. Trees rose out of sight, hairy-looking vines looped down, almost touching the moss-covered earth.

"You sure about this?" Xander asked.

David nodded. He tightened the helmet strap under his chin.

Xander said, "How long was I gone last night?"

David shrugged. "Twenty minutes?"

"So, it's probably all in real time. A minute over there is a minute here. If you're not back in fifteen minutes, I'm gonna get Dad and come after you."

David nodded. He stepped through.

The door pulled out of Xander's grip and slammed shut.

thirty-three

David watched the door waver and fade away. The moist heat drew sweat from his face and neck. The plants seemed to quiver, but whether from wind or some kind of ground tremor, David didn't know. The cushy grasses and moss prevented him from feeling much else under his feet. A bird cawed in the distance. It was a sound like an alarm that set David's nerves on edge. He was already thinking about how he would get back. If the door had vanished, where would he find the portal to home? He did want to experience this world, but he would have felt a lot better knowing where the exit was. He trusted that *somehow*—either with Xander's help or as Dad had said, through some signal from the items he held—the portal would reveal itself.

He stepped to the fern where the door had shimmered and ceased to be. He was moving the leaves around when a centipede—as long as his arm and as thick as a hotdog—scuttled up the frond toward his hand. Its front half rose up, as if to look David in the eyes. Its many legs wiggled and waved. Huge pincers, coming off its head, clamped and opened, clamped and opened. Unsure if the thing could leap or how fast it could move if it decided David looked like a tasty treat, he reversed another few steps. His heel crunched on something. A brown and yellow beetle, as big as an egg, oozed yellow guts from its shattered shell. Three others, bigger, moved quickly toward David, perhaps intent on avenging their friend. He gingerly danced away on tiptoes.

Should have put on the boots, he thought. He backed into something that moved easily under David's touch: a long, fat snake, hanging from a branch. David yelled, then laughed at himself: it was only a vine. He sighed, then spotted a real snake, slithering down the vine in his direction. Having already yelled, he bit his tongue and backed away.

His heart was a ferret, caged within his chest, panicky to get out. It seemed to jump and twirl and bang against his breastbone and his ribs. Its frantic beats made little room for the expansion of his lungs, and he found breathing to be difficult.

Well away from the snake and centipede and beetles, he stopped. He scanned the area, saw no immediate threats. He closed his eyes and forced himself to take a long, deep breath. He lifted Xander's camera off his stomach, where it had been bouncing at the end of its strap. He made sure the Record light was on, then held it to his face. He zoomed in on the vine and snake, panned to the plant where the centipede had been. He didn't see it now, in the camera's little LCD screen.

Nearby, something roared. It was a big animal, a wild cat. David lowered the camera. It roared again, and he wondered if it had caught his scent and was crooning its excitement about finding an exotic meal.

As if in answer, a second animal roared, in the opposite direction, but seeming just as near. The next roar came from a third beast—between the first two, but farther off. That ferret in his chest had found his throat and was pushing up into it.

David shook his head. Considering Xander's experience, it was just like that house to drop him into big-cat territory. From the roars, he figured he was in their favorite feeding zone and it was dinnertime. For all he knew, the portal issued a frequency only tigers could hear—the big-cat equivalent of a dinner bell. He had thought *tiger*, but he didn't know their roars from any of the other big cats. At one time or another, he had heard them all at the San Diego Zoo, but he wasn't nerd enough about animals to distinguish the difference. He thought he had read somewhere—or maybe it was from the singing animals in *The Jungle Book*—that the only big cats in jungle settings were leopards, panthers, and tigers. The roars were throaty and loud. Had to be tigers.

Whatever they were, he didn't want to hang around to find out. He unsheathed the machete. Its weight felt good in his hand. He admired its gleaming edge.

One of the beasts roared again. Almost immediately, it received an answering call. Both seemed closer, and David realized how awfully true his statement to Xander had been: the machete was a tool, not a weapon.

He held still, willing it or the hat or the utility belt to show him the way to the portal. He felt nothing, no tug, no weightiness in one direction or another. Maybe he had to move, get closer to the portal before the items started drawing him toward it.

He swung the machete down into a leaf the size and thickness of a bath towel. It fell away before him and he smiled. He sliced again and again, stepping forward each time.

Blazing a path, he thought. *Isn't that what they say?* So he blazed. He had no clue where he would end up, but he believed he was putting ground between him and the tigers. He swung the machete diagonally, lopping away a leaf and a branch. They fell to the ground, revealing the snarling face of a tiger. Its head was huge, twice the size of David's. The cat was pulled back onto its haunches. One paw up, ready to strike.

Its claws were curved blades: a single one could cause butcher-knife damage; five would take off his face and open him up.

He jumped back, but amazingly did not scream. He could not even breathe. He raised the machete over his head and turned it so the big cat could see it. It hissed, baring teeth the size of railroad spikes. Its eyes watched David intently.

He had heard something about what *not* to do with great predators. If he remembered right, turning and running would be the end of him. Rather, he backed slowly away. The animal did not move. Reversing along the path he had blazed, he moved around a bend and lost sight of the beast. Almost directly behind him, lost among the heavy leaves, another tiger roared.

Certainly not the same one. It could not have—

Finishing his thought for him, the tiger in front roared.

The third tiger joined in, off to his left. David's entire body shook in fear.

Dang it, Xander, he thought, *you could be wrong sometimes, you know.*

With no other place to go, he turned right and pushed through the tangle of vines and branches and plants with their stupid bath-towel leaves. He avoided using the machete, thinking its rhythmic chopping would bring the tigers more quickly, the way a thrashing fish drew sharks. For just a moment, he thought of the centipede and snake and wondered if he'd run into more of *them.* Just as quickly, he dismissed the thought. Those things were just pests in a world of true killers. He *wished* the creepy-crawlers were all he had to worry about.

Unable to cross a particularly dense spot, he chopped at it with the machete. A tiger roared. It sounded close. Leaves rustled nearby. Something was moving alongside him, twenty feet away. He pushed forward and it moved again, pacing him.

He realized he had been hearing the thunderous sound of a waterfall. For a time, he had mistaken it for his own blood rushing past his ears. Hope welled in him. A waterfall meant water, and cats didn't like water. He pushed toward it, chopping and cutting when he had to. He hoped none of the cats realized what he was doing and cut him off.

Something moved, heavy and fast, behind him. He spun, machete raised, expecting to see only the gaping maw of a tiger as it leaped at him. Instead, furry striped hindquarters and a tail flashed past. The thing had run right past him. He didn't know if tigers tormented their prey or if they were simply cautious hunters.

He *felt* tormented and he *felt* hunted.

Then the jungle stopped—just like that. It gave way to the granite edge of a cliff. Way down below, a river sparkled. The waterfall he'd heard was a half-mile away. The other side of the chasm was a long way off.

And the tigers were very close.

Like a gift from heaven, only a stone's throw away, was a bridge spanning the chasm. It was made of rope and wooden planks. If he beat the tigers across it, he could cut the ropes on the other side, separating them from their meal.

A tiger roared . . . David thought it sounded like a laugh. He hurried along the rock ledge to the bridge.

Movement behind him. A snapped twig, leaves flung aside with the sound of a wind-rippled sail, the pounding of heavy paws. He stepped onto the first planks, testing them. The wood felt solid, but the bridge was wobbly. He took another tentative step, ready to run if the tigers appeared, but they were nowhere in sight.

What did appear were men on the other side of the bridge. They were dark skinned and scantily dressed. Some kind of aboriginal tribe, David guessed. He did not know where in the world he was or what these people might be called. The three he had first noticed became triple that as they poured from the dense brush. Certainly they were hunters and would want the tigers. In fact, they carried spears and bows and arrows. He hurried toward them. Two of the archers took aim.

David looked back. No animals. Perhaps these hunters had spooked them. One archer released his arrow. David had to duck to avoid being skewered through the head.

"Hey!" he yelled. The camera swung against his chest.

The other archer fired. The arrow sailed a few inches from David's right arm. A spear came next, in a shallow arc designed to impale him. He dropped straight down onto the planks. The camcorder—he'd forgotten all about it—struck him hard in the chin. The machete flipped out of his hand and pinwheeled into the abyss. The spear clattered on the wood behind him. The bridge began to shake. David closed his eyes and gripped the edges. More shaking. The hunters had mounted the bridge and were running toward him in single file.

He lifted a shaking hand to one of the ropes that acted as a handrail for crossers. He pulled himself up and tore quickly away from the approaching hunters.

Ahead, a section of tall fronds whipped back and forth violently, then stopped. A tiger roared.

An arrow whizzed across his shoulder, slicing his T-shirt. It continued on to *thunk* into a tree, where it quivered as though furious about missing its mark.

David stepped off the bridge. He darted left along the rock ledge. A spear struck the ground three feet ahead of him and snapped in two. Each piece spun off in a different direction. Abruptly, he turned and plunged into the jungle. One of the big cats snarled nearby. It thrashed through the underbrush as big and heavy as a car. David veered away from it. Ahead of him a tiger roared.

He stopped. The thrashing continued for another few seconds, then stilled.

Breathing. Panting. Under it was a rolling *rrrrr*, almost a purr. Not friendly or loving. This was more of a satisfied sound. The creature knew it was going to get what it wanted.

More rustling in front of David. The inhalation and exhalation of a second beast reached his ears. Farther off, the pattering of bare feet on the wood-planked bridge, growing louder. A fat raindrop struck David's head.

Rain, he thought. *Just what I need right now.*

Another drop splattered on his shoulder. He felt it: sticky. He looked up. The third tiger was crouched on a branch high above him. At least for now, it seemed content to watch. He thought that was a particularly feline trait: to watch or play with its food until it grew bored and then the banquet started. He believed his only choice was to break through the jungle and leap off the cliff. He really didn't think he would survive the fall, even if he hit the water far below. But he would rather have that one chance in a million than no chance at all with these tigers and hunters.

But it was too late.

He could barely see over the top of the greenery in front of him. A dark gap, like a thick crack in the surface of a frozen lake, was moving directly for him—a beast was approaching fast, flattening the grass and plants as it came. Behind him, a branch cracked loudly. The breathing became a growl. It grew louder with each pounding step of the beast. From *two* sides, he thought. Three, if the one above gets involved.

I'm going to be torn apart.

He screamed.

Eyes wide, jaw set, Xander pushed out of the bushes in front of David. He grabbed David by the head and yanked him back. The bushes engulfed them.

"Xander! What are you—"

"Shut up and come on." Xander began crawling on his hands and knees. Every few feet he'd stop to pull David closer. The camcorder dragged on the ground, snagging on things, making David yank it with his neck.

Behind them, the tigers were going crazy, growling, roaring, and by the sounds of it, swiping at the jungle with their claws.

"What are we doing?" David whispered, his voice harsh, almost guttural. "Where are we going? There are three tigers—"

"I know," Xander said. He pulled David alongside him, threw his arm over his back, and gave him a squeeze. "Do you feel it? That tug Dad talked about?"

"No, I—" Then he did: a gentle tug on the utility belt as though Xander had his finger looped into it, but he didn't. The helmet too seemed a bit heavier on the upper right side, the same direction the belt was yearning to go. "That way!" he said.

"Right. It has to be close. I *just* stepped out of the antechamber."

They crawled through the underbrush. The tigers roared and hissed and pawed. They knew where their meal was. They were taking their time, enjoying the hunt.

David's helmet grew heavier, pulling his head suddenly to the side. The belt almost yanked his hips past his body.

Xander said, "Here! Hold on!"

The brothers rolled as one and fell into a hole.

CHAPTER

thirty-four

SUNDAY, 12:50 A.M.

They crashed onto the wooden floor of the antechamber. The door slammed against David's legs. He shifted them out of the way, and it banged shut. Xander was suddenly on top of him. He had fistfuls of David's T-shirt, and he was shaking him.

"See?" Xander said. He was so close, David felt spit spray his chin. "See? You didn't listen to me and see what happened!"

Tears ran from the corners of David's eyes into the hair at

his temples. He gritted his teeth. He wasn't gonna cry, he wasn't. He wasn't so sure about Xander, though. His brother stopped yelling, but kept his double-fisted grip on David's collar. They stared into each other's eyes. Xander shook his head.

The ferret in David's chest was settling down. It scampered around and around, more slowly with each revolution. He squeezed his eyes shut, expelling the last of his tears. He could weep, probably should. He had almost died in the most horrific way. From the time he crossed the threshold to when Xander pulled him back, he had been terrified. Stalked by tigers. Hunted by humans. Almost knocked off a bridge. By all rights he should be dead.

But he wasn't. He *wasn't*. That's what he held onto. Air filled his lungs. Blood flowed through his veins. His brother was spitting on him. He was alive.

He smiled, a big toothy grin. Into Xander's gaping-stunned-frightened face, he said, "Can I do it again?"

Xander pulled him up several inches, just so he could toss him down. David's head conked against the floor.

Xander said, "Idiot." He pushed himself off of David. He picked up the camcorder, pulled the strap over his brother's head, and dropped onto the bench.

David lay on the floor, breathing hard. He said, "I'm kidding."

"You're still an idiot."

David said, "Thanks for saving me. How much did you see?"

Xander closed his eyes. "I put on the boots and the compass to open the door. At first, it was just colors, greens and browns. I leaned through the door a little more, just until I felt something trying to pull me in, and I could make out trees and leaves and stuff. It was like the portal was stuttering through the jungle, moving in little jerky motions. All of a sudden, I was right next to a *tiger!* I could smell it!"

"There were three of them," David said.

Xander nodded, his eyes still closed. "I could tell there was more than one. I saw a flash of your shirt, but I wasn't sure it was you. I waited to see if it would come around again. But then I was afraid I'd lose you completely, so I stepped through. Not far from you, as it turned out." He examined the camera. It was dirty and scratched. He picked a leaf off it and tossed it to the floor. Immediately the leaf flipped in the air, as though caught in a draft, and fluttered away through the gap at the bottom of the portal door.

David felt a shooting pain in the top of his shoulder. He touched his fingers to it, winced. When he looked, his fingers were bloody. And here he'd thought that arrow had missed.

Xander said, "I was thinking. What if Dad *hadn't* saved me last night?"

"Yeah?"

"Let's say I died or for whatever reason I didn't come back." He looked down at David. "What would happen to me?"

"You're *dead*?"

"Or gone forever."

David's brow furled in thought. "I think . . . if you're dead, you're dead." He pursed his lips. "If you're gone, you're gone."

Xander pointed at him. "That's what I'm saying."

David shook his head. "I don't get it."

"What happened to the family who lived here before us?"

"The dad killed everybody and—" David had a light-bulb moment. "Ahhh . . . You're saying maybe that's *not* what happened."

"What if they went over and died or couldn't find their way back?"

"*All* of them?"

Xander shrugged. "I'm just saying. As far as anyone here would know, they disappeared." He went back to fiddling with the camcorder.

David closed his eyes. "You're making my head hurt."

"No, listen. What if we just solved the biggest mystery in Pinedale's history, and we just don't have the details?"

"Or evidence."

"I'm not saying we can clear anybody's name. Just . . . wouldn't it be cool to figure it out? To know the truth?" He held up the camera and made a disgusted face. He said, "Nothing . . . just static."

"How can that be?" David rubbed his chin where the camera had cracked it when he was on the rope bridge.

Xander pushed a few buttons. His voice came through the

tiny speaker: ". . . might not want to burp or do anything too embarrassing . . ." He fast-forwarded, turning the voices into incomprehensible chipmunk-chatter. David remembered what he'd said after that: "Like scream?" Yeah, he'd done a bit of that, hadn't he? Xander got the video rolling at normal speed again: ". . . gonna get Dad and come after you." A moment later: the rude hiss of static.

"As soon as you stepped through," Xander said. He set the camcorder on the bench and unstrapped the compass from his wrist.

David rolled over. Groaning, he pushed himself up onto his knees. "Achy," he said. "All over."

Xander nodded. "Take a shower. You'll feel better." He tugged off one of the boots.

David grabbed hold of the bench, lifted himself onto it. He put his head back against the wall. "What you said? You know, finding the truth about that family?"

Xander had the other boot off and was positioning them neatly on the bench. He said, "Solve a mystery, win a prize."

David said, "There's something else about that. If what you say really did happen to that family . . ." His stomach turned over on itself. "What's gonna stop it from happening to us?"

thirty-five

As Dad had done for him, Xander waited in the bathroom for David to shower. He tried being like Dad, saying comforting things and generally trying to get his brother's mind off of nearly being eaten—by beast *and* man, to hear David tell it. His brother did seem better equipped to leave his horrifying experiences in the past than Xander had been. Now that it was history, and he was alive, David didn't mind talking about it. Then again, David hadn't seen the mutilated bodies, a dead boy who was about his own age.

Twenty minutes later, Xander was sitting on his bed in the dark, listening to David ramble on about tigers and hunters and a centipede as thick as a hotdog and four times as long. David's words became slow, and he started having a hard time finishing sentences. Then, he was asleep. Xander climbed into his own bed, exhausted. He had crashed almost three hours ago only to get up again because of David's insatiable appetite for adventure. He hoped . . . he hoped *something* about David, but he was too tired to remember what it was. He fell asleep.

He jolted awake. Sirens in his ears. A noise from his dreams was his first thought, but then David was pushed up in bed, staring frighteningly at him. Smoke alarm? No, they had not installed them in this house yet. The clock on the nightstand between the beds said 2:21.

"Toria," David said, throwing off his blankets.

Xander propelled himself out of bed, letting his sheets and covers find their own way off of his body. He leaped over the footboard and landed on his feet hard enough to rattle something on the dresser.

Toria screamed. It was long and piercing, broken only by her need to fill her lungs. Then, more screaming.

Xander bounded into the hall. A dark figure bolted at him from the other end. It raced by a night-light, and he saw it was Dad, with Mom right behind. Xander arrived at

Toria's room first and rushed in. By the glow of her own night-light—*Shrek*'s Princess Fiona in full ogre mode—he saw she was sitting up in bed, eyelids clamped tight, screaming for all she was worth. He skidded to a stop beside her bed. He wanted to grab her but was afraid to. He gripped her leg through the blankets. Xander would have thought it impossible, but her screams became louder, more piercing.

"Toria, it's me! Xander!" It didn't seem to matter.

Only then did he think to scan the room for an intruder. He squinted into the dark corners and at the closed closet door.

The overhead light snapped on, vaporizing the shadows and exposing not a hint of a boogeyman. Dad crashed into him. He plucked Toria out of her bed. Squeezing her to him, he said, "Honey, honey, what is it?" Then soothingly: "It's okay; it's okay."

Xander wasn't sure it was, wasn't sure of anything. But it was a parent's job to say that. Hadn't Dad spoken those words to *him* only the night before? He wondered if David had been so tough earlier because Dad hadn't been there to quash a breakdown. Kind of a survival thing, conscious or not.

Mom was at Dad's side, brushing Toria's hair away from her face. She kept saying, "Sweetheart, what is it?" David stood in the doorway, his mouth a perfect *O* in the whiteness of his face.

"A-a-a . . ." Toria tried to speak.

Xander, kneeling by the bed, reached out to stroke Toria's hair. He half-expected his touch to ignite another fit of screaming.

Instead, Toria leaned her head back into his hand, as if wanting to feel it more firmly. She stopped trying to speak and concentrated on catching her breath. Three sharp little inhales, a single long breath out. At last, she raised a finger in David's direction, said, "A m-m-man . . . there was . . . there was a man in my d-d-doorway."

David stiffened, glanced over his shoulder, then hurried into the room.

Mom said, "A man, honey? What do you mean?"

Xander caught David staring at him. His eyes were wide with fear.

"I heard a n-n-oise and woke up," Toria said. "There was a man standing in my room, at the door."

"What did he look like?" Dad asked.

"Big. He filled it up, the doorway."

"What did he look like," Dad repeated. "Did you see his face?"

Toria concentrated. She made a sour expression.

"It was *dark*," she said apologetically.

"That's okay," Dad said.

"I think . . . he was hairy. He had rags for pants." She started to weep quietly.

Mom said, "Ed, call the police."

"And say what, G? They'll say she had a nightmare. Maybe she did."

Mom looked unsure.

"Daddy," Toria said.

He squeezed Toria tighter. He said, "It's okay, sweetheart. We can talk about it later."

She pushed back from him to see his face. "The man said something, Daddy."

Xander felt the skin on his forearms and the back of his neck pull taught and tingle.

Mom said, "What did he say?"

Toria shook her head. "I didn't understand it. It was rumbly, like thunder." It frightened Xander simply to hear about it. He might have screamed too. Xander gave her hair a final stroke, then moved around their parents. He tapped David as he walked by. His brother followed him out of the room.

In the hall, Xander whispered, "The big figure we saw!"

David said, "You think it was the same person?"

"It'd better be. Do you want a bunch of those things roaming around?"

"Where did he come from? We checked the whole—"

Xander stopped him with a hand on his shoulder. "I think I know. Sort of. The *rooms*."

David looked startled. "He's coming *from* one of those . . . those . . . *other worlds?*"

"Where else? That has to be it."

The implications of that swirled in David's head. Xander could see it in his eyes.

David said, "Can anything from those worlds *come through?*"

"Are you thinking about the tigers?"

David's bottom lip trembled.

Xander said, "I don't know. So far, it seems to be that big guy we saw, the one who scared Toria tonight."

David nodded. "The footprints."

They both turned their attention down the hall to the base of Toria's doorway. The floors were too clean now to pick up traces of the big man's passing.

"What does he want?" David whispered.

Xander had no answer for him.

"What if *we* stirred him up?" David said.

"You mean . . . by going through?" Xander shook his head. "Mom found the footprints in the dining room *before* we found the doors upstairs."

"But think about it. He never spoke before. He didn't *want* to be seen." David squeezed his eyes tight. "I never should have gone through. I just thought—"

"Gone where?" Dad said, coming up behind them.

The boys jumped. Dad's face grew stern, his eyes flicked between his son's faces. "Did you visit those rooms again?"

Xander bowed his head.

David said, "Yes, sir. I just wanted—"

His dad interrupted. "I thought I made it clear. Stay away from them." He shook his head. "I should have locked it up." His eyes found the bandage on David's shoulder. "That happen tonight?"

David nodded. "It was an arrow. I went—"

"Tell me tomorrow." Dad closed his eyes, then opened them slowly. He seemed tired and worried.

Probably a little more than disappointed in his boys, Xander thought. He said, "How's Toria?"

"She'll be okay. I'm gonna sleep in her room. She *could* sleep with us, but if we decide to stay in this house—"

"*If?*" David asked, sounding a little panicked.

Dad glared at him. "David, this is serious. But if we decide to stay—and that's a big *if*—I don't want her afraid of her own room. I almost have her convinced it was a dream."

They all knew better. Silence fell over them. Then Xander said, "Dad, let me do it, stay in Toria's room."

Dad shook his head. "No, I . . ."

"Then you can stay with Mom. I want to, really." He shrugged. "Least I can do."

"What about me?" David asked.

Xander said, "You can help with something else."

"I mean, I don't want to be alone. In our room. In the dark."

Xander gave him a little push. "What happened to Mr. Tough Guy?"

"He's going to sleep in Toria's room too," David said. "Double protection."

Xander said, "For you or her?"

"Ha ha."

Dad said, "Xander, are you sure?"

"I can do it."

"Me too," said David.

"Okay," Dad said. "Just till we figure out what we're gonna do." He nodded over their shoulders, toward their bedroom. "Go get your stuff. I'll tell the girls what's going on." He turned around, then back to his boys and raised his eyebrows at them. "And remember, those rooms upstairs are off-limits."

They nodded like twin bobbleheads.

CHAPTER

thirty-six

SUNDAY, 2:57 A.M.

David had talked Toria into letting him sleep with her in her bed. Xander knew it had nothing to do with providing better protection for her, as David had said. He just hated sleeping on the floor.

Xander didn't mind it. He had his pillow and his blankets. The area rug beside Toria's bed took the edge off the wood floor's hardness and chilliness. He lay there now, considering the pattern of shadows the trees in the moonlight cast on Toria's ceiling. So different from the ones in his and David's room. For one thing, they were much less distinct, washed out by Toria's night-light.

Again, he thought about *The Shining*, how the house had made Jack Nicholson go crazy. What if it could happen to a whole family? What if none of this was real and they were all going crazy? Seeing things, hearing things, *experiencing* things. With Toria seeing the man—*claiming* to see the man—it was like each member of the family was slowly getting pulled in.

Xander didn't like this train of thought. It was his exhaustion talking. He made his mind think of something else.

David and Toria had fallen asleep quickly. The rhythm of their breathing was not quite in sync with each other. Toria's was a little faster and a lot quieter. Together, they sounded like distant waves breaking against a beach. Xander listened, thinking of that beach. His eyelids grew heavy. He rolled over to his left side. He adjusted his shoulder, trying to find a comfortable position. Across the room, illuminated by the Princess Fiona light, Wuzzy stared at him.

Stupid bear.

His eyes closed and he was back on the beach. He could almost feel wet sand squishing between his toes.

In the next second, he pushed himself up, fully awake. The alarm in his head had been so loud he was surprised it hadn't woken David and Toria. But there they were, shoulder to shoulder, the blankets over their chests rising and falling, almost in unison.

Wuzzy, he thought.

He stepped quietly to the bear and picked it up. Then, to the open doorway. He leaned through and peered down the hall.

Dad was there, at the junction of the two hallways. Sitting on boxes, leaning back against the wall. He was fewer than fifteen feet from the master bedroom door. Mom was probably asleep inside. Twenty feet down the other hall was the false wall, beyond which the big man presumably dwelt. Dad clutched an aluminum bat in both hands. The business end rested against his shoulder. He spotted Xander and nodded.

"Bathroom," Xander whispered. He wasn't sure Dad heard him way down there, but his father nodded as though he had. Holding the bear, Xander walked to the bathroom, turned on the light, shut and locked the door.

At the small of Wuzzy's back was a panel of controls at the small of his back. The On/Off switch was in the On position. Xander had suspected it would be, since it seemed to capture everything the family said. Toria would play back the funniest, most embarrassing, or most irritating sound bites. The bear stored half a dozen snippets at a time. Each could be up to several minutes long, Xander thought. He did know it was sound-activated and would fill its memory chips in sequence: first, memory chip number one, then two, and so on. After number six, it returned to memory chip number one. It would replace what was on that chip with a new sound. A pressure-sensitive switch in Wuzzy's right paw caused it to play back the most recent recordings. That's how Toria had driven him crazy on the trip from Pasadena to Pinedale. Now, Xander changed Wuzzy's setting from Record to Playback.

Xander squeezed Wuzzy's paw. The bear whispered, "Bathroom," in Xander's voice. Dad may not have heard, but Wuzzy had. Xander hoped he hadn't recorded over what he was looking for. He gave the paw two quick squeezes—the first returned the playback head to the beginning of the current memory chip ("bathroom"); the second brought it to the previous memory chip.

His own voice again: "Good night, guys." It was louder than he had expected. He scrambled to turn on the water. It helped mask the rest of the recording:

David answering, "Night."

Toria sweetly saying, "Good night, Xander. Thanks for watching over me."

David again: "I am too."

Toria: "Thank you, David."

Xander heard the rustle of bedding, the squeak of a spring in Toria's mattress, a bang—and he remembered bringing his head down against the night table as he settled in. Hearing it made his head hurt again, and he felt the bump on the back of his head.

Two more quick squeezes of Wuzzy's paw: Xander, David, and Toria talking.

Two more: Mom and Dad saying good-night.

Again: Dad explaining that Xander and David would sleep in Toria's room.

Xander was becoming concerned that Wuzzy had already erased the recording he was most interested in. Or . . . he remembered what had happened when David took the camcorder over: nothing but static. He hoped for something better now.

Again: His sister screaming. Pounding footsteps. Xander saying, "Toria, it's me! Xander!"

Again: Toria saying, "Who is it?" Sounding sleepy. He scrunched his brow in concentration. He held Wuzzy close to his ear. There was a creaking sound—the bedspring—followed by another. Xander thought it was a floorboard. Toria started to call again: "Who—"

A deep, rumbling voice said: "*Sas ehei na erthete na paiksei.*"

Xander's stomach tightened into a knot. Toria started screaming. Xander quickly flipped the Off button.

Xander set the bear on the counter and took a step away from it. Wuzzy appeared as sweet and innocent as a little girl in a Sunday dress, but the deep-throated voice it had recorded and shared was sinister. He did not know how he knew it, he just knew.

Toria had not been dreaming. The family was not going crazy. Their problem was different. It was much, much worse.

CHAPTER

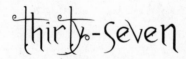

thirty-seven

SUNDAY, 3:25 A.M.

Now that Xander knew Wuzzy had recorded Toria's encounter with the man, Dad had to hear it. Before, when he didn't know if the bear had captured any important sounds at all, he didn't want to get Dad's hopes up or give him another reason to suspect his son was paranoid.

Xander approached him, bear in hand.

"What is it, Son?" Dad whispered. He shifted on the

box. The bat gleamed in the hallway lights. It made Xander feel better, how solid it appeared, how firmly his father gripped it.

Xander said, "We're not going crazy."

His dad offered a thin smile. "I know."

"I mean, I had kind of thought, you know . . . with the last family disappearing . . ."

"Mass hysteria?" his father asked. "You thought we were all going crazy together?"

Xander felt his face flush. It sounded ridiculous coming out of his father. "Well, I was starting to think the house was like . . . I don't know . . . like, driving us crazy, I guess." He shook his head. "Stupid, I know."

Dad slipped off the box. He touched Xander on the arm. "Not stupid. Say the house really is able to do all these weird things—drop intruders in our midst, even send you back to fight a gladiator. If it could do all that, then simply driving a whole family crazy doesn't seem like such a big deal, does it? What's more impossible: a house that makes you *think* crazy things, or a house that really *does* crazy things?

Xander nodded. "Either way, it's way off the charts, right?"

One of Dad's eyebrows curved up. "Way off," he agreed. "What's with the bear?"

Xander gave Wuzzy a little shake. He said, "Evidence we're not crazy." He turned it on and squeezed the paw. Toria's voice came through. "Who is it?" *Creak. Creeeak.* "Who—?" Then the booming voice: *"Sas ehei na erthete na paiksei."*

As soon as the last syllable came out of Wuzzy, something overhead banged. Maybe a slamming door. Or a body hitting the floor up there. The ceiling joists creaked. Footsteps.

Wuzzy screamed in Toria's voice.

Xander turned it off. His heart pounded like a lowrider's bass speaker: *Ba-boomp! Ba-boomp! Ba-boomp! Ba-boomp!* He stared at the ceiling. No more sounds. He lowered his eyes to his Dad's face. There was fear there. *Fear.* When your dad was frightened, there was something to be frightened about.

"What was—" Xander started.

"Shhh." Dad held up one hand. With the other, he kept his grip on the bat. His eyes roamed the ceiling, but he wasn't *looking*. He was *listening*. He cocked his head, held still.

No other sounds came from up there.

Dad brought his head down to stare at the false wall. It appeared to be completely shut. Xander could not tell where it ended and the real wall began. Dad had piled boxes in front of it chest-high. Still, Xander would not have bet on their ability to keep something from coming through.

Dad watched the wall for a long time.

"Dad?" Xander whispered finally.

Slowly, Dad turned his gaze away. He snapped his head back like a pitcher trying to catch a steal, before settling his eyes on Xander. He wasn't smiling.

Xander said, "What was that?"

Dad shook his head. He said, "That was the last straw. We're out of here in the morning."

Xander felt a mixture of relief and regret. Of course, he didn't want anything to happen to his family. But he knew he would never experience anything like this again.

Dad turned and picked up a box. "Now, give me a hand." He carried the box to the false wall and added it to the others.

Xander found a safe place for Wuzzy, then started hefting boxes.

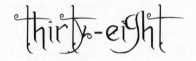

SUNDAY, 4:38 A.M.

Xander was back on the floor next to Toria's bed. The night's excitement had kept him going, but now his mind and body ached for a week of sleep. His eyes felt like they were made out of hot steel, his muscles nothing more than Silly Putty. He rolled onto his stomach and eased his cheek into the relaxing softness of his pillow. His head was full of images that would love nothing better than to keep him awake or give him nightmares:

his gladiatorial fight, the big man roaming their house, even all the things he'd left in Pasadena. He forced himself to once again hear the surf in his brother's and sister's breathing. He was on that beach, kicking at the water, smelling the salt, feeling the breeze . . . when the screaming started again.

He grabbed the edge of the mattress and pulled himself up. Groggy, not yet with full vision, he reached for Toria. He said, "What is it?" He felt Toria rise into a sitting position. He made out her face in the glow of the night-light—more puzzled than scared.

Beside her, David moaned, rolled over. He propped himself up on his elbows. "What's going on?" he said.

It hit Xander an instant before Toria said it.

"Mom!"

He spun and rose. He cracked his shoulder on the door frame, then crashed into the hallway wall opposite Toria's bedroom. He sprinted toward his parents' bedroom, trying to make sense of what he saw. Dad's aluminum bat lay on the floor. Boxes were scattered everywhere. His parents' door was open. No, not open—ripped from its hinges, on the hallway floor.

Xander crashed over a box. He fell on the unhinged door, got up, and grabbed the door frame of his parents' room. Only then did he realize the screaming was not coming from the room. Rather, around the corner. He spun, catching a glimpse of David beating it toward him. Xander paused long enough to hold up his hand. "No, David, stay here."

Toria came out of her room and ran toward her brothers.

Xander yelled, "David, stay with Toria. I mean it." He turned and scooped up the bat. He rounded the corner. The wall was wide open. Heavy footsteps climbed the stairs beyond, nearly lost under the sound of his mother's screams. So intent was Xander on reaching her, he nearly tripped over a pair of legs sticking out of the guest bedroom. He jumped over them, slid to a stop, crawled back. The bat clacked against the wood floor.

It was Dad. On his back. Not moving. Xander released the bat. He moved up his father's body, hand over hand. His palm pressed against his father's chest, his eyes reached his father's face, scanning for signs of life. He felt it: a heartbeat under his hand.

"Dad?" he whispered. He pushed his other hand under his father's head to lift it. It was warm and wet and sticky. He pulled his hand back, covered in blood.

"Dad!"

His father groaned. Xander heard fast footsteps.

David grabbed the door frame and almost swung through. He stopped himself, yelled, "Dad!"

Xander said, "He's alive. Mom—"

But David was already gone. He jumped over Dad's legs and pattered away, bare feet slapping on the floor.

"David, wait." Xander clutched the bat. He rose, turning away from his father. At the opening in the wall, he looked back, and braked hard. Toria had just come around the corner. He pointed at Dad and told her, "Take care of him. Stay

255

here!" He went through the next threshold and started up the stairs.

David was at the top, hitting the landing. He turned and pushed up the breaker that powered the corridor's lights.

"Mom!" he yelled and darted into the corridor.

"David, wait!" Xander yelled, almost at the top. He turned into the corridor in time to see the big man rotating around to face David, who was running all-out toward him.

Judging by his proportions in the hall, the man was not merely big, he was *massive*. He was almost naked, wearing only a tattered pelt like a diaper. He was simultaneously fat and muscular—Arnold Schwarzenegger going to pot. Broad shoulders, barrel chest, Buddha's belly. It was a body hewn and honed by strenuous and long-lasting labor, but insufficiently nourished by whatever the man could find. His flesh was covered in scars that both furrowed the skin and left ridges of discolored tissue. Dark smudges of dirt obscured even more flesh. And everywhere, sweat glistened. A long beard, seemingly made of rusty wire, burst from his face, hiding his mouth. From the tops of his sideburns, his head was bald as a rock. Fierce, dark eyes looked out from holes under a thick and bony brow.

Their mother was bent over his left shoulder. Her feet kicked in front; Xander could see her arms flailing behind the man.

As David plunged unheedingly toward the man, Xander bellowed, "No—!"

The man's cantaloupe-size fist shot forward. It hit David's head with a *crack!* David's momentum propelled his legs forward as his head flew back. His arms flung out and he went straight down. He landed on the carpeted runner with a sickening thud.

"David!" Xander yelled, almost to him. "Mom! Mom!"

Her screaming stopped long enough to yell Xander's name. Her feet kicked and kicked. Her hand kept rising and falling against the man's shoulder and back. Her efforts appeared to make no difference.

The man watched Xander approach. His face was impassive. Xander's eyes dropped to his brother, lying unmoving.

Be alive, be alive, was all he could think.

He was mentally dusting off the steps required to administer CPR—compliments of the American Red Cross and Mom's insistence that her children know the process. Could he revive David before the man stepped in to finish him off or before he carried their mother away? Didn't matter. Xander had seen the battering ram that had clobbered his brother, and he would not leave him to die on the floor.

His heart danced when David's arm rose shakily off the carpet. It reached up like a drowning man's grasp for the surface, then bent at the elbow. David's fingers found his face. He groaned.

Xander hurtled past his brother. He came down four feet from the brute. Without hesitation, he hiked the bat over his shoulder, stepped in, and swung it into the side of the man's head.

The head snapped sideways, catching Mom's hip. She began

screaming again. A bright red mark sprang up like a racing stripe across the man's temple and ear. He showed Xander his teeth. Not pretty. The man's leg-sized arm shot forward. His hand grasped for Xander's head. Xander stepped back and brought the bat down on the man's hand. The man hissed and pulled his fist to his chest. His eyes widened and seemed to sparkle with fury.

If looks could kill, Xander thought, *we'd both be dead.*

"Let her go!" Xander screamed. He stepped in, feinted another swing, then reversed out of reach. "I said, let her go! Now!" When the man didn't move, Xander swung the bat into his side.

The man grunted and heaved forward.

Xander made a grab for Mom's leg.

The brute was faster than he looked. He seized Xander by the neck with his injured hand. His fingers were like cables, cinching Xander's throat. Xander gagged, dropped the bat. The man seemed unable to squeeze harder, though his straining face reflected his desire to do so. Xander believed his neck would have already been crushed like a straw had it not been for the strike to the man's hand he had gotten in.

The man, appearing frustrated now, tossed Xander aside. Xander's head hit one of the wall lights. He crumbled to the floor. The heavy lamp lost its grip on the wall and fell on Xander's head. Everything faded. The hallway shrank in Xander's vision. Ahh . . . he was finally going to get the rest he needed. *And why not?* he thought. He knew there was a reason, but it kept slipping away.

His mother screamed.

The room swam back.

Xander remembered.

His eyes focused on the man lumbering away with Mom over his shoulder. She was looking back at Xander, her eyes so full of fear. She was pounding and scratching at the man's back, weakly now. She was giving up.

"Mom," Xander called. He tried to rise. The world spun around his head. He plopped down again. He ran his fingers over his forehead, through his hair. The same sticky warmth he had felt on the back of Dad's head. His hand came back coated in red, some of the blood his, some his father's. He was so *tired*. He just wanted to . . . he leaned back on his elbow. If he could just close his eyes for a second . . . just a second . . . then he would have the strength to get up and rescue his mother.

His mother! Had to get up now.

"Xander!"

He forced an eyelid up. David was crawling toward him. A big black-blue-yellow bruise almost radiated from his face. His left eye was not quite open, the skin around it swollen and dark blue. Blood drizzled out of his left nostril.

Xander blinked, coming back to the world. He ground his teeth together. Somebody had pounded on his little brother.

What was that joke? Nobody beats up my brother except me.

"Dae," he said.

"Xander, he's got Mom! He's got Mom!" Tears rolled over David's cheeks.

"Mom," Xander said. It felt like he was just waking up. He rolled over, got on his knees, stood. He could feel his pulse in his head, each beat feeling like a fist pounding on the inside of his skull.

Okay, he thought. *Use the pain.*

He remembered Arnold Schwarzenegger in *Collateral Damage* and Sigourney Weaver in *Aliens*—battered senseless and using their beatings to get *mad*, to get *focused*.

He stooped and picked up the bat.

The man was near the end of the hall. Only two or three doors left. He would enter one of them.

Mom's head had slumped. Xander could not see her face. He bolted for them. Each step tightened a vise around his skull. His brain throbbed.

Self-pity later. Right now: Mom.

Hoping to draw strength from it, hoping to distract the brute, Xander let go with his own piercing, animal-caught-in-a-trap scream.

Mom looked up. She appeared as stunned by Xander's primal outcry as he hoped the man would be.

The man spun around. Xander was on him again. He

ducked low and cracked the bat into a knee. The man grabbed at him, and he pulled his head back—too slowly. The brute seized a fistful of Xander's hair. The man pulled him closer. Xander lifted his foot and planted it in the man's stomach. He kicked off. Hair ripping out of his scalp. He landed on his back. The man reached for his ankle, clumps of long, brown hair falling from his fingers. Xander pushed back, pushed back. Beyond the man's reach, he rose again. Gripping the bat in both hands, he cocked it behind his head.

"You're going down," he said between clenched teeth. He was trying to psych himself up as much as anything.

He stepped in, aimed for the man's clavicle, and swung the bat over his head. It cracked against the ceiling, bringing down a plume of plaster dust. Xander felt the vibration of the sudden stop in his arms. He stumbled forward. The bat found an overhead light fixture and shattered it. Glass cascaded over Xander's head and into the man's face.

The enemy blinked against the falling glass.

Xander stepped closer. From its starting point touching the ceiling, he swung the bat backward, bringing it around like a clock's hour hand. At the six o'clock position, the tip of it pendulumed across the fuzz of the carpet, gaining speed. He brought it up between the man's legs. The jarring strike reverberated up the bat into Xander's hands and arms. The man buckled at the waist. His head came down, almost cracking into Xander's. Xander backed away; the man stumbled forward.

His hand shot up and shoved Xander in the chest. Xander flew backward. The man grabbed the bat and shook it. Xander lost his grip. He crashed into something that gave way behind him—gave way and cried out in pain. He landed on top of David, who had come up behind him to help. Xander put his hand down into David's stomach and pushed off. The boy *oophed*.

"You 'kay?" Xander yelled.

He did not wait for an answer.

"Go!" David wheezed, breathless. "Get Mom, Xander! Get Mom."

The man had recovered. He must have felt the goal was too near for these children to keep him from it. Instead of attacking while both boys were down, he had continued his trek down the hall. As Xander regained his feet, the man selected a door—second from the last. He bowed his head to clear the threshold. He stepped through.

Mom grabbed the door frame on both sides. Her straining hands made her knuckles, tendons, and veins push out against the skin.

"Mom!" Xander yelled. He reached the door. He punched his fist into the man's spine. He could have been striking a brick wall for all the good it did. He reached up to seize his mother under her arms. For just a moment, mother and son were face-to-face, inches apart. Staring into Mom's eyes, he was staring into his own—hazel and wide open with terror.

He felt her breath on his face. A tear dropped from her eye and struck his cheek.

She whispered, "I love you. I love all of you."

It was the proclamation of someone who thought she would see them no more.

"No," Xander said back at her. "No," he growled. He closed his eyes and pulled on her.

His efforts and his mother's grip on the door frame kept the man from progressing farther into the room. The man kicked back. A hammer-blow to Xander's thigh. Xander yelled but would not let go. Another kick and he had no choice. Pain crumpled him. He fell to his knees, losing his grip. Mom's hands slipped off the door frame. She moved away from Xander, as the man crossed to the second door.

Xander sprung up, reaching for her. She stretched her hands toward him. Xander's bruised thigh crippled his effort. He fell without touching her. The portal door clicked open. Daylight filled the room. A frigid breeze carried in swooping coils of snow.

Xander grabbed the man's right ankle. The brute kicked back at him. Xander ducked his head against the assault. The heel, as solid as a statue's, beat against him. Once. Twice. Three times. Xander's grip loosened.

"No," he groaned. "No."

The man snapped his leg out of Xander's hands. He stepped away and out the door.

"Mooooom!" He raised his face to see her. She was smiling back at him. *Smiling*. Saying it'll be okay.

But it won't, he thought. *It won't.*

More snow blew in. The door swung past his head. He caught it in both hands. For a moment, he held it there. Then it continued its arc toward the threshold, pulling Xander across the floor on his stomach. He pulled himself forward. He got one leg in front of him. The bottom of his foot came up against the wall next to the door frame. His other leg was bent and canted back painfully. He had no time or leverage to change its position. He clasped onto the edge of the door and strained back. The door kept closing. Stuck in that aching inclination, weakened by the struggle to save his mother, he knew he could not hold on much longer.

This was a battle lost.

The door closed farther. His knee buckled. It slammed up against the wall, twisting his ankle, lifting him off the floor. He had to let go or risk losing his fingers and possibly breaking the bones in his legs.

Something bumped up behind him. David leaned over his shoulder. He stuck the bat between the frame and the edge of the door, above the door handle. Xander let go. The door cracked into the aluminum Louisville Slugger. Pinched by the door, the tortured metal screeched as if in agony. The bat pivoted forcefully to point almost straight back at the first door. It struck David's arm and spun him around. He fell on the floor next to Xander. As they watched, the door closed on the bat. When the door was one inch from closing, it stopped. The bat quivered, then the door banged shut. The severed bat fell to the floor with a ringing clang.

Xander immediately rose and clasped the handle. His arms strained to turn it. It would not budge.

The snow whipped around his legs. To the sound of a sharply inhaled breath, it disappeared through the gap under the door.

One last time, he found the strength to yell for his mother—not just his mother: his friend, a woman he adored, not only because she gave him life, but because he knew what she was all about. Anyone who knew her so well would have felt the same. She was a good person to know.

David pushed his body into Xander's side. He hugged him. He started to cry.

They both did.

thirty-nine

SUNDAY, 4:51 A.M.

For Xander, the tears did not last long. In their place came resolve. He gently pushed David away. The items hanging on the hooks gave him an idea of where they went. A fur-lined parka. Goggles. Gloves. On the bench was a pair of snowshoes. Someplace cold . . . wintry.

He snatched down the parka. He pulled it on. It was heavy and frumpy, floating like a cloud around his body. He tried the door, still locked. He didn't know how many items were required to unlock the door; only that you did not need all of them. He plucked the goggles from the hook and slipped them onto his head. The door was still locked.

"What are you doing?" David asked.

Xander threw him a glance.

David knew perfectly well what he was doing. What David meant to ask was: have you *thought* about what you're doing? So that was the question Xander answered. He said, "If I can get through quick enough, I can get her. I can bring her back."

"But that guy was *unstoppable*."

"I'll think of something," Xander said, "once I'm there." He reached for the gloves. Holding them, he tried the door again. It opened easily and he looked through. Blinding whiteness everywhere. Snow swirled in. A blast of freezing air. Wind—or *something*—howled in the distance. He told David, "Come find me in twenty minutes."

David grabbed his arm. His tears were wet on his lids, his cheeks. "I want Mom back too. But, Xander, you can't—"

Xander jerked his arm away from David's grasp. "Don't try to stop me," he said.

"But you don't know—"

A muffled scream. Undoubtedly Mom's.

The brothers looked through the threshold to the unknown world beyond, then at each other. The scream had not come from there.

In the hallway, a door rattled and clicked open. Mom's scream was loud, clear, and horrified.

Xander and David bolted across the room. The door behind them slammed shut. They pushed each other through the first doorway into the hall. They looked at the last door, then down the hall toward the staircase. Halfway there, a door was open enough to see their mother's face. Her fingers were clutching, clutching, the edge. Xander yelled for her, ran. She screamed again. Her fingers disappeared. The door slammed. When Xander burst through, the second door slammed. There was water on the floor, mist in the air. The smell of the sea. He ran to the door, almost slipped. The handle was locked.

David hit the door frame behind him. "The ocean," he said.

The mist vanished into the gap under the door. The water on the floor turned into rivulets and shot into the gap, leaving not even the slightest moisture where it had been.

Xander's head pounded. Each pulse brought a new wave of pain and nausea. His eyes stung as though someone had rubbed pepper into them. He was frustrated, sad, and angry. He cast a grim expression at David. He threw the gloves onto the floor and yanked the goggles off his head. He ripped off the parka. He stepped to the bench and surveyed the items as a hunter might consider the perfect weapon.

"Don't do this!" David yelled. He was stepping up beside him.

Xander did not respond. There was a long, curved sword with a big hand guard and a rusty scabbard that might have once been covered in leather. It reminded Xander of a pirate's sword. *I definitely want that.* He pulled it down, saw that a thin, long strap ran through an eyelet in the scabbard. He looped it over his head so it hung off his shoulder. There was a three-cornered Jack Sparrow hat. Beside it, a simple scarf for tying around your head. He thought this would be less encumbering than the hat. He snapped it off of its hook.

David grabbed his arm. "You can't go like this! We don't even know if she's still in the world past that door." When Xander said nothing, David shoved him hard.

Xander sidestepped to keep from falling, and his hip hit the frame of the portal door. He lost his grip on the knot he was trying to make in the scarf. It slipped off his head. He made a grab at it, missed, and watched it settle on the floor.

He snapped his attention to David. The muscles in Xander's face were tight, his body trembled with emotion and the need to *do something*. His vision blurred, turning David into indistinct colors. He blinked, sending tears streaming down his face. David came back into focus.

The boy continued his tirade. "You can't do this!"

"*Someone* has to!" he yelled, as if it were David who had caused all of this. He knew it wasn't. The most blame lay on *his* shoulders. He shouldn't have let David go through earlier that evening, should have told Dad about David's intentions so they both could have prevented it. He shouldn't have let Dad keep watch alone; he should have done a better job helping him block the stairwell and hidden wall. He shouldn't have gone to sleep, not with all that had already happened. He shouldn't have let the man take Mom; he should have held on to her, to the death, if necessary.

All the things he had failed to do . . . all the things he had done wrong . . . They washed over him like scalding acid.

"Not like this!" David yelled back into Xander's face. "You're beat up! You're tired! You're ready to fall over!" David's head drooped. Everything about him seemed to sag, to lose its vitality. Softly, he said, "If you go over like that, you won't come back. I know you won't." His voice cracked on the second *won't*. He shook his head, knuckled away some tears. He plopped onto the bench, bowed his head. "You don't even have any clothes on. Just your boxers. How stupid is that?"

Xander's trembling subsided. He could not be mad at David for telling the truth. If he went looking for their mom now, he probably *wouldn't* come back. But he was so . . . frustrated. He knew what had to be done. He just did not possess the strength— mentally, intellectually, physically—to do it. It was like seeing a loved one trapped under a burning car that would explode at any second. Everyone has heard stories of adrenaline-fueled feats of inhuman strength, but the reality is: human muscles are no match for two tons of sheet metal.

Loved ones die. Fact of life.

But his mother *wasn't* dead, and he was not helpless. He was simply not up to the task at that moment.

"David, we *have* to get her. We have to rescue her."

David looked into his face. "I know," he said. "But we have to do it smart. We can't die trying, can we? Then who'll be here to bring her back? We'll be like that last family. *Gone.*"

Xander's shoulders slumped—with them, his spirit and whatever had been keeping him going despite injury and exhaustion. He was heartsick and discouraged. It was unimaginable to him that he didn't simply fall over dead. Were his organs really slipping over one another to pool in a heap at the base of his torso, or did it just feel that way? This must be how people lost in the wilderness felt: At what point do you muster the strength to keep going, against all odds, even after using up every ounce of energy in yourself? When do you admit defeat and lie down to die?

To Xander, David represented the logical side of the equation. Not that David didn't love their mother and want her back. He did, maybe even more than Xander did, if that were possible. For some reason, however—maybe his youth or that he had not looked into his mother's eyes as she was taken away—he was able to set aside the pure gut reaction of rescuing her immediately, at all costs.

Xander looked from David to the remaining items on the hooks. They were the other side of David's coin. They would allow him to continue the pursuit, to chase until his heart exploded. He would die in some frozen wasteland; or on the deck of a pirate ship three hundred years ago; or—if these rooms allowed it, he did not know—some moon base in the distant future. Perhaps one of those deaths was already written for him.

He knew David's way—to rest and go again—gave them the best chance of finding Mom, of bringing her back, of all of them growing old *here*, not *there*.

On the other hand, he could put on the headscarf and another of these high-seas-faring items. He could open the door—the portal—and plunge through. He could find his mother or die trying. Wasn't stopping now abandoning her? *Live to fight another day* was an expression that did not take into account the loved ones who would die because you didn't continue fighting *today*.

Feeling every movement in his body—stretching muscles, bending ligaments, the pressure exerted on every bone—Xander stooped to retrieve the scarf. He pulled it over his head and began cinching a knot in the back.

"Xander," David said, sadly. He shook his head, bowed it.

Xander heard a sniff, saw a tear fall from David's hidden face to his thigh. He was wearing pajama bottoms that were not his favorite anymore. These depicted characters from *Avatar: The Last Airbender*. He had abandoned them in favor of a more mature plaid pattern when he'd turned twelve a few months ago. Xander could not believe only one day had passed since they'd lost David's favorite pjs to the gap under the door. One day from discovering the rooms to losing their mother.

Xander leaned over David and selected a brass spyglass dangling from a hook by a leather thong. He stepped back, saw another tear fall.

"I have to," he said.

David looked up. "She went into one room, but came out another. We haven't even found out how to get back to the room we started from. We don't know enough about this for you to do any good."

"I have to," Xander repeated.

"It's stupid!" David stood up and stepped in front of the portal door. "It's killing yourself for no reason."

"Get out of my way, David."

His brother tightened his lips, scrunched his brow in determination. He widened his stance for more stability. He pressed one palm to the door behind him, the other to the wall beside the door. The doorknob was directly behind him.

"Okay," Xander said, equally determined. He stepped in to toss his brother aside.

Something banged in the hallway.

David's eyes flashed wide. "Mom!" he yelled.

Before David could dart past, Xander spun and ran into the hall. His eyes scanned for an open door or evidence of one having just closed. A voice from the other direction turned his head.

Dad was stumbling, touching his fingers to one wall for balance. Behind him, a wall fixture rocked back and forth. Dad must have knocked it as he passed. On his other side, Toria moved with him. She walked sideways, so she could press one hand to his back and grip his arm with her other. He appeared dazed.

"Dad," David called. He ran for him. The boys reached their father at the same time.

Dad's eyes stared past them, down the corridor. Xander could tell he was seeing something way beyond. He said something Xander didn't catch.

"Dad, what is it?" He leaned closer.

"Not again," Dad said. "Not again."

Xander squinted at him. "What do you mean, 'not again'?"

"Not again." Dad's face reflected something falling apart. His mouth quivered, then his cheeks, his forehead. His eyes grew big and focused on Xander.

Xander saw his father's attention coming back from that far-off place he had been. Dad's eyes focused on him, then squeezed shut. He began to moan, his shoulders heaving up and down. He was sobbing. He collapsed into a sitting position on the floor.

David stepped up behind him. His fingers caressed his father's head. He pulled his hands away. He glared at the blood on them. Then he wiped this fingers on his pajama pants. Xander witnessed his brother pulling himself together, regaining composure that he had not entirely lost. David asked, "Xander, what is it? You know what Dad's talking about?"

Through his tears, his wrenching sobs, Dad said, "I didn't mean for this to happen. Not again. Not this time. Not *her!*"

Glaring at his father, Xander said, "He *knew* this would happen!

It's happened before and he knew it." He dropped to his knees before his father. "You knew, didn't you? You could have stopped her being taken. Was this your secret? Was this your *plan*?"

Toria began to cry.

"What are you saying, Xander?" David asked, voice trembling.

Xander stood. He didn't know what to say. Had too many thoughts in his head. He turned and walked slowly down the corridor. He pulled the pirate scarf away. He let it fall from his fingers. He slipped the sword and scabbard off his neck. It clattered to the floor.

From behind him, someone called out. Dad's voice stopped him, but he did not turn around. He could not. His father's first sentence validated what Xander had suspected. It felt like being shot.

"I did know," his father said. "About this house, about these rooms."

Xander turned then. He stormed toward his father. "You *knew*? So when you said I should trust you, *this* is what you meant? Trust that our mother was going to be kidnapped, that she would be taken into some time- and space-bending place where she's all but gone forever?"

"No," their father said. "I meant things would work out. I thought they would."

Xander reached his father, still sitting on the floor. His anger frightened David and Toria—he knew and he didn't care. What their father had done was awful and it demanded his fury. They had been betrayed; their mother had been betrayed. She was gone, and his father had orchestrated the whole thing. He wanted to strike out, to punch him. He felt his fists tighten, hardening to stone. He was ready to do it, to pull back and throw his fist into his father's face.

Dad said, "I thought I could protect you. I thought I could make it different. I *locked* the door!"

Xander's anger did not know what to do with this information—his father talking protection, not harm. His putting a lock on the door at the base of the stairs did not jibe with the malicious intent he had ascribed to his father.

Xander said, "What do you mean, 'this time'? Why did you bring us here?"

Dad lowered his head. He was thinking, considering his words. His faced returned with a tight smile. He turned soft eyes on Xander. Sorrow there, regret. He said, "I thought I would be able to find my mother."

Xander jabbed a pointing finger at the door where he had last seen his mother. "Find her?" he said. "She just—" He had not really heard what his father had said, but it caught up to him at that moment. He said, "*Your* mother. What are you saying?"

The pain in his father's face was obvious. This was an agony he did not want to share. Dad said, "Thirty years ago, I watched my mother get kidnapped by someone who had come out of these rooms. I came back to get her."

CHAPTER

forty

SUNDAY, 5:48 A.M.

"I was seven at the time," Dad said. "My father brought us here."

The four of them were sitting at the dining room table. Toria and David were tending to Dad's and Xander's head wounds. David had a nasty black eye and a bruise on his cheek and forehead that approximated the shape of the big man's fist. Dad had given him Tylenol. When Toria went for the first-aid kit, David had said he felt well enough to help her.

"Grandpa Hank?" Toria asked. She dabbed at the back of Dad's head with a Bactine-soaked gauze. It came away bright red. She wrinkled her nose at it and frowned. She tossed it in a wastebasket and stepped from behind his chair to the table where the supplies were neatly arranged.

He touched his wound and grimaced. "Yeah, Grandpa Hank," he confirmed. "We came here when he got a job at the lumber mill. He had come out earlier and found the house for us." His eyes became unfocused as he remembered. He shook his head. "It was just a house. I didn't notice anything weird. Not for a long time."

"The *noises*?" Xander said, across the table from Dad. His voice was sharp as broken bones. "How sounds here aren't right? You're saying there was none of that?"

"It was a year, at least, before I noticed anything weird."

"But you did . . . *eventually*."

Dad agreed. "I—" But Xander didn't let him finish.

"So you knew!" Xander said. He hissed and pulled his head away as David parted his hair. He was after the laceration caused by the wall light that had fallen on Xander's head. "Stop!" Xander said, pushing his brother away.

"There's a lot of blood," David said.

"Let David clean it, Xander," Dad told him. "Who knows what kind of bacteria that hallway's got?"

Xander scowled at him. "Like I should listen to you."

"I'm still your father." He stared Xander down unapologetically. He was firm about his role in his family's lives.

Regardless of mistakes, Xander thought. He said, "Could have fooled me. You lied about coming here for a job . . . and when you were acting like you'd never seen the house before . . . even going to the real estate office! It was all a big scam!"

"Xander!" Toria scolded. Xander would have snapped at her as well, trying to take over for Mom already. But just as quickly, Xander knew that was wrong and unfair. Toria had often been like that, a mini-Mom. If Toria fully understood what had happened the way Xander did, she wouldn't be playing Nurse Nightingale for their father. She would be too angry and, even more, too distraught over the loss of their mother. Upstairs, Dad had said, "We'll get her; we will," and Toria had believed him.

"Wait a minute," David said. "You're the little boy in that picture?"

Dad nodded.

"That was *your* lightsaber I found?"

Dad smiled, more sad than happy. "I was a *Star Wars* freak."

"My bedroom was your bedroom!" Toria said.

"Whoa," David said, thinking. "You were that family that disappeared. So the father didn't kill his wife and kids and then himself."

"Grandpa Hank couldn't put down an old dog. After Mom was taken, he tried finding her. Every chance he could, he'd go through one of the doors and come back. Each time he got more depressed and worn down. And the house wasn't content to have taken my mother. The weird sounds continued, even got worse. When the big man started showing up again, that was it. My dad said he was afraid he was gonna go insane or that your Aunt Beth and I would be kidnapped next."

Xander noticed his father had been referring to Grandpa Hank as "my dad"—the first time Xander could remember him doing that. Xander believed his dad was back there, seven years old and reliving his experiences in this house.

Dad continued, his voice more strained. "I know it was the hardest decision he ever made, but he took us away. For our sake and his sanity, we left this house and never returned. He made us promise to never come back. I was so young, and as I got older, he kept reinforcing how important it was that we stay away."

"You should have listened," Xander said. His words were as cold as the glare he cast on his father.

Dad nodded. "Deep inside, I knew that someday I would come back and look for her, my mother. If there was no finding her, then I would at least discover what had happened and make sure it never happened again. When my dad—Grandpa—died last year, I felt released from the promise I'd made him. I couldn't stop thinking about this house."

Xander practically screamed. "So you bring us into it, your family? How stupid is that? Why would you do that?"

Dad gazed at Xander for a long time. At last he said, "I *am* sorry. I thought I could control it. Keep you guys away from the rooms. Keep *them*—" He looked up at the ceiling as if seeing "them." "Keep them out of the house. As I said, when I had lived here before, it was a long time before we realized there was something weird about the house. I thought I would have time to secure everything. I thought even if you kids found the false wall, you couldn't get up the stairs. I thought finding my mother was something I could do on my own, without anyone finding out."

David squirted ointment onto the top of Xander's head. He said, "Did you know about the rooms before your mother was taken?" Xander, David, and Toria had been told their paternal grandmother, Grandpa Hank's wife, had died in a car accident many years before. They had not talked about her much.

Dad said, "We discovered them right before she was taken. When we started hearing noises at night and finding footprints on the floors—around then is when I think my father found the rooms."

"So your mother gets taken and the rest of you up and *leave?*" Xander said accusingly.

"I didn't want to, Xander. I cried and begged to stay. And, for years afterward, to come back. I hated my father for a long time. I was an adult before I fully realized why he had given up."

Xander's face was pinched. He said, "Oh, sure. Gotta get on with your life. Can't grieve forever."

"It wasn't like that. He feared for all of our lives. And for his sanity. He came very close to losing it: he'd lost his wife, and the things he experienced in those . . ."

Xander stood abruptly. His chair flipped over backward. His head and shoulder knocked into David's arms. The gauze and tape David had been holding flew out of his hands. Xander said, "Well, *we're* not leaving! Do you understand? We're not going anywhere. I don't care what excuses Grandpa had, he never should have left his wife, your mother! I'm not leaving *my* mother here!" Tears erupted from his eyes, instantly wetting his cheeks. "You can talk all you want about saving the rest of the family, about getting away from this house before it makes you go crazy . . . But we're not leaving without her. We're *not!*" He bolted toward the dining room entrance. He shoved David so hard the boy fell, plopping down hard.

Dad stood. "Xander!" he called. "That's not what I'm saying! I—"

Xander went through the front door and slammed it on his father's words.

•••••••••

Xander had no idea how long he paced the woods in front of the house. Through the trees, the sky had lightened to steel gray, then caught a bit of the approaching sun's orange fire. He dropped onto the front porch steps. Behind Xander, the door opened and closed. His father sat beside him, too close.

When he put his arm across his back to drape his hand over his shoulder, Xander pulled away.

"I'm not saying we have to leave," Dad said.

"Not yet, you aren't."

"Not at all, Xander. Not until we have your mother back. I've made some mistakes, some horrible mistakes. I endangered all of you. Your mother, my wife, has suffered, *is* suffering, because of my . . . *stupidity*. I just hope—"

The way his voice broke, the wet sounds he made, made Xander look. His father was trying to be tough, resolute. His grief was getting in his way. At that moment, it was impossible to hate the man. As terrible as his actions had been, he was right; he was still Xander's father. The grief in his face was as clear as the grief in Xander's heart. His father had not wished this on them.

Dad swallowed hard. "I hope you can forgive me, and that you'll help me set this right."

"Set it right?" Xander squinted at him.

He nodded. "Help me *work* this house. Work those rooms. Figure it all out. Get her back. Xander, *get her back!*"

Despite it all, the pain, the loss, the anger, Xander found himself smiling. There was nothing okay about any of this, but Dad's words sounded so good. They were exactly what he wanted to hear. Several sentences formed in his mouth, but he bit them back. Finally, he said, "Now you're talking." He brought his hand up around his father's back and hugged him.

Dad showed him an expression of utter relief. It said, *Thank you for not making me lose my son on the same morning I lost my wife.*

Behind Xander, the door opened again. Two pairs of feet. Toria came down a step and sat next to Dad. She leaned her head into his side. David brushed against Xander, stopped halfway down the stairs. He leaned back against the railing. Xander knew it did his brother and sister good to see him and Dad friends again.

Xander smiled at David. He said, "We're going to rescue Mom."

All of the emotions Xander was feeling crossed over David's face: sadness and worry, doubt and fear, and, finally, hope and determination. David's eyes scanned the front of the house, as if seeing it differently. Then, he took in Toria and Dad before his attention settled on Xander.

David nodded. He said, "Let's do it."

NOT THE END . . .

READING GROUP GUIDE

1. None of the King kids is particularly happy about leaving everyone and everything they know back in Pasadena to move to Pinedale. Have you ever had to move away from a place you loved? How did you cope?

2. Pasadena is part of a big metropolitan area. Pinedale is small and secluded. What can you do in big cities that you can't do in rural towns? How about the opposite: What can you do in rural towns that you can't do in big cities? Which do you prefer?

3. Xander loves movies—to the point that he relates a lot of what happens around him to something he's seen in the movies. Do you ever do that with movies or books or something else? Does it help you understand situations better? Why?

4. When the Kings first find the big Victorian house, Xander gets an uneasy feeling. Have you ever had a bad feeling about something that you couldn't explain? What did you do about it?

5. "Victorian" architecture became popular during and after the reign of United Kingdom's Queen Victoria from 1837 to 1901. "Cape Cod" homes were named after an area of Massachusetts where they were popular. Do have a favorite house style? Do you know what style house you live in?

6. The Kings discover footprints in their new home. They search for an intruder or a place where people could slip into their house, but they find nothing. What would you have done if you were in their situation? What else could they have done to protect themselves?

7. Xander and David discover that the upstairs linen closet is more than a closet. What would you do if you found something so strange? Would you tell your parents? Why do you think the King boys decided to keep it secret?

8. Why do you think the guards in the Roman Colosseum threw spears at Xander? Was there anything else Xander could have done to save himself?

9. After Xander's bad experience in the Colosseum and Dad's making the third-floor portals off-limits, why was David so insistent about experiencing "going over" for himself? What do you think of his actions?

10. When David goes over, he runs into three tigers and a tribe of hunters. Where do you think he was? If you could go anywhere in history, where would you go? What would you do there? Who would you like to meet?

11. Why do you think the *Dreamhouse* portals to other worlds exist in the first place? In other words, what is their purpose?

12. The portals seem to continually shift around—for example, the first antechamber may lead to an Arctic world one time, but a pirate world the next time the Kings look. Why do you think the portals change?

13. The King children find out that Dad knew a lot more about the house than he had let on. Why do you think he kept his knowledge of the house secret? Xander and David have very different reactions to their father's lying about the house and their real reason for moving to Pinedale. Would you have responded angrily, like Xander, or more calmly, like David? Why?

Watcher in the Woods

"*You watched these people go through their lives and just had a feeling that they existed outside the usual laws of nature.*"

—CHARLES SPALDING

"*I'm watching you, always watching.*"

—ROZ, *Monsters Inc.*

one

At twelve years old, David King was too young to die. At least *he* thought so.

But try telling that to the people shooting at him.

He had no idea where he was. When he had stepped through the portal, smoke immediately blinded him. An explosion had thrown rocks and who-knew-what into his face. It shook the floor and knocked him off his feet. Now he was on his hands and knees on a hardwood floor. Glass and splinters dug into his palms. Somewhere, all kinds of guns were firing. Bullets zinged overhead, thunking into walls—bits of flying plaster stung his cheeks.

Okay, so he wasn't sure the bullets were meant for him. The guns seemed both near and far. But in the end, if he were hit, did it matter whether the shooters meant to get him or he'd had the dumb luck to stumble into the middle of a firefight? He'd be just as dead.

The smoke cleared a bit. Sunlight poured in from a school-bus-sized hole in the ceiling. Not just the ceiling—David could see attic rafters and the jagged and burning edges of the roof. Way above was a blue sky, soft white clouds.

He was in a bedroom. A dresser lay on the floor. In front of him was a bed. He gripped the mattress and pushed himself up.

A wall exploded into a shower of plaster, rocks, and dust. He flew back. Air burst from his lungs, and he crumpled again to the floor. He gulped for breath, but nothing came. The stench of fire—burning wood and rock, something dank and putrid—swirled into his nostrils on the thick, gray smoke. The taste of cement coated his tongue. Finally, oxygen reached his lungs, and he pulled it in with loud gasps, like a swimmer saved from drowning. He coughed out the smoke and dust. He stood, finding his balance, clearing his head, wavering until he reached out to steady himself.

A hole in the floor appeared to be trying to eat the bed. It was listing like a sinking ship, the far corner up in the air, the corner nearest David canted down into the hole. Flames had found the blankets and were spreading fast.

Outside, machine-gun fire erupted.

David jumped.

He stumbled toward an outside wall. It had crumbled, forming a rough, V-shaped hole from where the ceiling used to be nearly to the floor. Stumps of bent rebar jutted out of the plaster every few feet.

More gunfire, another explosion. The floor shook.

Beyond the walls of the bedroom, the rumble of an engine and a rhythmic, metallic *click-click-click-click-click* tightened his stomach. He recognized the sound from a dozen war movies: a tank. It was rolling closer, getting louder.

He reached the wall and dropped to his knees. He peered out onto the dirt and cobblestone streets of a small village. Every house and building was at least partially destroyed, ravaged by bombs and bullets. The streets were littered with chunks of wall, roof tiles, even furniture that had spilled out through the ruptured buildings.

David's eyes fell on an object in the street. His panting breath froze in his throat. He slapped his palm over his mouth, either to stifle a scream or to keep himself from throwing up. It was a body, mutilated almost beyond recognition. It lay on its back, screaming up to heaven. Male or female, adult or child, David didn't know, and it didn't matter. That it was human and *damaged* was enough to crush his heart. His eyes shot away from the sight, only to spot

293

another body. This one was not as broken, but was no less horrible. It was a young woman. She was lying on her stomach, head turned with an expression of surprised disbelief and pointing her lifeless eyes directly at David.

He spun around and sat on the floor. He pushed his knuckles into each eye socket, squeegeeing out the wetness. He swallowed, willing his nausea to pass.

His older brother, Xander, said that he *had* puked when he first saw a dead body. That had been only two days ago—in the Colosseum. David didn't know where the portal he had stepped through had taken him. Certainly *not* to a gladiator fight in Rome.

He squinted toward the other side of the room, toward the shadowy corner where he had stepped into . . . wherever this was . . . *whenever* it was. Nothing there now. No portal. No passage home. Just a wall.

He heard rifle shots and a scream.

Click-click-click-click-click . . . the tank was still approaching.

What had he done? He thought he could be a hero, and now he was about to get shot or blown up or . . . something that amounted to the same thing: dead.

Dad had been right. They weren't ready. They should have made a plan.

Click-click-click-click-click.

David rose into a crouch and turned toward the crumbled wall.

I'm here now, he thought. *I gotta know what I'm dealing with, right? Okay then. I can do this.*

He popped up from his hiding place to look out onto the street. Down the road to his right, the tank was coming into town over a bridge. Bullets sparked against its steel skin. Soldiers huddled behind it, keeping close as it moved forward. In turn, they would scurry out to the side, fire a rifle or machine gun, and step back quickly. Their targets were to David's left, which meant he was smack between them.

Figures.

At that moment, he'd have given anything to redo the past hour. He closed his eyes. Had it really only been an hour? An hour to go from his front porch to here?

But in the house where he lived, stranger things had happened . . .

CHAPTER

63 MINUTES AGO
SUNDAY, 6:48 A.M.
PINEDALE, CALIFORNIA

Following Toria, his nine-year-old sister, David stepped through the front door onto the porch. Xander sat there on the steps next to Dad, watching the sun wash the nighttime out of the sky. Toria went down a step and sat on their father's other side, leaning her head into him.

Dad put his arm around her and squeezed her close.

David looked at his brother.

Xander had stormed out of the house, furious at Dad for not telling them he had known all along that the house they had moved into four days earlier was dangerous. He didn't look quite as angry now, and David's heart lifted when Xander smiled.

"We're going to rescue Mom," Xander said.

Mom. David's concern for her was like a knife in his chest. Less than two hours ago she had been taken—kidnapped into one of the other worlds that lay hidden within their new house. He had watched a man carry her away. He and Xander had tried to stop him, but the intruder was too big, too powerful.

Then Dad had confessed that his own mother had been taken into a portal the very same way, when Dad was only seven years old. They had never found her. His father, Grandpa Hank, had feared for his children and his own sanity and taken the family away. Xander had gone through the roof. He'd screamed that he wouldn't leave until they'd found Mom, but David was afraid Dad wouldn't let them stay, knowing it wasn't safe. Now, it seemed Xander and Dad had agreed: they would stay.

David scanned the front of the house.

She's not yours, he thought. *We're coming for her, you hear?*

His eyes dropped to his sister's face, then over to his dad's. They felt it too, he could tell. They were up to this challenge. He looked at Xander's eyes and saw hope there, and determination.

David nodded. "Let's do it."

Xander reached for the railing and pulled himself up. "Good idea, Dae," he said, and bolted up the stairs.

David was right on his heels.

"Whoa, whoa, guys," Dad called out. "Xander!"

Xander kept moving. He pushed through the front door and took the stairs three at a time. David rushed to keep up.

Behind them, Dad yelled, "Xander! David! Stop!"

Xander turned on the landing, fire in his eyes. "*What?*"

David stopped two steps from the top.

"Where are you going? What are you doing?"

"Rescuing Mom," Xander said in the same tone he would use to explain that water was wet.

"We're going to do that, son, absolutely. But we need a plan."

"I *have* a plan!" Xander yelled.

It scared David how forcefully Xander said it.

"I'm going over," Xander continued. "And I'm going to keep going over until I find her."

Going over.

Since moving into the house, their lives just kept getting weirder and weirder. It had begun with the discovery that the second-floor linen closet was more than a storage place for towels and bedsheets: it was a portal to a locker at the Pinedale Middle and High School. Then he and Xander had followed an intruder in their home through a secret door in the wall.

There they'd found a flight of stairs to a third floor—a twisting hallway with doors on either side. Beyond each door was a . . . well, that was another thing. The new world they lived in came with its own vocabulary: an *antechamber* was what lay beyond each of the twenty doors in the upstairs hallway. It was a small room containing a bench and a selection of items—clothing, tools, weapons.

Set in the opposite wall of each antechamber was another door, always locked. Unlocking it required putting on or picking up some of the items. Beyond that door was a *portal*, a passageway from their house to one of the other worlds and back.

World was the word they used to describe the different times and places they could step into from their house. Xander had done it first. He had put on a helmet and chain mail, picked up a sword, and stepped into the Colosseum—right in the middle of a gladiator fight. Their father had barely managed to rescue him.

And *going over* or *crossing over* was the term he and Xander had begun using to describe stepping through a portal to a different world.

"It's not that simple," Dad said.

"It *is* that simple," Xander shot back. He ran down the hall toward the secret door.

"Xander!" As Dad flew past David, he said, "Stay here." He disappeared around the corner.

David threw a quick glance at Toria, who was standing in the entryway. He knew her expression mirrored his own:

open mouth, wide eyes. He thought of saying something, then he turned and bolted after his father and brother. He reached the hidden stairway to the third floor and clambered up. Toria was right behind him.

The first antechamber door was open. David could hear Xander's and Dad's voices:

"Let me go!"

"Just wait! Wait, I said!"

David slammed into the door frame. Xander was on his back on the floor; Dad was sitting on him, gripping Xander's shirt in his fists.

Tears streamed out of Xander's eyes. "You don't care!" he yelled. "You *let* her get taken!"

Dad pulled Xander up so they were nose to nose. Dad opened his mouth, then snapped it closed, pressing his lips tight. He stared into Xander's eyes, and slowly his face softened. He whispered, "Don't you think I want to do exactly what you're trying to do? Don't you think I want to go in after her too, just snatch her back? I do, Xander, I do. It's just . . ." He looked up at David and Toria, standing in the doorway. "It's not that easy. I've done this before. If we have any chance to find your mother—"

"*If?*" Toria said.

Dad looked at her sadly. "If we have any chance, any chance at all, it lies in being smart about it." He lowered his hands until Xander's head was back on the floor. "We can't just go crashing over. It's too dangerous. Your mother wouldn't want that." Dad stood and extended a hand to Xander.

Xander glared at it, pushed himself up, and stood. He wiped the tears off his face, then he sat on the bench and looked at the floor.

When neither of them spoke, David said, "So . . . what do we do?"

"Now," Xander said. "Not later—*now*."

Dad took a deep breath and looked around the room. "What did you see when the guy took Mom? In the room, I mean?"

"It was *snowy*," David said. "There was a white parka . . . and snowshoes . . . gloves . . ."

"Goggles," Xander added.

"Okay, so maybe the Arctic," Dad said, thinking.

"But she didn't stay there," Xander said.

Their father cocked his head. "What do you mean?"

"She didn't stay there long," Xander said, sounding frustrated.

David said, "We heard her in the hall. We ran out and she was trying to come through another door. Something . . ." A lump in his throat choked his words. "Something pulled her back in."

Dad stepped over to him and combed his fingers through David's hair. "A different room? Not the Arctic one?"

"We went in the antechamber," David said. "There were pirate things. A sword and a three-cornered hat."

"Like Johnny Depp's in *Pirates of the Caribbean*," Xander said. Leave it to him to put it in movie terms

Their father's puzzled look deepened.

"What's it mean?" Xander asked.

Dad shook his head. "Grandpa Hank said he thought there was a way to go from world to world without coming back through the house each time."

"Other portals?" David asked.

"I don't know. If so, he never found them. But if it's true, she could be anywhere, in any world."

"We already figured that out," Xander said.

"And if there are other portals," Dad said slowly, thinking it through, "it'd be like a combination lock. Every new portal would make the number of possible worlds she could have gone to increase exponentially."

Xander looked at him hard. "What are you saying? That it's impossible?" He stood. "We haven't even started, and you're *giving up?*"

"No, no," Dad said. He reached out and laid his hand on Xander's shoulder. Xander pulled away, but Dad continued: "It's just that we have even more work ahead of us than I thought."

"So what do we do?" David said again.

"Let's look for those worlds," Dad said. "The Arctic one and the pirates. She's probably not in either one, not anymore, but it's a place to start."

Xander said, "It'll be faster if we split up. David and me. You and Toria."

Dad studied him. "Xander, look at me," he said. "Can I trust you?"

David watched Xander meet Dad's gaze.

"More than I can trust *you*," his brother said.

three

SUNDAY, 7:55 A.M.

"Why are you being so mean to Dad?" David asked.

Xander didn't look away from the items hanging from hooks in the antechamber they stood in. Dad and Toria had left to find notepads and pens to catalog the rooms. "What do you mean?"

David mimicked his brother: "'More than I can trust *you*.'"

"It's true," Xander said.

"Dad made a mistake, that's all."

"His mistake got Mom kidnapped. Don't you understand? We may never see her again."

"We will," David said quietly. His heart felt like a cannonball in his chest. He surveyed the things in the room. "Doesn't look like any big deal," he said.

There was a leather jacket, a beret, a sheathed knife, a belt of rifle cartridges. On the bench lay a rolled-up paper and a crumpled pack of cigarettes.

"Hard to tell," Xander said. He elbowed David's arm. "You should know that, going over the way you did."

Xander was right. You couldn't judge a world's safeness by the items in the antechamber. After Xander's trip to the Colosseum, David had wanted to try it. They had chosen a room with clothes and tools that had seemed even more harmless than the ones here. And David had stepped smack into the middle of three hungry tigers and a tribe of fierce hunters.

He lifted the leather jacket off its hook. It was heavy, old, and wrinkled. He slipped it on.

Xander smiled and said, "'No man left behind.' That's from *Black Hawk Down.*"

"No woman left behind," David amended. He snatched the beret off the hook in front of him. It was big on his head, but he left it propped there, tilted down over one eyebrow. He said, "Xander, you know Dad feels the same way. He won't leave without Mom."

Xander didn't respond.

David said, "He loves Mom."

"He should have thought of that before bringing us here."

"He didn't think it would happen so fast. He thought he could protect us."

"He was wrong."

"He said when he lived here as a kid, the weird stuff didn't start happening for months. He thought he had time to make it safe, to figure it out."

The muscles in his brother's face seemed to tighten. David didn't like to see him looking so stern, so angry.

"He loves Mom," David repeated, whispering.

Xander sat on the bench. "Look," he said. "I know he does, and I know he didn't mean for any of this to happen. But it did—because of him. He loves us, too, and that's why he might try to get us out of here, thinking it's best. But it won't be, not without Mom."

David picked up the pack of cigarettes. He said, "This is *open*. And there are cigarettes missing. Weird."

"Why is that weird?"

David turned the pack over in his hands. The cigarettes inside felt like bones underneath a thin layer of skin. "It makes me wonder whose they were. What does he think happened to his pack of smokes?"

Xander shrugged, clearly not interested.

"And look," David said, holding the package up. "What language is that?"

"*Flor belmonte . . . extra-vergé,*" Xander read. He shrugged again. "Italian?"

David examined the pack, then slipped it into the jacket pocket. He looked at the door leading to the world where the jacket, beret, and cigarettes belonged. Had he picked up enough of them to unlock the door? Hadn't they determined that it took only three items from the antechamber to open the portal door? He looked sideways at Xander, who was reaching for the roll of paper.

Giving in to curiosity, knowing he shouldn't, David gripped the door handle and turned it. The door flew open as though pushed from the other side. A whoosh of warm air swept in.

"Hey!" Xander said. David sensed him stepping up behind him. He felt a tug as Xander's hand grabbed the collar of the leather jacket. "*David!*"

"I'm just looking," David said. But really there was nothing to see. Sometimes what lay beyond the doorway was fairly clear, as when they were able to see the jungle floor before David stepped through. But before Xander found himself in the Colosseum, they had seen the world on the other side as indistinct shapes. It was like that now, like peering through a steamed-up shower door.

A blurry object flashed past, causing David to jump. "Whoa!"

Another figure passed by on the other side of the threshold. This one was more distinct—dark hair framing a white face, dark clothes.

"People," Xander said.

"Doing what?"

More and more figures went past, moving right to left. A child went by, everything about him clear as tap water. David saw fear in the boy's eyes as he turned to look back over his shoulder. And yet, the person whose hand he was holding was blurry and indistinct.

"It's like we're seeing it through a camera lens," Xander said. "And somebody is playing with the focus."

The sound coming through was no better. Most of it was a garbled murmur. Now and then words came through. The syllables were sharp, but David didn't understand the language. A low *boom* sounded like the beating of a drum.

"A parade?" David wondered out loud.

"Shut the door," Xander said. "Wait for Dad."

More faces—in and out of focus.

"Hold on," David said. "I want to see more. Maybe I can figure out what they're doing."

"Don't move," Xander said, releasing David's collar.

David glanced back to watch Xander step into the hallway. "Dad!" his brother called.

Dust and smoke drifted into the little room. It smelled like fireworks on the Fourth of July. The angle of the view through the doorway seemed to be getting higher. David could see more people, mostly their heads now, not their bodies. He remembered Xander telling him that he had watched the jungle moving past the doorway before he jumped in to rescue David from the tigers. Whatever these portals were, they were not locked in one place. They moved, as though with a breeze or caught in an ocean current.

A face came into focus and immediately blurred. David's heart jumped into his throat. The glimpse had been enough.

"Mom," he whispered. Then he shouted it: "Mom! Xander! I saw Mom!" He leaned his shoulder into the door frame, hoping for another glimpse.

Xander raced up to him. "Where? David, where?"

"She went past! Xander, it was her!"

"Are you sure?"

"I'm sure! I'm sure!"

Xander went back into the hallway and yelled, "Dad! Dad!" His voice was shrill, panicky. His eyes were wide. He was shifting his gaze down the hall, back to David, down the hall again. David realized Xander was as clueless about what to do as he was.

He watched the throng of people in the other world start to thin out. The perspective of the doorway rose higher and farther away. He could no longer see the spot where he thought his mother was.

"Xander, I . . . she . . ." He turned his head.

Xander was looking at him, reading him perfectly. "No!"

"Wait for me!" David said and stepped through the portal.

CHAPTER

four

And so he found himself staring over the crumbling wall at an approaching tank.

Click-click-click-click-click.

Its turret rotated toward him. When the big barrel was pointed directly at him—all he could see of it was a black hole—it stopped. Fire and smoke erupted from it.

David dropped to the floor, knowing the wall would be like wet paper to the incoming shell. He squeezed his eyes shut.

Here lies a boy named David King, he thought, the image of his headstone filling his mind. *Food for worms because he did a stupid thing.*

He heard the whine of the shell as it cut through the air over his head. The explosion was farther away than he expected. The floor shook and dropped down a foot. Plaster and rock rained over him.

He cracked open an eye. The shell had gone through the bedroom's crumbled exterior and interior walls, sailing right through into the attic beyond. Two feet lower and he'd be as gone as the section of roof above his head, through which he could see the blue sky beyond.

The hum of the tank's turret started again. It was turning its cannon away from him! He brushed the debris off his face and shoulders, then took off the beret and slapped at his hair, kicking up thick plumes of white powder. He draped the beret back over his head and lifted his eyes over the top of a shattered wall. Men were crouched behind rubble and smoldering vehicles, shooting at the tank and the soldiers following it. Beyond this scattering of ragtag combatants, a bullet-pocked door cracked open and a woman peered out. She was not his mother, but he could see people crowded in the room behind her. This must be where the fleeing villagers had wound up. Maybe his mother was among them.

The tank boomed out a shell. David watched it flash into one of the cars the resistance fighters were hiding behind. It exploded. He saw bodies fly but quickly told himself that they were just parts of the car. The explosion rattled the façade of the building nearest it: a section of it, from ground to roof and ten feet wide, crumbled and fell, exposing the joists of the second floor and attic rafters. He caught a glimpse of an upper-floor bedroom similar to the one he was in, before smoke and dust obscured it.

Keeping low, he pushed away from the wall, then ran out of the bedroom and down a narrow flight of wooden stairs. They emptied into what used to be a pub. Most of the front wall was gone, pounded to dust. So were half the bar, tables, and chairs. A corner of the upstairs bed, the one that was burning, poked through the ceiling. Swatches of fiery bedding fell through. The heavier pieces plunged down like meteorites; lighter ones floated gently down like leaves from a flaming tree. Already the wood floor had ignited in a dozen spots. Smoke churned against the ceiling, filled the space with gray fog.

David coughed and coughed again. His throat was raw from the heat and smoke. His eyes stung. His lungs demanded fresh air. He dropped to his hands and knees and scampered across the floor, giving the flames a wide berth. He jumped over the rubble at the front of the building. Twisted rebar caught his foot, and he crashed down. He fell on top of jagged chunks of concrete and flipped over, landing in the street. By the time he caught his breath and blinked away the smoke and tears, three rifles were trained on him.

He threw up his hands. "Don't shoot me, please."

The faces behind the rifles twisted in confusion.

"*Qui êtes-vous? Identifiez-vous!*" one of the men shouted.

Oh, crap. David shook his head.

One man turned to the others, "*C'est seulement un enfant.*"

Enfant! David recognized the word from French class. It meant *child.*

"Yes, yes!" he said, nodding his head vigorously. "*Oui . . . enfant, enfant.*"

The tank belched out another round. The three men hunched down. David bowed his head, covering it with his arms. The explosion was a good fifty yards away. Still, debris zinged past David like buckshot. Something hit him in the calf. He grabbed it in pain, sure that he would find his flesh ripped open. It felt intact, so he opened one eye and looked. His jeans were not torn. No blood.

The fighters had forgotten him. Two of them were firing their rifles from around the back of a wrecked truck. The other had stepped onto the twisted bumper to get the barrel of a machine gun high enough to shoot over their own barricade.

David scrambled up. He limped down the block and across the street toward the door he had seen the woman open. Gunfire popped behind him. Divots of plaster ripped from the building on his right. Bullets sparked off the cobblestone on his left. He slammed into the red painted door. The thumb lever of the handle would not depress. He pounded on the door. Thinking of nothing else to say, he cried, *"Enfant, enfant!"*

The door opened an inch. An eye inspected him. Then it swung wide, and he was pulled inside. The air was stuffy and hot. There was an awful odor, which David knew must be sweat, but the first thing that came to his mind was *fear*. The room was crowded with women, children, and old men. Several people asked him questions he didn't understand. He shook his head and nodded, all the while moving to take in every face.

Then he saw the back of her head, the familiar color of her hair—golden yellow, like turning leaves. But this woman wore a dress. His mother had been taken in her nightgown. Of course, she would have found other clothes by now. He stepped around an old man whose shaking hands wanted to touch him, around two children not much younger than himself. Their cheeks were wet with tears. One of them was glassy-eyed, his face slack with shock. The other spoke to David urgently, repeating a line over and over. David frowned at him and shook his head.

His mother was huddled in a group of women.

"Mom!" David yelled. He supposed the word was similar to the one these other children would use. Many heads turned his way, all offering blank or hopeful stares.

His mother noticed the gazes the other women were giving him. She turned. As she did, she spoke rapidly to someone he could not see. His heart sank. She was speaking in French.

Her resemblance to his mother was undeniable, and his heart

skipped for a moment as he let himself think that he had been right. But he wasn't.

The woman responded to the disappointment on his face with sadness of her own. Softly she said, *"Avec qui êtes-vous, fils? Est-ce que je peux vous aider?"*

The ache in David's chest made him feel that his heart had turned into a plastic lump. It radiated out, transforming him into a plastic boy. He could not speak, he could not move; he didn't know if he was breathing or blinking. He had been so sure. . . . Deep in his mind he had already embraced her, told her how much he missed her, had taken her hand and brought her home.

A tear rolled down his cheek, and he knew his bottom lip was quivering.

The woman's frown deepened. *"Vous êtes si triste."* She held out her arms and stepped toward him.

He backed away, turned, and ran for the door. He was only half-aware of pushing people out of his way. He collided with the boy who had spoken to him. The boy yelled and went down. At the door, an old woman blocked his way. She shook a gnarled finger at him, scolding him with words he didn't understand. He shook his head back and forth, back and forth, trying to rid his mind of his lost hope, his sorrow, and even his being there.

One word formed out of it all and bounced around inside his skull like a racquetball: *Stupid . . . stupid . . . stupid . . .*

He shoved his shoulder between the old woman and the door. He flipped a dead bolt, pulled the door open, and went through.

Gunfire, screams, oily smoke. Behind him, voices rose in alarm. Several women called out to him: "*Enfant!*" and "*Garçon!*"

He stumbled into the street. Blinking hard to clear his vision, he looked back. The old woman scowled at him, cold to his feelings, calloused by the disrespect of youth. Faces behind her expressed worry and concern. More of them joined in a chorus, calling him back to safety. The old woman held on to the door. She gave him one last scowl and slammed it shut.

CHAPTER

five

The tank had come off the bridge. Now it was rumbling toward David on the town's main street. Under massive splatterings of mud and grime, it was painted in a camouflage pattern. On the front, where an emblem would have been on a car, was painted a white and black cross—David recognized the symbol of the German army.

I'm in World War II, he thought. *More than half a century before I was born.*

While the tank headed directly toward him, the gunners inside and the soldiers behind were occupied by something off to the side. Machine guns and rifles spat bullets in that direction. The tank's turret and cannon barrel slowly rotated toward the conflict. Bullets pinged against the side of the tank, kicking up tiny sparks.

Over the shooting and the rumble of the tank—sounds much louder than movies made them out to be—a voice reached his ears: *"Vous, là, sortez de la manière! Déplacez-la, garçon!"*

He turned away from the tank to see a man waving at him from farther up the street. The man wore a beret like his own and held a rifle. Beside him, behind a wall of rubble, more faces peered. The man waved his free hand high in the air as if swatting at flies. *"Sortez de la manière!"*

David was standing between the oncoming German army and the French Resistance. A breeze passed him. He felt it in his arms and hair, but it had not touched his face, and he realized it was not a breeze. The jacket and beret were exerting a gentle pressure all their own. Nudging him toward the portal home, as his father said they would. They urged him to cross the street, to the side opposite from where the women and children had taken shelter. He ran.

A scream stopped him. He looked back toward the tank. A woman had apparently run across its path, toward the shelter. She was lying in the street, trying to push herself up with her arms. As David watched, she slumped and stopped moving.

He took a step back toward where the portal must be waiting. He could take no more of this. No more suffering, no more death. With a deep sadness, he realized what, besides death itself, they were risking in trying to rescue their mother. They would be witnesses to events that would change them forever.

He saw the woman in the street stir and felt a spark of hope. A toddler in a white dress pushed out from under the woman's arm. She stood and looked down at the woman, who must have been carrying her. She reached a small hand to the woman's blouse and tugged at it. Then, confused and frightened by the loud noises, the little girl tottered away.

Go, David thought. Then he said it out loud: "Go!"

The tank was rumbling toward her. It was thirty feet away, closing fast.

A French soldier shouted and ran toward her. A small barrel set into the front of the tank rattled, spitting flame. Bullets kicked up dirt at the man's feet. He dived and rolled under a partially crushed truck. Round after round plunked into the truck's sheet metal. The machine gun panned to the wall of rubble. It blasted the concrete into clouds of dust, keeping the fighters cowering behind.

David looked over his shoulder, down the side street he believed his beret would tumble into if he let it. The portal. It had to be close.

He ran . . . not toward the portal, but into the path of the tank. The machine gun kept spraying bullets at the fighters. He hoped the gunner would either not see him at all or would recognize his intention to get the little girl and that he would not mow him down. The turret and barrel of the big gun were still aimed off to one side. David was not sure the driver even knew what he was about to run over.

Fifteen feet. The metal treads rolled on, grinding cobblestones. The tank was five feet from the child when David snatched her up, reversed himself, and darted toward the nearest building.

He ducked inside and immediately knew he could not stay. It was the pub, with the burning bed falling through the ceiling. Most of the lower floor was now engulfed in flames. David and the little girl coughed in unison. She tried to cry but could only cough more wretchedly. David peered out at the tank. Soon it would be even with him and then past him. The German soldiers crowding behind it seemed to be looking for something to shoot.

Clutching the child to his chest, he rolled around the edge of the broken wall and back outside. Someone near the tank yelled at him. The language was different, harsher and scarier than the French he had heard earlier. He did not stop—did not *halt*, to use the word hurled at him. He stayed close to the buildings and hurried toward the French fighters, who had moved farther down the street. At a side street he stopped. Across the town's main road, beyond the first block of buildings, he saw the old men, women, and children from the shelter. They were pouring from a back door to escape the advancing army.

A hand gripped David's shoulder and pulled him backward. It was the Frenchman who had beckoned to him when he was standing in the street. The man eyed him from under a furled brow. "*Que faites-vous? Où appartenez-vous, fils?*"

David gaped at him. "Uh . . . uh . . ."

The man slung his rifle over a shoulder. He held his hands, rough and bleeding, out to the little girl.

David twisted away. At first the man appeared surprised; then a smile pushed at his stubbled cheeks. His eyes flicked to the little girl, and he said, "Marguerite." He nodded. "Marguerite."

She held a hand up to the man. David handed her to him.

The man whispered something soothing to the little girl. He trotted down the side street, away from the tank's approach. At the corner, he turned back to David. "*Venez, garçon!*" He gestured with his head for David to follow him.

David took several steps. When the man disappeared behind the building, David stopped. If his father was right, and he understood the meaning of the strange, subtle tugging from the jacket and beret, the portal home was in the burning building right beside him.

The tank was near. Another ten seconds and he would be in its sights again. A dozen paces away on the main street, bullets flew in both directions. He aimed himself at an open doorway and ran toward it. Its frame was on fire, but David raised his arms over his head and plunged through.

CHAPTER

Six

David burst into the antechamber as though he were falling down the stairs. He took a step and, not finding solid ground, fell to the floor on his stomach. As it had done when he ventured into the world of French resistance fighters and Nazi tanks, the air burst from his lungs. This time, however, he was able to pull it back in without any trouble. He heard the door slam behind him, and he rolled over to see it solidly shut. Smoke filled the room, and he realized it was coming from him. Flames danced on his sleeves, and he felt heat on his neck.

"Aaahhggg!"

He felt hands slapping at him. In a few seconds the fire was out. He cringed away until he recognized Xander and his father. They were calling his name, asking if he was all right.

Wind whipped around him, stirring the smoke and sand and whatever else from the other world had been clinging to him. The wind pulled all of it into the gap under the door and was gone.

All the fear he had pushed aside to survive the German onslaught rushed into his consciousness as fast and furiously as flames igniting gas fumes. Simultaneously, relief washed over him, dousing those flames even as they sparked to life. He squeezed his eyes shut and began to weep. He heard his father and brother's words, felt their hands stroking his hair, squeezing his shoulder. His breath hitched in and out as he let the tears flow.

He wasn't even sure why he was crying: Was it the death he had seen or that he had pulled free from its skeletal fingers? He remembered Xander's response coming back from the Colosseum, and his own—although it was less pronounced—when he'd come back from the jungle.

He wondered if their experiences with the portals were like extreme booster shots of powerful emotions, or if the crossing over itself somehow touched the emotional receptors in their brains. He had heard that surgeons could touch parts of the brain with electrical probes, causing the patient to feel emotions that had nothing to do with his current experiences or memory. He'd also heard that electrical shocks could force a person to lose control of his bathroom functions. He was really glad that hadn't happened to him. It made shedding a few tears less embarrassing.

"I'm all right, I'm all right," he said.

They were lifting him, setting him on the bench. He sniffed, rubbed his forearm across his eyes, under his nose.

"I'm all right."

"What happened?" Xander said. His face was right there, big worried eyes, trembling bottom lip. He had one hand pressed to David's back, the other on David's chest, as though he was still trying to grasp that David had returned . . . or making sure David didn't suddenly flutter away and zip out of the room through the crack under the door, like the other debris from the faraway world.

Dad had taken a step back. He had his arms crossed in front of him and was scowling at his younger son.

"I'm sorry," David said. "I thought . . . I thought I saw Mom."

"*Did* you?"

David bowed his head, thinking of his encounter with the woman in the room full of scared people. "No . . . it wasn't her."

"And you almost died, too, didn't you?" Dad snapped. His voice was hard, angry.

"Dad!" Xander said.

"He did! He almost died! David, am I wrong?"

David nodded his head. "You're right," he said weakly. "There was this battle . . . I was in some French town, I think. The Nazis were invading. I . . . I . . ." He shook his head.

"It's okay," Xander said. He was kneeling in front of David, still holding him, rubbing his back through the leather jacket.

David looked up at his father: *Is it okay?*

Dad held his stern composition, then softened under David's gaze. He skewed his mouth into a semi-smile. He stepped forward, knelt beside Xander, and leaned in to be close to David. His big hand engulfed David's shoulder.

"You scared me," he whispered. He blinked slowly, seeming to reselect his words. "I mean . . . I was scared for you."

David threw his arms around his father's neck. He thought he was going to cry again, but the tears didn't come. Instead, he felt Dad's warmth, his heart beating against his chest. He felt stronger, as though drawing energy from his father.

Dad said, "When I was a kid, I crossed over a few times without permission." He looked intently at David. "Twice I thought I saw my mother and, well . . . I did what you did. I just went."

David was grateful for Dad's telling him that. He knew how stupid he had been to just go. It was the kind of thing that would make his father take them all away from the house, regardless of Xander's determination to stay. It helped to know that Dad understood.

Then Dad pointed a stiff forefinger at David. "That

doesn't mean what you did is okay. It jeopardizes everything we're trying to do. If this is how it's going to be—"

"It's not!" David said. "I won't do that again. I promise."

Dad looked at Xander, who nodded. "Well," Dad said, "I think I'm going to put some locks on these doors, just in case."

"How are we going to find Mom?" Xander asked.

"That's the question, isn't it?" Dad said.

"We *are* going to find her," Xander said.

Dad squeezed his knee. "I said we would."

Xander stood. He slapped David on the leg. "Come on," he said. "We've got other rooms to check."

David's mouth dropped open. Did his brother really believe he was up to doing anything other than collapsing in a heap? Trying not to whine, he started, "Xan—"

"They can wait, Xander," Dad said. "Look at Dae. He's ready to fall over. We were up all night—Toria screaming about seeing the man in her room, then . . . Mom. And none of us has slept since then."

Xander said, "You crash. I'm going to find Mom."

Dad stepped close to him. "Xander, I know how you feel. But you have to bring it down a few notches. Your heart's probably beating a thousand times a minute. Your mind's racing. I know, I can see it in your eyes, in the way you're acting. Keep it up, and you won't be around long enough to find your mother."

Xander made an exasperated noise and started to turn away, but Dad grabbed his arm.

"I mean it," Dad said. "This isn't a sprint, Xander. It's a marathon. If we use up all our energy at the beginning, we won't cross the finish line. Pace yourself, son."

Xander looked ready to fight. Then David saw the wisdom of Dad's words reach his brother. Exhaustion and resignation washed over Xander like a sudden downpour. His shoulders slumped, his face slackened. He nodded and said, "Ready for bed, Dae?"

"Oh, man," David said. "Who needs a bed?"

CHAPTER

Seven

MOTHER OF MERCY NURSING HOME
LAKE FOREST, ILLINOIS

The old man's eyes snapped open. For a moment he did not know where he was. Then his surroundings came back to him: the pillow beneath his head, the thread of sunlight outlining the window where blackout blinds almost did their job, the *beep—beep—beep* of the machine that monitored his heartbeat. The beeps were coming fast as he sorted out what had woken him. It was not uncommon for him to lie awake all night, but his ninety-two years of living had earned him the right to doze when the day's brightness bothered his eyes. He could not remember the last time he had seen the midday sun, even what little of it seeped around the edges of the blinds.

What was it? he thought.

His eyes snapped back and forth as he separated dream-thoughts from memories, memories from false memories. No, not *false* memories: *changed* memories.

That's it!

The beeping picked up pace, rabbit quick now. The man tried to sort it out. *What* had changed? Dreams bumped into memories, memories shifted away. He was too old for this. Or was it simply that sleep was still whispering? Whispering mumbo jumbo in his ears. Was it that the change was too small to easily grasp, a shift in knowledge that affected others more than it ever had him? He scrunched his eyes shut, feeling the wrinkles of his face crowd together like the folds of a rumpled blanket. The beeping came loud and fast, and now he could feel his heart in his chest pounding, pounding.

It had been too long, decades since he'd sensed the change in memories, the shift in knowledge that he felt at that moment. It didn't matter *what* had changed, only that *something* had changed. All the implications of that added to his jumble of thoughts. Already crashing into themselves on the freeway of his mind.

It was coming to him, what it all meant.

The beeping was like an alarm now, urgent and demanding attention. He realized it *was* an alarm. His racing heart had crossed some threshold in the machine, which was screaming for help.

The door of his room burst open, and help ran in with clicking heels and wide eyes. The nurse ran to him and leaned her face close to his. He felt her hands gripping his shoulders, bony shoulders that had once been layered with heavy muscle.

"Mr. Wagner!" the nurse called, louder than was necessary. "Mr. Wagner!"

"They . . . they . . ." His voice was dry and thin, the vocal equivalent of a piece of straw. His hand came up and clutched at the nurse's uniform, her collar. He looked into her eyes, needing to share, needing to let someone else know.

"They've come back!" he said.

"Who?" the nurse asked.

She scanned the room, clearly not getting his meaning. How could she? He noticed that an unsure smile had found her lips and realized it was in response to his own shaky grin.

"They've come back," he repeated. It was not for her benefit anymore, but for his. He liked the sound of it. He liked what it meant.

He looked past the nurse, thinking, thinking. His smile fell away. Something else dawned on him.

"They don't know," he said. His eyes found the nurse's face again. He wanted desperately to communicate, to get this one thing across.

"What don't they know?" the nurse asked. She shook him gently. "Jesse, what don't they know?"

"The killer," the old man said. "He's still there. He doesn't want them in the house."

CHAPTER

SUNDAY, 9:01 A.M.

David had closed the curtains over their bedroom windows, but the room was still bright. Part of his mind screamed to hop up and do something: find Mom, make a plan, *something*.

The rest of him wanted nothing but sleep. His muscles felt heavy. When he closed his eyes, it felt as though he were sinking into his mattress—slowly, like quicksand. From time to time, all the things that had happened in the last few hours made his eyelids snap open. He'd notice the sunlight on the ceiling, the shadows of the leaves, and his lids would droop again. He started drifting, floating away on shadows as though on currents of water . . .

"David, you awake?"

His eyes sprang open. Back in his bedroom. Had Xander said something?

"Dae?"

He turned his head. Xander was on his own bed, his head propped up on his arm.

"How can you sleep?" Xander asked.

"I'm tired." The words came out as though his tongue were too big for his mouth.

"Mom's gone. We need to get her."

"We will," David said. He blinked slowly at his brother, some of what had been on his mind coming back. "We gotta work together. Stop fighting Dad."

"I'm not *fighting* him. It's just . . ." Xander dropped his head onto the pillow and spoke to the ceiling. "It's just that Dad and I have different ideas about how to get her back."

"Different how?"

"Like now. Look at us, in bed when we should be searching for her."

"Even soldiers sleep, Xander. I can't even think straight."

Each time his lids came down, David forced them open again, waiting for Xander to say something else. But he didn't.

His brother just kept staring up at the ceiling. Finally David's eyes closed, and he let them stay that way. Xander's breathing grew louder, more steady. David thought he heard a snore. And then he was out.

CHAPTER

nine

734 BC

OUTSIDE SIDON, ASSYRIAN EMPIRE

The assassin lost sight of his target. Smoke from the burning city behind him roiled in the sky like mud kicked up from the bottom of a pond. It blotted out the sun and cast shadows over the land. The assassin squinted at the last place he had seen the fleeing man and spotted him: There! *He was halfway to the distant mountain range, where the assassin knew the man hoped to find refuge in one of the many caves.*

The land between the two men was hard-packed earth, cracked like snake scales from a long season of drought and heat. Why his king wanted this barren country, the assassin did not know. But then, he was often commanded to kill for reasons known only to people more favored by the gods than he. His duty was to kill, not to ask questions. It was for this labor that he had been taken from his family on his eighth birthday and trained for over a dozen years. During this time, his abilities of stealth, resourcefulness and, he learned later, ruthlessness, set him apart from the other boys. So his masters had sent him away for special training under the tutelage of Gilgamesh, a man whose skills in the art of death were legendary. The assassin had discovered they were also very real.

He looked back at the crushed city. Against the shimmering blue backdrop of the Mediterranean Sea, the clay walls of its buildings rose out of the desert like a mirage.

From the city itself, smoke rose in columns like the blackened trees of a long-dead forest. The vast Assyrian army had pushed against the walls and poured into the streets. He was not part of that powerful force, though he worked to accomplish the same goals of protecting the empire and conquering new peoples and lands. If the army was a battering ram, he was a dagger. The army crushed whole cities, while he sliced at the few men who could rally those cities' legions or rebuild them from afar.

The prince he was after was just such a man.

The assassin had slipped into the city well ahead of the army. His task: to kill the king and his two grown sons. He had found the father and one son together, planning their response to the approaching invaders. Their deaths had been easy. The second son had been with his commanders, who had fought the assassin gallantly. In the end, the commanders had succumbed to the assassin's superior skills. Their efforts, however, had allowed the prince to escape.

The assassin's arrows had found the prince as he bolted away. But his own injuries had kept him from moving in for a quick kill.

He took a step and felt every one of those injuries. A heavy gash through a muscle in his thigh threatened to topple him. A puncture in his side, just under his ribs, made breathing difficult. He knew it needed attention, but he could not spare the time—not as long as the last prince drew breath. His forearms above the wide iron cuffs he wore for protection were bruised and cut, as was the back of his right hand. He tightened his grip on his knife, thankful to have not lost his hand's power and mobility.

Another step, and he did topple. His knees struck the dirt, as hard as tiles. He slouched down, needing to rest. His head felt like it was baking in his tight, cowhide cap. He pulled it off, letting his hair fall to his shoulders, over his eyes. He used the tip of his knife to flick it back off his face. He hitched in a breath and felt the wound in his side flare with white-hot pain. He tasted blood and spat it out. The reddish-pink glob evaporated on the scalding desert floor. He let his head roll back on his neck until he was staring up at the smoke-filled sky. There was no breeze to cool his skin, no water to quench his thirst. He closed his eyes.

He imagined himself as a king. Instead of blood, his fingers would be stained with wine. Instead of death, he would dream of life, the people of his empire stretching to the horizon, honoring him for letting them live.

His eyes snapped open, and he shook such imaginings out of his head.

It was not his destiny to wear gold, but to wield weapons. He did not have the power to grant life, only the duty to take it. To think otherwise would lead to weakness and insanity.

Gritting his teeth, gripping his knife, he forced himself to rise. His eyes found the prince, and his heart leapt with hope. The man appeared to be down, sprawled against the unkind earth. The sight put strength in his legs. He stumbled on, after his target.

When the assassin was fifty yards away, he saw the two arrows he had let fly. They were jutting from the prince's back. Their feathered ends swayed slightly, as though in a breeze. The assassin knew better: it was the prince's breathing that moved the arrows. His muscles tightened with determination to finish the job.

The prince stirred. His head lifted, and he pushed himself up onto his elbows. He turned and saw the assassin. His eyes flashed in terror. He got to his feet, every movement punctuated by a gasp of pain, a groan of effort. He lurched on toward the mountains.

The assassin let out a heavy sigh. Didn't the prince know it was over? Death was too near to hide from it any longer.

The man of death followed. He tried to pick up his pace, but his injuries were taking their toll.

On with it, *he thought.* End it now.

Ten minutes on, he figured he had closed the gap by only a few paces. He forced his legs to move faster. He switched the knife into his left hand, so his right could hold the wound in his thigh.

A scratch, *he told himself.* Is man defined by flesh and blood, or is he everything he has learned to be? I am an assassin because of my skills, my determination to perform well. My bones and sinew do not make me an assassin. My wounds cannot stop me from being one.

The sounds of the invasion behind him had faded. The smell of smoke had left his nostrils. A slight breeze swept down from the mountains, carrying the musty scents of eucalyptus and juniper. He was alarmed to realize how far they had walked from the city. There was no chance of the prince escaping, but he wondered if he himself would make it back before succumbing to his own injuries.

Great fissures came down from the foothills and carved jagged cracks into the desert floor. As the two men approached the first of these gashes in the earth, the assassin smiled. It was impossible to cross. The prince was as trapped by a rent in the ground as he would have been by a wall.

The prince stopped at the edge of the ten-foot-wide crevasse. He seemed to appraise it, then shifted his gaze back toward the assassin. With no other choice, he stepped forward and fell out of the assassin's view.

The assassin shook his head. Of course the man would not make this easy. He did not want to even think about having to climb back out of the fissure once he delivered the prince to Charon, Hades's ferryman.

At the edge, he looked down. The crevasse was barely deeper than a man, but no man lay at the bottom, as he had expected. He looked to the left and right, able to see a good distance in either direction. No one. No footprints. No blood. No deeper holes in which to hide. Directly below, something shimmered. He squinted at it. The light and shadows were playing tricks on him. Was that a pool of water? The entrance to a cavern? He couldn't tell, but something . . . something was there.

He stepped off the ledge to the first foothold. The dry ground crumbled under him. He slid down, tried to hold something, found nothing. He dug in his heels, skidded, and stopped.

He balanced on the edge of the pool, but it was no pool. The earth wavered at his feet. A mist stirred, obscuring whatever it was that caused the sight. He crouched and passed his hand over the fog. It cleared, and his knifed hand shot up, ready to plunge down.

There was the prince! Down in the pit—but he did not appear to be whole. To the assassin's eye, there was blood and body, not all together. An arm here. A torso there. Was it a trick of the air, the way it shimmered and moved? Or had an animal moved in on the prince?

A fast, silent animal, *the assassin thought.*

The assassin plunged his knife down. Coldness gripped his arm. It tugged at him. He tried to move back, but the earth under him gave way, and his feet went into the hole. More coldness, pulling . . . pulling. With one arm and both feet ensnarled by this trap, he knew he was going in.

He raised his face to the sky and yelled—not in fear, but in defiance and effort: He would not die easily. Whatever pulled him would feel his blade, his teeth, his determination.

Then, in a flash, he went in.

And vanished.

CHAPTER

Sunday, 3:33 p.m.

Sitting on the front porch steps, David bounced his soccer ball on a lower step between his legs. He had planned on practicing his dribbling and making some shots into a makeshift goal while waiting for Dad and Toria to return from the hardware store, but he didn't feel like it now. He squinted up at the sun through the trees. His eyes were achy, and he felt groggy and ready for bed, even though it was midafternoon.

"Not used to sleeping during the day," he said.

"Sleep's sleep," Xander said.

David lowered his eyes to find his brother, but saw only his own ghostly image reflected in the lens of Xander's camcorder. Xander paced in front of him, pulling in and out with the camera. Stooping almost to the ground to get weird—Xander would say *artistic*—angles.

"Quit stalling," Xander said. "What happened in that World War II village you went to this morning?"

"I don't want to talk about it."

"Just a little," Xander coaxed. "We've gotta document what we're doing here."

"Why?"

"Come on, Dae. How many people can say they rescued their mother from time-traveling thugs?"

"We haven't found her yet."

"We will, and we'll have the story of it on tape. We'll be millionaires, I'm telling you."

"Are you filming my sneaker?" David kicked at the camera, connecting with it harder than he had intended.

"Hey!" Xander yelled. He turned the camera to look at the lens. "You're going to break it, and you almost jabbed it through my eye."

David just frowned at him. He had sat through Xander's walking completely around him, filming and saying things like, "This is the boy who fought off a Nazi tank" and "Ladies and gentlemen: the wound." Here Xander zoomed in on the place where David's hair had been singed at the back of his neck and the collar of his shirt had caught fire. He hadn't been burned, and there was no wound.

Then Xander had started asking questions about his time in the French village, and David had realized that it wasn't such a fun memory. He hadn't found his mother as he thought he would, he was almost killed, and death and terror had been all around him. It wasn't just this last jaunt to World War II that bothered him.

"I know I was all gung ho about checking out these worlds. I mean, I insisted on going into that jungle where the tigers almost got me. And when I thought I saw Mom, I just went. But, I don't know . . ." He shook his head. "I'm starting to think there's nothing good about those worlds. It's just death . . . and danger."

Xander said, "We gotta find Mom, Dae."

"That makes it so much worse, that we *have* to go through."

He examined his brother's face, looking for any sign that he was as worried and reluctant as David. But Xander's expression was unreadable. Since Mom's kidnapping, Xander's determination to find her made all of his emotions—anger at Dad, sadness for Mom—look the same.

David said, "After you came back from the Colosseum, you didn't ever want to see those doors again. Aren't you still afraid of what's on the other side?"

"Of course I am."

"You don't act like it."

"We gotta find Mom," Xander repeated. "That's all that matters. That's all I think about."

"But you're out here with your camera, talking about making a documentary. We're getting ready for school tomorrow. Mom can't be all you're thinking about."

Xander sat on a lower step and twisted to look up at David. "I've been thinking about what Dad said, that our best chance to find her is if we have all the time we need to do it and none of us gets hurt. I want to find her today, *right now*, but what if it takes longer—a month or even a year? We can't have people curious about what we're doing, why we're not in school, why we've become recluses. We need to look like a normal family."

"Even if we're not," David added with a half smile.

"*Especially* because we're not," Xander said. "People will leave us alone if they think there's nothing special about us. And Dad needs to make money. We need to live, eat. We might need to buy things to help in the search."

David thought about that. "Like what?"

Xander shrugged. "Like rope," he said, unsure. "Like the locks Dad's getting now. There's always something. I've seen movies where people lost wars because they couldn't afford to keep fighting. If we want to keep looking for as long as it takes, we need money, and that means Dad has to work."

David pictured Dad going into his office at the school, listening to parents complain, disciplining students, hiring teachers . . . whatever else principals did. He imagined himself grinning at teachers, raising his hand to answer a question, making new friends. All with Mom gone—*kidnapped*. "I don't think I can do it," he said. "Just pretend everything's okay?"

Xander set the camcorder on a step and gripped David's knee. "I don't want to either. I wanna be up there now, going through every door, but that would be like jumping in the ocean to rescue a friend when you can't swim. You both end up dead. Better to find a lifeguard or throw in a life preserver. That's how Dad wants to handle it: smart and safe." He smiled. "So be the gloomy kid, if you have to. Just don't be the weirdo who never showers and always rambles about living in a haunted house."

David said, "It *is* haunted . . . in a way."

"Sort of," Xander agreed. His eyes took in the front doors. "The past lives here, doesn't it? I mean, *really*."

"I wish it didn't," David said. "And I wish we didn't have to keep visiting it."

"Maybe we'll find Mom right away."

"You think so?" David asked.

Xander didn't answer. He didn't have to.

They heard the SUV's engine and its tires crunching over the dirt road, and turned their heads to wait for its appearance around the bend. The sun flashed brightly off its hood and windshield, reminding David that it was a sunny world away from the woods in which they lived. The 4Runner swung around and stopped at the end of the road.

Toria climbed out and waved. She waited for Dad to come

around from the other side. She took one of three heavy-looking plastic bags from him, and the two of them trudged into the forest toward the boys.

"Been out here the whole time?" Dad asked.

"You told us to," Xander said, a little whine in his voice.

Dad's eyes roamed the front of the house as he approached. It seemed to David that he was expecting to see something he hoped he wouldn't. When Dad was close enough, David tossed him the ball.

Dad grabbed for it, but the bags hindered his dexterity, and he knocked the ball into the trees. He shrugged and hefted the bags. "I'll feel better once we have these locks on the doors." He looked from David to Xander and frowned.

David thought he was going to comment on the mopey expression on Xander's face, which he was sure matched his own. But Dad simply shared their sadness. How could they feel any other way?

He set the bags at the base of the stairs and sighed. He said, "Come on, all of you. I want to show you something."

"What?" David said.

Dad began walking toward the side of the house. "You'll see."

The kids threw puzzled looks at each other. Then Xander pushed off the steps to follow. Toria dropped her bag with the others and fell in behind him. David considered staying right where he was. He'd seen enough for that day . . . for that *year*. But curiosity got the better of him. He jumped down to the ground and hustled to catch up.

CHAPTER

eleven

Dad led David, Xander, and Toria to the clearing. It was way behind the house, through an especially dense area of forest. David and Xander had been there before, and its strangeness came back to David as soon as he stepped into it. It was an almost perfect oval carved out of the woods. The ground here was flat and grassy. The tall trees around it bent in, forming what looked to him like a naturally domed arena. Stranger than its physical appearance was the way it affected people: it made David's stomach feel funny, like plunging a long way down in an elevator; it seemed to allow them to run slightly faster than normal; and it caused their voices to be higher pitched, as though they were talking with their lungs filled with helium.

Everyone but David stopped at the edge of the clearing. He continued toward its center. He said, "Dad, we already know about this place. Remember, you found us here the other day?"

As he walked farther into the clearing, his voice rose in pitch until "the other day" was as squeaky as Mickey Mouse's. Despite the sour mood he had carried with him from the porch steps to the clearing, he laughed. It came out like a little girl's giggle. That got him laughing harder, which made his voice seem even more distorted and ridiculous.

The others began laughing as well, but at the edge of the clearing their voices sounded normal. Xander laughed so hard, tears streamed down his face, and he fell to his knees.

Toria managed to say, "Why are you . . . why are you talking like that?"

David beckoned her to him. "Come here!" he squeaked.

When she was near, she said, "What?"—as high-pitched as a rusty hinge. Her eyes went wide, and her hand flew up to cover her mouth.

David cracked up again.

"Was that me?" Toria squealed.

Xander rose and walked into the clearing, wiping at his face.

"Dad," he said. The last part of the word was higher pitched than the first. "Dad. What's this about? Do you know?"

Dad shook his head and joined them. "I know what this clearing *does*, but not why." Even his deep voice was no match for the squeakifying power of the clearing.

"Is this why you brought us here?" Xander asked. "For a . . . I don't know, a *break* from the doom and gloom?"

"It worked," David said. "I've been frowning so much, my face hurts."

It was about four in the afternoon. He could not believe that his mother had been gone for only twelve hours. He knew he shouldn't feel as lighthearted as he did, but he couldn't help it. He wondered if the laughing gas some dentists used had the same effect: making you feel like laughing when you should be crying.

David smiled at Toria. She was holding her arms out from her body and rising up on her tiptoes and down again, rising up . . . she was feeling the lightness, the *bounciness* David and Xander had noticed the first time they were here.

Dad said, "This isn't the half of it, guys. Watch." He moved deeper into the clearing and stopped near its center. He faced them, but his attention was on something they couldn't see. He looked around as though tracking a flying insect. Holding his hands out, seemingly for balance, he rocked up onto his toes. He took a step, rocked up again.

Xander and David exchanged a look of complete bafflement.

"Hold on!" Dad squeaked. His foot rose high, but instead of coming back down, the rest of him rose up to its level.

David gasped. Toria made a noise that might have been a startled scream. Xander spat out a word: "*What?*"

It was as though their father was standing on an invisible platform—an unstable platform. His feet wobbled around beneath him. He kept shifting his knees, his weight whipping his arms this way and that, apparently to keep from falling. Instead of coming down, he slid sideways and rose higher. Still wobbling, his eyes came off his feet to take in his startled children. A wide grin stretched across his face. His hair rose and fell as though blown by a breeze. He said, "What do you think?" The act of speaking seemed to distract him from whatever concentration he needed to—

To what? David thought. *Fly? Float?* The way Dad was balancing himself, David would say Dad was grinding a rail on a skateboard.

Dad wobbled and went higher.

"You've got to be kidding me!" Xander said, stepping forward. "Are you . . . are you *flying?*"

"I don't know what it is," Dad said. He shifted his hips, moved sideways and up.

Correction, David thought. *Not grinding a rail—more like riding an escalator. An invisible escalator that isn't very stable.*

The smile never left Dad's face. He said, "We discovered this when I was a kid. There are like . . . air currents or something. But more than air. If you find them, you can kind of step on them, *ride* them." He suddenly sailed thirty feet through the air, going sideways, straight up, then plunging down a little. His body wobbled as he tried to stay balanced. He let out a long, high "Aaaah!" and laughed. "Not so much a ride as it is like *surfing* on whatever currents are moving through this clearing."

David stuck out his foot, feeling for something he could not see, hoping to feel it. Nothing, just that same lightness everywhere. He called, "How? Can we do it too?"

"Sure you can!" Dad said. He zipped higher and came closer to the kids. He hovered over them, smiling down at David.

David could see the bottoms of his shoes, a spot of gum stuck on one of them. For some reason, this more than anything drove the point home: his dad was flying. And he seemed to be getting more comfortable in the air, less wobbly, more in control.

Their father shot backwards and stopped. He was still looking down at David, but not between his feet. He said, "It has something to do with attitude, with *wanting* to do it. It's like flexing a muscle to find the currents. I'm not saying you're willing yourself to do it—more like you're *allowing* yourself to do it."

David lifted his foot again, tapping his toe in the air. He *did* feel something, a kind of resistance. He moved his whole foot. The air felt spongy, as though he were stepping on a balloon. He heaved himself up onto it and came straight down. He lost his balance and fell back onto the ground.

Xander and Toria laughed.

From high above, Dad called, "That's it, Dae! You can do it. It takes some getting used to."

David leaned back on his arms to look up at Dad, and he realized something. "You did this before," he said to his father. "I mean recently. When you found Xander and me here the other day, you'd been doing this, huh?" He remembered that Dad had been out of breath, his hair all messed up.

Dad shrugged. He zipped around in a tight circle, rose even higher, close to the level of the treetops now. "I confess," he said, and laughed. "I wondered if the clearing still allowed it and if I could do it. After you guys found the portals, and Xander went to the Colosseum, I needed a break. This place takes your mind off everything."

David lay back, feeling the soft grass under him, tickling the back of his neck. The trees arched over the edges of the clearing, leaving an oval of blue sky directly above. Nothing indicated that the imaginary dome created by mentally extending the treetops to the center of the opening was the highest you could go, but he suspected that was true. His father was just below this upper limit, weaving around. Instead of standing straight, he was starting to lean over. This made what he was doing appear even more like flying.

"Whoa! David, look!"

It was Xander. When David looked, his brother was standing four feet above the grass.

CHAPTER

Xander laughed. His feet, well off the ground, were slipping and sliding around under him, but he somehow stayed up.

"Check it out!" Xander yelled.

"Oh, man," David said, getting to his feet. If Xander could do it, he'd better be able to. He walked to the center of the clearing, thinking that the currents, whatever they were, would be stronger there. Toria was closer to the edge. She was lifting her feet and hopping, but not getting any air.

She'd better not do it before me, David thought.

He closed his eyes and patted the air around him. After a moment he felt the resistance he had noticed earlier. Again, he lifted his foot and moved it around, as though feeling for a stair. More resistance, but nothing else.

Come on, come on! he thought. *Fly!*

Sponginess under his feet, under his hands. Squeezing his eyelids tighter, he imagined the air holding him, lifting him.

"David!" Xander called.

David looked.

Xander was *way* above ground now, grinning like a madman. "Yeah, man!"

David felt his feet almost slip out from under him, as though he were standing on ice. At the same time, he realized he was not looking up at Xander. He dropped his gaze straight down and saw the grass ten feet below his shoes. His stomach rolled. His muscles tightened. His feet *did* slip out from under him. He fell back, his arms pinwheeling, his legs shooting up over his head. But he didn't drop. He saw the ground below him and then Xander again as he came back around. He had done a backward somersault in midair.

"Way to go, Dae!" Xander said. He threw himself backward. He spun his arms and kicked his feet until he had executed a similar move.

David watched with amazement. He felt pressure under his feet and arms, as though invisible hands were keeping him afloat.

He brought his arms down and kicked as he would under-water. And what would happen underwater happened here: he rose higher. As frightening as it was to watch the ground get farther away, David felt a lightness that went deeper than his skin and muscles. It reached his spirit. It was like he was free of more than the laws of gravity; all the garbage that had been dumped on him recently didn't seem so heavy.

He was still aware of his mother's absence and how awful it was. But at this moment, he felt able to deal with it. He was sure it was temporary, as though she had gone to the store and would return soon. He laughed at that, kicked his legs, and shot higher. Bending at the waist, he leaned diagonally over the ground. This—staring directly at a forty-foot plunge—was even more exhilarating. His heart raced faster. His mouth twitched from a joyful smile to a worried frown and back again. His father called to him, and when he turned to look, his body rotated with his head.

Dad was standing—if that's what you called it, when there was nothing to stand on—as high as David thought he could go, at the center of the opening to the wide blue sky.

"What do you think?" Dad said and laughed.

David meant to answer, but only an excited breath came out. He swallowed and tried again. "Great!"

Just under the arcing canopy of leaves, Xander hovered. He

was reaching up to touch the branches. He was being careful, as though any connection with reality would send him crashing back down.

"I can't do it!"

Toria's voice reached David, sounding thin and far away. He looked to see her jumping in place on the grass.

Dad said, "I think you're trying too hard, honey." He moved his arms and legs and began descending toward her.

David swiveled away and "swam" toward the canopy at the edge of the clearing. How cool would it be to get a leaf from up here and save it as a memento of his first time flying? He still had trouble thinking of it as *flying*. It wasn't like *Peter Pan*: hadn't Wendy, John, and Michael Darling needed fairy dust? And they had flown away to Neverland.

David, Xander, and Dad weren't flying, and they would never go anywhere this way. But that was all right. This was enough.

He was near the edge of the clearing and reaching up to a leaf bigger than his hand, when something outside the clearing caught his eye. His eyes widened, and his heart felt squeezed into a tight knot. Through the trees, on the ground, a man stood looking at him. He was in shadows, but David could tell the man's expression was grim. He had long hair that was blowing around his head. He wore a dark overcoat, and his hands were stuffed into his pockets. The whites of his eyes seemed to glow in the darkness of the woods.

David hitched in a breath and tried to yell for Dad, but his mind would not form the words he wanted to use. He moved his mouth without saying a thing.

He suddenly realized he was still moving, fast and out of control. He saw a heavy tree branch seconds before he crashed into it. His face hit first, then his chest. The pressure or currents that had been holding him up suddenly evaporated, and he fell.

His hands clawed for the trees and grabbed a branch. His descent jerked to a stop, then the branch snapped and he kept falling. His fingers tore at leaves and twigs. Like a freight train, the ground rushed at him.

David screamed.

thirteen

The assassin tumbled over the body of the prince. He realized instantly that the man was intact; it must have been a trick of the light, the shimmering, that had made him think the prince had been torn apart.

The assassin crashed down against a wood-planked floor. His ankle twisted; the puncture in his side flared with fresh pain. He ignored it. Instead, he rolled away from his adversary, away from any slicing blades the injured man might swing at him. A wall stopped him short. So he twisted and spun and plunged his knife into the prince's back, cracking through the left shoulder blade to reach the heart. The prince did not utter a gasp of death. He did not spasm in a final effort to retain life. The man had been dead before the assassin's knife—from the arrows, surely. But the assassin was trained to consider all possibilities before a normal person would think of even one. Could someone else have killed him, someone now hiding?

He looked around. He was in a small room with doors on opposite walls. A wooden bench, some items hanging on the wall above the bench—a helmet, tunic, an archer's bow. One door was open, revealing the walls of the crevasse into which he had jumped in search of the prince. Beyond the crevasse, black smoke streaked through a blue sky.

The door slammed shut. The assassin leaped for it. He tugged and pushed at a circular metal protrusion, but the door did not budge. Light glowed from a torch mounted on the ceiling, but it did not flicker with flames, and when he held his palm up to it, the light did not warm it. He squinted suspiciously.

A banging noise came from the other door. Quickly, he pressed his foot against the back of the prince and extracted his knife. He swung it toward the door, crouching, ready to spring. With no place to hide, he would simply have to fight whatever confronted him.

The banging continued, and he realized it was not coming from the door itself, but somewhere beyond. He stepped silently to the door and listened.

Bang, bang, bang.

It was not at this door that someone pounded. Perhaps, he thought, the people here knew an intruder had entered their midst. Maybe this banging was an alarm.

He must have stumbled into secret caves the Sidonians used to escape from their enemies. But why would they have put so much effort into the construction of a subterranean hideaway? The room was a perfect box, its walls smoother than he had ever seen outside of a king's palace. That's it, he thought, this place must be a sanctuary for Sidon's nobility. That's why the prince, and not commoners, had fled to it. Only a select few knew of it.

Bang, bang.

And one of them was beyond the door, obviously deeper into the cave. He put his fingers on the metal knob and pulled. The door remained shut, as he had expected it would. Like the other door, its latch was hidden. Then his hand moved, and the knob turned with it. He heard a click, and the slab of door came loose from the wall. He inched it open and peered through the crack. He saw a corridor stretching out of sight. It was narrow, as a tunnel should be. Like the room, however, the walls had been carved smooth and shaped into a rectangle. Fifteen feet away, a man studied the frame of another door on the other side of the corridor. While the assassin watched, the man slammed a tool into it: bang, bang.

What would he be doing at a time like this? Certainly, he knows about the city's besiegement.

But the man's relaxed posture and casual movements indicated no knowledge of the war outside or of the assassin's intrusion.

Good, the assassin thought, the man will be dead before he realizes his ignorance.

At that moment the first door blew open. Blinding light flooded in, along with a wind that carried stinging grains of sand and swirling smoke. The wind whipped through the small room and back out the door from which it came, like a genie's invisible hand reaching for the assassin. He squinted against the light and the blowing sand, and his hair flapped like a flag pointing at the wide-open door.

When he looked, the man in the corridor was staring back at him. The wind pulled the door out of his hand, opening it all the way. The wind was pulling everything. The hem of his chiton, which hung from belt to mid-thigh, snapped up and down and then pulled tight toward the open door. He thought again of a hand tugging at him.

The body of the prince began sliding along the floor. The shafts of the arrows extending from his back bowed in the fierce wind. A gust howled in and, as it departed, took the prince's body with it. The assassin watched the prince fly through the door and vanish in the light. The wind pulled at the assassin's feet, and he fell. His knife was ripped from his hand. It disappeared into the bright void beyond the threshold. The assassin would have gone through next, had he not gripped the frame of the other doorway.

The man in the corridor rushed toward him, his expression changing from bafflement to alarm.

The assassin was powerless to defend himself. It was all he could do to hold on to the frame and resist the force that pulled at him. Everything in him screamed out against being taken through that other door. Before the wind had come, he had seen the crevasse and smoke-filled sky on the other side. Now there was nothing but light and wind. Perhaps his nation had angered the gods by attacking this land. Or maybe he had stumbled into the lair of some beast unknown to his people. At that moment all he knew was that he must not go back through that door.

He pulled with all his might toward the hall, but the wind's grip on him was too strong. The other man reached him, grabbing for his arms. He seemed suddenly to become aware of the storm. He lurched forward, and the assassin thought this man, too, was going to fly right past him and out the door. But the man jammed his feet into the corridor wall on either side of the door's frame. Over the howl of the wind the assassin could hear the man yelling in a strange tongue. The man held firmly to the assassin's arms.

The assassin noticed the man's clothes and hair were flapping only slightly and realized the pull of the wind was not as fierce outside the small room. He had to get out. Seeking to gain more leverage, he released one hand from the door frame and gripped the man's clothes under his neck. The man canted his body backward, pulling the assassin with him.

The wind grew even stronger. The assassin's sandals came apart and flew away—first one, then the other. Near panic now, he tugged hard on the man in the corridor, putting him off balance. The man flipped forward, over the assassin and into the blinding light beyond the other door. The assassin squinted back, watching the man disappear. As soon as he vanished, the door slammed shut, and the wind died.

The assassin gripped the door frame and kept his eyes on the closed door for a long time. When it didn't burst open again, he pulled himself into the corridor, rolled away from the room, and stared up at the ceiling until his breathing and his heartbeat slowed to normal. Finally he sat up. The corridor was dimly lit from vessels of light attached to the walls. Like the light in the ceiling of the small room, they did not flicker with flame. Everything about this place was strange.

He nodded to himself. He had thought a beast resided here. The strangeness seemed to confirm that suspicion.

Grunting, feeling his wounds and aching muscles, the assassin stood. With the caution and stealth that was as natural to him as breathing, he approached the open doorway to the little room. It was cleared of everything he and the prince had brought into it: no sand, no weapons, no clothes. Even the blood they had shed was gone.

Strangely—but no stranger than the rest of this place—the items still hung from hooks over the bench. He remembered them rattling against the wall as the wind tugged at them, and he wondered how they survived its devastating pull.

He stepped into the room, just far enough to reach his fingers around the edge of the door. He pulled it shut as he backed into the corridor and stood quietly. He kept his eye on the door, expecting something to lurch out at him. His ears, accustomed to hearing the slightest scrape or breath, sensed nothing. He scanned the corridor one way and then the other, and the skin on the back of his neck tightened as he realized that the door he had just shut was only one of many. Who knew what monsters lurked behind the others? If they were anything like the wind-beast he had survived, he was in no hurry to meet them. A wall blocked one end of the corridor. Set into the other end was an opening. Shadows lay beyond. He was used to darkness. He thrived in it. He walked toward it. Leaning against the walls for support, he stumbled past the doors, determined to find a way out of this labyrinth of ghosts and monsters.

fourteen

SUNDAY, 5:55 P.M.

David sat on a treatment table in the Pinedale Community Health Clinic. Every time he shifted his weight, paper crinkled under him. He frowned at the newly plastered cast encasing his left arm. A nurse had given him pills for the pain, but it still felt like someone was twisting the point of a knife into his forearm. Dad ran his fingers over David's head, sweeping the hair off his face.

David wrinkled his nose at him. "It still hurts," he said.

Dad brushed his fingers over David's cheek. "I'm sorry. Nothing like that ever happened to me, just falling like that."

"I lost my concentration. That man . . ."

David had already told his father about the man he had seen in the woods. While Dad was checking him for more injuries and scooping him up to carry him to the car, Xander had run into the woods for a look. By the time Dad pushed through the dense vegetation surrounding the clearing, David in his arms, Toria holding on to his pants pocket, Xander had returned. He had not spotted anyone or seen any signs that someone had been there.

"But he was there! I saw him!" David had insisted. He had not wanted his father to think that the excitement of flying had caused him to be reckless. Plus, Dad should know that somebody had been there. Somebody had *seen* them.

Dad had given him a squeeze and said, "Let's not worry about him right now, Dae."

That had made him feel better, but now that he knew he was going to be all right, the man's presence concerned him again.

"You're sure he saw you?" Dad whispered.

David nodded. "He was looking right at me. Just standing there."

"You've never seen him before?

David thought about it. "I don't think so."

"Long, dark hair? How old?"

"His face was in shadows, but I think he was old . . . older than you."

"Wow, he must've been ancient."

David smiled. "Sorry."

Dad stroked David's head again. He said nothing.

David looked up at him. "What does it mean, someone seeing us like that? I mean . . . it can't be good, right?"

Dad frowned. "I don't know." He leaned closer to whisper. "David, you're sure he wasn't the same man who . . . the one who took Mom?"

David shook his head. "No way. The guy who took Mom was bald and *big*. The guy in the woods was a lot skinnier. The one who . . . who . . ."

As soon as Dad had mentioned Mom, David felt his chest tighten. His eyes stung with unreleased tears. Getting hurt bad enough to go to the emergency room was just the kind of thing that brought out the best in his mother. She would be here comforting him, assuring him that everything would be all right. Dad had been there for him, saying the right things, coming to his rescue. But he wasn't Mom.

When he'd fallen, and all the way to the clinic, David had yelled and groaned. He had gritted his teeth and essentially handled the scariness of the fall, the pain of his arm, and his concern over having been seen. Now, with the thought of Mom thrown into the mix, it was more than he could bear. His father's face swam out of focus as tears filled David's eyes. He lowered his head, and fat drops fell onto the hospital gown covering his lap.

Dad pulled him close and hugged him. The paper under him crinkled again. It reminded him that he was in a strange place—not just the hospital, but Pinedale and the house itself. They were away from everything and everyone they knew, and bad things had happened. He wanted to go home, to his bedroom in Pasadena, to the familiar walls and smells and faces that would come to smile at him and wish him well.

He hitched in a breath. "I . . . I . . ." He let the tears come. Then he caught his breath and tried again: "I don't like it here. I want to go home."

"I know," his father said, pulling him closer. David took some comfort from Dad's big hand on his head.

He sniffed. "I want Mom!"

"Me too," Dad said. "We'll get her, Dae. We'll—"

"Mr. King?"

Shiny black shoes came back into David's view. David didn't want to look up at the doctor, not with his face all wet and his nose running. He sniffed again and told himself to stop with the waterworks.

"Is he still in pain?" the doctor asked.

Dad rubbed David's back. He said, "I think the scare of falling out of the tree caught up with him."

"Are you all right, David?" the doctor asked.

His voice was smooth and calm. David wondered how

many times a day he used those words. David nodded, then sniffed again. He wiped at his face with his fingers.

The doctor stepped away. He returned, holding a handful of tissues where David could see them.

"Mr. King, could we speak in private a moment?"

"Of course."

The doctor's shoes clicked against the tiles as they left the room.

Dad leaned close to David, gave him another squeeze. He whispered, "I'll be right back."

He wiped his face and looked up to watch his father step into the hallway, look both directions, then step off to the right.

He wondered what the doctor needed to say in private?

David slid off the table, cringing at the crinkling paper, ignoring the throbbing of his arm. The nurse had helped him remove his shirt—taking extra care to slip it off his injured arm—and given him the gown. He still wore his own pants and sneakers, which was a good thing now: he knew how to walk quietly in them. He crept to the open door and listened. Dad and the doctor were talking in the hall. Their voices were hushed, but David could make out the words.

Doctor: " . . . just asking if everything is okay at home."

Dad: "And I'm asking what that has to do with my son falling out of a tree."

Doctor: "I know that's what you said happened, but—"

Dad, his voice getting louder: "What do you mean, *I said?*"

Doctor: "The boy has other injuries, older, not consistent—"

Dad: "What injuries?"

Doctor: "Mr. King . . . he has a scabbed-over cut on his shoulder."

Boy, these guys catch everything, David thought. He had completely forgotten that the tribesmen had shot arrows at him when he'd gone into the jungle world. The three tigers that had wanted him for dinner had made the armed men seem like nothing big. But one of their arrows had cut his shoulder.

Doctor: "He has a black eye, a bruise on his cheek. It looks like—"

Dad: "Like *what*? What are you saying?"

Doctor: "I just want to make sure David is safe."

Dad: "From what? From *whom*? Are you suggesting that someone at home is hurting him? That *I'm* hurting him?"

Doctor: "I'm simply—"

David stormed into the hallway. The doctor's eyes grew big at something he saw in David's face, and he tried to smile.

"You think what you want," David said, his voice loud against the tiles and smooth walls. "My dad loves me and has never hurt me!"

He stopped beside his father, who put his hand on his shoulder. "It's okay, Dae."

"No, it's not," David said. He never took his eyes off the doctor. "We came here for help, and you just accuse my dad of something . . . something . . . *horrible*." Folding his cast close to his body, he pointed at his bruised cheek with his other hand. "For your information, my brother did this. We were playing, and it got a little rough, okay?" David threw a glance up and down the hallway, but Toria and Xander had wandered somewhere else. "He's around here somewhere. You should see *his* head."

Dad stepped between him and the doctor. He gave David a look that was both stern and compassionate. He said, "That's enough, David, I can handle this."

"But—"

"I got it," Dad said. "Really."

David opened his mouth to continue, then pressed his lips together, sealing his words inside.

Dad smiled at him—the same smile that had comforted David many times: when David had not made the top-ranked soccer team, whenever nightmares had awakened him. He realized that he had been wrong before. They had not left *everything* familiar behind. They still had each other.

Dad turned back to the doctor. "Are we done here?"

"I just . . ." The doctor seemed to change his mind about what he wanted to say. "The nurse will get David a sling, and you'll be all set. We'll need to see him back here in a week."

Like everything is normal, David thought. *Like you didn't just accuse Dad of beating his kids.*

"Thank you," Dad said, playing the game as well. He turned David's shoulder to lead him back to the room.

David gave the doctor his fiercest scowl.

He hoped the man felt ashamed, but he just nodded at David and turned away.

CHAPTER

fifteen

In the car on the way home, David was still brooding. He was in the front passenger seat. Toria sat in the back with Xander, complaining that all Xander had done at the hospital was sit in the waiting room and text his friends. Even now, he was clicking away on his cell phone.

Dad moved the rearview mirror to see his elder son. He asked, "Is that Dean you're text messaging, Xander? How is he?"

Xander shook his head. "It's Danielle."

"So how is *she?*"

Xander's thumbs tapped out a message. He let out a disgusted sigh, flipped the phone closed, and dropped it onto the seat beside him.

"Problem?" Dad asked.

"*Girls,*" Xander said. He crossed his arms and glared out the window.

When he didn't continue, Dad said, "Is she giving you a hard time for moving?"

"It's not that. Just . . . I don't know. She's being nice, I guess."

"But . . . ?"

"But she's acting like we didn't spend almost every minute together this summer. She says the weather's been nice. She saw the new Matt Damon movie last weekend. Chitchat."

Dad nodded. He caught David's eye and raised his eyebrows in a *what's-a-guy-to-do?* way.

The sling the nurse had given David was blue and took the weight of the cast off his arm. The white plaster extended from his elbow to his hand, where it covered his palm and ran between his thumb and forefinger. He doubted he was ever going to get used to it.

"Can I sign your cast?" Toria chimed from behind him.

"I didn't like that guy," David told his father.

Dad gave him a puzzled look. "Who?"

"That doctor, what he was saying."

"What'd he say?" Xander asked. He sounded glad to shift his thoughts away from his ex-girlfriend.

"I wanna sign it," Toria repeated, louder.

"He didn't mean anything by it," Dad said. "It's his job to look out for his patients, especially children."

"You didn't seem too happy about it."

Dad shrugged. "He caught me off guard."

Xander said, "What? What'd he say?"

David twisted in the seat, bumping his injured arm and sending a bolt of pain into his shoulder. His words came out sounding angrier than he intended. "The doctor practically accused Dad of beating me."

"He said Dad *broke your arm*?" Xander's eyes grew wide in disbelief.

David said, "We told him I fell out of a tree, and he said, 'So you say.' He asked if everything was okay at home and how I got this bruise on my face."

Xander was leaning forward as far as the seat belt would let him. "What did you say?"

David smiled. "That you did it."

"Well," Xander said, sizing up the bruise, "it is in the shape of a fist."

Now David's cheek was starting to ache, just thinking about how the man who had taken Mom had punched him. He touched his fingers gently to his face. He said, "Yeah, but about twice the size of *your* fist."

"Okay, then," Dad said, "can you blame the doctor for asking?"

David scrunched his face at him. "But, Dad, come on! You beating us?"

Dad frowned. "It happens, guys. Not everyone should be a parent."

They rode in silence for a minute.

Finally Dad said, "This is the kind of thing we have to anticipate. We've got injuries we can't explain . . . your mother's absence . . ."

"*Flying!*" David said, dramatically.

"We can't do much about what people actually see," Dad said. "But, David, when we told the doctor you fell out of a tree and you said Xander had caused the bruise on your face, those were lies."

"What else was I supposed to say?"

Dad held up his hand. "I know, I know. What I'm saying is . . ." He paused, struggling with his words. "It's just that . . . I think we're going to have to get used to lying for a while."

Toria gasped. "Daddy!"

"Just for a while," Dad said. "If we tell the truth about Mom and everything else, they'll either think we're crazy and lock us up, or think that we're hiding something and start an investigation."

"We *are* hiding something," Toria said.

Dad glanced back at her. "They'll think we hurt Mom."

"Like they think you hurt me," David said.

Dad nodded. "The truth is too weird."

"We can show them," Toria suggested.

"Oh, yeah!" Xander said. "The government would move in and take the house. Then we'd never find Mom."

Dad turned the SUV onto the narrow dirt road that ended at their property. He said, "We have a secret. Sometimes you have to lie to keep secrets safe."

"*You* know all about that," Xander said.

"Xander!" David snapped. It would be a long time before his brother forgave Dad for bringing all of them to the house in the first place. He was about to say something else, something about letting it go, when Dad spoke up.

"You're right, Xander, I do. And I regret it. But until we get Mom back, we're going to have to make up a story about where she is. I'm thinking we should say she's back in Pasadena, wrapping things up—you know, with the house sale and stuff. How's that sound?"

None of them replied.

To David, coming up with an explanation for Mom's absence felt like turning a page and leaving her behind. He knew Dad was right and they had to do it, but he didn't have to like it.

Dad stopped at the end of the road. In the woods, the house seemed to be waiting for them. It was barely visible in the shadows, with its green paint now weathered to a dull gray. David felt it, though. It was like waking up at night and knowing someone was in the room with you, even when you couldn't see him. You just *knew*.

Dad killed the engine and turned to look at each of them. He said, "Well? Can we keep what happened to Mom a secret?"

Xander looked like he'd been asked to swallow a slug. He nodded.

"Toria?" Dad said.

"For how long?"

"Till we get her back."

"What if they make me tell? What if they torture me?"

Dad thought about it. "If they torture you, you can tell them the truth."

That seemed to satisfy her. "Okay."

Dad smiled at David. He said, "I know *you* can do it, Mr. My-Brother-Punched-Me-in-the-Face."

David said, "If it will help get Mom back."

"It will."

"All right then." He had the feeling that this was an important moment, a decision they would always remember. He hoped it was the start of a successful rescue and not something he would have to talk about in court someday. He squeezed his eyes closed, trying to push from his mind all the courtroom dramas he had seen on TV. There seemed to always be a time when someone made the decision to start lying, and everything went downhill from there. This had better not be that moment for them.

Moving on—because his heart *had* to move on—he said, "What are we gonna do about dinner? I'm starving." He opened the car door and hopped out.

On the way to the house, Xander moved in close to him. "Ever see *Spy Kids?*" he asked.

"You know I have," David said. "We have it on DVD."

"So you know the story. Some kids save their parents from a bad guy who imprisoned them."

David stopped walking. "What's your point?"

Xander shrugged. "The kids weren't always up-front about what they were doing. If they were, someone would have stopped them from rescuing their parents."

David rolled his eyes. "Xander, I hate to break this to you, but that was a movie. This is real life."

Xander chuckled. "What's the difference, Dae?"

CHAPTER

SUNDAY, 7:07 P.M.

While Xander helped Toria start dinner, David and Dad put locks on all the third-floor doors. David kept the screws in the sling with his broken arm, along with a snack-sized bag of Fritos. When Dad needed a screw, David would pull it out and hold it in place. As soon as Dad's power screwdriver drove it into the wall, David released it and watched it shrink shorter and shorter until it was all the way in. They had been working in the third-floor hallway for about a half hour. Six doors were now padlocked shut. Fourteen to go.

At the first door, David had cracked it open and peered in. A fishing rod and thigh-high waders rested on the bench. From the hooks hung a tackle box; a vest with pockets everywhere and fishing flies hooked into a patch of thick, yellow wool where ribbons went on a military shirt; and a floppy, wide-brimmed hat.

David had said, "Fishing stuff."

"Shut the door, David. Let's stay on task." When David hesitated, he added, "These rooms have a way of drawing you in. We've got to be careful."

"Draw you in? Like how?" He popped the last of the Fritos in his mouth.

His father dug around in the shopping bag of hardware. "Haven't you noticed? You kind of *want* to go over?"

David thought about when he had gone into the jungle world. He had threatened to go with or without Xander's help—he wanted to go that bad. And hadn't he decided a little too quickly to go into the World War II village in search of Mom?

"If that's true," he said, "it's scary."

"Like a shark posting signs on the beach saying the water's fine," Dad agreed. He snapped a lock through a ring in the hasp and gave it a couple of quick yanks to make sure it was secure. They moved to the next door.

"What's with these wall lights?" David said.

They stopped in front of one that depicted two warriors in

combat. One was thrusting a spear through the other's chest. The figures stuck out slightly from the surface of the shade, which seemed to be made of stone—a *relief*, his father had called it.

"I don't know," Dad said. His hand reached out toward it but stopped short. He held his fingers inches from the warring figures, as though he was resisting a temptation. "I think they show things from the worlds beyond the doors."

"There's one down there with metal leaves and eyes peering through them," David said. "It could be a tiger."

"And you saw the one with the gladiator?"

David nodded, then something occurred to him. He said, "You know how the items in the antechambers change, and then the worlds beyond change too?"

Dad nodded.

David asked, "So do these wall lamps change?"

Dad raised his eyebrows and looked up the hallway at the lights. "Now that you mention it . . . I don't know. Most of the time I've been here, it's been pretty chaotic. A lot of the lights appear the same until you look closer." He put his hand on David's shoulder and nodded. "Good question."

While he was holding a screw for the next hasp, and Dad was positioning the screwdriver over it, David thought of another one: "What if Mom tries to come back and the door's locked?"

Dad lowered the screwdriver and looked at him for a long moment. "Well . . . my mother never did. I don't think the portals work that way."

"But you don't know."

"No."

David grew quiet.

Finally his dad gripped his arm. "Your mother's a strong woman. I'm sure she's all right."

"She's all right," David repeated, "but she's not *here*."

"She's not here," his father agreed.

It took them another forty-five minutes to put locks on the rest of the doors. When it was done, they stood on the landing and looked down the twisting hallway at their handiwork. The hasps and padlocks attached to every door seemed almost an insult to the old-hotel décor. They were ugly and stark, like a scar on the face of a baby.

His father rattled a fat ring of keys and said, "I'll hold on to these."

"Dad?" David said. "Are the locks supposed to keep us out or keep them in?" He didn't have to say who he meant by "them." They knew about only one person who'd come into their house from another world—the big guy who'd taken Mom—but they all wondered if others could and would.

"Both," Dad answered. "Still hungry again, yet? Something smells good."

"We have to eat *Toria's* cooking?" David asked.

"She's always helped in the kitchen." He shrugged. "Guess we'll see how she does."

David nodded, and Dad started down the stairs. As David

was about to follow, he heard something in the hallway softly *clink*—metal on metal. He looked, but didn't see anything. Then his eye caught a lock about halfway up on the left side. It was swinging back and forth.

Seventeen

Sunday, 8:15 p.m.

As long as David could remember, they had come together as a family for dinner. It didn't matter how scattered they were during the day—Dad at work, Mom on errands, Xander with friends, David playing soccer, Toria at some music lesson or other—dinner reunited them, like bees returning to the hive.

While Mom liked to make it nice, David thought it was Dad who wanted the coming-together in the first place. He called it an "anchor"—keeping them moored together despite their far-flung adventures—and an "island"—a place to see each other and rest from each day's "struggle to stay afloat."

Those were Dad's words on tough days. On better ones, it was something like "a romp in the surf" or "backstroking through the day's travails." When David had asked him what that meant, he had said, "It means staying calm when troubles hit."

After that, David had sometimes found himself actually rotating his arms in a backstroke way to remind himself not to get too freaked-out. Odd thing was, it worked. Pop quizzes, bullies, not doing so well on the field—they lost some of their scariness with a couple pinwheels of his arms. He'd even come to enjoy the puzzled looks the gesture drew.

He raised his right arm now and brought it back and down. He began to lift his left arm, but felt the extra weight on it and the dull pulse of his blood rushing through it, and remembered the cast. He raised it as high as his shoulder, then switched back to his good arm. Sitting next to him, Xander gave him a knowing smile.

Toria had put a place setting in front of their mother's chair. *Sad*, David thought . . . *and a little creepy.*

His sister came in with water glasses, which she set precisely at each plate's one o'clock position. The glass she placed by her mother's plate was the only one that was empty. She gave it a little nod and glanced at the empty chair, as though seeing someone there that David did not. Then she strode back into the kitchen.

Dad, sitting at the head of the table, opposite Mom's place, caught the boys' unease. He said, "It was my idea. In many cultures, families would keep a place at the table for a missing loved one, a son who'd gone off to war or someone who'd . . ." He let the rest of his thought trail off.

David watched him. Dad didn't want to say, "Someone who'd *died*," and David didn't want him to say it.

More quietly, Dad continued, "It reflected that person's place in their hearts. They were gone, but in a way still with them."

Toria came back with a tureen. A ladle rose from steaming yellow liquid. "Chicken noodle soup," she announced.

"You made it yourself?" Xander asked.

"Smells great!" David said, trying to make his enthusiasm sound less forced than Xander's.

She dipped her head. "It's Campbell's." She sat and ladled soup into her bowl, then passed the tureen to Dad. She leaned toward him and whispered. "The *candles*."

"Oh, sorry," Dad said. He stood, patted his pockets, found a lighter. He leaned to light the candle nearest him, then walked around Toria to reach the one on the other side of the table. Between the two candlesticks, Toria had placed an arrangement of flowers and what looked to David like weeds from their yard.

Back in his seat, Dad smiled at each of his children. He held one hand out to Toria and the other to Xander. David was glad to see Xander accept it without hesitation. He and Xander gripped hands as well.

David rested his cast on the table near Mom's place setting. He knew if she were there, she would stretch to grip it. He locked eyes with Toria and could tell she was feeling the same thing he did. Sadness, for sure, but something else: it was some- how more *active* than that, like having a wound poked. It was a stark reminder that Mom *should* have been there, but she wasn't.

Without a word, both David and Toria lifted off their seats to clasp hands across the table. It seemed right to David that it was awkward and uncomfortable. A link in their family chain was missing; they weren't supposed to fit right without it.

After that, they bowed their heads, and Dad prayed. "Dear Heavenly Father, thank You for this food and this family. Please be with our wife and mother. Keep her safe." He was silent for a long time, perhaps searching for words that wouldn't come, or maybe talking privately to God. Finally he said, "Amen," and the kids repeated the word.

"Remember last Sunday?" David asked. "You told Mom we'd go to church this Sunday—'no excuses.'"

Dad frowned. "I wasn't expecting such a doozy of an excuse. But no more. Next week for sure."

David smiled weakly. "That's what Mom said."

"I know. And I mean it. Your mother will kill me if I let things fall apart here."

They ate their soup in silence. Their spoons clinked against the bowls. David didn't intend to slurp his soup, but did anyway. Xander probably intended to and did. David had heard expressions like "the silence was deafening" and someone's "absence filled the room." They had never made sense to him. But now he understood.

"David?" Dad said, startling him out of his thoughts.

David felt something on his cheek and touched it. He had not realized he was that close to crying. *Close?* He *was* crying. He used his napkin to wipe his eyes. "I'm okay."

Toria set down her spoon, walked around the table, and wrapped her arms around him.

Dad found and held his gaze. David had always thought his father resembled the perfect knight. His face was lean and strong, almost muscular; he had a broad forehead, direct eyes, and a slightly cleft chin. David had inherited that cleft, unlike his siblings. He sometimes studied his features in a mirror, wondering from which parent each came and if all of them together made him look strong or weak, like a man or a wuss. His father definitely did not look like a wuss.

As though he had read David's mind, his father said, "It's not unmanly to cry, son." His eyes flicked to Xander, including him, then back to David. "If we didn't have strong feelings, how could we love or fight? When our flesh is cut, we bleed. When our heart is broken, we cry. There's nothing wrong with that. It only becomes a problem when it gets in the way of what you have to do. You can't crumble when others are counting on you."

David sniffed and nodded.

That's what he means, he thought. *He's protecting us. He probably wants to cry himself, even now. But he has a family to protect and a wife to find.*

Dad said, "Do I smell something besides soup, something good?"

"Meat loaf," Toria said with a smile. She released David and ran off to get it.

Dad looked compassionately at his boys. "We'll be okay," he whispered. "You know that, don't you?"

Xander shrugged.

David thought about it, then he smiled and nodded.

"Ta-da!" Toria said. She was wearing oven mitts and carrying a casserole dish. So much steam rose from it, David couldn't make out her features. Then the dish shattered on the floor before he even realized it had slipped from her hands. Toria screamed.

Dad, David, and Xander jumped up from their chairs.

David said, "Did you burn yourself? Are you all right?"

Then all three of them realized she was staring at something. They turned their own gazes toward the door that opened into the foyer.

A man was standing there, smiling.

CHAPTER

eighteen

"Hey! Hey!" Dad said. He stepped over the broken casserole dish and ruined meat loaf. As he strode toward the man, Dad's hands came up, as though he intended to physically toss the guy out on his head.

David wanted to shout out a warning. It was the man he had seen in the woods, the one who had watched them fly.

The man raised his palm to Dad, his own warning to keep

397

Dad at bay. He said, "I'm sorry. I didn't mean to startle you." His voice was deep and smooth.

Despite the urgency his sudden appearance had put into all of them, his words came out slowly. David detected a slight accent he couldn't place.

Dad stopped inches from the man's outstretched hand. He said, "You walk into my *home* and—what?—oops? I don't think so." He stepped closer. His hand touched the man's arm to nudge him toward the door.

"It was unlocked," the man said. "My coming in was . . . habit, I supposed you'd say."

"Habit?"

"You see . . ." The man's voice trailed off. He had scanned the faces of the King children, stopping on David's. His eyes appeared gray and slightly too large for his face, which was lean and muscular. He had thin lips, which seemed to be perfectly horizontal: they offered no hint of a smile or a frown. The man's hairline had ebbed back from his face, giving him a large forehead. His hair, black with threads of silver, was swept back and fell to his shoulders. It looked wiry, like the Brillo pads Mom used to clean their iron skillet.

The man's gaze seemed to reach past David's eyes to examine his thoughts. David fought the urge to run, to get away from his piercing stare, but he couldn't move. The man's eyes held him in place the way a pin holds a bug to a cardboard display.

"Sir!" Dad nearly yelled.

The man pushed his lips into a twisted smile, then snapped his gaze away from David.

He continued talking to Dad, as though he hadn't paused to scare David spitless. "You see, I used to visit this house. I've always found it lovely. Are these your children?"

"What do you mean, 'visit'?" Dad said.

"Your boy," the man said, gesturing toward David. "If I may ask, what happened to his arm?"

"Little accident," Dad answered.

The man nodded knowingly. "Boys will be boys."

"I didn't catch your name," Dad said.

The man's raised palm turned so it became a hand extended in greeting. "Taksidian," he said. "You may call me Jim."

Dad ignored the man's gesture. "Mr. Taksidian, the door is this way. . . ."

Taksidian frowned. "I was hoping we could talk."

"About what?"

"You are Edward King, are you not?"

"You know I am."

"And you own this house?" While he spoke, the man's gaze drifted again to David. Slowly, the man winked at him.

David felt himself on the verge of either passing out or peeing his pants. He mumbled something that he had intended to be "Excuse me," but it didn't come out that way at all. Forcing himself to break away from the man's stare, he walked into the kitchen.

As soon as he knew he was out of sight, he put his back up against the wall and edged close to the doorway. For the second time that day, he found himself eavesdropping on his father's conversation.

"I have to confess to a bout of foolishness," the man said.

"How's that?" his father prodded.

"This house," the man said.

His deep voice reminded David of hypnotists he'd seen in movies. The tone of their voices alone made people want to do what they asked.

"I've admired this house for a long time. I kept telling myself to buy it, but—and here's where I've been foolish—I never thought I needed to hurry. Here you are, proving me wrong."

"Well, Mr. Taksidian, if—"

"Jim, please."

"Jim," Dad said. His voice was softening.

David knew his father would give the man the benefit of the doubt. As though walking into someone else's home could ever be an accident!

Don't cut him any slack, Dad, David thought. *This guy meant to scare us. He knows more than he's letting on.*

Dad went on: "If it's any consolation, this house has been in my family a long time. It was never for sale."

"Really?" the man said. "What about now?"

"I'm sorry?" Dad said.

"I'm willing to make a most generous offer."

David could almost hear the man smiling. He felt something touch his arm, and he jumped.

Toria stood in front of him. She whispered, "What are you doing?"

"Shhh."

She leaned closer. "What's the matter? You don't look so good."

"I'm okay," he said. "Come on." He walked back into the dining room, trying not to look at the man. He stopped at his dad's side and gripped his arm.

"I'm sorry," his dad was saying. "This house is not for sale."

David stared at the man's hand. It was powerful looking, veined and wrinkled. Scars marred the skin, slashing across the knuckles. A thick welt of scar tissue ran up the back of his hand and disappeared into the sleeve of his overcoat. His fingernails were longer than they should have been. *Dracula hands*, he thought.

"Is that something you and Mrs. King have discussed? Perhaps *I* should talk to her. I have a . . . *way* with women."

David felt the muscles in Dad's arm tense up. He tightened his grip. As much as the man deserved it, he thought Dad hitting him was a very bad idea.

CHAPTER

nineteen

Holding onto Dad's arm as Dad spoke to Mr. Taksidian, David's heart stepped up from a gallop to a headlong run.

Was it his imagination, or had the man's voice taken on a threatening tone when he mentioned Mom? As much as he'd have rather avoided the man's piercing eyes, David looked up to his face.

Dad said, "Your *way* with women' has nothing to do with my wife, sir."

The man was looking up toward the second-floor landing, as though expecting to see Mom standing there. He said, "I meant only that she should hear my offer. As I said, it's quite generous."

"She's not here right now."

Dad's voice had taken on a hard edge. David wondered if it was from the stress of having to lie about Mom or because the man's pushiness had made him angry.

"Oh? When will she return? Perhaps I can wait."

Dad said, "She's away. Maybe a couple weeks."

"I see," the man said. His Dracula hand slipped inside his overcoat. It reappeared holding a small pad of paper, which he opened with a flick of a fingernail. His other hand dropped into an outside pocket and produced a pen. He said, "If you'll tell me how to reach her, I'll give her the details directly."

"The house is not for sale," Dad repeated. "Now, if you'll please . . ." He nodded toward the door. "We were just sitting down to dinner."

The man didn't budge. He stood like a statue, casting his awful gaze at Dad's face. David realized that Dad had leaned closer to the man. He was staring him down, not blinking.

Way to go, Dad.

"Houses like this," the man said, "are always more than most people can handle."

When Dad did not respond, the man continued: "You know, not as stable as they look on the surface. A wall might collapse. Other surprises. I would hate . . ." He took the time to look at Xander, then Toria, finally coming to rest on David. "I would *hate* to see anything happen to your lovely family."

"Good night, Mr. Taksidian," Dad said.

The man closed his eyes. He sighed heavily. "Will you at least hear my offer?"

"No."

His eyes opened slowly. He nodded and turned. He opened the front door but did not step through. Without looking back, he said, "Mr. King . . . I have a nasty habit of getting what I want."

Again, Dad said, "Good night, *sir*." The "sir" sounded as sharp as a fist striking a skull.

The man stepped out, and the door closed behind him.

The family didn't move for a long time. They just stared at the door. David wondered if anyone else expected the man to come back through.

Finally Xander went to the door and turned the knob that engaged the dead bolt. He looked at Dad. "What just happened?"

Toria said, "Who *was* that?"

Dad told her, "If you see him again, don't go near him."

"Dad," David said, near a whisper. He was still gripping his father's arm, tighter now. "That was the man I saw in the woods."

"What?" Xander said. "When we were flying? When you fell?"

David looked up at his father and knew right away that Dad had suspected as much.

"But wait," Xander continued. "If he saw David flying or

hovering or whatever it was we were doing, why didn't he say anything about it? I mean, that's gotta be, like, the weirdest thing anyone has ever seen, right? You don't just ignore it."

Toria said, "Maybe he didn't really see David."

"He did," David said, remembering the eyes watching him in the forest. They were the same eyes that had stared him down just now.

Xander stepped closer. "This can't be a coincidence. We move in, Mom gets taken, this guy shows up wanting to buy the place? What's going on?"

Dad didn't answer right away. When he did, his words came slowly. "I don't know who he is or what he wants with this house. But you're right, his showing up isn't a coincidence. He's here because we're here, and he doesn't want us to be. We've got to watch out for him."

"Like we don't have enough going on?" Xander said. "We've gotta find Mom while pretending everything's all right, we gotta watch out for the guy who *took* Mom, and now we have to watch for *this guy*?!"

"What else are we gonna do?" David said.

It was too much for one day. Stepping into some French village during a Nazi attack. The flying—or *whatever* it was they had done in the clearing. Breaking his arm. The doctor's accusation. And now this guy: his sudden appearance, his low measured way of talking, his *eyes*.

David didn't want to let go of his dad. And his other arm

was in a sling. But in his mind he did the backstroke. Just trying to be calm when he had every reason to go crazy.

"I'm not going to pretend this doesn't change things," Dad said. "We'll have to be more careful, we may have to work faster, and we've got to keep our eyes open for dangers coming at us from outside the house."

"Taksidian," Xander said.

Dad nodded. "But in some ways, nothing's changed. We still have to do everything we can to avoid drawing attention to ourselves. Maybe that's more important than ever now."

David said, "Is that your way of saying we still have to go to school tomorrow?"

"No!" Xander said.

Dad smiled. "First day of school. I'm the principal. I think we have to, don't you?"

Xander said, "I say we do nothing but look for Mom. Eat when we have to, sleep when we can. Get Mom, get out of here, and leave this house for Taksidian or whoever else wants it."

Man, that sounded good to David.

But then Dad said, "That would be fine if we knew for sure we could find Mom quickly. My dad spent weeks looking for my mother and never found her."

"That was one person," Xander said. "With all of us working together—"

"And that's why we're going to find her," Dad interrupted. "But I don't think it will be easy . . . or quick."

"If it takes a year, ten years," David said, "I'm in."

"Me too," Toria said.

Xander frowned, but he was nodding. He said, "Okay, we pretend everything is great, and that buys us the time we need to find Mom."

"School tomorrow, then," Dad said. "So let's get to bed early. Toria, how about the two of us rounding up something else for dinner?"

Toria headed down the hall toward the kitchen.

"Xander," Dad said, "would you and David mind cleanup duty?" He nodded his head toward the mess on the floor.

"Awww," David said. "The meat loaf smelled good. We can't have any of it?"

Dad laughed and gave him a push, then went to join Toria in the kitchen.

David touched his arm to stop him. "What about the man? Taksidian?"

Dad squeezed David's shoulder reassuringly. "He's going to do what he's going to do, Dae. Right now all we can do is wait and see what that is."

"He said he was in the house. Do you think he knows about the third floor, the portals?"

Dad thought about it. "There's a reason he wants this place. I imagine it has something to do with this place being special—and what makes it special are the portals."

David bit his lip. "But . . ." He didn't know how to put his feelings into words. It was like having the messiest room in the world: he didn't know where to start to sort it out in his head.

Dad touched his cheek. "Don't worry about it, son. Together, we'll get through whatever we have to. Okay?"

David nodded.

Dad walked down the hall and disappeared into the kitchen.

David stood watching, thinking. *He's going to do what he's going to do.* David didn't like the sound of that.

CHAPTER

Sunday, 9:00 P.M.

Mr. James Taksidian—he was used to the name now—stood in front of the house among the trees. Moonlight played against the clapboards, stirred by the shadows of countless leaves. He could still see the oldest boy in the foyer, his back to one of the narrow, leaded windows that flanked the front doors. Absently, he rubbed at the heavy scar on the back of his right hand.

The meeting had not gone as well as he had hoped. A

few more weeks without their wife and mother, a few more encounters with household intruders, and they would have jumped at the opportunity to abandon the house. Ah, but Taksidian was growing older, and less patient. He had fewer years left to do all the things he wanted to do. He didn't have time for pests like the King family.

He had hoped to find more despair and disillusionment. When he started to push them—frightening the boy, implying knowledge of what had happened to the woman—he had witnessed more anger and determination than the fear he had hoped to instill.

One important fact had come from the meeting: he had verified that they were not some random family who had somehow weaseled their way into the house. They belonged. This meant they would not scare so easily. But he had no doubt that he could get them out. If one method did not work, another would. Seeing the resolve in their faces, hearing it in their voices, had convinced him that he had to step up his efforts. The pressure he would apply could crush a . . . He searched for the right metaphor and laughed when he found it. The pressure he would apply could crush a king.

He spun away from the house and headed toward the car he had parked down the road. He laughed again, sure that he knew the outcome of this latest little adventure with the house.

They would run or they would die—he didn't care which.

The last one had fled, and for almost thirty years had left Taksidian alone to do as he pleased. It had been a time of great prosperity.

And he would have his time with the house once again.

CHAPTER

twenty-one

TUESDAY, 11:28 P.M.

Something woke David from a sound sleep. He saw that
Xander was sitting up in bed and thought that his brother had
called to him.

"What?" he said to Xander's dark profile.

"Shhh."

Bam!

David jumped. "Was that a gunshot?" The noise seemed to come from the hallway, but who really knew?

Bam!

"Xander!" David had *felt* the noise that time, coming up through the floor into his bed.

"Daaaaad!" It was Toria. David and Xander threw back their blankets at the same time and hit the floor running.

Bam! Bam!

The vibration shot up into David's feet. Before they reached it, the hallway light turned on. Xander charged through the doorway, with David right behind.

"Daaaaad!"

Bam! Bam! Bam!

Dad was running down the hall toward Toria's room. He reached it ahead of Xander and swung through. Xander and David stopped at the threshold.

Bam! Bam!

David not only felt it in his feet, but also in his arm, which was pressed against the door frame. Toria was sitting up in bed, eyes wide. She reached out and grabbed her father's neck. He lifted her out of bed and scanned the room wildly.

Bam!

Not from this room.

"What is it?" Toria squealed.

Dad said, "I don't know, honey. It's okay." He walked toward the door. David and Xander stepped back into the hall.

Bam!—followed by a crash.

At once, their faces turned toward the ceiling. David touched his father's elbow. "The hallway upstairs."

Dad began walking with Toria in his arms toward the far hallway and the false wall. He stopped in front of his open bedroom door to hand Toria to Xander.

Dad disappeared into his bedroom, then reemerged with the ring of keys he and David had made earlier in the day.

"Stay here," he told them.

"No way!" Xander said. He reached out and grabbed hold of his father's T-shirt.

"Daddy, no!" Toria said.

Bam! Bam! Bam! More crashes. Something *thunked*. The lights in the hall flickered with each sound.

Dad thought about it. He scanned the ceiling.

Bam! Crash!

"Stay behind me," he said. He walked around the corner and stopped.

The false wall was shut tight. The two padlocks they had attached earlier were locked and hanging from their hasps as they had left them.

Bam! Bam!

The lights flickered. The locks swung slightly from the vibration.

Dad strode to the wall. He checked the number on the top lock and started flipping through the keys.

"We should have bought a gun," Xander said. He stooped to set Toria down on her feet. "Why didn't we buy a gun?"

Dad got the first lock off and squatted in front of the lower one.

The bat Dad and Xander had used against the big man who had taken Mom had been destroyed when one of the portal doors shut on it. Not that it had done any good, David thought. Still, he would have felt better if one of them carried something, anything more than keys.

The boxes that had been piled up against the wall and then scattered when the man had come for Mom were still there. Some were turned over, none of them neatly arranged. It looked as though the boxes themselves had been running from the sounds and stopped when the humans arrived. David looked in one and found only clothes. Another contained books. Not quite sure what he was looking for.

From the third box he pulled a toy rifle. He hadn't played with it for at least a year, but he hadn't wanted to toss it out, either. The stock and forward grip were made of wood, the barrel of steel. At one time it had been a cap gun, but that part of it hadn't worked for a long time. David held it by the barrel, feeling its heft. He caught Xander looking at him, and David nodded: *Yeah, this'll clock somebody good.*

Dad had the false wall open and was stepping through to the next door. David hurried through the opening and over the next threshold to follow his father up the stairs.

Dad was tiptoeing now, so David did too. He had forgotten Xander and Toria were behind him until he heard the creak of a step and his brother's breathing close behind.

Bam!

Toria let out a yip.

David jumped. He almost lost his balance and fell backward down the stairs. Xander's hand pressed into his back and righted him.

The noise had been earsplitting. Definitely a gunshot.

Their father was crouched low at the top of the stairs, not quite on the landing. He was trying to peer around the corner and down the long, jagged hallway.

"What is it?" David whispered.

"Can't see. Too dark." Dad edged up onto the landing, gesturing for them to stay back. He moved toward the hallway on his hands and knees, stopping when his head was just below the light switch. He stayed like that a long time, perhaps listening or hoping his eyes would adjust to the dark.

David expected another gunshot at any moment. For some reason, he didn't think Dad would be hit, but he would jump back to get out of the way and crash into the three of them. The whole family would tumble down the stairs and land in a heap at the bottom. The flight did not have a handrail, so he crouched low and gripped the edge of the landing. Xander crowded up behind him.

In the murky light of the staircase's single dim bulb, David saw his father's hand finally rise to the switch. The hallway lit up in that strange way that was becoming familiar to David: it was somehow different from other light, seeming to flicker like fire, without actually flickering at all.

Dad made a noise David didn't understand, kind of a surprised moan.

"Dad?" he whispered. When his father didn't answer, David reached out and touched his foot.

Dad startled and swung his head around to look back. David didn't like what was in his eyes.

"What is it?" David whispered.

Dad shook his head. Slowly he stood, staying close to the wall.

Can't be some madman with a gun, David figured, *but what would scare Dad without chasing him away?*

He rose and stepped onto the landing behind his father. He looked past him and gasped.

Every lock and hasp they had installed that day was lying on the floor. They were closest to the wall opposite the doors they had secured, as though ripped from the doors and frames with great force.

He heard the others coming up behind him. He stepped around Dad for a better look. Across from the first door the wainscoting was damaged. Farther up, opposite the second door, one of the wall fixtures had broken. A large piece of it—featuring the prancing legs of a horse—lay on the floor.

Sawdust, splinters, even pencil-sized strips of wood fanned out from each door.

"The locks just blew off," Xander said behind him. "Look. They hit the walls hard enough to break the wood. That light fixture is higher than the lock was. The lock must have come off with so much force it actually *flew*."

"Did someone kick the doors open, you think?" David asked. He looked back at his dad.

Dad's eyes roamed the hall, taking in the locks and splintered wood. He whispered, "The doors don't open into the hall. They couldn't have been kicked open."

Toria spoke up, her voice shrill. "Is somebody here? Are there people behind the doors?"

That creeped David out. He felt his stomach tighten. His eyes darted from door to door, as far as the crooked hallway would let him. He caught a glimpse of something. He said, "Dad? About halfway up on the right—one of the doors still has a lock."

"Not only that," Xander said. "It's moving."

CHAPTER

Xander was right. The lock was vibrating. It seemed to move faster and faster. Then the sound of it rattling against the hasp reached them: *click-click-click-click-click-click* . . .

Xander said, "What does that mean?"

Dad just shook his head.

David pressed up close to him and stayed there as they moved closer to the door. He felt Xander's hand on his shoulder. David was doing the same thing with Dad: it was a way of staying close without having to pay attention: all of their focus was on that door.

As they drew nearer, Dad lifted the keys.

"*Don't,*" David said.

"Let's go downstairs," Toria agreed.

Dad hesitated. "Look, guys," he said. "Maybe there's a reason this door and only this door still has a lock on it."

David's head began to hurt. He squeezed his eyes shut and said, "Just do it."

Keys rattled, and he opened one eye to see this father select a key and let all the others drop away from it to settle at the bottom of the ring. Dad took a step closer. David went with him. Xander kept his hand on David's shoulder.

The vibrating of the lock became faster: *clickclickclickclickclickclick.*

Toria said, "Is there something on the other side of the door doing that?"

Dad pressed his palm to door. He said, "I don't think so. I don't feel it coming through the door."

David was between his father and the door. He leaned his shoulder to the door and felt nothing.

Dad reached out with the key. David saw that Dad's hand was shaking, almost as quickly as the lock. David heard the key tap against the lock as Dad tried to find the—

Bam!

The lock and hasp flew away from the door—so fast David

saw only a blur marking its trajectory. It struck Dad's hand. He yelled and pulled his arm back.

"Go!" he yelled. "Back! Back!" He swung his arms out and reversed, forcing David, Xander, and Toria to move back toward the landing as well. His hand grazed David's cheek.

David felt warm wetness and wiped at it. His fingers came away bloody. As they continued moving away from the door, he focused on Dad's hand, held out to corral his children: blood poured from a gash along the back of his hand. David could see that the skin around it had already turned dark—black-and-blue, people called it, but this was mostly black.

"Dad—" David said. "Your hand!"

"Go, David! Go!"

At the landing, they stopped.

Dad continued holding his arms out like a guard keeping back a crowd. David stared at the wound. It was leaking like a broken bottle of ketchup. But it wasn't ketchup, and David's stomach turned.

"What happened?" Xander said.

"It just flew off," Dad said.

Toria said, "It hurt my ears."

"Your scream hurt mine," Xander said.

"That was David," she said.

Dad hushed them. They stood quietly in the hall, watching the door, listening.

Finally Xander whispered, "If that lock had hit somebody, they'd be dead."

"Xander," David said, "it did." He turned his eyes back to Dad's hand.

"Dad!" Xander said.

Toria made an "Oohhh" sound.

"I'm all right," Dad said.

Xander said, "That doesn't look all right."

Dad inspected his hand and tucked it close to his chest. "It looks worse than it is." He glared down the hall. "Are there any more locks?"

"Daddy," Toria said, "can't we check tomorrow? Your hand . . ."

David saw the struggle in Dad's face. He wanted to know what was going on. He wanted to know *now*.

After a moment, Dad said, "Okay, we'll see what's up tomorrow. After school."

"We still have to go?" Xander said.

"We've already been through this, Xander," Dad said.

Dad stayed on the landing until David, Xander, and Toria were at the bottom of the stairs. He took a last look into the hallway, flipped off the lights, and came down. His hand had soaked his T-shirt, making it look to David like he was holding together a hideous wound in his abdomen.

CHAPTER

twenty-three

MONDAY, 12:01 A.M.

Together they washed and dressed Dad's hand in the master bathroom. When Dad stuck his hand under the faucet, David wanted to turn away. He expected torn muscles, veins, and bones. But Dad had been right. It wasn't as awful as it had looked. A deep, long gash, lots of bruising.

David and Xander were almost back to their bedroom when their father called to them. Dad was on the other end of the second-floor hallway, in front of his own bedroom. Toria stood with him, holding his hand.

"What?" Xander said.

"Let's stay together tonight," Dad said.

"*Sleep* together?"

"Sounds good to me," David said.

Dad said, "We'll make beds for you in here." He gestured toward his bedroom. "Come on, Xander."

Xander shook his head. "Hold on."

The boys went into their bedroom to gather their pillows and blankets.

"This is nuts," Xander grumbled.

"Why?" David said. "You know what they say: safety in numbers."

Xander scowled at him and stormed out of the room. David hurried to catch up, and the two of them, laden with bedding, marched down to the master bedroom.

Toria was already under the covers in the big bed. David dropped his pillow and blankets beside the bed, on Dad's side. Xander kept hold of his stuff, as though setting it down would mean he was cool with their all staying together, which he obviously wasn't. Dad pushed a bit of blanket under Toria and came around to help David set up his sleeping area.

"How long are we going to have to sleep in the same room?" Xander asked.

"We've got to watch out for each other," Dad said.

"Can't you and Toria stay in here, and David and I sleep in our own room?"

Dad positioned David's pillow, sat on the floor beside it, and crossed his legs. He sighed. "It's better this way, Xander."

"How is it better?"

Dad said, "Safety in numbers."

Xander rolled his eyes. "Yeah, I heard. So what, are we going to stay together *all* the time?"

"As much as possible," Dad said. "At least at night."

"So who's gonna go to the bathroom with me?"

"Xander," Dad warned.

"No, really." Xander dropped his bedding on the floor. "We're going to be like prisoners!"

"Shhh," Toria said and rolled over. She flipped her pillow, covering her head with it.

Dad closed his eyes, opened them again. "I was thinking more like the buddy system."

"Okay," Xander said. "The buddy system means two people together, right, Dae? Isn't that what they told you in your scuba classes?"

"Yeah," David said quietly. He didn't want to get in the middle of this argument.

Dad just looked at him.

"See?" Xander continued. "Two people. David and me. You and Toria."

Dad leaned back, propping himself up with his undamaged

hand. He rolled his head in a complete circle. He looked as tired as David felt.

"I don't know, Xander. The guy who took Mom. This new person, Taksidian. The locks not helping one *bit!*"

David could tell it was all getting to him. He wanted to tell Xander that they should just do what Dad said. Give the man a break. But Xander was as stressed as Dad was. And he did have a point. In the end, David bit his tongue and busied himself with ensuring his makeshift bed was laid out just right.

"Dad," Xander said, "I just don't think it's practical. You said that thing about safety in numbers, but there's also something about getting more done in teams, isn't there? When we're here, when we're not out pretending everything's okay, we have a lot to do."

Dad groaned and got to his feet. He put his hands at the small of his back and bent backward. "All right," he said. "If I had my way, we'd lash ourselves to each other and never be separated again." He stepped closer to Xander. "I can't stand the thought of something happening to one of you. Overprotective, I guess."

Xander shrugged. "I suppose you have good reason to be."

"Stay in here tonight," Dad said. "Humor me. Tomorrow, you and David can go back to your own room." He waggled a finger at Xander. "But you're buddies, you hear? You stay together."

Xander smiled. "Gotcha."

"David, you hear?" Dad said.

"Stick with Xander," David confirmed. Then he watched with relief as Xander wrapped his arms around their father and hugged him.

twenty-four

MONDAY, 12:40 A.M.

David came out of sleep slowly. Like rising from deep under water to the surface. It was rough seas, and the waves jostled him back and forth. Then he realized it was Xander, shaking him gently. In the glow of Toria's night-light, he could see Xander smile.

"What do you want?" he grumbled. "I'm tired."

"But, Dae, I have to go to the bathroom. Don't you want to come?"

"No, go yourself."

Dad had not really meant buddying up for bathroom trips, and Xander knew it. Even if Dad had meant for them to stay together for everything, even this, Xander would not have obeyed. He was just trying to get back at David for not supporting him in front of Dad.

Or something . . . like that . . .

David was going back under, into that dark deep, leaving the surface way behind.

Then up again he went, waking once more under Xander's shaking hand.

"Xander! I said *no*. Go yourself."

"I did," Xander said. "I saw something! You gotta come look." He was whispering, but his tone was excited, maybe even scared.

David rose up on an elbow. "What is it?"

Xander touched his lips with a finger. "Shhh."

They both looked at Dad's sleeping form on the bed. Heavy, rhythmic breathing said he was fast asleep. Xander jerked his head toward the bedroom door, rose, and crept toward it. David followed. When they were in the hallway, Xander leaned back in to pull the door closed.

"Now what?" David said.

"Come here." Xander walked down the hall, then began to descend the staircase.

"Xander, wait!"

"It's out front," he said.

"What were you doing out front?"

"I just looked out the window. I thought I heard something." He went the rest of the way down and peered through a window next to the door. "Yeah," he said. "Look."

He moved away.

David touched his nose to the glass. Beyond the porch, the mist swirled lazily over the forest floor, glowing slightly in the moonlight. The trunks of the trees, their branches and leaves were blacker than the shadows they cast. They made David imagine that the house was in the palm of some giant hand, and the trees were fingers.

"Xander, I don't see any—"

But then he did: there was a man out there. He was standing halfway to the dirt road, the trees rising all around him. The mist glowed behind him, making his silhouette stand out.

"He was in that exact spot when I first saw him," Xander said. "I don't think he's moved at all."

David could not take his eyes off the figure. "Maybe he's dead."

Xander stepped to the window on the other side of the door. "Dead? Standing up?"

Just then, the figure did move. One shoulder seemed to come up as the other went down, as though the person had shifted his weight from one foot to the other. Both Xander and David pulled in a sharp breath.

"Do you think it's Taksidian?" David wondered out loud.

435

"I bet."

"Why? What does he think he'll see?"

"Maybe he's waiting for us to leave so he can do something to the house," Xander suggested. "Or he's just trying to freak us out."

"It's working," David said.

"This place is so weird, maybe it attracts weird people."

David thought about that. He said, "It attracted us."

Xander said nothing. The boys watched the watcher for a couple minutes. In that time, he appeared to shift or sway twice.

David said, "Do you think he can see us?"

Xander looked back around them, at the dark foyer and the upstairs landing. "Not unless he has cat eyes."

"Should we tell Dad?"

"Let him sleep. What's he going to do?"

"Chase the guy away," David said. "Call the cops."

"They won't do anything."

"He's on our property," David said.

"So they make him back up thirty feet. Would that make you happy?"

David imagined the guy thirty feet farther away, but still out there, still watching. He said, "I guess not." He turned away from the window to look at Xander. "So what do we do?"

"Go back to bed."

"What if he's there in the morning?"

"We'll make him an omelet," Xander said.

"I mean it."

Xander pushed away from the glass, shrugged, and headed up the stairs. "Dad will be up then. He'll figure out something."

That wasn't the answer David wanted. He looked back through the window. The mist appeared to be crawling up the figure's legs, like snakes or flames. David felt a chill streak up his spine. Getting to sleep again wasn't going to be easy.

He turned away and started up the stairs, thinking he could still feel the man watching.

CHAPTER

twenty-five

MONDAY, 6:40 A.M.

David couldn't even think of the word that described the
nightmare he was about to face: new school, new kids, new
teachers, new town . . . his mom had just been kidnapped . . .
and they were supposed to act like everything was normal.
Just another day on planet Earth. Isn't the weather lovely
today?

Dad and Toria whipped up a breakfast of French toast

and sausage. They took their sister to her elementary school, and Dad went in to meet the teacher. Xander sat in the front passenger seat, looking tired and glum.

"You all right?" David asked.

"What do you think?" he answered.

They arrived at Pinedale Middle and Senior High a half hour early. Dad wanted to greet the parents as they dropped off their kids. His hand was bandaged, the yellow of ointment, the red of blood barely showing through. He joked about telling the parents he'd hurt his hand disciplining one of his kids. "But nowadays," he said, "we'd better not go there."

David frowned. "Especially after what the doctor said."

Dad looked at his hand, one side, then the other. "If anyone asks, I'll tell them I hurt it fixing up the house. How about you boys join me in saying hi to everyone?"

"Like some kind of don't-we-make-a-cute-family thing?" Xander said. "I don't think so."

"Great way to meet your classmates."

"Dad." Xander rolled his eyes.

"David?" Dad looked at him hopefully.

"I'm with Xander," David said. "I don't wanna get beat up my first day."

"Go, then, go," Dad said, waving them away.

Without saying another word, the brothers walked through the front doors and turned right. There was a sign on a portable stand telling them they were heading toward the grade 6–8 classrooms. Through the windows that lined the wall on their right, they could see Dad standing on the curb, waiting for cars and students. On their left were lockers and classrooms. At the end of the hall, they could go through double doors into the cafeteria or turn left into another hall-way. They turned and approached locker number 119. It didn't look like anything special.

Say that after portaling to and from the linen closet, David thought.

Neither of them could believe they hadn't told Dad about it. Between Mom's abduction and trying to deal with it, the linen closet had slipped their minds.

Xander said, "Maybe subconsciously we don't *want* to tell him."

"Doesn't he already know?"

"He's never said anything."

David nudged Xander. "Want another sausage link?"

Xander gave him a puzzled look, then smiled. He eyed the locker. "I don't know . . ."

"There and back, no big deal."

Xander glanced toward the main hallway and its wall of big windows. "Uhh . . ." he started.

David followed his gaze. Across the grassy courtyard, beyond the picnic benches and flagpole, was the student drop-off point. Dad was standing at the curb, grinning right at them. He raised his bandaged hand and waved.

The boys waved back. David said, "I guess maybe later, huh?"

•••••••••

When he got there, David's homeroom was empty. A brown
lunch bag sat on the teacher's desk, next to a stack of papers
and spiral notebooks, so he guessed she'd been there and gone
off somewhere. Mrs. Moreau, according to the class schedule
Dad had brought home. He unslung his backpack and leaned
it against the side of the desk. In Pasadena, backpacks were
banned from classrooms, but Dad had said they were still okay
here—just more evidence that Pinedale hadn't caught up with
the rest of the world.

The windows at the back of the classroom looked out onto
an athletic field. Three older boys were on the track that circled
a large grassy area. Two were jogging; the other was either in the
middle of some extreme stretching exercise or was hoping to
replace a contortionist next time the circus came through town.
The room was smaller than the ones David was used to. He
counted the desks: four rows of five desks each. In Pasadena,
only private schools limited their class size to twenty. He supposed Pinedale was too puny to have big classrooms.

He walked around the teacher's desk to a bulletin board on
the far wall. There were notices about the hot-lunch program;
chess and computer club meetings; a list of fund-raisers—
entertainment books, popcorn sales, cake walk: it was enough
to make David wonder if they were supposed to be students or
salespeople. Sports announcements—once again, it grated on

him that the school didn't sponsor an eighth-grade soccer team. Supply lists. Emergency exit procedures. Where to park. How to drive. When to eat. If David had to read all this, if he had to *know* it, he would go out of his mind.

Walking past the teacher's desk again, something caught his eye: his father's name on a piece of paper. Not unusual, given his position at the school. But this wasn't a memo from him or about him. Someone had handwritten his name—Edward King—in the margin of a newspaper. Next to it was a drawing of a face with mean eyes under a V-shaped brow. Horns poked through the hair, and the mouth was full of fangs. A balloon speech box started at his mouth and disappeared under a stack of papers.

He reached to move the stack away so he could read the words. Before his fingers touched the stack, a voice startled him.

"You must be David."

He spun to see a woman pressing a sheath of papers to her chest with both hands, glaring at him. She was in her forties and birdlike—not in the dainty way, but angular and severe. She was thin and tall and slightly stooped, reminding David of a vulture. Adding to the image was the fuzzy gray sweater draped over her shoulders. The dress underneath was bright red.

Her frown disappeared so quickly, David wasn't positive he had seen it at all. In fact, her whole countenance seemed to change in a heartbeat from cruel to kind, but maybe it had been a trick of the light. He wasn't sure her grin was any better than the scowl he thought he'd first seen. It reminded him of a

T-shirt Xander had once owned: a wicked, beady-eyed troll rubbing his scaly-clawed hands together. The slogan under it read *Trust me*.

"Yes, ma'am," he said, thinking he sounded pretty together. Her eyes flicked to the desktop, compelling him to add: "I was just . . . um . . ."

Think!

" . . . looking for information about . . . the chess club."

Her eyebrows went up. They were bushy things more suited to Russian presidents. "Oh, do you play?"

"I try."

"What's your favorite opening move?"

"Pawn . . . to . . ." He felt himself smile. "I'm just starting, really."

"Well," she said, striding toward him. He took a step back. She set the sheath of papers down, covering the cartoon figure of his father. "Mr. Campbell runs the chess club. He'd love to have you. I can introduce you, if you'd like."

"I'll find him when I have more time, thank you."

She held out a long, bony talon. "I'm Mrs. Moreau. Nice to meet you."

David didn't think the hesitation he felt showed as he reached for her hand. It was cold, and he could feel the bones through paper-thin flesh. "David King, ma'am."

He went to withdraw his hand, but she wouldn't give it back. Instead, she put her other hand over his as well.

She said, "I met your father. Such a nice man. How are you liking our little slice of heaven?"

All kinds of images went through David's mind. First, he thought of the piece of Boston Cream pie at the diner last week. Hadn't the waitress called *it* a slice of heaven? Then he guessed she was talking about the school, but who in their right mind would use the word *heaven* to describe a school?

His confusion must have shown, for she added, "Pinedale. Don't you just love it?"

David brightened. "Ah, yes. It's . . ."

Far from Pasadena. Isolated. Smaller than the mall I'm used to. Creepy.

" . . . lovely!"

She leaned toward him, as if sizing up the meal he'd make. She said, "I can't wait to meet Mrs. King."

David opened his mouth and shut it again. "Uh . . . that would be nice," he said lamely.

She released her grip on his hand, and he pulled it back quickly. She said, "Whatever happened to your arm?"

"Fell out of a tree."

She aimed her beady eyes at his arm for a long time, as if reading the truth from it. She pressed her lips together and nodded. Her not saying anything was worse than questioning him about his fall or even flat-out calling him a liar. He felt the urge to blurt out what had really happened . . . and along with it all the weirdness he'd seen since coming to her little slice of heaven . . . and what had happened to Mom too.

You wanna meet Mrs. King? he thought. *Pack your bags, lady, cause it's a long trip.*

She laughed, snapping him out of his . . . what was that? *Freak-out time* sounded about right.

"You have that deer-in-the-headlights look," she said. "I don't blame you. New town, new school, and you go and hurt yourself." She fixed her eyes on him. Slowly she said, "And I hear you're moving into the old Konig place."

CHAPTER

twenty-six

MONDAY, 8:22 A.M.

"Ma'am?" David said.

"Your house, the Victorian outside of town?"

David nodded. He thought, *Let's not talk about the house, okay?*

She smiled and moved her attention to the papers on her desk. "Lot of work, old house like that. But once it's fixed up, it'll be lovely."

Words and laughter, the squeak of sneakers on tile, drew

their attention to the classroom entrance. Three boys were barreling in, pushing each other, breaking their conversation off when they saw Mrs. Moreau and David.

"Boys!" she said. "How was your summer?"

They nodded, mumbled, "Good" and "Okay."

"Ben, Marcus, Anthony—this is David. He's just moved here from . . ." She swung her gaze back to David. "L.A.?"

"Pasadena."

The boys gave him "hi's" and nods, and he returned them.

One of the kids—David thought his name was Anthony—whose broad shoulders and solid chest would make him prime linebacker material in a few years—said, "What happened to you?"

David raised his elbow in the sling. "Fell out of a tree." Each time he said it, it got easier. Maybe he'd believe it someday as well.

"And that shiner," one of the other boys said. "The tree beat you up too?"

That got them all laughing.

"Uh," David said. He touched the bruise around his eye. It was still tender. "I . . . my brother punched me."

"Why?" Another of the boys asked. This one was Ben, if Mrs. Moreau had said their names in the order they stood. He wore glasses and looked like the sort of kid who said "why" a lot.

David shrugged. "Just playing around."

"Is he bigger than you?" Anthony asked. They moved closer, totally ignoring the teacher now.

"He's fifteen."

Ben said, "Does he beat you up a lot?"

The boy who hadn't yet spoken, Marcus, said, "I have a big sister who beats me up all the time."

Anthony pushed him. "She's a girl, dude! You baby!"

The tallest of the three, Marcus didn't look like a baby. He looked big enough to give Xander a hard time. David wondered what kind of monster his sister must be.

More kids streamed in—a guy and four or five girls.

Mrs. Moreau clapped her hands and said, "Everyone find a desk. Anywhere's fine for now. Mr. King, it would do me a great honor if you would sit up here by me." She gestured toward a desk that was front and center. The other kids laughed and stumbled over each other getting to the back of the room.

"Yes, ma'am," David said. He wasn't sure whether he wanted his disappointment to show or not. He didn't want to get on her bad side, but if she knew he wasn't happy there, she might let him move. He retrieved his backpack and took his seat.

Mrs. Moreau sat behind her desk and began squaring the piles of papers. For a few moments she seemed intent on her work, not much interested in the students filling her classroom. Without looking up she tugged the newspaper with his father's caricature on it out from under the stacks of paper, folded it, and dropped it into a desk drawer. Only then did her eyes venture beyond her desk.

"Ladies. Nice to see you," she said. Then, looking beyond David, "Gentlemen, welcome back."

David glanced around shyly, nodding when he caught someone's eye. Several girls had their heads together, glancing at him and giggling. He turned back to find Mrs. Moreau watching him from the corner of her eye. He looked away quickly, not sure if he should acknowledge her attention or pretend he hadn't noticed.

Before he realized it, the classroom had filled up. A bell sounded to mark the beginning of the period, and a few students, who had been standing, rushed to their desks.

Six hundred miles from the last school he had attended, but still so many things were the same: the glare of the fluorescents, competing with the daylight; the little noises of chair legs scraping on the floor, cleared throats, the tick of the clock; the mingling odors of a dozen different shampoos and laundry detergents, sweat. He heard the murmur of persistent whispering and wondered if it was about him.

The teacher used her palm as a gavel against a stack of handouts. "Quiet down," she said. "We have a lot to go over and a lot of papers to distribute, some for you and some to take home to your parents. Let's start with roll call." She began with "Abernathy, Jennifer" and proceeded down an alphabetical list, last name first.

David tried to pay attention, tried to remember each name, though he wasn't turning to see which student it belonged to.

Another reason sitting up front stunk.

Mrs. Moreau called "Jennings, Anthony." David thought the guy responding "here" sounded like the Anthony he had met.

"King, David."

"Here," David said.

The room around him erupted in quiet laughter and whispered comments: "King David? Ohhh."

"Did you kill Goliath?"

"Isn't that the naked statue?"

The last one brought a new burst of giggles from the girls and a few *harr-harrs* from the boys.

David felt the eyes of his classmates on the back of his head like raindrops blowing into him. He almost cringed, tucking his head down into his shoulders, but stopped himself.

Just wait it out, he thought. *Don't say anything. You'll just give them more to laugh about.* He was only glad his name wasn't Arthur.

"Hey! Hey!" Mrs. Moreau snapped. Her palm had become a gavel once more. "We do *not* poke fun at people's names. David's name has a rich and regal legacy. When the David you're thinking of was just a boy, he killed a lion with his bare hands."

Several "oohs" around him.

Shhh, he thought, *you're making it worse.*

But she continued: "And he was probably no older than any of you, than *our* David himself, when he slew the giant Goliath with a single stone."

Several kids went, "Ooohhhh!"

451

Someone asked, "Was he *naked* when he *sleeeeew* him?"

The entire class cracked up.

David felt his face flush. No doubt his face was as red as Mrs. Moreau's dress. His head got heavier, and it was harder not to let it sink between his shoulders.

Mrs. Moreau's hand slammed down with a *bang!* She stood up from her chair and said, "Clayton!"

Don't do it . . . don't do it . . .

She did it. "You can take that smart mouth to the office right now."

David let his head drop. She had just made sure that Clayton's comment about nakedness and "slewing" giants would be passed on to every student in the school, and David would be reminded about it the whole year.

"What?" Clayton protested.

"You heard me, young man."

From the heavy sigh and banging, David knew Clayton was obeying, but was not happy about it. From the corner of David's eye, Clayton came into view. He was a stocky kid, brown hair, freckles. He wasn't mean-looking, just a twelve-year-old kid. When he was almost to the door, Mrs. Moreau stopped him.

"And Clayton?" she said, almost sweetly. "Do you know whom to ask for?"

Oh no! David felt his eyelids stretching until he thought his eyeballs would fall out onto the desk. He shook his head *no* at Mrs. Moreau, but her attention was on Clayton.

Clayton glared at her, his lips tight.

Her thin lips pursed before opening them to squawk, "Ask for *Mr.* King, our new principal."

Clayton's eyes grew as wide as David's and snapped over to him. Shocked whispers filled the air like buzzing bees.

"Yes, Clayton," Mrs. Moreau continued, "David's father. You may call him King Edward if you're still feeling smart when you get there."

Clayton frowned, shook his head, and pushed out of the door.

David was certain his face would remain red forever.

Mrs. Moreau took her seat again. She cleared her throat, checked a sheet of paper in front of her, and said, "Krakauer, Amy."

CHAPTER

twenty-seven

SUNDAY, 4:10 P.M.

"And after that, everyone kept calling me King David!"

In the front seats of the 4Runner, Dad and Xander nodded knowingly.

"It's embarrassing," David said. He made a face at Toria, who was sitting in the backseat with him.

She tilted her head and stuck out her bottom lip, feeling for him.

"Get used to it," Dad said.

Xander twisted around in his seat. "Nobody's said that to you before, back in Pasadena?"

David shrugged. "Sometimes, but it wasn't mean. These guys are mean."

"Mean how?"

"You know, little-kid-giant-killer and . . ." His voice trailed off.

"What?"

"The . . . Michelangelo thing."

Xander laughed. "You're too sensitive, Dae."

"It's embarrassing," he repeated.

"What Michelangelo thing?" Toria asked.

Xander said, "It's a statue—"

"Nothing!" David said. "Can we drop it already?"

Xander grinned. "You're just—"

"Okay, that's enough," Dad said. He slapped Xander's thigh. He moved the inside rearview mirror to find David's face. "Otherwise, how was it, Dae?"

"All right, I guess."

"I'm Star of the Week in October," Toria said brightly.

"Your birthday week?" Dad asked. He moved the mirror off of David to find her.

"No . . . some other kid has a birthday that week too. They gave it to him."

"That's not fair," Xander declared. "You're a girl; you should've got it."

"Tell that to Mrs. Varley," Toria said. "She doesn't believe in girls first or any of that. She even said there's no difference, so there should be no special treatment."

Dad braked at a crosswalk. He signaled for a couple of kids to cross. To Toria he said, "Do you believe there's no difference?"

"Well, of course there is!" She could have added: *Duh*.

"I mean beyond the obvious," Dad said. "Should boys treat girls special?"

"We *are* special."

"And boys aren't?" David asked.

Toria stuck her nose in the air. "Mom says boys would be like rocks if it weren't for girls."

"*Rocks?*" David said.

"God made girls special, so we can teach boys how to feel."

David shook his head. "I don't need girls to teach me how to feel."

"Guys fight and girls *looove*." Toria strung out the last word in a swooning, romantic way and batted her eyes.

"I *know* Mom didn't say *that*," Xander said.

"I said that," Toria said.

David liked talking about Mom. It kept her with them, in a way. He said, "I wonder what she would have put in our notes today."

Toria beamed. "Oh, yeah! Mom always put notes in our lunches on the first day of school."

Xander crinkled his nose. "Mushy, corny ones. Half the note

was *I love you this* and *I'm proud of you that.* The other half never made sense."

David grinned. "Like last year. She told me not to rip my pants or try to open doors with my face." He shook his head. "What was that about?"

"She told me not to put Skittles in my nose," Toria said.

Xander said, "And she never even *tried* to explain them. She'd just look at you like *Whatta ya mean, you don't get it?*"

They all laughed. That was Mom. She wasn't very good at *telling* jokes. She either forgot the punchline or said it too soon or set it up all wrong. But her lunch-box notes had always made David smile, and they'd all laugh about them later.

"You know," Dad said, "she gave me notes too."

Xander looked surprised. "She did?"

Dad tilted his head. "Once, a long time ago—Xander, you were just a baby, David and Toria, you weren't born yet—she sent me off to my first day on a teaching job with a brown-bag lunch. I put it in the refrigerator in the faculty break room. There were half a dozen brown bags just like it, and one of the other teachers got mine by mistake. He found the note, and it said, 'Honey, don't forget to glue on your hair.' I had a big ol' mop of hair back then, but from that day on, I could never convince anyone that it was really mine. I would pull on it and invite them to yank on it, too, but they would just laugh and say I must use good glue."

They all laughed. Xander lifted his own hair on both sides to show both its volume and authenticity.

"Let me tell you," Dad said, "for a guy with lots of hair, that was devastating."

Toria pulled at her hair with both hands; David did the same with his one good hand. Together they said, "I must have used the good glue!"

Dad remembered more. "At the faculty Christmas party, I tried to get her to admit she was joking, but she played it straight. She never actually said I was bald, but she said things like, 'There's nothing wrong with male-pattern baldness. Look at Sean Connery.' As sweet and innocent as can be."

"Is that when you started calling her Gee instead of Gertrude?" Xander asked.

David added the line he'd heard his dad say so many times: "Because she definitely isn't a *Gertrude!*"

"Nah," Dad said. "She'd been going by Gee since she was a little girl. She was named after her grandmother, but her parents knew right away that she wasn't going to live up to the old-fashioned prim and properness that name brings to mind."

"What do you think she should have been named?" Toria said.

Dad smiled. "Honey."

As the SUV progressed up Main Street toward home, their laughter faded. David knew that the others were thinking of Mom, just as he was.

After a minute Xander said, "What are we going to do? About getting her back?"

"I was thinking," Dad said. "We're going to need a central place to figure out that house, to gather everything we know and everything we learn about those rooms upstairs."

"A war room," Xander said.

"A mission control center, like NASA's," David suggested.

Dad nodded. "You've got the right idea." He pulled off the main drag into a drive-in diner. It was the kind of place where you ordered from your car and they hooked your tray of food onto the car window. He smiled at them and raised his eyebrows. "Who's up for an ice cream?"

twenty-eight

MONDAY, 5:18 P.M.

"Okay, where?" David asked.

The whole family was in the library. Boxes from their old house were stacked there, waiting to be unpacked—the movers had come on Friday, and Mom had been kidnapped Sunday night: almost everything they owned was still boxed up and would probably stay that way for a while. Dad had identified the cartons that would be most useful to their task, the ones from his home office.

David had spotted a dry-marker board and pulled it out from between a wall of boxes and the built-in library shelves. Now he needed to know where to take it: what part of the house would become their mission control center?

"How about this room?" Xander said. "It's got shelves. It's close to the kitchen."

"Nah," David said. "If we have to go back and forth between the control room and the portals, this is too far away. Two flights of stairs and the other end of the house."

Dad said, "Besides, it's open to the foyer. Anybody coming over would see it. We don't want that."

"What about in the hallway on the third floor?" Toria chimed, apparently stunned by her own brilliance. "Right there next to the doors and everything!"

"That's a little *too* close for me," David said. "The way those locks came off, and everything that's happened up there . . ."

"It'd be like having a war room right on the front lines," Xander agreed. "Bullets zinging around—you'd never get any planning done."

"How about the servants quarters'?" Dad said. "Big room. Has its own bathroom. Right at the base of the stairs leading up to the portals."

"Perfect," Xander said.

"I like it," David agreed. He walked out of the room with the dry-marker board, heading for the stairs.

Xander lifted a box that had the word *Mac* scribbled

on one side. "I've got the computer," he said, hurrying after David.

"Yea," David said. "I've got a computer class and have to get online."

Xander said, "Not in our control center, dude. It's only for things that will help find Mom."

"We only have one computer," David complained.

"Tough."

They had reached the top of the stairs. David called over the banister, "Dad! Can I use the computer for school?"

"We'll see," Dad called back.

David yelled, "We only have one!" He showed Xander a sour face.

Xander scowled back at him and leaned close. He whispered, "We only have one mom."

It felt like a punch to David's stomach. He frowned and carried the dry-marker board toward the room that would become their control center. As he was leaving, Xander caught him by the arm.

"I'm sorry," he said.

David looked at the floor. "You can *try* not to be mean, you know."

"I'll try." Xander punched him gently in the shoulder, on the uninjured side.

David stomped him on the foot and ran down the hall, laughing.

Over the next half hour, David, Xander, and Dad carried boxes up to the room. Toria followed them with a notepad. As they thought of things they needed, they called them out to her: bulletin boards, index cards, dry-erase board markers, pushpins, Sharpie markers in different colors, binders, a first aid kit.

Xander thought the computer needed upgrading. "For sure a bigger hard drive and flat-screen monitor," he said. "Maybe *two* screens."

David thought it would be cool to link the notes they would make about each world with possible connections to other worlds or things. He imagined an index card about his time in the French village during WWII linking somehow—he didn't know how yet—to Xander's adventure in the Colosseum.

He asked Toria to add colored string to the list.

Dad dug into the boxes from his days as a teacher and found a time line of all the major events in history. Only a foot tall, it ran some thirty feet long. He mounted it high up along two walls in the mission control center—or MCC, as they were already calling it.

To David, it was the coolest thing so far. After all, the portals apparently were doorways into the past. That got him thinking. He said, "Dad, do the portals ever take you to the future?"

"Not that I've seen, Dae," Dad said, rummaging through a box. They were all in the old servants' quarters now, cleaning, unpacking, setting things up.

"Why not?"

"I don't know. Maybe it has to do with the laws of time travel, or . . ." He shrugged. "Whatever."

"There was that antechamber with things that looked like they were for space travel," Xander said. "Remember, Dae?"

David nodded. "But people do that now," he said.

"Neil Armstrong walked on the moon in 1969," Dad reminded them.

"The *moon?*"

The way Xander said it made David's stomach squirm. Dad scowled at Xander and pointed a finger at him. "Stay away from the rooms with space stuff. At least for now."

"Well, the portals do take you to different times and *places*," Xander said. "We'll need a big wall map of the world."

"I think I have one," Dad said.

"My string-connection idea is gonna work perfect," David said.

As they became more involved in the task, ideas for making it more useful struck each of them like beads of water in a storm.

Xander said he would draw up a large chart of the hall-way and antechambers. They would write down the items they found in each and keep doing it as the rooms shifted and the items changed. "Maybe there's a pattern to the way they move around that we haven't noticed yet," he said.

"We can link your lists of items to the worlds they lead to, to the map and time line," David said.

Dad added, "So we'll have links from rooms to items, to

historical times, to geographic locations." His grin stretched wide, and he nodded. "This is gonna work. I know it."

David caught his excitement. He said, "Whatever's happening, whoever's behind it—they haven't seen anything like *us* before."

"We'll take 'em by storm," Xander said. "We'll be Bruce Willis in *Die Hard*."

David added, "Aragorn in *Lord of the Rings*."

"Aragorn?" Xander said. "No, no . . . Legolas."

"You're both wrong," Dad said. "Gandalf!"

"I know," David said. "Arnold Schwarzenegger in *Terminator!*"

Xander's eyes got big. In his best deep voice, he said, "I'll be back," and ran out the door.

twenty-nine

MONDAY, 5:59 P.M.

They listened to Xander's footsteps pounding down the hall—
toward their bedroom, David thought. But in that house you
could never be sure where any sound came from. It was unsettling,
like detecting the faint smell of smoke without ever finding out
what was causing it.

Toria said, "Dad, did you say flip chart?" She was consulting her list, tapping it with the tip of a mechanical pencil.

"And a stand for it," Dad agreed. "It's like a big tripod."

"For what?" David asked.

"Rules. We'll start a list and refine them as we learn more."

David wrinkled his nose. "Rules? Like what?"

Dad came off the step stool he had been using to reach the time line and smooth out a section. He sat down on the stool. "I've been thinking about this." He held up two fingers. "Two kinds of rules: one are things that we impose on ourselves for safety and to learn the most about the worlds."

"Like the buddy system?" David asked.

"And that we always debrief within an hour of coming back from a world."

"Debrief? What's that?"

"It's sharing everything you learned from a mission—writing about it, talking about it—so you and others can learn from it. If we do it right away, we won't forget anything."

"Like what?"

"Take your trip yesterday to World War II. I'm sure there are things you've already forgotten: what people looked like, any signs that you saw, exactly what you did and the order in which you did it."

David shook his head. "How would any of that help?"

"Until we know what we're dealing with, *anything* could help. What if we realize that we're seeing the same people in different worlds?" He gave David a look that said, *Yeah, huh? What about that?*

David felt something in his head pull painfully tight, like getting a charley horse, but in his mind. He said, "The same people in different worlds? You mean like *us*?"

"Travelers like we are, maybe . . . or not." He looked at David's bewildered face. "Never mind. What I'm saying is, we just don't know what we'll learn once we start recording our experiences, comparing them to each other. That's what debriefing will let us do."

David sat on the floor and leaned his back against the wall. "And debriefing is a *rule*?"

"Well, yes. It's SOP—standard operating procedure. Rules that we implement to help us reach our goal and keep us all on the same page. Like the rule that we never talk about what we're doing here to anyone else. And not to each other in public. And never over the phone. Things like that." He stood and started to pace. "I can think of dozens. We need to write them down and all agree to them."

"Okay," David said, letting out a weak laugh. "I get it. Lots of rules."

"Those are just *our* rules," Dad said. "Then there are the rules of the worlds, the time ripple or whatever it is." He looked at the room around him. "The house."

"The house has rules?" David said.

"The same way everything does," Dad said. "Like the rules of gravity and physics." He leaned over and touched David's bruised cheek. "You cut yourself, you bleed, right?"

"The house doesn't *bleed*."

Dad raised his eyebrows. "As far as we know. But it does do weird things with sound, right? And it doesn't like to have the doors upstairs locked. The antechamber won't change as long as someone's in it or in the world beyond. These are all 'rules,' and I'll bet there are many more we don't even know about yet. We need to make a list of them so we know what we're dealing with, what we can do and what we can't do. Maybe we'll see a pattern that will help us figure this whole thing out."

Dad paced to the end of the room, turned, and came back. "And I think we should try to understand the reason for each rule in the first place."

David lowered his face into his hands. "You're making my head hurt."

"No, Dae, this is good. For example, why can't you bring a camcorder into another world and film your time there?"

David thought about Xander's camcorder that had dangled around his neck the entire time he was playing keep-away from hungry tigers. When he'd come back, all that had been recorded was static. He said, "How are we supposed to find out why the camera didn't work?"

Dad spread out his hands. "I don't know! But that's part of what we're doing here, part of what this room, the MCC, is all about, right? Figuring stuff out, maybe even conducting experiments to learn more."

David frowned. "Experiments" made him think of science class and failing more times than succeeding. He was already trying to get his head around "rules"—two sets of them!—and the very idea that this control center was an attempt to understand something that to David was not understandable: you've got a house with doorways to other times and places, people from those places who can step through and take your mom, and doors that can apparently shake off the locks you put on them—how could you *understand* any of that?

Dad started tapping his chin, thinking. He said, "Let's get a big wall calendar too. We can—"

"How do you spell *calendar*?" Toria asked.

Dad told her, then continued: "It'll help us keep track of what we've already done, how long everything takes to do."

"Like what?" David said.

"Like . . ." Dad thought for a moment. "Like we came to Pinedale on August 13. We found this house the next day."

Because you knew about it before we even started looking, David thought. Instead of rubbing it in, he said, "And we moved in a few days later."

"Right," Dad agreed. "The seventeenth. Last Wednesday."

"Just last Wednesday," David repeated to himself. He could not believe how much had happened since then. It felt like months.

Dad said, "And three days later, yesterday—" He stopped.

David finished for him: "Yesterday morning is when Mom got kidnapped."

Dad shook his head. "So quickly . . ."

Xander rushed into the room, out of breath and holding

an armful of white tubes. David recognized them as rolled movie posters.

"Check it out," Xander said. He dropped the posters on the floor and selected one, then smoothed it open against a bare spot of wall. It displayed a fierce warrior flexing his torso and arms of rippling muscles, gritting his teeth and obviously ready to fight.

"*300?*" David said. "What's that got to do with—"

"Think about it," Xander said. He flashed a big grin over his shoulder. "We're going to be heading into worlds that so far haven't been very friendly to us. We need *guts!* We need to be ready to *fight!* Doesn't this psych you up for that?" He released the poster, which snapped back into a roll, and snatched up another one. He spread it out against the wall.

"*Gladiator!*" David announced: Russell Crowe looking bad and ready to take on the world.

"Yeah?" Xander said, nodding his head with enthusiasm.

"I don't know," Dad said. He was studying the poster with narrow eyes, as though judging a science fair project.

"We can play some music too," Xander said. "I've got tons of soundtracks. Stuff that will really get your blood pumping, you know? We can get one of those clock radios you connect your iPod to. Toria, put that on your list."

She scribbled it down.

Xander nodded toward the posters. "I got *Commando, Die Hard, Matrix . . .*"

"I like where you're going with this," Dad said. He was using his teacher voice. "What bothers me is"—he put his finger on Russell Crowe's breastplate—"we're not these people. We don't have their training, their physical attributes . . ."

"That's not the point, Dad!" Xander said. "These help us get jazzed up for going over. *Mentally*, we're these guys. We're ready! We're tough! We can do it!"

Dad nodded but said, "I understand the mental part. I just don't want us to go diving headlong into a situation we're not ready for."

"All right, look," Xander said. He released the poster and quick-stepped to the far end of the room. "How about if right here"—he turned in a circle, indicating the floor under him—"we *train* to be like those guys? We get in physical shape, and we learn whatever skills we might need in whatever world we're heading to."

Dad shook his head. "Xander—"

Xander cut him off. "Dad! Even if I never learned how to wield a sword or hold a shield, just having the never-say-die warriors of *300* on my mind would have made me better at fighting that gladiator in the Colosseum. Maybe if you hadn't rescued me, I could have fought him off long enough to have found my own way back home, I don't know. But I do know soldiers in war get psyched up like this."

"And soccer players," David chimed.

"Right, athletes!" Xander said. "You're a history teacher. You've studied war. You told me once that battles are won in the mind long before they're won on the battlefield. Isn't *this* what you meant?"

Dad walked to where Xander stood on the other side of the room and looked around, as if trying to see it with Xander's eyes. After a time he smiled and nodded, then said, "Toria, put free weights and exercise mats on the list. Xander, get those posters up on the wall. David, don't you have some killer video game posters?"

David jumped up. "*Halo, Metroid, Call of Duty.*"

"Do they make you want to kick some butt?"

"Oh, yeah!"

"Go get 'em." Dad clapped his hands together. "Come on, guys, let's do this!"

CHAPTER

MOTHER OF MERCY NURSING HOME

Jesse Wagner fidgeted in his wheelchair. He looked at the clock for the thousandth time. Where was Keal? If anyone there would listen to him, it was Keal. To most of the staff at Mother of Mercy, he was just an old man. Heck, he was just an old man to the other old men and women who frittered away their final days in that depressing place. But Keal Jackson was different; he treated people with respect. He was an attendant at the home and knew who still had a light burning in the attic and who didn't.

Shafts of light from sodium vapor lamps in the parking lot streamed through the dirty windows of the community room. Little flecks of dust floated in the light like tiny insects with nowhere to go and nothing to do.

But Jesse did have something to do. Trouble was, he had no way of doing it. Not alone, not by himself. It'd been decades since he could walk without a cane, and eight years now that he'd needed a wheelchair.

He hunched over to stare at his slippered feet. "What good are you?" he yelled at them. "Can't keep a body standing. Can't even shuffle one in front of the other. What good are you!"

A booming voice came from behind him: "You talking to yourself again, Jesse?"

Finally!

Jesse straightened and craned his head around. He said, "'Bout time, Keal. I been waiting for you since yesterday! Don't you work anymore?"

"Gotta have a day off sometime," Keal answered. He came around and dropped into the sagging, cracked vinyl chair in front of Jesse. "Stop being such a grouch." He smiled, a creepy, Cheshire cat thing straight out of *Alice in Wonderland*. The man's skin was so dark, all Jesse's aged vision could make out were Keal's eyes and teeth.

Jesse leaned forward to place a shaky hand on top of Keal's

and gave the attendant his most intent stare, trying to appear as serious and urgent as the task for which he needed Keal's help.

Keal misread the expression. "You suffering from gas today, Jesse?"

"No!" Jesse yelled in his loudest voice, which wasn't loud at all these days. The nurse at the desk in the corner didn't even look up from her magazine. He snatched his hand away and flapped it at the big black man. "I've got urgent business, Keal! Life-and-death business!"

"You don't say." Keal leaned forward.

Jesse sighed with exaggeration. "Listen to me," he said, taking time to make his words clear and strong sounding. "You've known me for what, six years?"

Keal nodded. "Since I started here."

"Have you ever seen me lose my grip on reality? Have I ever rambled about dragons the way ol' Charlie Hobbs used to, God rest his soul? Have I ever thought the cafeteria was a sandy beach in Hawaii, the way Mrs. Thompson does?" He shook his head. "Always taking off her shoes and trying to hang ten on the tables. Have you ever had to restrain me because I thought the night nurses had come to kill me like . . . well, like half the people here? Have you seen me do *anything* crazy?"

Keal flashed his teeth at Jesse again. "I always said you got it together better than most of the staff, Jesse. I hope I'm half as aware when I'm your age . . . if I ever get to be your age."

"So you got to listen to me now, Keal. I mean it. I ain't crazy, even though what I have to say will make me sound that way. Give me the benefit of the doubt, okay?"

Keal's teeth vanished, and the whites of his eyes narrowed. Jesse knew he was frowning.

Good, he thought. *He's listening.*

"I need you to take me somewhere," Jesse said. "Someplace important."

"Like . . . where? If it's the restroom, Jesse, I got you covered, man. Any farther than that, we got a problem."

"California," Jesse said firmly.

Another flash of teeth, and Keal boomed with laughter. "Oh, Jesse, Jesse . . . you know I can't take the residents outside the building, less'n it's to the hospital, or maybe an occasional field trip to the park."

Jesse let him laugh. When it was all out of Keal, and the aide had caught his breath, Jesse said, "People will die if I don't get there. Lots of people."

He felt Keal's big hand on his knee.

The attendant said, "Jesse . . . I . . . I don't know what to say. You know—"

"I know what I know," Jesse snapped. "I have to get a message to someone, a message so important I have to do it in person. He may not believe me, otherwise. And I have to show him . . ."

"Show him what?"

Jesse closed his eyes. "I have to show him how to . . . to . . ."

He didn't know how to say it differently, but he also knew how it would sound. "I have to show him how to save the world."

"Save the world?"

"I know how it sounds."

It was Keal's turn to sigh. He said, "Who is it you think you have to see?"

"I don't know who, exactly." Jesse shook his head. "I mean, I *do* . . . but . . . but it's been so *long*. It could be almost anyone. No, not *anyone* . . ."

Keal gave his knee a gentle squeeze. "Calm down, Jesse. It's okay. So this guy—whoever he is—he's going to save the world?"

"Yes, yes, but he doesn't know it yet. I have to tell him." He squeezed his eyes closed again. His lungs didn't work the way they used to. He had to pull hard just to get enough air. "His father, or his father's father, was supposed to show him, but I know he didn't. It's been too long. He didn't do what he was supposed to do. He left his post."

"Post? Jesse, I have to say, man, you might as well be ranting about dragons and surfing on the tables, for all the sense you're making."

Jesse gripped Keal's hand in both of his. He squeezed, but knew Keal hardly felt it. "His *post*," he repeated. "The house. They left the house . . . for *years* they left the house." He squinted at the whites of Keal's eyes. "It's not a house you want to leave. It's too special, it's too *important*."

"A house, Jesse?" Keal said. "You're talking about a house?"

"Like no other house, like no other place."

"And that's where you want to go? To this house? In California?"

Jesse pulled in air. He wasn't getting enough. He nodded.

"How do you know about this house, Jesse? Did you live there?"

Jessie smiled at a memory. Then other memories flooded into his head, wiping the smile away. He said, "I more than lived there." He glanced around and leaned closer. Then he whispered, "I built it."

CHAPTER

thirty-one

Xander King had walked completely around the outside of the house. He had to plow through bushes and scale trees to do it, but he finally managed to film the entire exterior. He planned to upload the footage to their computer and print still pictures of every angle. He imagined a wall of house photos in the war room, David's "MCC."

He stood midway between the house and the dirt road,

where their 4Runner was parked. He squinted up at the second-floor windows above the porch roof and wondered if he should try to get a few close-ups of them. But it was early evening, and he was losing his light. The sun was already gone from the sky, leaving only a reddish-purple glow. Even that was fading fast.

The term "false twilight" came to him. It was when darkness came earlier than it should have, usually from a solar eclipse or because the shadows in a canyon grew dark with the slightest dropping of the sun. The woods around the house were like that, near-black despite the sky's luminance.

He didn't want to be outside much longer. Besides, they'd gotten up early and had to go to school again tomorrow. Dad would want them all to go to bed before too long.

A clatter came from the house. Xander's heart jumped as the front door burst open. Then he recognized David bounding off the porch without touching a single step.

"Xander!" David called.

"What?"

"Dad wants you."

Xander pushed a black cap over the camcorder's lens.

"Now!" David said, insistent.

"Hold your—" He registered the urgency on David's face. He brushed past him, heading for the door. "What is it? Is he all right?"

"He went through," David said. "He's in a world!"

Xander stopped to look at his brother. "What? Why? Did he see Mom?"

"No. We were cleaning up the locks upstairs. He looked in one of the rooms and laughed. He said he remembered it from when he was a kid and wanted to show it to you. He said he was going on ahead and told me to come get you."

"Why me? Why not you?"

"He said I can go later."

David pushed him, and Xander hurried up the porch steps.

David continued: "He said he'd been wanting to talk to you, and this was the perfect place."

"He went on alone?" Xander couldn't believe it. "Without anyone even in the antechamber?"

"What holds the room in place, he said, was being in the *world*, not the antechamber." David added: "I propped the door open with a picnic basket. Just in case."

They went through the door, and Xander pushed it closed.

"Lock it," David said. "Dad wants to keep the house battened down." He smiled. "That's what he said: *battened down.*"

They started up the stairs.

Xander said, "Where's Toria?"

"Playing in her room. I'll wait for you guys in the antechamber."

In the second-floor hallway, heading for the hidden stairwell, Xander stopped again. He turned to David. "Did you say *picnic basket?*"

483

•••••••••

Xander's sneakered feet stepped onto the softness of tall grass. A light breeze blew past. The air felt warm, but he saw no sun in the sky, just a uniform pinkish glow. Dawn or dusk, he couldn't tell. Thin tendrils of clouds swooped in long arcs, as though fingers had raked across the sky. He looked over his shoulder to see the wavering image of David standing in the little room. Then the door slammed shut without a sound. The image broke apart like dandelion fluff and disappeared.

He reached up to tug at the rim of the wool cap he'd taken from a hook in the antechamber. It was checkered, with a little pom-pom on the top, like ones he'd seen some serious golfers wear. At his hip, hanging by a strap over his shoulder, was the picnic basket David had told him about. It was empty, but that didn't stop it from helping him unlock the portal door. In his left hand he carried a net at the end of a yard-long pole. SpongeBob used one like it to catch jellyfish; Xander had had no idea it was something people actually owned.

Scoping out his surroundings, he started to understand the items. He was standing in a meadow at the top of a gentle hill. The grass rose as high as his knees. It swayed one way and then the other, reminding him of rolling swells in the open ocean. Wildflowers swirled among the grass: white and yellow, blue and red. Butterflies fluttered over the petals. Several flitted past him on their way from one patch of flowers to another. As far as he could see, the land around him rose and fell like a rumpled blanket. Woods occupied some of the space, covering one hill but not another.

Movement at the edge of the meadow caught his eye. A family of deer stepped from the shadows of trees. A buck with huge antlers stepped forward, studied Xander, then stooped to chew on the grass.

At the bottom of the gently sloping meadow, a river ran across the pristine landscape. It was about a mile away, but he could see his father sitting on a blanket near the glistening ribbon of water. He was leaning back on one arm and tossing something over the grassy bank into the river.

Xander started down the hill. From the woods, birds chirped. He heard an eagle's cry and looked up to see two of the majestic birds sailing in circles overhead. More animals—a fox, a couple of rabbits, a coyote—ventured from different places in the woods. They sniffed the air, looked at Xander, then went about their business. None seemed concerned by his presence.

He filled his lungs. The air tasted *fresh*, like it contained more oxygen than he was used to. He wondered if he was high up. The Rockies, maybe or . . . what were the other big mountain ranges? The Alps, the Himalayas, the Andes . . . But he didn't see any of the jagged, snowcapped peaks he would expect if he were in any of those places.

He could hear the river now. The water rushed over rocks, poured over short drop-offs.

His father looked relaxed. He sat with one knee cocked up, the other leg stretched out before him. While Xander watched, he turned his head, appeared to select a pebble from the ground beside the blanket, and casually tossed it into the water.

"Hey!" Xander called.

Dad looked back over his shoulder and waved.

Xander spread his arms out. "What *is* this?"

"Nice, huh?"

Xander set the net and picnic basket down. He dropped onto the blanket. His dad tossed another pebble, and Xander followed it with his eyes. He watched the water rushing by, tumbling and churning. He realized that flowing water could be as complicated and interesting to watch as flames. The two shared a kind of orderly chaos.

He said, "I don't get it."

"What don't you get?"

"This." Xander looked around. "I thought all the worlds were violent and dangerous."

"Most are," Dad said. "In fact, this is the only one my father found that wasn't like that."

"So why's it here? What's it about?"

Dad shook his head slowly. "Maybe it's a respite from the insanity of the other worlds, a peaceful break. Grandpa thought of it that way. I think this was one of the reasons he gave up the search and took us away."

That jolted Xander. "*This* place? I thought it was the dangers of the other worlds that made him think he would go crazy. Or that he thought he'd die and leave you and Aunt Beth alone in the house. Or that someone would take you and—"

Dad nodded. "Those things were the raging storms he weathered every day. *This*—" He took in the landscape around him, a satisfied smile on his lips. "This was his break from those horrors."

"So why would it drive him away?"

Dad looked at him from the corner of his eyes. "Because he was afraid he'd come here and stay."

Xander thought about that. He said, "Wow."

"If he didn't have other responsibilities—kids—maybe he would have done just that."

"And no one would ever know," Xander said. He found a pebble and tossed it in. "It *is* nice."

"When I looked in the antechamber and saw the items—the basket and blanket—" He nodded at the cap Xander wore. "The tam-o'-shanter."

"So that's what it's called." Xander touched the pom-pom and smiled.

"Snazzy," Dad said, winking. "When I saw them, I remembered the world that lay beyond. My father took me here a couple of times. I wanted you to see it."

"Yeah, why me? David was with you."

Dad watched the river. His face was expressionless. Finally he said, "Because as much as David loves Mom and misses her, he doesn't blame himself for her being gone."

"*What?*" Xander snapped, surprised. "You think I blame myself? If anybody, I blame—"

"Me. I know." Dad looked directly into his eyes. "But I think you believe you should have stopped that man."

"I . . ." Xander started.

But Dad was right. Xander had never admitted it even to himself, but his inability to stop the man from taking Mom had been haunting him. He felt shame and anger at himself.

Dad patted Xander on the knee. "You have every right to be mad at me. I don't blame you, and I'm not going to tell you to feel otherwise. Not about me. But you did everything you could to help her. That man was twice your size and experienced at doing what he did. You can't punish yourself for not stopping him."

Dad blurred in Xander's vision, and he thought the portal was materializing right there between them. Then he realized that tears had filled his eyes. He blinked, spilling them down his cheeks.

Dad turned to press his body to Xander and wrap his arm around his neck. Xander expected him to say again how sorry he was, but Dad simply held him. After a few moments, Xander lowered his head and cried on his father's shoulder.

He let it all come out, all the sorrow and fear he'd been trying to pretend he didn't feel. When it was over, he straightened. He saw that he'd soaked Dad's shoulder. He laughed a little and brushed at it.

Dad's eyes were red too. "I wanted . . ." he said. His voice broke, and he had to stop. He pulled in a couple deep breaths, then said, "I wanted you to see this so you'd know it isn't all bad. Your mother could be somewhere like this."

"You believe that?" Xander said.

Dad nodded thoughtfully. He studied Xander's face. He said, "You look so much like her."

Xander wiped the back of his hand under his nose. "But *am* I like her?"

"You mean independent, resourceful, tenacious? Oh, yeah."

Xander chuckled. He pushed the wetness out of his eye sockets. "This family is way too weepy," he said.

Dad pointed at him. "No more of that!" He sniffed and slapped Xander's knee, then stood. "Come on. We'd better get back."

"I can feel it," Xander said. "The pull."

"The more sensitive you are to it, the better."

"But I'm not feeling it this way," Xander said. "It's tugging me back toward where I stepped into this world."

"Me too," Dad said. "I just want to do one thing first." They headed for a big tree.

"Dad?" Xander asked, watching his sneakers kick down the

footlong blades of grass. "Why did this happen? I mean, why did God *let* this happen?"

His father stopped. He gave Xander a long, serious look. "I don't know, Son. But I trust that He has His reasons."

"You *trust*? After He let Mom get taken?"

Dad bit his lip, thinking. Finally, he touched his chest. "It's here. I don't know how to explain it."

Xander shook his head. Whatever it was Dad felt, it wasn't the same in Xander.

Dad gripped his shoulder and gave it a squeeze. "Give it time, Xander. You'll see."

"I doubt it."

They stood like that for a while, then continued their trek to the big tree. Dad produced a pocketknife and unfolded it. He began scraping the point against the bark.

"What are you doing?" Xander asked.

"You know when we were talking about your mother leaving notes in our lunches?"

The mark on the tree started taking on a shape Xander recognized. "Sure."

Without pausing the blade, Dad said, "That got me thinking. I'm leaving a note for *her*."

It was "Bob," the cartoon face both parents often doodled on notes and cards to each other and the kids. Xander sometimes found the face on a scrap of paper among his homework paper or stuck in his shoe. It told him someone was thinking about him. Dad said it had started with Grandpa Hank, and Dad had scribbled it since he was a kid.

Xander said, "Bob?"

"Bob," Dad confirmed, starting on the bulbous, heavily lidded eyes. "It'll let her know we're looking for her, that we've been here."

"But no one else will know it's from us or to her," Xander concluded.

"Exactly," Dad said. "You never know when a message could cause problems. If no one else recognizes it as a message, it won't stir anything up."

"Except in Mom."

Dad stepped back to appraise his handiwork: one goofy face carved in a tree trunk.

"Will it stay?" Xander asked.

"Stay?"

"I mean after we're gone. Does time get weird here? Will it suddenly be the past and Bob will never have been here, or will it become the future and Bob will be long gone?"

Dad scowled at him. "I never thought of that." He looked at Bob. "I don't know."

"I hope he stays," Xander said. "I want her to know we're looking for her."

Dad folded up the knife and dropped it into his pocket. He put his arm around Xander's shoulder and steered him toward the portal, according to the pull of the antechamber items. "She knows we are, Xander. Even without Bob, she knows."

thirty-two

MONDAY, 8:05 P.M.

David sat on the bench in the antechamber, backstroking with one arm. His right hand rose up and descended, palm down as though pushing water past his body. His left elbow rose as far as the sling would allow. In his mind, he finished the stroke. Then the process started all over again with his right hand rising above his head.

He watched the door Dad and Xander had gone through. His

eyes flicked to the other door, the one that led to the hallway and the rest of the house. He'd been hearing noises for some time now: creaking floorboards, thuds. Once he thought he heard a door slam. It was nearby, one of the other doors on that floor. Then there was the telephone downstairs. Every few minutes, it would ring and ring and ring. *Why didn't Toria answer it?*

His mouth was dry, and his stomach hurt from rolling over on itself every time he heard a noise or imagined something creeping around in the hallway.

He heard a loud drawing of breath, like someone sucking air in through his teeth. He jumped, staring at the hallway door. Then he realized it was coming from the other door, the portal door. Air hissed through the gap underneath it. He couldn't tell if it was blowing into the little room or being sucked out of it. The last thing he wanted to do was get close enough to feel for the wind's direction.

Dim light appeared under the door and quickly grew in intensity until it was blindingly bright. Squinting at it, he saw the light trace a line around the entire door. Shadows flickered through the light as though something was moving past the door on the other side. The handle began to turn. David stood and backed into the hallway door.

The portal door burst open. Wind whooshed in, carrying leaves and grass and a meadowy fragrance. The portal itself looked like a churning cauldron of dry ice, backlit by flood lamps. The smoky air swirled around and around. It thinned and blew away, off to either side of the door. In its place was an out-of-focus image of greens and browns. The colors shifted and came together, forming a human figure.

Xander stepped into the room, coming down hard on his feet as though stepping off a foot-high platform. He fell to the floor, grunting.

David fell to his knees beside him. "Xander! You all right?"

Xander raised his head. His hair was a mess. There was a leaf stuck in it. "Yeah," he said. "Gotta remember to watch that first step. It's a doozy."

"Where's Dad?" David said. He looked through the portal just as another figure formed out of the colors.

Xander rolled out of the way as Dad came crashing through: "*Oomph!*"

Dad saw Xander beside him and touched him. "You all right?"

"Took you long enough," David said.

Dad swung around to him. "What's wrong?"

"I've been hearing noises in the hallway, and the phone keeps ringing."

"What noises?"

"I heard creaking, and a door slammed."

Dad scrambled to his feet. He tossed down the blanket and said, "Xander, put the items back. Let's go."

Halfway to the staircase, the phone began ringing again.

Dad said, "David—?"

"Got it!" David ran ahead, clomped down the stairs and into

the master bedroom. Toria was sitting on the bed, an array of dolls and their clothes splayed across the bedspread. The phone on the nightstand started into its fourth ring.

"Why didn't you answer it?" David said.

"I'm not supposed to."

David snatched up the wireless receiver and thumbed a button. "Hello?"

"There you are. Mr. King. I need to speak to Mr. King." The woman's words rattled at him, fast as machine-gun fire.

"One moment, please." He ran into the hall and met his father coming through the secret panel in the wall. He held the phone out to him.

"Sounds important," David whispered.

Dad put the phone to his face. "Hello? . . . Yes?" He continued down the hall.

David turned to Xander. In a hushed voice he said, "It sounded like my homeroom teacher, Mrs. Moreau."

Xander made a face. "What did you do?"

"Nothing. It wasn't me, it was that kid I told you about. Clayton. She sent him to the office."

"Boys!" Dad called. He had walked around the corner into the main upstairs hallway. Now he stepped back into view. "Come on! We gotta go!"

"Where?" Xander said.

Dad vanished again, his footsteps clumping away. "City hall. Toria, grab your shoes."

"City hall? Why?" Xander called as the brothers raced around the corner.

Dad came out of the master bedroom, pulling their sister along by the hand. His face was tight with worry. He said, "Someone's trying to take the house!"

thirty-three

MONDAY, 8:37 P.M.

In the 4Runner, Dad explained that someone had claimed that the house was unsafe. "The town council convened an emergency meeting to consider evicting us."

"Just because someone said our house was unsafe?" Xander said. His voice was high in disbelief.

"Apparently somebody is trying to convince them that you guys are in danger," Dad said. "They got the doctor who set

David's arm telling the council about his injuries. Someone's claiming he was hurt in the house because it's so dilapidated."

"What's that?" Toria said.

"Rundown," Xander answered.

"You keep saying *someone*," David said. "Who is someone?"

Dad's eyes caught his in the rearview mirror. "That's what I asked. The woman on the phone said she didn't know."

"Or didn't want to tell you," Xander said.

David thought about the doctor's line of questioning at the clinic. He said, "No one said it was *you* who hurt me?"

Dad shook his head. "Not yet, but that doesn't mean they're not going to. I have a feeling this is just the beginning."

"Or the end," Xander said, "if the city council believes them and kicks us out. Dad, you can't let that happen!"

Dad said, "There's something else I don't get . . . why is this a city council matter? You'd think the safety of children would go to social services or even the police department."

Xander said, "They do things differently in small towns. Do they even *have* social services here?"

"Still, calling in the city council just feels like overkill to me," Dad said. "Like using a nuke when a penknife would do. And why wouldn't they just come out and look for themselves?"

In the rearview mirror David could see his father's brows getting closer together as he thought about it.

Dad said, "I think something bigger is going on."

"Bigger?" Xander said. "Like what?"

Dad just shook his head. He said, "The mayor will probably be there. He was one of the people who interviewed me for my job." His eyes found David in the mirror. "Dae, the woman on the phone hung up when I asked who she was. Any idea?"

Xander spoke up. "He thinks it was his teacher."

"Teacher? Who?"

"Mrs. Moreau," David said.

Xander said, "Dad, what if the phone call was just a way to get us out of the house?"

That made Dad's eyebrows actually touch. He said, "What makes you think that?"

"We saw somebody watching our house last night."

"When?"

"After the thing with the locks. I got up to go to the bathroom."

Dad said, "Maybe it was that Taksidian guy. Why didn't you tell me?"

Xander threw up his hands. "It was late . . . I just thought . . ."

"Listen, guys . . ." Dad shifted his head around to make eye contact with each of his children. His attention returned to the road before he continued: "With all that's going on, *everything* is important. And somebody watching the house!" He scowled at Xander. "How could you think that wasn't important?"

"I didn't say it wasn't important!"

"But you didn't tell me!"

Xander's shoulders slumped. Instead of explaining himself, he turned away to look out the window. David knew what he was thinking: with school, setting up the MCC, Dad and Xander going into another world—when was there time to even *think* of anything else? Maybe it was this kind of thing that the control room was meant for, a place to record things and keep everything straight. He knew Dad was right. With so much at stake, everything was important.

"Here we go." Dad said, braking to a hard stop.

They were on Pinedale's main street in front of the city hall. The front doors were open and people were coming out, descending the stairs, talking to one another. They all seemed to notice Dad at the same time. David thought they were trying not to look guilty of something.

Dad opened the door and hopped out. He beelined it for an older man who was halfway down the concrete steps.

Xander unsnapped his seat belt and swiveled around to face Toria and David. "That's the mayor. His picture was on the wall in one of my classes."

David said, "His picture? Weird."

"Welcome to Pinedale." Xander opened his door and scrambled out.

David and Toria did the same. They all came together on the steps around Dad and the mayor. The other people who had come out of the building were watching from safe distances in both directions of the street.

Dad was saying, " . . . this isn't right, and you know it."

The mayor said, "Now, Ed, our only concern is for the children."

The way he spoke made David think of a glazed doughnut, all soft and sugary.

The mayor glanced at each of the King kids in turn. He paused on David, taking in, David was sure, his black eye, bruised cheek, and broken arm. Turning back to Dad, he said, "When we get reports like this, of course we have to investigate."

"Reports like what?" Dad snapped.

"Well . . . uh . . ." His hand rose to indicate David.

Dad continued: "I think *investigation* is the right word here. But it sounds to me like you've already investigated—or have no intention of ever investigating."

"Ed, we *know* that house. It's been rundown for years."

"So?" Dad's volume rose a notch. "That doesn't automati-cally make it unsafe. Are you questioning my judgment when it comes to keeping my family safe? I can't believe all these people are going along with this." Dad looked around at the men and women who were watching from the sidewalk.

Suddenly he froze, and David saw the muscles in his jaw tighten, his eyes narrow. He looked over his shoulder to follow his father's gaze. David's heart jumped into his throat.

Across the street, in an alleyway between two stores, stood a man. Though the figure was partially hidden by shadows, the light from a streetlamp crossed over his face, revealing Taksidian. As David watched, the man took a step back and vanished in the darkness.

"Oh, I see," Dad said. "Tell me, Steve, did your report happen to come from Mr. Taksidian?"

The mayor swallowed, his eyes darting to the people standing around. He said, "It was . . . uh . . . anonymous. But I'll have you know, Mr. Taksidian means a lot to this town. He is considering relocating several of his businesses to Pinedale. What that means to us, economically, at a time when businesses have been closing, people moving away—"

Dad held up his palm. "I get it," he said. His hand became a pointing finger aimed directly at the mayor's nose. "Let me tell you. Whatever you do, make sure you can support it in a court of law, because that's where you're going to end up."

For just a moment the mayor's eyes focused on Dad's finger. He actually looked frightened—though David thought something like *I'll hunt you down like a dog* would have worked better.

The mayor composed himself and said, "Mr. King, is that a threat?"

Dad's finger didn't waver. David was awfully glad it wasn't pointed at him.

"I'm just telling you, Steve, don't mess with me, my family, or my house." Dad turned and descended a few steps toward the car.

The mayor cleared his throat and said, "Speaking of your family, Ed, where is the missus? We heard another report that—"

Dad spun around, and his index finger came up again. "Don't mess with us. I mean it," he warned. "Come on, kids."

He climbed into the SUV and slammed the door.

David ran around and was the last one in. The car pulled forward before he had his door shut. As they drove past, David looked hard into the alley where Taksidian had stood, but the man was gone, leaving only darkness.

CHAPTER

thirty-four

MONDAY, 11:57 P.M.

That night, the day's events kept replaying in David's head. He was exhausted, but he wasn't sure he'd ever again get a good night's rest. Even being in his own bed didn't help. *If you can't turn off your thoughts,* he said to himself, *who cares how soft your pillow is?*

Xander's whispered voice reached him from out of the darkness: "You awake?"

"Yeah," he whispered back. He looked over toward

Xander's bed. The moonlight coming through the windows was enough to show his brother sitting up. He looked at the clock on the nightstand. "Almost the witching hour," he said.

"No such thing," Xander told him.

"I'm not sure about anything anymore," David said. "What's real, what's not . . . this house has confused everything."

When Xander didn't say anything, David realized he had been hoping his brother would laugh at his words, say they were crazy. He wanted somebody to tell him the world was essentially the same as he thought it was before coming to Pinedale, but it wasn't. Their mom was gone, and they lived in a house that messed with time and space. The past was supposed to be the past—unreachable, unchangeable. Here, however, things that belonged in history books were as easy to get to as the bathroom.

See? he thought. *Thinking again. Why can't I let it all go, at least until morning?*

Xander said, "I've been thinking."

"Join the club. I can't turn it off."

"No, listen." Xander shifted from his bed to David's. "They're trying to take our house or kick us out or something."

"I know," David said. "It's that Taksidian guy."

"It doesn't even matter who's behind it. If they kick us out, who knows what will happen? They'll probably chain the doors, board up all the windows. Maybe even tear the whole place down."

David sat up and scooted back against the headboard. "They can't do that. It's our house."

"Dad Googled Taksidian. He's some rich bigwig. Owns all these companies. People like that can do anything they want."

"Not *anything*," David said. This was another way the world was not as David had always imagined. Maybe it didn't involve ripples in time or monsters, but it was equally scary.

"Just about," Xander said. "Don't you think a man like that can take any house he wants?"

David thought about it. With enough money and lawyers, dishonesty and meanness, of course he could. David's chest felt tight.

"What—" he started to say, then realized how close he was to crying. He took a deep breath and tried again. "What's going to happen to Mom?"

"That's what I've been thinking about," Xander said. "The MCC is cool, but Dad's taking too long. He's so concerned about appearances and keeping people off our backs so we have all the time in the world to find Mom . . ." He shook his head. "But we don't *have* all the time in the world. We may not even have a few days."

"There's nothing we can do about that, Xander."

"We can start looking for Mom *now*. Forget playing it safe. Forget debriefings and motivational seminars. We gotta just do it, Dae. We gotta find Mom."

"What are you saying?"

Xander leaned closer. He squeezed David's leg. "Come with me! Now!"

"What, just . . . *go over?*"

"Between the two of us, we can cover the same ground in half the time."

"Xander, I don't know. I promised Dad I wouldn't."

"Come on, David, what do we have to lose?"

"Our *lives?*"

"Think about it. The faster we go, the more worlds we see, the better chance we have to find Mom."

This is it, David thought. As much as he wanted to find Mom, as much as he'd gone along with setting up the control room and making plans for searching through the various worlds, somewhere inside he had hoped it would not be necessary. Maybe Mom would just show up. Or Dad would decide that he was too young.

The first time he went over, he had almost been killed by tigers and tribesmen with spears. The second time, he had almost been killed by Nazis. Two times through, two close calls. He didn't like those odds. They had cured him of his desire for that kind of adventure.

He looked at the clock again. It was exactly midnight. With far less enthusiasm than usual, he said, "Let's do it."

CHAPTER

thirty-five

"Why are they shooting at me?" David screamed.

There was a *crack!* in the distance, and the earth beside him erupted in a mini-geyser of dirt. They had stepped into a nightmare battlefield where bodies littered the ground, the injured howled in pain, and David had become a target before drawing his third breath. Though Xander and he were near each other, it was clear the shooters wanted David. One man who had aimed a rifle at him lowered it when Xander darted into the line of fire. That did not stop others from plugging away at him.

"Get down! Get down!" Xander said, waving his arms at David. Xander was sidestepping in circles around his brother, trying to spot and dissuade the next would-be shooter. It seemed every time he circled around one way, a shot rang out from the opposite direction, and a bullet would sail past so closely they could hear it, or it would hit the ground at their feet.

A thick plume of smoke drifted past, hiding Xander from David's view. David panicked. "Xander! Xander!"

"I'm here, Dae, stay down."

David felt warm wetness on his cheeks and thought for sure he had been hit. He wiped at it. Only tears, and they were flowing as heavily as blood would have from a head wound. He dropped to his hands and knees and yelled again, "Why are they shooting at me?"

The smoke cleared. Xander was standing ten feet away. "Your uniform!" he said. "David, your uniform."

David looked at the jacket he had put on in the antechamber. One side was draped over his cast. It was gray, like the kepi he wore on his head. To gain passage into this world, he had also carried a rifle. Xander had recognized it from *Glory, The Patriot,* and other Civil War movies: it was a Harper's Ferry rifle, single shot and muzzle loaded. He had confirmed that it was unloaded, with the gunpowder and musket ball nowhere in the antechamber.

"All the better," Xander had said. "You'd end up shooting your foot off, or worse, shooting me."

David had forgotten all about it as soon as the first bullet zinged past his head.

He looked up from the gray wool of his uniform to see that Xander was wearing dark blue. In his hand, he held a sword—the only other weapon in the room after David had gotten dibs on the rifle.

"They think you're a Confederate soldier, David!" Xander yelled. He glanced around. "We're on the Union side of the battle." He looked back at David and saw something that made his eyes grow even wider. "And you've got that rifle! Throw it away! David, throw the rifle away!"

David heaved it off to the side.

A shot rang out, then another. Dirt kicked up into his face. Another round passed so closely over his head he thought for sure it had taken off his kepi, if not his scalp. He reached up and felt the soft cloth of the worn hat. He spat dirt out of his mouth. "*Xander!*" he screamed with everything he had in him.

"Lie down! Lie down!" Xander yelled, running to him.

David did, and Xander lay down on top of him. Xander's breaths were loud and quick in his ear. David couldn't help it: his weeping became full-out crying.

"I told you . . . I told you," he repeated. It was all he could say, over and over.

"Shhh," Xander whispered into his ear. "It's going to be okay."

Nearby, the ground exploded. Hurled into the air was a thousand times more dirt than the musket balls had kicked up.

"What . . . what . . . what . . ." David screamed, pulling in a short breath between each word.

"Cannonball," Xander said. "I think the Confederates are advancing. We can't stay here."

When David had awakened that morning with the first day of school on his mind, it had never occurred to him that he would die that same night in the dirt by a Union soldier's musket ball. He squeezed his eyes closed. He tried not to think about the rifle fire and the screams, the smoke that stung his nostrils and scorched his throat.

He forced himself to think of home. He would have liked to have tasted Toria's meat loaf, to have kicked the mayor of Pinedale in the shin, to have used their mission control center at least once. That got him thinking about something he wanted to write on Dad's flip chart: *What is it about these worlds and WAR?* In his mind, he underlined *WAR* three times. WWII. The Civil War. He would even say Xander's battle with the gladiator was a form of war. What else would you call it when people tried to kill you—whether it was a single person or many—and other people approved.

The chorus of gunfire they had been hearing in the distance grew louder, closer. Another cannonball slammed down, too close for comfort.

"We can't stay here," Xander repeated.

"What are we supposed to do?" David gasped. "As soon as I stand up, they'll shoot me."

Xander was quiet for what seemed like a long time. Finally he said, "I'm sorry I got you into this, Dae."

"I don't want to hear it, Xander," David said. "Don't apologize; just get me home."

Xander squirmed above him, apparently looking for something that would save them.

"Xander, Xander," David said. "Listen, you go. I'll stay here and play dead."

"I can't do that," Xander said loudly into his ear. "Anything could happen." He paused. Then: "Wait, wait, wait." He rolled off of David and vanished into a wall of drifting smoke.

"Xander!" David rose up onto his elbow. "Xander!" The barrel of a rifle jutted straight toward his face. He screamed and dropped his head into the dirt. He covered himself with his good arm as if it could protect him from a musket load. He wondered if he would hear the gunfire, or if the next thing he heard would be angels welcoming him into heaven.

When neither an explosion nor heavenly voices reached his ears, he lowered his arm and looked up. The opening of the barrel was big and black and six inches in front of his eyes. At the other end stood Xander, staring off to the side. Xander swung his attention back to David.

"Come on!" Xander said, "Didn't you hear me? Get up."

"Xander, what—"

Xander's eyes flicked around, then he said, "Don't say my name. You're my prisoner, understand? That's how we're getting out of here. Let's go."

David fought back a smile. He wiped the sleeve of his troublesome jacket under his nose, leaving a streak of snot and dirt. He rose and noticed that the other soldiers in blue were moving backwards, firing in the opposite direction. He turned to head the same way, raised his good hand, and began walking.

Behind him Xander said, "Take off your hat so they can see you're just a boy."

David pulled it off and held it above him in his hand.

"Don't hold it up like that," Xander said. "Let's not give anybody a gray target to shoot at."

"Don't we need it to find the portal?"

"Stick it in your belt," Xander instructed.

David lowered his hand to do that. He thought that having his arm down out of a surrender position made him fair game for anyone who wanted to shoot. He got his hand back in the air as fast as he could. He said, "Xander . . . ?"

"Don't use my name!"

"What if the portal home is on the Confederate side? I'm not feeling the items pull me yet."

Xander said, "Back when I was lying on you, I thought I felt my jacket pulling in this direction. But it might have been the wind . . . or you. Wherever it is, David, we'll get to it. I promise."

David believed his brother. On a list of character traits, Xander's top two would be determination and stubbornness.

David said, "Don't use my name."

thirty-six

They marched for a long time. They went over one, two, three hills, past the slow-moving injured and those who would never move again. Some soldiers ran by on their way to the front lines. They frowned at David. The anger in their eyes seemed to change to sadness when they registered his age. One man nodded at Xander and said, "Good job, private."

Dutifully, Xander replied, "Thank you, sir."

Finally, tents and groups of scurrying soldiers came into

view. As they drew closer, an older man with a closely cropped black beard broke away from a small group of soldiers to walk toward them. His jacket had a high collar and two rows of brass buttons running down his chest. Patches embroidered with stars were sewn to the top of each shoulder. He stepped in front of David. His eyes roamed down to David's feet, then back to his face.

"How old are you, son?" the man said.

David pulled his jacket closed in front, making sure his cast was hidden. He said, "Twelve, sir."

"And those cur dogs got you fighting?"

David thought fast. He figured an officer wouldn't take kindly to an enemy combatant regardless of age. He said, "No, sir. I'm only a drummer boy."

The officer narrowed his eyes at David. "Caught without your drum?"

David said, "Taken from me, sir."

The man said, "You know what I hear about young recruits?"

"Sir?"

"If they want to fight, they scrawl the number 18 on a piece of paper and put it in their shoe. When enlistment officers ask them if they're 'over eighteen,' they can honestly answer, 'Yes, sir, I am.' Those dogs are so desperate for soldiers, they take them at their word even when they know they're putting a child on the battlefield." The man stepped closer. "What concerns me are all the Southern children who do that in order to put musket balls in my men. You didn't do that, son, did you?"

Every organ in David's body felt shriveled to the size of a pea. It was all he could do to keep from passing out. He said, "No, sir. Just a drummer boy."

The man squinted down at David's sneakers. He said, "Son, those are the strangest shoes I've ever seen."

"Sneak—" David started, then backed up. "I mean, sir, my mother made them."

"No offense to your mama, but I think she could use some lessons."

"Yes, sir."

The man looked past David to Xander. "Oh, no," he said. "How old are *you*?"

"Fif—" Xander's voice suddenly grew deep. "Eighteen, sir."

The man frowned. "Beauregard hit our blind side. What's your take?"

"Pretty bad, sir. We saw . . . uh, *I* saw lots of casualties back there."

The bearded man nodded. He said—more to himself than to Xander, David thought—"Retreat is not dishonorable. *Unnecessary* retreat is. I don't believe it's time to shoot the horse."

"No, sir."

The man scowled at Xander. "You know where the stockade is?" Conveniently, he pointed down the camp's center aisle.

"Yes, sir."

"Carry on, then." The man stepped aside.

David felt the barrel of the rifle poke his spine. His feet felt like they were made of cement, but they moved on down the middle of the encampment.

"What was that 'shoot the horse' stuff?" David whispered.

"I think it's his version of throwing in the towel. Do you know who that was?"

"A guy who almost shot me," David said flatly.

"Ulysses S. Grant."

When David said nothing, Xander went on: "He became president of the United States. He's on the fifty-dollar bill."

Xander seemed more impressed by this last fact than by the first.

David simply nodded. As they moved toward the back of the camp, he finally spoke up. "How come I got the gray uniform?"

"Luck of the draw, Dae." After a few moments, he added, "And I am sorry about this."

"I know." He walked a few paces. "Xander—"

"Don't use my—"

David said, "Xander, Xander, Xander."

Xander sighed and said, "What?"

"I don't see any way we could look for Mom like this. And I just want to go home."

"Yeah," Xander said. "I have an idea. Come on." He grabbed David by the collar and tugged him toward a tent.

"Hey!" David said. "What are you—?"

"Just trying to make it look real. You're my prisoner, remember? Now, *shhh.*"

Xander pulled the tent flap back. Past his brother, David saw a man getting dressed. Xander said, "Excuse me." He let the flap fall back into place and pushed David on.

"What are we doing?" David whispered.

"I'm looking for something."

"What?"

But they had reached the flap of the next tent. Xander had his ear close to the canvas, listening. Inside, someone was screaming in pain.

"Xander, let's go to the next one!" David said.

Xander pulled back the flap and gasped. David couldn't keep his eyes from looking. A man lay on a table, convulsing. Blood jutted from a wound in his neck. His screams became gurgles. A woman in what David assumed was a nurse's hat and covered in blood held a cloth to another injury in the man's chest. She looked up quickly.

"Boy!" she yelled. "You must fetch Dr. Scott. Two tents down. Hurry!"

"I . . . just . . ."

"Now!"

"Yes, ma'am." Then something caught Xander's eye. He let go of David and stepped into the tent.

"*Xander!*" David whispered harshly.

"Didn't you hear me?" the nurse said. "Two tents down!"

"Yes, ma'am," Xander repeated, but he continued into the tent. David saw that he was heading for a row of bodies lying near the side of the tent. A swath of tan canvas covered each body; only bare feet and hands protruded. On each covering was written a name: A. Powell, J. Davis . . . Xander bent and picked up the piece of charcoal beside the bodies.

"What are you doing?"

Yeah, David thought. *What are you doing!*

The nurse had reached the end of her patience with Xander. She screamed, "Help! Dr. Scott! Help!"

Xander darted to the tent flap and pushed David through it.

"What was that about?" David said. Then he realized that the nurse's yells were largely muffled by the tent material. With the yelling of commands to the soldiers and cries from the other wounded, no one would be able to hear her.

David pointed. "This way, I think. Dr. Scott, she said?"

"Hey," Xander scolded. "You're a prisoner."

They headed toward the tent she had indicated. Before reaching it, David felt a strong tug on his body, like a surf's undercurrent. Just as he realized what it was, Xander grabbed his shoulder.

"David!" he said. "The portal. My clothes are pulling me that way. The rifle too."

"I feel it too," David said. "Just go tell the doctor—"

"Are you crazy? We gotta go now. The portal moves. We can't risk losing it."

"But, Xander, that man."

"We're not supposed to be here," Xander said. "If he dies, that's the way it's supposed to be. Now, come on."

He grabbed David's collar again and yanked him toward where they both knew they would find the portal—beyond the row of tents opposite the ones Xander had been looking into.

David looked back at the tents. What if that man died because they didn't get the doctor for him? The nurse had not asked Xander for a glass of water but for a doctor, a lifesaver. He felt he was walking away from something important. The dying man was out of sight. And they weren't doctors. They couldn't *really* help the guy, could they? But did these things— that they couldn't see the person who needed help, that their help was limited to getting real help—mean they didn't have to try as hard as when David had saved the little girl from being run over by the Nazi tank?

Then again, Xander was right. They knew from watching the worlds through the doorways that the portals drifted around. It was as though they were caught in a river current. And they didn't know enough about how they worked to know for sure they wouldn't simply drift away or vanish altogether. If they didn't reach the portal when they had a chance, they could be stuck in Civil War world forever. They might die there—and sooner rather than later. What good would that do?

He let Xander pull him more easily toward the portal. Then his legs were moving fast alongside Xander's, and he pushed the dying man from his mind.

"Do you feel it?" he said. "Is the pull getting stronger? I can't tell."

"I think so. Come on." They ran between two tents. David thought he saw it: a hundred yards away where the field met the woods, the base of a tree seemed to shimmer and ripple, as though he were seeing it through the heat waves of fire.

"There it is!" David yelled and picked up his pace.

Xander grabbed his arm and stopped him. "Hold on a sec."

He ran back toward the front of the tent.

"Xander, come on! What are you doing?"

Xander disappeared around the edge of the tent. When David reached the corner, he found Xander drawing on the canvas of the tent with the charcoal he had picked up. David recognized the cartoon face that was his family's inside joke. The way he was drawing it, it would be four feet up, right on the front of the tent.

"What are you *doing*?" David yelled.

"I'll explain later," Xander said. "Go to the portal."

David looked back through the tents. His heart sank. The portal was gone. Then he saw it again, deeper into the woods. It was drifting. He knew at any moment it could just . . . float away.

"Hey, you!" someone yelled.

David turned to see a soldier standing in the camp's center aisle pointing at him—or at Xander, who was still drawing on the tent. Either way, this kind of attention wasn't good. Several of the pointing soldier's comrades turned to look. Whether they didn't like Xander defacing the tent or a Confederate soldier standing in their camp, unshackled and unguarded, he didn't know. But that something disturbed them was clear: two of the soldiers raised their rifles.

"Xander!" David yelled.

His brother's eyes darted toward him, then around to the object of David's concern. Xander dropped the chalk and bolted around the corner of the tent, slapping David on the back as he did. They ran for the woods.

Was the portal getting smaller or just farther away? Didn't matter—David would keep running until he reached it, and if he had to, he'd squeeze into a space the size of a mouse hole to get home.

Behind them someone yelled again, more insistently.

David's cast bounced against his ribs, causing jagged bolts of pain in both his arms and his ribs. The side of his jacket that had been hung loosely over his cast slipped off. It flapped behind him as he ran as fast as he could, staying right on Xander's heels.

A shot rang out. The musket ball tore through the woods ahead of them, sending branches and pine needles flipping through the air.

David would not have thought he could run any faster, but he did. He pulled even with Xander, then passed him.

Another shot, but he didn't see where that one went. A sickening thought crossed his mind. He yelled, "Xander?" He could not hear his brother's footsteps or breathing over his own.

He was ready to stop when Xander answered right behind him: "Go! Go!"

They hit the line of trees. David leaped over a tangle of branches. He came down on a small bush, almost fell, stayed up.

Without pausing, he ran directly into the shimmering, swirling portal.

CHAPTER

thirty-seven

TUESDAY, 1:22 A.M.

David was still running when he burst into the antechamber.
He hit the far door at full speed. His cast hit first, then his
knees and forehead. He began falling backward, when Xander
came through the portal, just as fast. Xander slammed David
back into the door. Both of them crashed to the floor.

"Ahhhg!" David screamed. It felt as though his entire left
arm was on fire. The pain was so intense he saw nothing but

a bright, blinding light in his head. He felt a hand clamp over his mouth.

"Shhh! You'll wake Dad."

"I . . . don't . . . care," David said through clenched teeth and Xander's hand. "My arm! My arm!"

Xander wrapped his arms around him, hugging him tightly, the way Dad would have done. "I know it hurts," he said, "but it's just your arm, Dae. You didn't get shot. You're alive."

It felt as though a sword had been run up the entire length of his arm. Slowly, while Xander rocked him, the agony diminished. The sword became a hot wire, then a throbbing pulse, like his blood was having a hard time traveling through the damaged highways of his veins and arteries.

After a while, David opened his eyes. They were sitting on the floor, leaning against the door he had crashed into. The portal door on the opposite side of the room was closed. Of course it was: it always slammed shut after a person went through. This time it had waited until both of them— Xander and David—had reentered the antechamber.

"Okay," David said, pushing Xander off him. "I'm okay." But he wasn't sure it was true. Each time his arm throbbed—which kept perfect time with the beating of his heart—pain shot into his shoulder and head. On the downbeats, when the pain took little breaks, his arm tingled. "My arm feels like it's asleep," he said. "When it's not—*uuuhhhgg*—killing me."

Xander scooted back on the floor and leaned into the bench. He was smiling.

"What's so funny?" David said. He was holding his teeth so tight against the pain, it felt like his molars would crumble.

"How many times did you get shot at?" Xander said. "And you wait till you get back home to get hurt."

"I got hurt *coming* home."

Xander shook his head, eyeing David. "You look terrible. Your face is covered with mud . . . where your tears didn't wash it away."

David touched his face. He had been in too much pain to even realize he had been crying about it. He kicked out at Xander's legs, striking him in the ankle.

"Hey," Xander said.

David said, "What was that, drawing Bob on the tent? We were almost free and clear until you stopped to do that."

Xander's expression grew solemn. "Something Dad thought of," he said. "It's a way of letting Mom know we were there. If she sees it, she'll know we're looking for her."

"But what if it doesn't last?" David said. "Does anything we do in those other worlds matter? Do they stay the way we left them?"

Xander thought for a minute. He looked at the portal door. "Maybe we should go back and see."

"No way!"

"I don't mean now. You know how the rooms change, how the things in the antechambers switch to something else?"

"Sometimes they're in another room. Sometimes they don't show up again until later."

"Same as the portals; the worlds are cycling through the house," Xander agreed. "There are twenty portals on this floor. What if there are a hundred different worlds? A thousand? It's like they move away from this house and then come back."

"Like a Ferris wheel," David suggested. "The seats move away from the guy who helps people get on at the bottom, then later on they come back down to him."

"Yeah, like that," Xander said. "But we don't know where the portals go when they move away from the house." He gestured toward the portal they had just stepped through. "Let's let it go away. When it comes back, we'll check it out, see if the world beyond is the way we just left it or if it reverts back to the way it was when we first found it."

David nodded, thinking. "So if it were a Ferris wheel and we left gum on the seat, would the gum be there when we saw the seat again, or would someone have cleaned it off?"

"Right," Xander said, smiling. "In this case, will Bob be there when we check again? It's exactly the kind of experiment Dad talked about."

David frowned. "How are we going to record what we learned if Dad doesn't even know we're doing this? You thought we could go over, take a quick look around, maybe find Mom. But, Xander . . ." He shook his head. "I don't think it's going to be that easy. Dad was right—we have to learn more about all of this. You can't take a quick look around when people are shooting at you."

"We're going to have to tell him, I guess," Xander said. He pointed a finger at David. "But he'd better get moving. I feel like we're dragging our feet."

David narrowed his eyes at his brother and said, "Don't talk about Dad like that. He's the one who thought up the control room. He's the one who knew it was going to take more than just popping in and out of the worlds to find Mom."

"Yeah, but we're the ones actually *doing* something."

That made David think of something his old soccer coach had said. "So we're the players and he's the coach," David suggested. "Together we're a team. We're in this together, right?"

"Together," Xander agreed. He smiled again at David. "You know how a hot shower feels so good after coming back from a world?"

"Like you're washing the bad stuff away," David said.

Xander gestured toward David's cast. "Let's wrap that in a trash bag. You *really* need a shower."

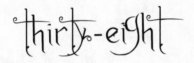

TUESDAY, 8:50 A.M.

In school Tuesday morning, David could hardly keep his eyes open. He needed more sleep . . . and they needed to find Mom . . . and they needed to keep up the appearance of a normal life. How could they do it all? Dad always said things looked bleaker when you're tired. David didn't really believe a good night's sleep would give him a better attitude. But it sure would help him keep his eyes open.

His arm continued to throb. Every now and then it would send a searing hot dart into his shoulder, neck, and head. He wondered if it needed resetting or even if he'd broken it in another place. He didn't want to tell Dad about it, though. Dad would insist on taking David back to the doctor, which would give the doctor, and the *town*, more reason to believe that he was in danger—either from his own family or from the house. He would suffer through it and hope it got better.

"King?"

He heard Mrs. Moreau say his last name and realized she had been calling on him for some time. He raised his head, forcing his eyes to open wide. "Ma'am?"

She scowled at him with her birdlike features. "Are we asleep, Mr. King?"

He glanced around. All faces were turned toward him, smiling at his being caught unaware. "Uh . . ." he said. "*I'm* not."

"Then I must be boring you."

"No, ma'am."

Her narrow lips bent into a tight smile. "Would you come to the front, please?" she said.

David lowered his head, miserable. This was all he needed. He pushed himself out of his chair and walked to the front.

Mrs. Moreau said, "Please summarize today's lesson for the class."

There was a lesson?

Facing his classmates, he waited for something to come to him.

Surely *something* his teacher had said during the past hour had made it into his head. He could tell his class about meeting a Civil War general, about being shot at, and how it feels to run into a door with your broken arm. But he didn't think that's what she wanted from him. After a full minute of her letting him stand there looking stupid, he turned the most apologetic eyes he could muster on her.

"I'm sorry."

"Don't apologize to me, Mr. King," said Mrs. Moreau. "It's your classmates who suffer when you don't pay attention. Look at all the time you've wasted."

David scanned the faces staring back at him. A few nasty smiles, but mostly he saw sympathy. Probably they were just hoping they weren't next. He looked back at Mrs. Moreau, hoping to be excused to return to his chair. He saw only sly expectation on her face.

What does she want from me? he thought. Then he realized that she had been serious. In a low voice he asked her, "You want me to apologize to the class?"

"That would be nice."

He turned back to all the faces. "I'm sorry."

Mrs. Moreau touched his back as though they were buddies again. "Thank you, Mr. King. Don't let it happen again."

On the way back to his seat, his eyes landed on Clayton, the boy who had been sent to the principal's office for ridiculing David's name. Clayton gave him a stern look and ran his finger across his throat.

Oh, come on! David thought and sat down.

CHAPTER

Thirty-nine

In his dream, the assassin was back home in Nineveh. He had just returned along with the Assyrian army from yet another conquest. Crowds filled the streets to cheer for the returning fighters and taunt the prisoners in their cages. Each of these cages was designed to hold a single person. They were small, even too small for children. But it was grown men and women who had been crammed into each of the hundreds of cages rolling into the city. Their howls of despair for their families, for themselves, rose above the cheers like the voices of a thousand souls condemned to Hades. Many

537

would be removed from their cages and skinned alive during the coming days of celebration.

The assassin paced at the edge of the crowds, recognized but never acknowledged. No one dared to speak his name or even allow their eyes to dwell on him for more than a couple of seconds. He knew that their collective voices thanked him for his role in the conquest. That knowledge and their fear were gratitude enough.

As he watched, a soldier drew his sword and held it high. The man pointed to the fingers of a prisoner, which were protruding from the iron bars of his cage. The crowd roared louder. The soldier brought down his sword, skimming it along the bars. Sparks flew up and the fingers came off. The soldier leaned over and used the tip of his sword to flick the fingers into the crowd. The citizens of the assassin's capital city scrambled for these treasures. They would be added to the ever-changing, ever-decaying "works of art" the citizens kept in their homes, art made exclusively of the body parts of their conquered enemies. It was their way of honoring the gods for their victories and their expanding empire. It reminded every Assyrian both of their power and the fragility of their mortal bodies. They had to stay strong, had to keep conquering, or they themselves would end up as artwork in another man's home.

Striding past a cart of caged prisoners, the assassin paused. The crowd was pointing to something just beyond him, urging him to act. Toes protruded from a cage. In one swift motion the assassin unsheathed his sword and brought it down on the toes. The woman inside the cage bellowed in pain and turned her face to the assassin.

He reeled back as he recognized his own mother.

Taksidian bolted straight up in his hotel bed, gasping for

breath. Sweat coated his body and drenched his sheets. They clung to him like a specter, trying to pull him back into the nightmare. He peeled them off his body and tossed them to the floor. He ran his fingers up his face, catching the strands of hair that were plastered there and pushing them back over his head. He leaned his head back and moaned.

Would the nightmare never leave him alone? For more than thirty years it had haunted him. Despite the wealth he had amassed, the luxuries to which he had grown accustomed, ever since he had stepped from the world of his birth into that house, his sleeping mind never let him forget. The world from which he came was violent and bloody, and indeed his mother, his whole family, had been slaughtered. But he had not taken part, except to know what happened as part of the process to harden his heart and prepare him for the life of an assassin.

He rose from his bed and stretched, feeling his joints pop, his muscles flex. Age was catching up to him, and he still had so much more to do. He strode to the curtains and parted them. Daylight streamed in, stinging his eyes. What little sleep he allowed himself he always got during the day. Night was too valuable to waste on sleep. It was for working without interruption. And for stealth.

He went into the bathroom and turned on the shower. While the water heated, he leaned against the countertop to stare at his reflection in the mirror. His face was still lean, his eyes bright. Had he remained in Assyria, had he gone back, he would have certainly been dead by now. No Assyrian lived past the age of forty, and the assassin who saw his thirtieth birthday was rare. Here he was, almost sixty and still kicking. Kicking hard.

He glanced at his watch. 1:13. Good. Still time to get to the house before that family returned from school. He had news to gather and instructions to give. He bristled at the thought of the King family. They were a thorn in his side.

No matter, he thought as he turned back to the running water and checked its temperature. Soon enough, he would pluck them from his flesh and flick them away—like fingers under the tip of a sword.

CHAPTER

TUESSDAY, 3:00 P.M.

Throughout that second day of school, David kept an eye on
Clayton. He watched him in the hallways between classes and
at lunch. When he saw David looking, the boy merely smiled.
It was not until the final bell rang that Clayton made his move.
As David was leaving his last class, Clayton slipped into the
room. He grabbed David's cast, sending a fresh bolt of pain
into David's shoulder.

"Let's talk," Clayton said.

"I don't think so," David said. He tried to shake his arm free, but Clayton had a good grip, and pain kept David's movements to a minimum. "Let go," David said, trying to look fierce.

Another boy, taller than either of them, stepped up beside Clayton. David knew his name was Joe.

He jerked his head to indicate the classroom behind David. "Get in there, King," he said quietly.

Other kids streamed past them and glanced back knowingly.

David took a step back. Clayton and Joe stayed right on him.

Clayton turned to the teacher, who was erasing the white marker board at the front of the classroom. He used his sweetest voice to say, "Mrs. Hammerstrom, Mr. Reid is looking for you."

"Oh," Mrs. Hammerstrom said, setting the eraser down and smoothing the wrinkles out of her blouse and skirt. She hurried out of the room, her heels *clack-clack-clacking*.

The sound was harsh in David's ears, which struck him as sadly appropriate for the situation he was in.

"Let's sit," Clayton told him.

"You don't want to sit," David said.

"I do, for a while," Clayton said, smiling. "At least until the school clears out a bit. We don't want your screams to draw too much attention."

"Clayton, it's not my fault you went to the office."

"Oh, really? Whose fault is it, then? Let's see, it was your stupid name that got me in trouble, and it was your stupid father I had to go see."

David stuck out his chest and bumped Clayton with it. "He's not stupid."

Clayton was taller than David by at least two inches. When he bumped back, David had to take a step to keep from falling.

"Stupid enough," Clayton said and laughed, as though he had said something clever.

"Look, you want to fight. I get it. But how tough are you, beating up on a kid with a broken arm? Wait until I get this cast off, and we'll make it fair."

Clayton's palm slammed into David's chest. David stumbled into a desk and fell backward hard. The desk fell with him, and the seat back cracked him on the head. He rubbed the spot, already feeling a knot starting to swell under his hair. He looked up at Clayton's and Joe's grinning faces and said, "Mrs. Hammerstrom will be coming back."

"Not for a while," Clayton said, laughing. "I saw Mr. Reid take off in his car after last period. He's the assisstant principal, you know. Her boss. She'll look everywhere before giving up." He slapped Joe in the arm with the back of his hand. "Shut the door."

David watched Joe lean into the hallway, look in both directions, then shut the door.

"Clearing out fast," Joe reported.

Clayton's grin grew wider.

"My dad's waiting for me," David said. "We pick up my sister right after school."

"He'll wait for you," Clayton said.

"Or he *won't*," Joe added and laughed.

"Either way, this won't take long," Clayton said.

David really didn't need this. He was tired. He was hurt. He just wanted to go home and find his mother. He said, "My father will send in my brother to look for me." He tried to make it sound like a fact, not a threat.

"*Oooh*, your brother. I'm scared. Joe, you scared?"

"Shaking in my boots," Joe said. He laughed again.

Clayton hardened his face into a mask of meanness. He said, "We'll just have to kick both your butts. Two Kings for the price of one."

David didn't like Clayton thinking he could own Xander. "He's fifteen, my brother. A lot bigger than you."

"I know who he is," Clayton sneered. "You don't think you can just move here without everyone knowing everything about you, do you?"

Not everything, David thought. *If you did, your little mind would explode.* He wanted to say it, but settled for saying, "You don't know *anything*."

"I know you moved into the old haunted house outside of town," he said.

David felt sick. "It's not haunted," he said.

"Everyone knows it is," Clayton said. "Right, Joe?"

Joe nodded.

"Last family that lived there, the father killed 'em all, then killed himself."

"Did not," David said. He warned himself to shut up, just shut up.

"Did too. Maybe your daddy's going to do the same to you too. Is that how you broke your arm? Daddy try to kill you?"

David lowered his head. Not seeing Clayton's sour face helped David bite his tongue.

"Yeah, that's what I heard. Your daddy broke your arm. That's what everyone's saying. Huh, Joe?"

"Twisted it until it just snapped like a twig," Joe confirmed. "Heard you cried like a girl."

Stay down, David told himself. *He wants me to fight. Then he could say I started it.*

Clayton said, "The whole town is so convinced your dad's banging you around, I can pound you to a pulp and no one'll believe that I did it."

"I fell out of a tree," David said quietly.

Clayton laughed. "Oh, is that the best you and your old man could come up with? Fell out of a tree?" He stepped closer, reached down, and grabbed a fistful of David's shirt.

David swung his good arm up, knocking Clayton's hand away.

Clayton looked surprised by David's boldness. He said, "That'll cost you another broken arm, dude." He circled around to David's left side, obviously looking for an easier angle of attack.

Outside, a car horn honked. Joe looked through the windows at the back of the room. "Clay, I think it's his old man."

Clayton crouched. "Get down! Get down! Did he see you?"

"I don't think so. He's out in the parking lot . . ."

The horn sounded again.

"Honking," Joe said.

"No kidding? Go look."

Joe waddled in a crouch to the windows. He peered over the sill. "He's just sitting—"

David lurched forward. Clayton grabbed for him. David swung his arm and smashed his cast into Clayton's mouth. The boy yelled and flew backward. David pushed himself up and darted for the door. Clayton was wailing behind him.

David didn't look back. He pulled open the door and ran into the hallway. He turned right, toward the main entrance, and beat his feet against the tile floor, wanting only to put distance between himself and Clayton. He realized too late that he'd made a mistake. He was heading toward the cafeteria, not the front entrance. He stopped to turn around and saw Clayton and Joe emerge from the classroom. Blood coated Clayton's lip and chin.

The boy saw him, spat on the floor, and smiled. He started toward David.

David ran for the cafeteria door and hit the bar that opened it. He would have been better off slamming into a brick wall.

He banged his cast on the door—*again!*—and bounced off. The doors were locked.

Man, they shut down early around here, he thought.

He scrambled to his feet. Clayton and Joe were ambling slowly toward him, knowing he was cornered, savoring his fear. The only other exit David knew about was on the far end of the hallway, past the boys who wanted to pound him to a pulp. He was near the short leg of hallway that had been his introduction to the building's interior—the first he had seen of the school when he had portaled from the linen closet to the locker.

The locker, number 119. It was right there, not fifty feet away. He could probably reach it before Clayton and Joe got to where they could see him go into it. Did he dare?

He thought about Clayton—madder than ever, bloody lip and all.

It wasn't a difficult decision.

He darted into the short hallway, directly toward the center locker, the locker that was the way out of this mess.

From around the corner, Clayton called, "That's a dead end, King David! You're stupid, just like your dad."

As he approached the locker, David's eyes focused on the latch. *Please, please, please*, he thought. *Don't be locked*. He saw that there was no lock on it yet, and his heart was thankful for the break. His sneakers squeaked to a stop in front of it. He had the latch lifted and the door opened before the momentum of his body had slowed. It was empty.

"Ollie, ollie oxen free," Clayton called.

Quickly he looked in their direction. They hadn't come around the corner yet. David climbed in and pulled the door closed behind him.

CHAPTER

forty-one

TUESDAY, 3:21 P.M.

David felt the sides of the locker move away from his shoulders. Instead of metal and pencil shavings, he smelled wood and fresh laundry. Instead of a thin steel floor under his feet, which buckled a little when he shifted his weight, he was standing on solid floorboards. Even the quality of the darkness had changed, reflecting the difference between the light that came through the locker vents and the dimmer illumination of his home's upstairs hallway as it seeped through the crack under the door. He opened the door and stepped into the hallway, pulling in a deep breath. As he released it, he released the tension of knowing he was about to get pounded. He smiled at the thought of Clayton and Joe coming around the corner and not finding him.

The possibility of their having witnessed his vanishing inside locker 119 brought a tinge of concern back to his stomach. But compared to the beating Clayton had promised, it was a concern he could live with. He would not be able to avoid Clayton forever, but at least this gave him time to figure out what to do about the school bully.

He shut the linen closet door and glanced around. Home. He had never been there alone before. It was a little creepy, the silence, the stillness. The only light came from the sun, filtered through the trees outside and the bedroom windows. It gave the house an unlived-in, museumlike feel.

He bit his bottom lip. Dad was waiting for him at school—honking for him to come out. He did not know about the portal from school to home. After Mom had been taken and Dad had come clean about having lived in the house before and knowing its secrets—though apparently not *this* one—he and Xander should have told him about the linen closet. David wasn't sure why they hadn't, except that it seemed everything had been moving a thousand miles a minute since Mom's kidnapping. They just hadn't had time.

He felt a pang of guilt, knowing there were other reasons as well: David and Xander *liked* knowing something about the house Dad didn't, and what if they wanted to *use* the portal sometime? They didn't want Dad restricting them or jumping all over them. And that they had kept it a secret this long would make telling Dad about it that much harder.

There was no way Xander would say anything, no way he would even suspect that David had used the portal now. He and Dad would just keep waiting for him. When he didn't come out, they would probably search the school. All the while, Toria would be waiting at her elementary school. Dad would be worried sick.

David would have to go back through and meet Dad at the school. Of course, he'd need to wait until he was sure Clayton and Joe had given up looking for him. That would give him time to think of an excuse for being late.

A murmuring reached his ears. It had the rhythm and alternating tones of human conversation. He wondered if someone had left a radio on. Dad liked to listen to what he called "talking heads" in the mornings.

David crept down the hall to the banister that overlooked the foyer. He leaned over the railing but could no longer hear the voices. Something creaked, and he realized it was overhead—from the third-floor hallway. His heart began to race as he thought of the big, bare footprints they had found in the house and the man who had taken Mom. Had he returned? Or was it someone else?

He detected the murmuring again: a deep rumbling of spoken

words, followed by more words in a slightly higher tone. *Two people!*

The footprints they had found had all been similar. They had assumed that someone—as in *one* person—had been in the house. But David was hearing *two* voices! He crept farther down the hall past the master bedroom door on his left. For just a moment he was terribly sure that he had misjudged where the creak and the voices had come from. After all, how could you tell in a house that played with sounds the way children played with marbles?

He was frozen in front of the master bedroom's open door, sure that if he turned to look, two people would be looking back at him. Then a man said something in a sharp tone. It was not as near as the bedroom, and David felt relief. He turned his head and saw no one in the room. He continued to the end of the hallway. Here, a second hallway branched toward the back of the house. The secret panel at the end was hinged open. He tiptoed toward it. The door to what was now the MCC came up on the right. But the voices were clearer now—and definitely coming from upstairs.

David reached the secret panel and leaned through the opening.

A rumbling voice drifted to him from the upstairs hallway. He furrowed his brow in concentration. He did not understand the words he was hearing.

As though reading his thoughts, a different voice said, "In

English. If I ever need your help outside this house, in this time, you will need to speak the language of the day."

As deep as this English-speaking voice was, the other man's was deeper. It rumbled like boulders in an avalanche, but much slower. It said, "Not . . . easy."

"I know. We'll work on it. I have another mission for you."

David heard the rustling of paper.

"This man . . . see, here? Must not reach his destination."

The boulder-voice said, "Want . . . kill?"

"Of course. Do what you do best."

Boulder-man grunted.

"You'll find him here . . . in this world. Look for the—"

Trying to hear, David stepped through the secret panel. His cast thunked against the door. He froze in place and held his breath. Silence. The men upstairs had stopped talking. Then came the sudden sound of footsteps—two sets of them, moving fast, growing louder.

David spun around, already moving out of the hidden panel's threshold. His cast hit the door again, louder this time. He didn't care. He shoved his shoulder into it. It flew open and crashed into the hallway wall. He was at the junction of the upstairs hallways when he heard a clattering of shoes on the stairs behind him. A more muffled pounding made him think of the barefoot giant who had taken Mom. A man with shoes, a man without: David had no desire to meet either one.

He moved as fast as he could, past the master bedroom, the

553

landing, Toria's room, the bathroom. Three doors lay ahead: his and Xander's room, the spare bedroom, and the linen closet. He had to reach the linen closet before his pursuers rounded the corner. He gritted his teeth and willed his feet to move faster. He reached the closet door, opened it, and stopped.

At the far end of the hallway, Taksidian came racing around the corner. He saw David and paused. The only sounds were David's panicked breathing and the footsteps of the barefoot man hurrying to catch up.

Taksidian said, "*Boy!*"

David scrambled into the closet and slammed the door. He felt the air change around him, the walls press in.

Come on, come on! he thought.

When light appeared before him, forming itself into the vents of the locker door, he pushed it open to step through.

It was only at this moment that he even considered the possibility of Clayton still looking for him in the short hallway.

Who cares? he thought. *Clayton or Taksidian? No contest.*

Still, it would be a disaster if Clayton found out about—

Hands grabbed his shirt and yanked him out of the locker.

forty-two

TUESDAY, 3:34 P.M.

"What are you doing?" Xander said. Gripping David's shirt, he gave him a shake. "What were you doing in there?"

David looked back at the open locker and said, "Taksidian's right behind me. He saw me go into the closet."

Xander's jaw tightened. "What? Why did you go through?"

"Clayton—"

"Never mind!" Xander said. He shoved David aside and reached for the locker door.

"Wait!" David said. "Does it work if the door's left open? What if he can't follow me here if we don't shut it?"

Xander flashed an expression at David that was part confusion, part frustration. He backed away from the locker. "And what if he just appears in the locker?" He snapped his fingers. "Okay, okay, I have an idea. Wait here." He ran out of the short hallway and around the corner.

"Xander!" David yelled. "Xander!"

"Wait there a sec!" He sounded pretty far away. "If Taksidian shows up—*run!*"

David backed away from the locker. He kept his eyes on its dark interior. Did something move in there? He squinted. Nah, just shadows. He heard footsteps, and his stomach cramped. Could sounds come through before a person did?

Then Xander came jogging around the corner. Reaching the locker, he said, "Okay," and slammed the door closed.

"Xander, no!" David said.

"I got it, I got it." Xander slipped a combination lock through the hole in the latch. He smiled at David. "See?"

Bang!

Something slammed against the locker door from the other side.

Xander jumped, and David screamed.

Bang! Bang! Bang!

David started to run, but Xander grabbed his arm to stop him. Xander whispered, "It's locked. He can't get through."

"He could break the lock," David said.

Bang! Bang! Bang!

Xander pressed his lips together. He stepped close to the locker and held his hand up to it, but didn't actually touch it. He said, "Leave us alone."

The banging stopped. Xander looked at David. David shrugged.

A voice came through the door. It was deep and echoey from the smooth metal walls inside. "Leave the house, and I'll let you be."

The words chilled David's skin. He stepped forward and said, "We want our mother back."

Silence. Then: "I don't have her."

David said, "Did you take her?"

More silence . . . longer. David was about to repeat his question when Taksidian said, "You should know by now, nothing about that house is as simple as that."

Xander slammed his fist against the locker door. "Did you take her or not?"

They waited for a reply. And waited.

David yelled, "Do you know about our mother?"

After a minute of silence, Xander whispered, "I don't think he's in there."

"How could he leave? I thought you had to open and shut the door?"

Xander shook his head. "Maybe he just made his point: nothing is as simple as that."

David said, "Want to look?"

"No way."

David stepped past him and pressed his ear against the door. He squeezed his eyes shut in anticipation of a *bang!* suddenly breaking his eardrum. He heard nothing inside. No breathing, no metal buckling under shifted weight. He squinted up into the vents. Only blackness.

"If he's not in there, he's in our house," Xander said.

"With the big barefoot guy," David agreed. To Xander's puzzled expression, he said, "I'll tell you later. Dad needs to hear it too."

Xander nodded toward the locker. He said, "Is there stuff in there? Books, a jacket, like someone's using it?"

"I didn't see anything."

Xander stepped closer. He licked his lips, then began slowly turning the dial on the combination lock.

"What are you doing?" David hissed.

"We don't know if this locker has been assigned or not. Either way, a lock will draw attention to it. And we had to give them our combinations, in case they want to open them and not use bolt cutters. I don't want any school officials even *thinking* about this locker. And I definitely don't want them thinking about *me* and this locker."

"Like someone's going to take the time to test every combination they have to see whose lock it is," David said.

"If they figure out the locker does weird things, they will," Xander said, leaning closer to the dial. The lock snapped open.

Before he could slip it off the latch, David grabbed Xander's fingers and the lock. He whispered, "What if he's in there?"

"Get ready to run."

With the care and slowness of a demolition expert snipping the wires of a bomb, Xander maneuvered the lock out of the hole in the latch. As soon as it was clear, he backpedaled away. David matched his steps, never taking his eyes off the locker door.

They waited. Finally, Xander nudged him. He gestured with his head and started for the bend in the hallway. They went around it and headed toward the double doors at the far end, snapping their eyes over their shoulders to make sure no one was following.

When it seemed safe to talk again, Xander said, "There were two kids roaming around when I came in looking for you. Are they part of this?"

David said, "I was trying to hide from them."

"In the locker?"

David nodded.

"And you ran into Taksidian? Your luck just seems to get better and better, doesn't it?"

"Tell me about it," David said.

•••••••••

By the time they reached home, David had told his father about the linen closet portal, his passage through it that afternoon, and his encounter with Taksidian. Xander confessed his role in keeping the linen closet secret and helped David explain the part about talking to Taksidian through the locker door.

Dad stopped the SUV at the end of the street in front of their house. He sat there with the engine idling, peering through the windshield. Xander turned in the front seat to exchange a worried look with David. Even Toria understood the significance of it all and remained quiet.

"Well," Dad said finally. "I can't say I'm happy about your keeping the closet a secret, but I understand." He reached out and gripped Xander's shoulder. "And I suppose I don't have the best track record for honesty myself right now. But no more secrets, okay?"

Xander nodded.

Dad threw his arm over the back of the seat and gazed at David. "Okay?"

"Um . . . Dad?" David said, wondering how his father was going to take the news of his sons getting shot at on some Civil War battlefield. "Last night—"

"I woke him up again," Xander interrupted. He gave David a quick scowl—there and gone. "We . . . looked for that guy again who was watching the house." He smiled, a little too broadly. "We didn't see anybody."

Dad looked from Xander to David, back to Xander.

He knows something's up, David thought, miserable.

But instead of quizzing them, Dad simply nodded.

David leaned forward and turned his head to peer at the house. "What if they're still in there?"

"Daddy?" Toria said, sounding frightened.

Dad looked through the window at the house. "Okay. We'll search the house together."

"With knives?" Xander suggested.

"No!" Dad said, pointing at his oldest son. "We'll just . . . grab something to defend ourselves when we get in there. No knives." He killed the engine, and they all got out.

As Dad unlocked the front door, David edged close to him.

"Dad?" He touched his father's arm. When he got no answer he said, more insistently, "Dad!" and gave him a push.

"What, Dae?"

Instead of answering, he pointed. Thirty or forty feet beyond the side of the house, a man stood in the woods. He wore a dark overcoat like Taksidian's, but it wasn't Taksidian.

"What the—?" Dad said. Without taking his eyes off the stranger, he descended the porch steps.

"Dad . . ." Xander said.

"I'm taking care of it, Xander," his Dad replied.

Xander said, "No, Dad, look."

Dad looked up at Xander; then his eyes followed Xander's pointing finger toward the opposite side of the house. There, deep in the woods, stood another man. Dad looked again at the first stranger and took a step toward him. He called out, "You're on private property! I'm calling the police." He went to the door and pushed it open. "Come on, kids."

"Who are those men, Daddy?" Toria asked.

"Just people trying to scare us."

"Why?"

"I don't know, sweetie. Xander, shut the door. Make sure it's locked. Let's take a look around."

"Are you gonna call the cops?" David asked.

Dad frowned at him. "Probably not. I'm not sure anyone in this town is on our side."

forty-three

TUESDAY, 4:31 P.M.

They searched the house and found nothing. Even the secret door in the wall was shut and looking just as it should. David was glad that Xander had heard Taksidian pound on the locker door. Otherwise, he would have wondered if his family really believed everything he had said about that afternoon. After the search, Dad and Toria went to the kitchen to start dinner. David and Xander found themselves in the MCC.

"Why didn't you let me tell Dad about last night, about going through the portal to the Civil War?" David said in a harsh whisper.

Xander squatted by the rolls of movie posters. He picked up one and unrolled it just enough to see what movie it advertised. "If we tell him now, he won't let us go back into it."

"What? To that same world? Why would we want to?"

Xander raised his eyebrows at him. "Because we're trying to find Mom, remember?"

"Dad knows that," David said. "He's not against us going over. He just wants to do it safely."

•Xander dropped the poster and picked up another one. "And what does that mean, exactly? I don't even think Dad knows. Why isn't he up here now, planning a trip through a portal to find Mom, instead of downstairs making dinner?"

"Xander, I almost got killed last night—again! I thought we agreed we can't just hop into these worlds, grab Mom, and bring her back. Not unless she happens to be strolling around right where we appear, and that doesn't seem very likely. And it's like everywhere we go, someone's trying to kill us. Xander, listen to me!" He waited for his brother to look at him. "I'm totally with you—but we need Dad too. We need to do this smart." David's shoulders dropped, and he couldn't help feeling a little sorry for himself and a lot sorry for Mom.

Xander dropped the poster and stood. "All right, but let's

do one thing that will show Dad we aren't just being . . . *rebel-lious*. Let's show him that our hearts are in the right place."

"How?"

"He's the one who suggested putting something in each world that Mom would recognize so she'll know we're looking for her."

"Bob," David said.

Xander nodded. "But Dad didn't know if it would stay there after we left. We don't want to be going through all these worlds, taking the time to leave a message for her in each one just to have it disappear from that world when we come back to the house. If we can just give Dad something solid, a positive yes-it's-still-there or no-it's-not . . ." He shrugged. "Then at least he'd know."

"A rule," David said. "Dad likes to know the rules. But how are we going to—"

"We go back and look. Right now. All we have to do is go in, see if Bob is still on the tent, and get out."

David glared at his brother. His stomach and throat were so tight he wasn't sure he could speak, but he did: "Xander, I *can't*. The bullets were like . . . I mean, I heard them zipping past my head. I . . ."

"Okay, okay," Xander said. "Then, just come up with me. Help me find the room and wait for me. In case I need you."

"Don't go."

"I have to, Dae." He stepped over the posters to grip David's good arm. "Look around. This room is *all* we've done to find Mom." He shook his head, obviously frustrated. "You stepped into that World War II village, but that was almost an accident. We're supposed to be *doing* something."

David bit his lip. "We promised: no more secrets. Dad's told us how many times, Xander? The portals are off-limits . . . at least when he's not with us. It's only been two days since Mom was taken. Give Dad some time—"

"We don't *have* time!" Xander said forcefully, but not with enough volume to warn Dad of their argument. "*Mom* doesn't have time." He closed his eyes, then opened them slowly. "Let's do this one thing."

"When does the sneaking stop?" David asked. "First Dad didn't tell us the real reason we moved here. Then we started sneaking through portals into other worlds, even after Dad told us not to. When does it stop, Xander?"

Xander held up his index finger. He said, "After this one thing. Dad would say, 'No, it's too dangerous. We don't know enough yet.' But maybe if he saw progress—you know, if we showed him that the way to learn things, to get closer to finding Mom, is to go over and not just talk about it—then maybe he'd get going and *do* something."

David just frowned.

Xander continued: "When you wanted to see for yourself what those doors were all about, when you thought Dad was going to take us away, you said you'd go over with or without me."

David's eyes narrowed. "So?"

"So, I'm going to do this whether you help or not."

"That's not fair. That was before Mom—"

"Are you in or out, Dae? That's all I need to know."

Xander was probably right that Dad would nix this plan in a heartbeat. It was also likely that handing Dad proof that they were learning about the other worlds would psych him up to take more action.

But they had *promised*. How many more broken promises would it take for Dad to completely lose his trust in them? Then he would definitely take them away, because he wouldn't be able to trust them to be safe.

In the end, it was the determination in Xander's face that made up David's mind. He said, "I'll help you this one last time. But I mean it, Xander. No more secrets. We do this as a family . . . or not at all."

Xander smiled. "Agreed." He stood there, waiting for something.

"What?" David said.

"I need to hear you say it, man. Come on, for me."

David gave him a lopsided grin. He said, "Let's do it."

•••••••••

David and Xander each took one side of the hallway. They moved from door to door, checking each antechamber for the Civil War items they had worn the night before.

"Dae," Xander said. He was clearly thinking something through. "If you see the items from when Dad and I went over—you know, the picnic stuff—let me know. We can find out what we need there too."

"Bob?" David asked.

"Yeah. Remember I said Dad carved him into a tree?"

David opened a door and saw a well-used painter's smock, a rosary, a wooden mallet, and some other things that were definitely not related to the Civil War. He closed the door and moved on to the next one. When he reached the end of the crooked hall, he started back, looking into the rooms he had seen just minutes before. It gave him an uneasy feeling to find that the items inside each one had already changed. Where the smock, rosary, and mallet had been were now a bridle, reins, and riding crop.

On the third lap through the doors, David said, "Dad's going to wonder where we are."

Xander opened and closed a door, then headed for the next one. "He's got spaghetti with meat sauce cooking. I can smell it. That always takes forever. Besides, when dinner's ready, he'll probably send Toria—" He opened a door and stopped, then smiled at David. "Bingo."

forty-four

MIDWAY INTERNATIONAL AIRPORT, CHICAGO

Keal looked like he was going to be sick. His face glistened with sweat. His eyes kept darting one direction, then another.

Jesse stretched out his fingers and patted the back of Keal's hand. The big black man actually jumped in his chair.

Jesse smiled. "It's okay."

"Okay?" Keal whispered. He lowered his head, even though they were the only people in the waiting area of Gate A19.

"I've *kidnapped* you, man." He snapped his head up and shot glances all around.

"It's not kidnapping if I asked you to take me."

"You don't understand," Keal said. "You're an old man in a nursing home where I work. They'll say I took you against your will or that I took advantage of your senility to talk you into coming with me."

"I'm not senile."

"You're *old*," Keal said, making the word sound like a disease. He tapped his temple. "They'll say you've lost it, even if you haven't."

Jesse shook his head. "Why would you want to kidnap me?"

Keal started to say something, then stopped. His eyes snapped to a police officer strolling casually along the concourse. He waggled a finger at Jesse, and his deep voice grew even quieter. "All I'm saying is you better be right."

Jesse pulled in a long breath. He frowned and scrunched his brows together, then said, "You're doing the right thing, Keal. I appreciate it."

"I mean," Keal said, "I don't want anyone to be in danger, but when we get there, there better be people to save, you know?"

"There will be," Jesse said. He got hold of Keal's big hand again and squeezed. "You wouldn't believe how many people you're saving by taking me home."

He leaned back in his wheelchair. A sign behind the empty

counter confirmed that the gate serviced a flight that would take them to Redding, California—a ninety-minute drive from Pinedale. It was scheduled to leave in just under two hours.

Jesse caught Keal looking at him with unsure eyes, and he smiled again. He whispered, "Thank you," then lowered his eyelids to catch a few winks before takeoff.

CHAPTER

forty-five

TUESDAY, 6:50 P.M.

David paced the little room. From the portal to the open hall-way door, he could take only five good steps. No wonder he had crashed so painfully into the door the night before. The other direction, from the bench to the wall, was only three steps. He supposed it was all the space that was required: pick up a map, throw on some clothes, maybe change your shoes. What more did you need to venture into a different world? He looked at the gray coat hanging from a hook. It was still dirty from when he had hit the ground, trying to keep a musket ball from taking off his head. Perhaps he should have gone over with Xander again, but every time he thought of those soldiers firing at him, he felt sick.

Just come back, Xander. Please.

David didn't wear a watch, but he felt his brother had been gone fifteen minutes or so. If he had stepped onto the same battlefield they had the night before, he should be able to reach the tents and find the portal home in about five more minutes.

He heard footsteps pounding toward him, and he froze. Someone was hurrying up the stairs.

Toria's voice reached him: "Xander! David! Are you up here?" Her voice was shrill with panic, and he realized she wasn't calling them for dinner.

He stepped into the hallway. "Here!" David said. "What is it?"

Toria bounded into the hallway and stopped. Her eyes were wide. "Cops!" she said, out of breath. "They're at the door. Dad's arguing with them. They want us to leave."

David looked back into the antechamber at the closed portal door. Could he just leave Xander? Would it be okay? He thought about propping open the hallway door—maybe that would keep anything from happening up here while he ran down to find out what was going on. But if he'd learned anything about the house, it was that it would do what it wanted to do. It didn't matter if they propped open a door or locked it or whatever. Maybe by the time David got downstairs, Dad would have taken care of the situation, and David could be back before Xander returned.

He strode toward Toria. "What's Dad doing?"

"Nothing, just saying they don't have the right to make us leave."

David darted around her and raced down the hidden staircase. Hearing angry voices, he paused at the secret doorway in the upstairs hall.

"I don't care what that piece of paper says," Dad said. "You can't just—"

"Sir, where are the children?"

"That's my business. Hey! Hey! I said no, you can't come in!"

Toria stepped up behind David. She whispered, "Where's Xander?"

"Shhh." He walked past the MCC and turned into the second floor's main hallway. The voices were booming up from the foyer. Stopping at the top of the stairs, he couldn't believe what was happening in the entryway below.

The door was open, and two uniformed police officers were grabbing at Dad. One seized his arm and twisted it, forcing him to spin around. They pushed him face-first into the wall. David saw a flash of bright metal and realized they were about to slap handcuffs on his father.

"Daddy!" Toria screamed and ran past David. He tried to

stop her, but she slipped out of his grasp and started down the stairs.

The handcuffs clicked, binding Dad's wrists behind his back. One of the cops pushed his hand into Dad's back, keeping Dad's cheek pressed against the wall as though it were glued there. Dad strained to get a look at Toria coming down the stairs.

"Stay there, honey!" Dad yelled.

"Come here, sweetheart," the other cop said, gesturing with his hand.

Toria braked before reaching the foyer. "Daddy?"

Dad's eyes rolled and found David. "David, where's Xander?"

"He's . . . uh . . ."

"Go get him!"

"But . . ."

The cop who'd spoken to Toria was looking at David now. He said, "Come down here, son."

"No!" Dad yelled. "David, go get your brother."

A movement in the open doorway caught David's attention. Taksidian stepped into view and leaned casually against the frame. He took in the scene, then his eyes flicked up to David. The man smiled thinly.

Dad caught sight of him. He said, "Is *he* why you're doing this? That man wants my house!"

The cop holding him spun him around. "We don't know about that, sir. We're just doing our jobs."

The other cop beckoned to David again. "Son, you'll have to come with us."

David backed away from the stairs. He was about to turn and run when he heard a sound. It was the *click!* of a door handle's latch. It had come from down the hall, toward Xander and David's bedroom.

Toward the linen closet!

Just as the thought came to him, the closet door swung open. Already beating impossibly fast, his heart went into overdrive.

Clayton stepped out of the closet and looked around, wide-eyed and openmouthed. He looked as though he thought he was dreaming. He squinted at David, and said, "King David?"

David was sure his own expression was just as stunned.

"Who's that?" asked one of the cops below—from the foyer, the closet was out of sight.

The other answered, "Must be the older boy. Both of you, come on down!"

David glanced over the banister at the men, their faces turned up, growing impatient. Realizing something was up, Taksidian's smile faded. He scowled at David.

Without a word, David headed toward Clayton. If he simply left him there, eventually the kid would find the cops or the cops would find him—then he'd start talking: *I stepped into a locker at school and wound up here! No, really!* David wasn't sure exactly what he could do to prevent that, but he had to do *something*. Should he take Clayton with him to get Xander?

What if he didn't want to come? The boy was bigger than David; it wasn't like David could just *drag* him—especially past the cops. Even if he could take him, that would mean showing Clayton the third floor. It was enough he'd found the locker-to-closet portal; did they really want him knowing everything?

The bully was standing in the closet doorway, his fingers on the handle. As David approached, Clayton's face twisted into a nasty smirk. "What kind of freak-thing you got going on here, twerp?"

David put his palm on Clayton's chest and shoved him back into the closet.

Clayton's eyes flashed wide as he fell back. "Hey—!"

David slammed the door shut. He heard a whoosh of air from the gap under the door: Clayton was heading back to the locker. David went into his bedroom, grabbed a chair, and dragged it into the hall. He wedged the seat back under the closet's door handle. He leaned close to listen. No sound from inside. It wouldn't take long for Clayton to figure out that he could return to the house by opening and closing the locker door. Then what? He'd start pounding.

At least this bought David some time. Maybe Clayton would be too freaked-out to come back. Maybe the cops would leave before he returned. Maybe Xander would have a plan.

Too many maybes!

David ran down the hall, intent on finding his brother. As

he passed the foyer, a cop yelled up: "Hey, kid! Stop! Hold it right there!"

David rounded the corner and shot through the passageway where the fake wall was hinged open. He turned and pulled it closed, tugging until he heard it click. Then he bolted up the stairs. Xander wasn't in the antechamber when he got there. Panting, David stared at the door, willing it to open, willing his brother to step through. Gritting his teeth, thinking of nothing else to do, he yanked the gray jacket off the hook and slipped it on.

Maybe I can take it off when I get there, he thought. *Roll it up under my shirt before they start shooting at me.*

His stomach lurched. His guts tightened in fear, and he had to close his eyes until the feeling passed.

Got to find Xander. As soon as I get there, I'll just run, run straight for the camp.

He reached up for the dirty gray kepi.

The portal door burst open. Blinding sunlight. A gust of wind blew in. Smoke stung his nostrils. Grains of dirt peppered his cheeks.

The door slammed shut again. The smoke and dirt whipped out through the cracks.

In the center of the floor, Xander crouched on his hands and knees, his shoulders rising and falling. His breathing was deep and fast.

"Xander!" David yelled. He dropped onto his knees in front of his brother, then reached out with his good arm and grabbed Xander's bicep. "Xander, downstairs—"

"Listen," Xander interrupted. He raised his face. It was scratched and filthy. His eyes were wide with excitement, rimmed with tears.

"We need you," David said. "Dad's—"

"Dae!" Loud. In his face. Xander rose up to grip David's shoulders. "I found her!"

David's lungs locked up. A tingling sensation coursed up his arms and over the back of his neck like electricity.

Xander leaned close. He said, "I found Mom!"

NOT THE END . . .

READING GROUP GUIDE

1. Xander wants to immediately plunge through the portals in search of Mom. Dad insists that they pace themselves; he says their search may take time, and he wants to make sure they have the energy and freedom to continue looking for as long it takes. Do you understand Xander's feelings? Do you see that Dad may be right as well? What can Xander learn from Dad's caution? What can Dad learn from Xander's impatience?

2. When David jumped through the portal, thinking he saw his mother, was he being reckless or heroic? What would you have done?

3. After David returns from the World War II French village, the old man Jesse wakes up realizing someone is in the house. What do you think happened that alerted him to the Kings' presence in their new home?

4. Why do you think Taksidian wants the Kings out of the house?

5. What's with that clearing? What do you think makes it defy the laws of gravity? Dad calls it a place to take your mind off everything. Do you sometimes need a mental break? What do you do to clear your mind?

6. Dad invited Xander into a calm, peaceful world, where they sat on a picnic blanket by a river. Why does Dad think that

this world may have contributed to his father's decision to give up their search and leave the house? What do you think this world is all about? Why is it relaxing when the other worlds seem to be so crazy?

7. Can you relate to David's experience at school that first day? Have you ever been the new kid in school? What did you do to adjust? Did anyone help? Why do you think bullies bully? What is the best way to handle bullies?

8. In the Mission Control Center, Xander puts up posters of tough-guy action movies to get them "psyched up" for their adventures into unknown worlds. What psyches you up to tackle difficult challenges?

9. David and Xander disobey Dad to go into the Civil War world. Xander says it's because Dad's search for Mom isn't moving fast enough. Do you agree that this is a good reason to sneak into the portals? With Mom's rescue at stake, what else could Xander have done?

10. Cops arresting Dad. Clayton coming into the house through the linen closet portal. Xander finding Mom (but he didn't bring her back!) What happens next?

11. Where would you like to see the Kings go? Your idea could end up in a future Dreamhouse Kings book. See the contest information page for more details.

BOOK THREE IN THE DREAMHOUSE KINGS SERIES

COMING
JANUARY 2009

THE DREAMHOUSE KINGS "DREAM THE SCENE" CONTEST

Xander and David have already battled a gladiator in the Roman Colosseum, dodged bullets in a World War II French village, and almost died on a Civil War battlefield. Now their mother has been taken *somewhere* in time, and the kids are determined to find her. Where do you think they should look? An Aztec temple at the height of the Spanish conquest? A pirate ship during a high-seas mutiny? On Admiral Peary's trek to the North Pole?

What do they find there? What clues to Mom's location? Who helps them? Who tries to stop them? Does Toria tag along? Does Dad?

HERE'S YOUR CHANCE TO LAUNCH THE KINGS INTO AN ADVENTURE OF A LIFETIME.

Author Robert Liparulo wants to know where *you* think the Kings should go and what they find when they get there. If he chooses your idea, he'll write it into a future Dreamhouse Kings book, making it a part of their story forever. The creator of each winning idea will be acknowledged in the novel that features the adventure, and also receive a new iPod Nano.

You have four chances to win, so find out all the rules and how to enter at www.DreamhouseKings.com. Submissions must be fifty words or less and must be received by August 15th, 2008, in order to be considered for the next book in the series.

Look for *Gatekeepers*—Book Three of the Dreamhouse Kings Series

COMING JANUARY 2009